SMOKE
JENSEN
THE BEGINNING

SMOKE JENSEN
THE BEGINNING

WILLIAM W. JOHNSTONE

with J. A. Johnstone

PINNACLE BOOKS
Kensington Publishing Corp.
www.kensingtonbooks.com

PINNACLE BOOKS are published by

Kensington Publishing Corp.
119 West 40th Street
New York, NY 10018

PUBLISHER'S NOTE
Following the death of William W. Johnstone, the Johnstone family is working with a carefully selected writer to organize and complete Mr. Johnstone's outlines and many unfinished manuscripts to create additional novels in all of his series like The Last Gunfighter, Mountain Man, and Eagles, among others. This novel was inspired by Mr. Johnstone's superb storytelling.

All Kensington titles, imprints, and distributed lines are available at special quantity discounts for bulk purchases for sales promotions, premiums, fund-raising, educational, or institutional use. Special book excerpts or customized printings can also be created to fit specific needs. For details, write or phone the office of the Kensington sales manager: Kensington Publishing Corp., 119 West 40th Street, New York, NY 10018, attn: Sales Department; phone 1-800-221-2647.

PINNACLE BOOKS, the Pinnacle logo, and the WWJ steer head logo are Reg. U.S. Pat. & TM Off.

ISBN-13: 978-0-7860-3642-4
ISBN-10: 0-7860-3642-7

First Kensington hardcover edition: February 2015
First Pinnacle mass market paperback printing: October 2015

10 9 8 7 6 5 4 3 2 1

Printed in the United States of America

Also available in an e-book edition:

ISBN-13: 978-0-7860-3643-1
ISBN-10: 0-7860-3643-5

PREFACE

Kirby "Smoke" Jensen became a legend of the old West, and has been featured in a series of books called "Mountain Man." But, as with many legends, it often becomes difficult to separate fact from fiction. This book hopes to clear up the many misconceptions about the Smoke Jensen novels, a series that began in 1985.

Some of the information will seem in contrast with what those followers of Smoke Jensen may have read earlier. That is because in the ongoing saga of Kirby Jensen, the legend grew to be bigger than the man. And, as the line in the movie *The Man Who Shot Liberty Valance* says, *"When legend becomes fact, print the legend."*

In this book, we will look at Kirby "Smoke" Jensen before he became legend.

SMOKE
JENSEN
THE BEGINNING

CHAPTER 1

Early October, Stone County, Missouri

Election season of 1860 was the most contentious election season in the history of the United States. Newspaper editorials and campaign speeches suggested that there would be major consequenccs, depending upon the results. Four candidates were running for President, the major two being Abraham Lincoln as a Republican and John Breckenridge as a Southern Democrat. In addition, two other candidates were in the race. Stephen Douglas was a Democrat and John Bell was running on the Constitutional Union ticket.

Several of the Southern states had already made the threat to secede if Lincoln won, and tensions were running high.

Missouri was a slave state with almost 120,000 slaves, but as of the latest count, only sixteen resided in all of Stone County. Emmett Jensen didn't have any slaves, but he did own a forty-acre farm of loam and rock adjacent to Shoal Creek. The farm required a great deal of work just to make it productive enough to feed a family of five. At twelve years old, Kirby was the youngest of Emmett and Pearl Jensen's three children. Janey was fourteen and Luke was eighteen.

The institution of slavery had an effect on the lives of almost everyone in Missouri and Kansas, a free state. The question of slave or free had gone far beyond mere debate, erupting into actual fighting between armed partisans of the two states.

The guerrillas from Kansas called themselves Jayhawkers. Their counterparts in Missouri were known as Bushwhackers, and for some time, shooting had been taking place between the groups. Led by Asa Briggs, the Missouri Bushwhackers called themselves the Ghost Riders. The Jayhawkers from southeast Kansas were led by Angus Shardeen.

Shardeen once rode with John Brown, and personally took part in the Pottawatomie Massacre in which several pro-slave sympathizers were murdered. Since John Brown's death, Shardeen had started his own group, and was making his presence known by burning homes and killing innocents in southwest Missouri, all in the name of abolition.

"There's a big war acomin,' " Tom Byrd told Emmett the afternoon he went to Byrd's farm to retrieve the two mules he had rented to his neighbor for the afternoon. "You mark my words. It's acomin'."

"Maybe not," Emmett replied, his response motivated more by hope than reason. "Maybe cooler heads will prevail."

"No, they won't. The Republican, Abraham Lincoln, is going to be elected, 'n that's all it's agoin' to take. Once that ape becomes president, there's going to be war sure as a gun is iron."

Emmett shared some of the conversation with Pearl and the rest of his family over supper that night.

"If war does come, Pa, which way do you think Missouri is goin' to go?" Luke asked.

"Well, seein' as Missouri is a slave state, I don't see it goin' any other way except for the South."

"Yes, sir. That's what I was athinkin' too," Luke said.

"But Pa, you said many times, that you don't hold with ownin' slaves," Kirby said.

"I don't hold with anyone holdin' another man like that, be the man black or white. But that ain't the only thing that's causin' the trouble. People ought to have the right to say what goes on in their state, and the federal government's got no right stickin' its nose into our business. I reckon if it comes to it, 'n all my friends and neighbors go off to join up with the South, why then that's the way I'll have to go."

"That's sort of what I was figurin' too," Kirby said. "If war comes, we'll be fighting for the South."

"There is no *we* about it, boy. You're too young to even be thinking about such things."

"I ain't always goin' to be too young," Kirby said.

"Well, you are too young now."

"Maybe Kirby is, but I ain't," Luke said. "If war comes, I'll be ridin' off to join up with the South. You can bet on that."

"I'm so tired of hearing everyone talkin' about the war," Pearl said. "Can't we at least talk about somethin' else here in our own home?"

"I hear what you're sayin', Pearl. But let's hope that it don't get no further than just talkin' about," Emmett said.

*   *   *

When Emmett first built the house back in 1841, it had only two bedrooms, one for him and Pearl, and one for the child he was sure they would have. Luke came along the first year, then four years later Janey was born, so Emmett put up a wall right down through the middle of the room, dividing it into two cubicles, each barely large enough to hold a bed. That arrangement gave Luke and Janey their privacy. Kirby came along two years after Janey. There was no place to put him, so Emmett built a small shelf just under the eaves of the house in order to make a sleeping loft.

It was a long time before Kirby was able to go to sleep that night. He was thinking too much about the supper conversation. Was it actually going to come to a war? Some might have said the skirmishes between the Bushwhackers and the Jayhawkers meant a war was already occurring, but that wasn't the kind of war he was wondering about. He was thinking of a real war, like the kind he had read about in books.

He knew about the Revolutionary War, the War of 1812, and the two Mexican Wars. The man that owned the leather store in town, Marvin Butrum, had been in both of the Mexican wars. He was with Sam Houston at San Jacinto during the Texas Revolution, and he had been with Robert E. Lee in the Mexican American War.

Kirby wondered what it would be like to be in a war. He pictured himself in a uniform astride a white horse, holding his saber high, and leading men into battle.

Well, it probably wouldn't really be like that. He was pretty sure that a twelve-year-old would not be entrusted to actually command an army. That realization caused the image he had projected in his mind to fade away.

He rolled over. But wait. The battle was in his imagination! While in his imagination, he could be anything he wanted, including a captain or a general or a sergeant; he wasn't sure enough about ranks to know what he wanted to be. But, whatever he was, he smiled as he remounted the white horse, lifted the saber, and gave the order to charge.

The next morning, Kirby and Janey went out to the barn to milk the two cows.

"You should be the one that does all the milkin'," Kirby complained.

"Why?"

"Because you're a girl, and milkin' cows is girl's work."

"What makes you think it's girl's work?"

"Pa don't never milk a cow, 'n neither does Luke. They plow and plant and harvest, but they don't milk cows."

"No, and they don't gather eggs either, but you do. Let's face it, Kirby. Pa prob'ly thinks you are a girl." Janey laughed at him.

"Yeah? Well, would a girl do this?" Kirby picked up a double handful of straw and dumped it on her.

"Don't do that! You'll get straw all in my hair."

Kirby laughed.

The cows, Ada and Bridget, were back to back in a

stall, waiting to be milked. Kirby and Janey put the milk stools in place, then sat down to milk.

"I bet I finish first," Kirby said.

"It isn't a contest, Kirby," Janey replied.

Kirby did finish first, then he got an idea. He had been milking Ada while Janey was with Bridget. Reaching over to grab Bridget's tail, he lifted it up, then did the same thing with Ada's tail. Using the hairy twitches at the ends of their tails, he tied them together.

Janey had been concentrating so much on the milking that she didn't notice what he had done.

"Want me to carry your bucket for you?" Kirby asked, diverting her attention.

"Well, that's very nice of you," Janey said, handing the bucket of milk to him.

They started back toward the house when the two cows began bellowing behind them.

"What in the world is wrong with those two?" Janey turned around. The two cows were trying to go in opposite directions, but couldn't because their tails were tied together. "Kirby! What did you do?"

"I don't know how it happened, Pa," Kirby tried to explain a while later. "As near as I can figure, they was just swattin' at flies 'n their tails musta got tangled up somehow. That's all I can figure."

"Are you trying to tell me they tied their own tails together?"

"Think about it, Pa. I mean, here are these two cows, just standin' there gettin' milked 'n all, and they sort of start swingin' their tails back and forth, not payin' no attention to each other. The next thing you know, why, their twitches has got all tangled up. Don't you think maybe it coulda happened that way?"

"I tell you what, Kirby. You go paint the barn, and while you're painting it, you might just come up with a lot better explanation than that cock and bull story you just tried to pass off on me."

"I thought you wasn't goin' to paint the barn till next summer."

"I changed my mind."

"All right, Pa."

Janey stuck her tongue out at Kirby.

Emmett watched his youngest son leave the house, and not until he was sure Kirby was well out of earshot, did he turn to Luke. "Who would ever think to tie a couple cows together by their tails?" he asked, laughing.

"Nobody but my little brother, I'm thinking," Luke answered, laughing as well.

McMullen School was a one-room school accommodating twenty-two students in grades one through eight. Kirby was in the sixth grade. He was naturally a big boy, bigger than anyone else in the school, including the two boys in the seventh, and the one boy in the eighth grade. In addition to his natural size, hard work on the family farm had made him strong.

In the eighth grade, Janey was a beautiful girl with black hair, dark brown eyes, full lips, and prominent cheekbones. But it didn't stop there. Her body was already fully matured to the point that visitors to the school sometimes mistakenly assumed that she was the teacher. Aware that her looks and body had an effect on men, Janey wasn't above being a sexual tease when she could do so to her benefit.

After completing the fifth grade several years ago, Luke had left school to help his father work the farm. After he completed the fifth grade last spring, Kirby had petitioned his father to let him do the same thing.

On the crisp fall day, Kirby was recalling that conversation as he sat at his desk, staring through the window.

"I can already read, write, and cipher," Kirby told his father and older brother. *"I don't see any sense in me staying in school any longer, when I could be helping out on the farm."*

"You are going to stay in school," Emmett insisted.

Kirby continued staring at a distant flight of geese. Very high in the sky, the geese were maintaining a perfect V formation as they headed south for the coming winter. He imagined himself down at Shoal Creek with a shotgun. He could bring home a goose, and his mother could—

"Kirby? Kirby, have you suddenly gone deaf?"

The others in the classroom laughed, and it wasn't until that moment that Kirby was even aware he was being spoken to by his teacher.

"I beg your pardon, Miss Margrabe?"

"I just gave you an assignment. From the *McGuffey Reader*, I want you to spell, define, and tell what part of speech is, the word *fluctuate*."

"*F-L-U-C-T-U-A-T-E*," Kirby said, spelling the word carefully.

"Very good, Kirby. And it means?"

"It means somethin' is moving back and forth, but it can also mean that somebody can't make up their mind about somethin', like if I'm tryin' to decide whether I want a piece of cherry pie or apple pie."

"And what part of speech is it?"

"It's an intransitive verb."

Miss Margrabe smiled and nodded. "Very good, Kirby. You were paying attention after all."

"Yes, ma'am," Kirby said.

"All right, children, I'm going to be working with the first and second graders now. The rest of you know what your assignments are, so please study at your desk."

The assigned work for the sixth grade was math, and Kirby was working on a problem of long division. He hated long division, particularly when the answer never came out even. The lesson was that it had to be carried out at least four decimal points. Kirby found such problems frustrating, and he was still working on them when Miss Margrabe stopped by his desk to look at his work.

"Very good, Kirby. You wouldn't happen to know if . . . uh . . . Luke might be—" Miss Margrabe stopped in mid-sentence, then gave what could only be described as a self-deprecating chuckle.

"Might be what?"

"Never mind. It was quite inappropriate of me to ask. Keep up the good work; you have an excellent math paper here."

"Thank you." Kirby smiled as Miss Margrabe walked away. He and Janey knew that their teacher liked Luke. Kirby would never say a word about it, but Janey wasn't above teasing her brother.

Returning to his work, Kirby finished the last problem, then turned his attention outside again. A group of riders were coming toward the school, riding fast and all bunched up. That alone was enough to arouse his curiosity, but one of the men was carrying a flaming torch. Because it was the middle of the day, that made their approach even more curious.

As they drew closer, the rumble of hoofbeats became a thunder and soon everyone in the school was aware of the galloping band of horses. They looked at each other in confusion, and Kirby got up from his seat and moved to the window.

"Kirby, take your seat, please," Miss Margrabe said.

"Somethin' ain't right," Kirby said.

"*Isn't* right," Miss Margrabe corrected automatically.

The riders came within twenty yards of the school building, then stopped. The leader of the band had red hair, a red beard, and a very prominent purple scar on his face. His description was well-known. It was Angus Shardeen.

"It's Jayhawkers!" Kirby shouted.

Several of the riders began shooting toward the school, and the bullets crashed through the windows. The students started screaming.

"Get down on the floor!" Kirby shouted as he ran to his sister and pulled her down, just as a bullet slammed into the desk where she had been sitting.

"Don't they know this is a schoolhouse?" Miss Margrabe cried.

"Miss Margrabe, no! You'll get killed!" Kirby shouted. Leaving Janey lying on the floor, he ran to his teacher and pulled her down as well, though not in time to keep her from being shot in the shoulder.

"Burn in hell!" someone shouted from outside. A second later a flaming torch came in through one of the windows that had been shot out. The other students screamed and shouted and ran away from the flames. Only Kirby had the presence of mind to grab the pail of drinking water and toss the water onto the torch, extinguishing it.

"They're leavin'!" a seventh-grade boy shouted. "They're ridin' away!"

With the fire under control, Kirby hurried over to Miss Margrabe, who was on the floor, leaning up against the wall under the blackboard. She was holding her hand over the shoulder wound, and blood was coming between her fingers, though she wasn't bleeding profusely.

"Janey, come look at this, will you?" Kirby called. When Janey didn't respond right away, he called again. "Come here and take a look at Miss Margrabe's shoulder. You can get up now. The Jayhawkers is gone."

"Are gone," Miss Margrabe corrected through clenched teeth.

"Yes'm they surely are."

Janey went over to them, then knelt beside the teacher and examined the bloody wound. The bullet hadn't actually hit her shoulder, but high up on her right arm.

"Kirby, use your knife to cut the sleeve off," Janey said.

"Must I bare my arm?" Miss Margrabe asked.

Janey nodded. "Yes'm. I'm afraid you're going to have to."

Kirby took a jackknife from his pocket and cut away the sleeve. He pulled the severed sleeve down across the teacher's hand, giving Janey an unrestricted view of the wound.

"It looks like it just cut a ridge in your arm, but I don't think the bullet is still there. Kenny, bring me some coal oil," Janey ordered one of the seventh grade boys. Boldly, she pulled up her skirt.

"Kirby, cut off enough of my chemise to make a bandage."

"Janey, that'll leave your legs bare," Kirby replied.

"Either cut enough for me to use as a bandage and bare my legs, or I'll take the whole thing off and bare my butt," Janey said. "Now do it."

Kirby took the bottom of Janey's chemise in his hands, but before he began to cut, he looked at the other boys in the room, all of whom had come closer for a look. "Every boy in here turn around, right now. If I catch any of you lookin' at my sister, I'll black your eye, and that's for sure and certain."

Reluctantly the boys turned away.

"Here's the coal oil," Kenny said, handing the can to Janey.

"You turn around, too," Kirby ordered.

A moment later, Kirby had cut a two-inch strip from all the way around the bottom of Janey's chemise.

"Now, cut a little piece off the end, so I can use it as a wiping cloth," Janey ordered.

After Kirby did so, Janey soaked the cloth in kerosene and used it to clean the wound. Then, pouring a little more kerosene over the wound, she made a bandage by wrapping the rest of the material around the teacher's arm, and tying it in place.

The sheriff and at least half a dozen other men came dashing into the school. Their sudden entrance frightened some of the other students until they realized who it was.

"We heard shooting!" the sheriff said. "What happened here?"

"It was Jayhawkers, Sheriff," one of the students said.

"Any of the kids hurt? We brought Doc Blanchard with us."

"Ain't none of the kids hurt, but they shot Miss Margrabe," Kenny said.

"*There aren't any children* hurt," Miss Margrabe corrected.

"Doc, get over here 'n look at the teacher, will you?" the sheriff asked.

"I'm real proud of both of you," Emmett said at supper that evening. "Kirby, the sheriff says that if you hadn't acted real quick, the whole school could have burned down. And Janey, Doc Blanchard said all he had to do was change the bandage. You did a fine job of nursin' Miss Margrabe."

"I stopped by to see Lettie," Luke said, speaking of Miss Margrabe. "Your teacher had nothin' but praise for the two of you."

"Praises for us, and kisses for you, I bet," Janey teased.

Luke smirked. "That's for me to know, and you to find out."

"I can't imagine any group of men so evil as to do something like that," Kirby's mother said.

"Never underestimate a man's capacity for cruelty," Emmett said.

"That's some real elegant words, Pa. Where'd you come up with 'em?" Kirby asked.

Emmett grinned. "I heard Governor Price say 'em durin' some of his speechifyin'."

"Pa, they's some fellas I know that's plannin' on joinin' up with Asa Briggs and ridin' over into Kansas to set things right," Luke said. "And I aim to go with 'em."

"No, you ain't," Emmett said.

"Pa, we can't just let 'em get away with somethin' like this."

"You ain't goin'," Emmett said again.

"It ain't like I'm plannin' on defyin' you or anythin' like that, but I'm full growed, Pa. And I reckon if I was to really take a mind to do it, there wouldn't be nothin' you could actual do about it."

"And I reckon you're right. But I would sure hope you wouldn't. It ain't our fight, boy."

"The hell it ain't! They attacked the school where Janey 'n Kirby was. They're family. They also shot Lettie. To my way of thinkin', it just don't seem right lettin' them Jayhawkers get away with doin' what they done."

"Thanks to your brother and sister, they didn't do much of anything. Kirby kept the schoolhouse from burnin' down, 'n Janey kept Miss Margrabe's wound from gettin' any worse. No need for you to be goin' over to Kansas with anyone when I need you here on the farm. Besides that, what do you mean when you say you plan to 'make things right'?"

"Just what it sounds like. Give 'em a taste of their own medicine," Luke said.

"You mean you plan to do the same thing to innocent folks over there, that the Jayhawkers have been doin' over here? Are you goin' to burn a few houses, and maybe shoot some women and kids? Because it's for damn certain that you won't be runnin' into any of the ones who actually done this."

"It just don't seem right, Pa, to let 'em get away with it and do nothin' at all."

"Two wrongs don't make a right, son, and if you'll think about it, you'll see what I mean."

"All right, Pa."

"I tell you what. If you're all that anxious to shoot somethin', there's a covey o' quail down in the south pasture. I thought maybe me, you, 'n Kirby could go down there just after dawn tomorrow mornin' and shoot a few of 'em. I'd love nothin' better 'n a mess o' fried quail, gravy, and biscuits. That is, if Pearl 'n Janey would cook 'em up for us." Emmett winked at his wife.

"I'm not a very good cook, Pa. You know that," Janey complained.

"It's 'bout time you learned, don't you think? You're 'most a woman now, 'n you'll be takin' on a husband afore you know it. When you do, you're goin' to have to cook for 'im."

"I'm not ever goin' to have a husband, because I'm not ever goin' to get married," Janey said.

"Why not?"

"I have no intention of being a farmer's wife."

"What's wrong with being a farmer's wife?" Pearl asked sharply.

"Nothin' at all is wrong with it, Ma, if all you want to do is stay home, cook for your husband, and raise a passel of brats. But no, ma'am. That just ain't somethin' I want to do. I don't plan on staying around here. I'm goin' somewhere exciting, like New Orleans, or St. Louis, or maybe even Chicago."

"Well, right now you are in Stone County, Missouri," Emmett said. "And, whether you ever get married or not, you're goin' to learn to cook, if for no other reason than I told you to. And you can start tomorrow."

"What makes you think you'll get anything, anyway? Arnold Parker and a couple of others from school went quail hunting last week, and they didn't get anything."

"They aren't Jensens," Emmett said easily.

The Ozark Mountains could have been an artist's palette, alive as they were with color—yellow, orange, red, green, and brown. A crisp coolness to the morning could be felt as Kirby, his father, and brother walked across a recently harvested cornfield. Somewhere a woodpecker drummed against a tree, the rapid staccato beat of its beak echoing through the woods.

Suddenly, a brace of quail flew up in front of them, filling the air with the loud flutter of their wings. Quickly and smoothly, Kirby brought the double-barrel twelve-gauge shotgun to his shoulder and pulled first one trigger, then the other.

The double boom of the exploding cartridges caused the sounds of nature to pale in comparison. Feathers flew from two birds as they tumbled from the sky.

"Good shooting, Kirby!" Emmett shouted as the boy started forward to retrieve his two birds.

An hour later, the Jensens returned to the house with nine quail, more than enough to make a fine meal. They cleaned the birds and turned them over to Pearl and Janey to prepare.

"While your ma and sister are cookin' our dinner, how about you two boys come on out to the front porch for a few minutes," Emmett suggested.

Once they stepped out onto the porch, Emmett and Luke filled their pipes.

"Boys, we had us a real good corn crop this year. We made sixty bushels an acre, which means we've got about twenty-four hunnert bushels gathered." Emmett sucked on the pipe until the tobacco caught, and a cloud of smoke wreathed. "Last I checked, we can get fifty-nine cents a bushel in Galena, which would bring in around fourteen hunnert dollars. That ain't bad for forty acres and a team of mules."

"I'll say!" Luke said enthusiastically.

"Pa, what about the seed corn for next year?" Kirby asked.

Emmett reached out and ran his hand through Kirby's hair. "Good for you, son, for thinkin' of that. I've already took out twenty bushels of the best lookin' seed corn."

"Seein' as we got only one wagon, it's goin' to take us three trips into town to get the corn delivered," Luke said.

"No it won't. Tom Byrd will rent us two wagons and two teams for ten dollars," Emmett replied.

"That still leaves us short one driver."

"Oh, I think Kirby could miss a day of school to drive one of the wagons." Smiling, Emmett looked over at Kirby. "That is, if you don't mind."

"Ha!" Kirby said with a huge grin. "I don't mind at all!"

"I didn't think you would."

"You men come on in for your dinner," Pearl called.

"There's only two men out there, Ma. Kirby's still a boy, remember." Janey smiled as she teased her younger brother.

"He does a man's work, and that makes him a man in my book," Emmett said.

"I hope you like the biscuits, Pa, because I made them," Janey said proudly.

Kirby picked one up and took a bite, even before the rest of the food was on the table. "Umm, umm. You did a great job! Yes sir, you're goin' to make some farmer a fine wife."

"You'll never see it!" Janey said, grabbing the biscuit from a laughing Kirby, and throwing it at him.

CHAPTER 2

"How are you doing, Miss Margrabe?" Janey asked when she went to school Monday morning.

"Well, I'm doing just fine, dear, thanks to you and your brother," Lettie replied. She looked around. "By the way, where is Kirby?"

"Him 'n Luke 'n Pa went to Galena to sell some corn," Janey said.

"*He and Luke,* dear."

"He and Luke," Janey said, correcting herself.

"I don't know if you know it or not, but Luke came by to see how I was doing. Wasn't that sweet of him?"

"Yes ma'am. But, seeing as he is sweet on you, I'd expect him to come calling on you," Janey said.

"Hush, now. You shouldn't be saying such things." Lettie smiled around a blush.

"I'm just saying what's true, is all."

"Well, as much as I'm enjoying our conversation, we do need to get class started." Lettie saw one of the boys standing near the window. "Kenny, would you ring the bell, please?"

"Yes, ma'am."

"I make it two thousand, five hundred, and seventeen bushels," Fred Matthews said after the corn was unloaded and counted. "At sixty-six cents a bushel that would be—"

"Sixty-six cents?" Emmett said.

"Accordin' to the telegraph sent out by the Chicago Board of Trade ever' day, corn's tradin' at seventy-eight cents, today." Matthews pointed to a sign on the wall behind him. "Like the sign says, we pay eighty-five percent of the price set in Chicago."

Emmett, Luke, and Kirby smiled at each other.

"It looks like we chose a good time to sell our corn," Emmett said.

Matthews grinned. "Yes, sir, I'd say you did. Twenty-five hundred and seventeen bushels at sixty-six cents a bushel comes to sixteen hundred and sixty-one dollars, and twenty-two cents. Do you want that in cash or by bank draft?"

"Cash, if you don't mind," Emmett replied. "I don't have a bank account, and the banks charge too much when they cash a draft."

"All right. Come on into the office and I'll count it out for you," Matthews offered.

Standing close by was a man named Roy Joiner, supposedly examining a wagon wheel. In truth, he was there to overhear conversations between the farmers who were selling their crops and the broker, hoping to happen upon an opportunity to put the information to good use.

Hearing the talk between the Jensens and Matthews was exactly the kind of information he was looking for. He watched the men enter the office, then hurried away.

"He's a dirt farmer," Joiner told Pogue Mason a few minutes later. Him and his two sons, one of 'em nothin' more 'n a boy. Hell, just the sight of a gun would probably scare 'em so much they'd piss in their pants."

"How much money did you say they would be carryin'?" Pogue asked.

"Over fifteen hunnert dollars. And it's all in cash. We'll hold 'em up out on the road. It'll be like takin' candy from a baby."

"Let's do it," Pogue said with a wide, nearly toothless grin.

About two miles north of Galena, Emmett, Luke, and Kirby rode in three empty wagons. Emmett was leading the little convoy, while Kirby was bringing up the rear. Aware that they were about to be overtaken by two men on horseback and thinking nothing was unusual about that, Kirby pulled over to one side of the road to give them room to pass.

They didn't pass. One of the men jumped into the wagon and put his gun against Kirby's head. "Call out to your pa, boy."

"What for?"

The man cocked the pistol, the hammer making a loud, double-clicking sound as it engaged the cylinder. "Do it, boy, or I'll blow your brains out. Maybe your brother will have more sense."

"Pa?" Kirby called. "Pa, we got a problem!"

Emmett and Luke stopped their teams and turned

to look back toward Kirby. They saw the two men, one of them in the wagon with Kirby.

"Mister, if you don't want to see your boy killed, you'd best do what we tell you," ordered the man on horseback.

Setting the brake on his wagon, Emmett climbed down and started back toward Kirby. "Luke, you be ready to act if you get the chance," he said under his breath as he passed the second wagon. "Don't hurt my boy!" Emmett pleaded, making his voice sound frightened.

"Just give us the money you got from sellin' your corn, 'n ever'thing will be just fine," stated the mounted robber.

"Pa, you want me to get the money and give it to 'em?" Kirby asked.

"You may as well." Emmett kept his voice as if he was resigned.

Kirby stood up.

"Here, what are you doin'?" the man in the wagon asked.

"I'm goin' for the money. Ain't that what you said you wanted?" Kirby replied.

The two robbers were looking directly at Kirby, which meant they had taken their eyes off Emmett. Suddenly, Kirby jumped off the side of the wagon, then quickly rolled beneath it. His action left the two would-be robbers totally confused.

That was all Emmett and Luke needed. Both men drew their pistols and fired, and the two outlaws went down.

Luke jumped down from his wagon and, with his gun drawn, hurried back to where the two outlaws lay on the ground. Emmett gave both men a hard kick, but neither responded.

"Kirby, you all right?" Emmett called.

"Yeah, Pa. I'm all right."

"Come on out, then. These two ain't goin' to do you no harm now."

Kirby crawled out from beneath the wagon, then looked down at the two men his father and brother had just shot. "That's the first time I've ever seen anyone get killed," he said in awe.

"The way things is in this world, it ain't likely to be the last time you'll sce it," Emmett said.

"What are we goin' to do with 'em, Pa?" Luke asked.

"Let's throw 'em in your wagon and you take 'em back into town. Me 'n Kirby will take Tom Byrd's wagons and teams back to him, then you can pick us up on your way back home."

"Take 'em to the undertaker?" Luke asked.

"No, take 'em to the sheriff. Let the county bury 'em. Besides, it's more'n likely that these two have dodgers out on 'em."

"What's a dodger?" Kirby asked.

"A reward poster. I suspect these two men may be wanted, and if they are, we'll collect some reward. And we'll split the reward money three ways." Emmett smiled. "You done real good, Kirby. I'm proud of the way you kept your head."

"Yeah," Luke added with a smile. "For a young whippersnapper who don't have no more sense than to tie a couple cows together by their tails, you done just real good."

Kirby beamed under the praise.

A reward of three hundred dollars on each of the two men was offered and Emmett, true to his promise, gave Kirby and Luke two hundred dollars apiece. It was the most money Kirby had ever had in his entire life.

Long after midnight, Kirby heard a rider galloping toward the house, shouting at the top of his voice.

"Jensen! Jensen! Turn out! Turn out! It's Gimlin's place! They've set fire to it!"

Emmett stepped out onto the front porch, wearing his long handle underwear. "What is it, George? What's goin' on?"

"Jayhawkers, Emmett. They've set fire to Gimlin's barn and house! I'm callin' folks to go give 'em a hand."

"Good for you. On your way, then. We'll be there," Emmett promised.

Fifteen minutes later, the entire Jensen family was in a wagon headed for the Gimlin farm three miles away. They could see the glow of the fire long before they reached the farm. By the time they arrived, the house that had been home to Marvin and Gail Gimlin, and their two young children, was completely engulfed in flames. Several neighbors were gathered around, but all they could do was watch the house burn.

Standing in the yard, five-year-old Mollie was crying and shivering.

Janey went to her, carrying one of the blankets she and her mother had brought from home. "Here Mollie, wrap this around you," she said, comforting the little girl.

"Janey, why did they do this? Why did those men come burn down our house?" Mollie asked between sobs.

"Because they are evil," Janey said. "Some people are just meaner than snakes."

"My doll got all burned up."

Janey put her arms around the little girl and pulled her close for a moment. "Wait here. I have a surprise for you."

"What?"

"Well, if I told you, it wouldn't be a surprise, would it?"

Janey walked back to their wagon where blankets, quilts, cooking utensils, and extra clothing were piled, just in case the Gimlins would have need of them. Thinking of Mollie, Janey had included the doll that had been hers when she was much younger.

She took it to the little girl. "You can have my doll," Janey said, handing a China doll to the little girl.

Mollie's eyes grew big. "I can have it?"

"Yes, I don't play with her anymore, and I think she misses having someone to play with."

"I'll play with her." Mollie held the doll in a close embrace.

"That was real nice, what you done," Kirby said when Janey joined the rest of her family in front of the smoldering house.

She shrugged. "It's just an old doll. I was goin' to throw it away some day, anyway."

"Still, he's right. It was good of you to give your doll to the little Gimlin girl." Emmett walked over to Gimlin, and put his hand on the man's shoulder. "I'm real sorry about this, Dewey."

"At least we all got out without any of us gettin' hurt," Gimlin replied. "But we ain't got a thing left to our name. No furniture, no clothes, no dishes, nothin'. And no house to put it in, if we did have them things."

"You will, and soon." Emmett turned to the friends and neighbors who had gathered and held up both arms. "Folks!" he called. "Let me tell you what we're goin' to do."

He pointed to what was left of the house which was nothing but glowing embers and fire-blackened wood. Though the flames were mostly gone, a great deal of smoke was still pouring from it and its heat could still be felt.

"As soon as that pile of burnt wood is cool enough for us to work with it, we're goin' to clear it all out. Then we're goin' to build another house for the Gimlins just like the house that the Jayhawkers burnt down. No, we'll build it even better."

"Yeah!" one of the other men shouted. "By damn, that's exactly what we're goin' to do."

"And ladies?" Pearl called out, stepping up beside her husband. "While our men folk are rebuilding the house, we're goin' to refurnish it. I know that between us, we can come up with furniture, clothes, blankets, quilts, and whatever it takes to get the kitchen put together again."

"Looks like we won't need a cookin' stove," one of the women said, pointing to the rubble of the house. "The one they had come through just fine. All we got to do is clean it up a bit."

By mid-afternoon, a large gathering of wagons was parked at the Gimlin farm. At least fifteen families had come to help. The men were constructing a new house. Three sides of framework were already up, and they were about to put the final side into place. Kirby, doing the work of a man, scurried up one of the ladders, then got into position. Half a dozen ropes were thrown to the men on top of the frame, and Kirby grabbed one of them, pulling with the others as the end frame was raised into position.

With so many men working, the framework of the house was in place with amazing speed. After the siding and roofing was completed, everyone grabbed a brush and bucket of paint and, before supper, the house had been erected and painted, and all the furniture moved in.

The stove had been cleaned but not moved, and even before the house was completed, some of the women had started cooking. A temporary table, long enough to feed forty people, had been put together using boards and sawhorses. By the time construction clutter had all been picked up, the meal was ready and the Gimlins, Jensens, and neighbors sat on make-do benches for supper.

Kirby was watching his sister. Merlin Lewis, who had left school three years earlier, was sitting beside Janey, and it was obvious that she not only welcomed Merlin's attention, she was inviting it. Kirby couldn't help but marvel at how easy it was for her to control Lewis.

The twelve-year-old glanced over at his brother to see if he saw what was going on, but Luke was lost in his own world. Lettie Margrabe was doing the same thing to him that Janey was doing to Merlin Lewis. Kirby laughed.

"What are you laughin' at?" Emmett asked.

"Nothin', Pa. I was just laughin' is all," Kirby said as he reached for another piece of fried chicken.

"Careful, boy. Someone's goin' to see you laughin'

at nothin' someday 'n they're goin' to think you've gone crazy."

Kirby turned his attention to another conversation going on near him.

"What I plan to do, 'n what I'm invitin' the rest of you to do, most especially the ones of you that ain't got a family to look after, is to join up with George Clark." The speaker was Lee Willoughby, a man who was the same age as Luke.

"Clark ain't nothin' but a murderer and an outlaw," someone said.

"That may be so, but he don't do none of his outlawin' in Missouri," Willoughby replied. "He does all of it over in Kansas. Luke, what do you say? Me 'n you was talkin' 'bout this the other day."

"We was talkin' about Asa Briggs, not George Clark."

"Briggs is an old woman compared to Clark. You want to come with me?"

Luke glanced over toward Emmett for just a moment before he replied. "I reckon not."

"Why not? You gone scared on me, have you?"

Luke stood up and glared. "Would you like to put that proposition to a test, Willoughby?"

A bit startled by Luke's response, Willoughby blinked his eyes and licked his lips for a few seconds before he responded. "No, no, I didn't mean nothin' by what I said. I don't want to fight you. I don't want to fight nobody from Missouri. All I'm lookin' to do is make things right. You folks has seen what kind of men the Jayhawkers are. They attacked the school, they come in the middle of the night to burn Mr. Gimlin and his whole family out of his house. Like I said, all I'm lookin' to do is set things right."

"I don't hardly see it as right, ridin' into Kansas and burnin' some farmer and his family out, like was done to me," Gimlin said. "I expect most folks over there are just like us. No line drawn on a map, especially one that you cain't even see, would make it right to go over there 'n start burnin' and shootin' and such."

"Yeah, well, a war's acomin', 'n I don't plan on missin' out on it," Willoughby said.

"If war comes, I expect a lot of us will get caught up in it," Emmett said. "And, in this state, I expect some, even some of us here, will choose up different sides."

"Which side would you choose, Jensen?" Willoughby asked.

"Well, sir, I don't have any slaves, 'n I don't hold with the idea of keepin' any. Besides which, I got a brother who lives up in Iowa, and he'll for sure be fightin' for the North. But the truth is, I can't see as the federal government's got 'ny right to tell a state what it can or can't do. I figure if it comes to it, I'll be pitchin' in with the South."

Emmett was normally a man of few words, and Kirby believed that may well have been the longest speech he had ever heard his father make.

Willoughby smiled. "Well now, that's good to know. I've always looked up to you, Mr. Jensen, 'n I've always figured Luke to be my friend. I'm for sure goin' to fight for the South and I wouldn't want us to wind up bein' enemies."

"I don't consider anybody here my enemy," Emmett said, "whether they wind up fightin' for the North or the South."

One month after Gimlin's house was burned and re-built, Abraham Lincoln was elected President of the

United States. As a result, South Carolina seceded from the Union, claiming independence. Six Southern states soon followed, eventually creating the Confederate States of America.

April 1861

A garrison of Union troops occupied Ft. Sumter in Charleston Harbor. South Carolina demanded that the troops be withdrawn, but the federal government refused to do so.

On April 10, Brigadier General Beauregard, in command of the provisional Confederate forces at Charleston, demanded the surrender of the Union garrison. Major Robert Anderson, the Union commander of Ft. Sumter, refused.

On April 12, Confederate batteries opened fire on the fort. Designed to repel invaders from the sea, Ft. Sumter was unable to withstand an effective defense against an attack from the land side.

At 2:30 PM the next day, Major Anderson surrendered and was allowed to evacuate the garrison on the following day. Not until then were there any casualties, as a Union artillerist was killed and three wounded when a cannon exploded prematurely when firing a salute during the evacuation.

Immediately after that incident, Lincoln called for 75,000 troops to be drawn from every state that had not seceded. That action caused four more states to secede. The Confederate government matched Lincoln's move by calling for 75,000 troops of its own.

*   *   *

Lee Willoughby came by the Jensen farm not long after that, wearing the gray uniform of a Confederate lieutenant. "Iffen you had come with me when I asked last fall, more 'n likely you'd be an officer, too," he said to Luke. "Now, if you come in, you'll have to come in as a private. There ain't nothin' I can do for you, 'cause it's too late."

"Privates'll be fightin' the war same as officers, won't they?" Luke asked.

"Well, yes. Of course they will."

"Then the way I look at it, it don't really matter all that much whether I'm a private or an officer. Fightin' is fightin', 'n now that the war has started, I reckon I'll get into it so's I can do my part."

"When you plannin' on comin' in?" Willoughby asked.

"Right away," Luke answered. "No, wait. Give me till tomorrow. I want to tell Lettie good-bye."

"We're gettin' up a wagon to carry men to the re- cruitin' office in Springfield. It'll be leavin' Galena long about noon tomorrow. If you're comin' with us, be to the courthouse before the wagon leaves." Willoughby slapped his legs against the sides of his horse and rode off.

Luke looked at his father. "What about you, Pa? What are you goin' to do?"

"I don't plan to rush into anything," Emmett said. "I plan to take the night thinkin' on it. I don't like the idea of the people in Washington sendin' seventy-five thousand troops into various states to tell the folks what they can and can't do. So, if I'm bein' truthful with you, I'd say I'm leanin' hard on goin' with you." As fate would have it, he did just that.

* * *

Lettie Margrabe lay naked in bed, staring at the leaf patterns the sun was projecting onto her bedroom wall. She had slept that way for the very first time. It was also the first time she had ever slept with a man.

Lying beside her, breathing the soft, rhythmic breath of sleep, was Luke Jensen. He was also nude.

Lettie had lost her virginity.

She was in love with Luke, and what they had done was no different from what lovers had been doing since the beginning of time. He had come to tell her good-bye, to tell her that he would be leaving for the war. It was Lettie who had asked him to stay, and not until he was sure that it was truly something that she wanted, did he agree.

As she lay in bed that morning she could still feel the exquisite pleasure of the night of passion they had shared. That sensual gratification, however, was tempered by the fact that she knew that if anyone ever found out about it she would lose her teaching position. Such exposure would mean she would leave the county, and maybe even the state, in disgrace. Despite that possibility, she had no regrets about what they had done.

They had made love several times during the night, and Lettie intended to do so at least once more before she let him leave.

Emmett did not own a horse, so he hooked the team of mules up to the wagon. The entire family rode into town with him to say good-bye. When they reached the courthouse, they were surprised to see so many men were going to Springfield to join up with the Confederate army, that it took three wagons. Like the Jensen family, other families were there as well to say good-bye to their husbands, fathers, sons, and brothers.

"Pa, I don't see why I can't go with you," Kirby complained. "I've read that both armies is takin' folks my age and some even younger. Drummer boys they'll be."

"Both armies, Kirby? Are you tellin' me that if I don't approve of you joinin' with the Gray, that you'd be willin' to join the Blue? You'd fight against me 'n your brother?" Emmett was not amused.

"No, sir. I ain't atellin' you that. I'm just sayin', I don't think I'm too young to go. You said yourself that I can do a man's work."

"That is exactly what I said, and that is exactly why you need to stay here. You'll be runnin' the farm, Kirby. The responsibility of the whole thing is goin' to be on your shoulders. You're goin' to have to get the crops put in and tend to 'em. Then you're goin' to have to get 'em out and get 'em to market. I don't want to come back home to a farm that's gone and a family that's most starved 'cause nobody was takin' care of 'em. I'm countin' on you, boy. So is you ma and your sister."

Kirby didn't reply. He knew that his father was correct. Someone would need to keep the farm going. With his father and brother gone to war, he was the only one who could do it. "All right, Pa. I'll do what you say."

Emmett was not a demonstrative man. The closest thing to affection he showed was to reach out and take

Kirby's hand in a firm handshake. "I know you will, son. That knowledge is what I'll keep with me the whole time I'm away."

"How long do you expect that to be, Pa?"

Emmett grunted and shook his head. "Truth is, this whole war is a foolish thing, us fightin' against each other. I expect the people in charge will come to their senses sooner than later. I'm bettin' we'll be back in time to help get the crops out, come fall."

"Emmett, you look after Luke now, you hear?" Pearl said. "He's my firstborn. It wouldn't sit good with me, if somethin' was to happen to him."

Emmett looked around. "Where is Luke?"

"He's over there, Pa," Janey said, pointing. "You didn't expect him to leave without sayin' good-bye to his woman, did you?"

Luke and Lettie were standing close together, and though they weren't touching, the expressions on both their faces all but gave away to the discerning what had gone on between them during the night.

"I thought he told her good-bye last night," Emmett said.

"If they really are sweet on each other like Janey says, you'd expect 'em to tell each other good-bye again this mornin', wouldn't you?" Pearl said with a smile.

"I reckon so."

"Recruits!" Lee Willoughby shouted then. "Load up into these here three wagons! It's time we was leavin'!"

"Boy," Emmett said before starting toward the three wagons. "Remember what we talked about. You take care of your ma and sister while I'm gone."

"All right, Pa. I will."

Kirby had no idea how long it would be before he saw his father and brother again, or even if he ever would see them again. He could see tears in the eyes of his mother and sister and felt a lump in his throat.

But he would be damned if he would cry. He had just taken on the responsibility of a full grown man.

Two months later, Kirby had the crops planted and was watching them carefully, taking pride in what he had accomplished in such a short time. On a trip to the barn to get a new bridle for the mule called Ange, he heard a sound coming from behind a pile of hay. Not sure what it was, he looked around for a weapon of some sort, and saw an axe handle without its head. Grabbing the handle, he approached the stack.

"No. Merlin, I said no." That was Janey's voice.

"Come on, Janey. You've let me get this far. You can't stop now!" Merlin Lewis's voice was demanding and edgy.

Kirby stepped around to the other side of the stack of hay and saw his sister lying on the ground with the top of her dress and camisole pulled down so her breasts were exposed. Merlin was pulling on the dress, trying to take it all the way off.

"She said no!" Kirby said firmly.

"What the hell?" Merlin gasped, jumping up quickly. "Where did you come from? Get the hell out of here!"

Kirby drew back the axe handle. "No, Lewis. You get the hell out of here . . . before I bash your head in."

"You talk big with an axe handle in your hand." Merlin sneered.

Kirby tossed the axe handle into the hay stack, then doubled his fists and raised them. "I don't have an axe handle now."

Although Merlin was three years older, Kirby was every bit as tall and a little more muscular.

Merlin looked at him for a moment, then waved his hand dismissively. "Nah, I ain't goin' to fight you. Your sister's nothin' but a slattern anyway." Merlin turned to leave.

"Lewis?" Kirby called to him.

Merlin stopped, but he didn't turn around.

"I don't want to see you on my farm anymore."

"Your farm?"

"Yes, my farm. I'm the one living here. I'm the one working it. Don't come back."

Kirby followed Merlin out of the barn and watched to make sure that he left. He also wanted to give his sister time to cover herself up. He had never seen her like that before and was embarrassed by what he had happened on to.

"Kirby?" Janey's voice was small and frightened.

"Are you decent?" Kirby called back.

Janey was always aware that she was older and a bit more sophisticated than Kirby was, and most times she didn't mind making him aware of that fact. Her voice sounded different from normal. "Yes."

Kirby turned and saw her standing a few feet behind him. He had never seen such an expression on her face before. It showed nothing of that self-confidence. On the contrary, it was an expression of contriteness and fear.

"What was that all about?" he asked.

"I told him to stop, and he wouldn't do it. I'm just

thankful that you came along when you did. If you hadn't . . . I don't know what would have happened."

"Janey, I've never been around a girl . . . like that . . . so I'm not real sure how things like what I saw here could happen. But it seems to me like it wouldn't have got that far if you hadn't let it."

"I admit I was . . . teasing him," Janey said. "But I thought I could control it. I thought that if I told him to stop, he would."

"Like I said, I ain't got that kind of experience, but I've heard enough talk to know that it don't always happen like that. You had to know that he's a lot stronger than you. You was playin' with fire."

"I was. I admit it now." She went over to Kirby and put her hand on his arm, then fixed him with a pleading gaze. "I don't know how to thank you. You came along just in time to save me. There's no telling what would have happened."

"Janey, Pa told me to look out after you 'n Ma. I'm goin' to ask you, please, don't be doin' nothin' like this again. You could get yourself in some serious trouble. And I don't know if I could even face Pa then."

"I promise I will be much more careful in the future. I've always had it in mind that I could control boys. Now I see that it isn't as easy as I thought."

"You can control boys. But you're of an age now, Janey that"—Kirby took in Janey's body with a wave of his hand—"it ain't boys you have to worry about. It's men. And you can't control men."

"You're right," Janey said contritely.

"Why don't you go on back to the house now?"

"Kirby?"

"What?"

"You won't tell Ma nothin' about this, will you?"

"I ain't goin' to say a word about it," Kirby promised.

The worry left Janey's face, and she kissed her brother on the cheek.

"Thank you, Kirby. Thank you for everything."

CHAPTER 3

Belle Robb was someone that the people of Galena euphemistically referred to as "a painted woman." She advertised her services by the very method that gave her the sobriquet by which she was called. Her red hair came from a bottle, her lips and cheeks from a paint pot. She wore fine, but revealing dresses and travelled around town in an elegant carriage driven by a free black man. She was the wealthiest person—man or woman—in the entire county.

Strange as it might seem, Belle and Lettie had developed a friendship when Belle began paying Lettie a great deal of money for private tutoring. For the last two years, Belle had been coming to the school on Saturday and Sunday afternoons for the lessons.

On this particular Saturday afternoon, Lettie was waiting most anxiously for her.

"Say, that *Pride and Prejudice* is one fine book," Belle said, returning the book to Lettie. "Thank you very much for lending it to me."

"I'm glad you enjoyed it," Lettie said, though her words were without animation.

"Lettie, what is it? What's wrong?"

"Oh, Belle, I'm so frightened. I . . . I have done something awful, and you are the only one I can talk to."

Belle reached out to put her hand on the teacher's shoulder. "Lettie, I know you, and I know that you can't do anything awful. Now, tell me what is bothering you."

"My womanly time . . . is late. I didn't worry too much about it, but . . . now I have missed it a second time. I'm two months behind, and it could only mean one thing."

"You're pregnant," Belle said matter-of-factly.

The way Belle spoke the words gave Lettie a sinking feeling. She had hoped someone like Belle might be able to come up with another reason. To hear her fears confirmed was devastating. "That's what I was afraid of."

"Does the baby's father know about it?"

"No, and I've no intention of telling him, nor anyone else."

"What are you going to do?"

"I . . . I've heard that there are ways of terminating a pregnancy," Lettie said. "I was wondering if you know anything about it. I mean, how would one go about obtaining such a thing?"

Belle shook her head. "I have known girls who did this, and I would advise against it."

"Why?"

"Because two of the girls I knew died undergoing the process. I wouldn't want to see anything like that happen to you."

"If . . . if the father was here, I would go to him and

tell him. I'm sure he would marry me. But he isn't here, and I don't know when he will return, or if he ever will return."

"He has gone to war?"

"Yes. If I have the child, and he doesn't come back for a few years, how could I ever convince him that the baby is his?"

"That could be a problem," Belle agreed.

"Oh, Belle, what will I do? What is left for me besides disgrace? I'll no longer be able to hold my head up among people who had once been my friends . . . among people who respected me."

"You can leave," Belle suggested.

"Leave and go where?"

"I have a friend, a gambler, who lives in Denver. I'll write a letter for you to give him. I'll tell him that your husband was killed, and you want to get away from sad memories. He'll do right by you."

"Oh, Belle," Lettie said, her eyes filling with tears. "Thank you. From the bottom of my heart, thank-you."

It was only a matter of a few weeks after Emmett and Luke joined the First Missouri State Guard Infantry, a Confederate company, that they were involved in their first battle. Union troops, under command of Brigadier General Nathaniel Lyon's Army of the West, were camped at Springfield. The Confederate troops, under the command of Brigadier General Ben McCulloch, formulated attack plans.

At 5:00 AM on the morning of August 10, the two forces met at Wilson's Creek about twelve miles southwest of the city. Rebel cavalry received the first blow and fell back, away from Bloody Hill. Confederate forces soon rushed up and stabilized their positions, attacking the Union forces. Three times they attacked that day but failed to break through the Union line.

The Union troops received a heavy blow when General Lyon was killed during the battle. Major Samuel D. Sturgis replaced him.

Meanwhile, Confederates routed Colonel Franz Sigel's column south of Skegg's Branch. Following the third Confederate attack, which ended at 11:00 AM, Sturgis ordered a retreat to Springfield. The Confederate victory buoyed Southern sympathizers in Missouri, giving the Confederates control of southwestern Missouri.

It was shortly after that battle that Emmett and Luke were split up. Emmett protested at first, but a colonel pointed something out to him that seemed to make good sense. "Suppose you and your son were in the same company. And suppose that company was engaged by such superior forces that virtually the entire company was killed. Your wife would lose a husband and a son, and your children, still at home, would lose a father and a brother. Wouldn't it be best for you to be separated, to lessen the chances of both of you being killed at the same time?"

Emmett nodded. "I reckon you're right, Colonel."

CHAPTER 4

Spring 1862

Kirby had been plowing for two weeks, averaging an acre and a half per day. By the middle of May he had the ground broken in twenty-one acres, which was just over half of the farm. What he would plant was entirely up to him, and he planned to do twenty acres of corn, ten of wheat, and ten of oats. He had already spoken with Mr. Matthews, who'd agreed to take his crops as soon as he could get them out.

"Truth is, they ought to bring a premium this year," Matthews had said. "What with the war goin' on an' all, there's a demand for the produce, and with so many men bein' off to do the fightin', not as much will be grown as in years past. It'll be a sellers' market, that's for sure."

Kirby had done some figuring and thought the chances were good that he would be able to bring in at least fifteen hundred dollars. He planned to save as much of it as he could to have for his father and brother when they came back home.

If they came back home.

Reports had already been received from a battle that happened in April at a place called Shiloh. Kirby had never heard of Shiloh, and he didn't know if his pa or Luke had fought in that battle or not. If so, he was reasonably sure that they hadn't been killed. The casualties for Stone County, including names from both participating armies, had been posted on the door of the courthouse in Galena. Neither Emmett nor Luke's name was on the list, but Lee Willoughby's name was.

So far, the family had received only two letters from Emmett. In one of them, he told them that he and Luke had been split up, and he had no idea where Luke was. They hadn't heard from Luke.

Kirby was thinking about this when he got the whiff of an awful smell.

"Hell's bells, Ange!" he swore at the mule. "Ain't you got no better sense than to fart in a man's face? Damn. You are the fartin'ess mule I've ever seen. Why ain't you more like Rhoda? She don't hardly ever fart. I guess she's more of a lady than you are a gentleman." Kirby picked up a clod of dirt and threw it at the offending animal.

He was just reaching the end of a row when he saw Janey approaching. "Whoa," he called.

Janey was carrying a canvas bag.

"Hi, sis. You're bringing water, I hope."

Janey smiled. "No. I brought you something better." She reached into the bag and pulled out a jar of tea. "It's sweetened," she said as she handed it to him.

Kirby had worked up quite a thirst during the plowing and he took the sweetened tea with grateful hands, then took several, deep, Adam's apple bobbing swallows, until more than half of it was gone. Finally, he pulled the jar away, wiped his mouth with the back of his hand, and smiled at Janey. "Damn, that was good. If you weren't my sister, I'd marry you," he teased.

"I told you. I'm never goin' to get married. And I wouldn't marry you, even if you weren't my brother. You're too onery."

Kirby drank the rest of the tea, but saved the last mouthful, and spit it out toward his sister.

"Kirby!" Janey complained to his laughter.

"That's what you get for calling me onery." He handed the empty jar back to her. "What's Ma cookin' for supper?"

"What difference does it make? You'll gobble it down like a hog. You always do."

Ange chose that precise moment to let go another fart.

"Oh, what is that awful smell?" Janey screwed up her face and waved her hand back and forth in front of her nose.

"You ain't plowed behind a team of mules a whole lot, have you?" Kirby asked, laughing again. He slapped the reins against the back of the team. "Gee!" he called, and the team turned to the right.

Janey stood at the edge of the field, watching as Kirby started back across the field. She was thankful to him for keeping secret the incident he had happened upon between her and Merlin Lewis. She also realized that he was faithfully fulfilling his promise to their pa to "be the man of the place." She couldn't help but feel a little guilty as she lay in bed every morning when, while still dark, Kirby would go out to harness Ange and Rhoda, then start a full day of plowing. If he found the work too strenuous, he never complained. If he ever had the urge to leave the farm, he never spoke of it.

Janey wanted nothing more in the world than to leave the farm. She hated farming and everything about it. The only reason she was still there was because she felt a sense of obligation to her mother and to Kirby.

She was sixteen but could easily pass for twenty. If she left home now, that's the age she would assume. She was fully developed by the time she was twelve. Although some of the other girls had envied her, it wasn't necessarily a good thing. She sometimes felt as if she were a full grown woman trapped in a young girl's body. She began to have fewer and fewer friends because the things that most interested them seemed childish to her.

The woman she most admired in town was Belle Robb.

She had never spoken to Belle. She knew that her ma would be mortified if she did. But she had watched the woman riding by in the back of a carriage, glancing neither left nor right, either oblivious of, or unconcerned about, the stares and gossip.

What would it be like to have so much money that she didn't care what others thought? Janey wondered.

She also wondered what it would be like to be with a man . . . not a boy like Merlin Lewis, but a real man.

As Kirby started back toward the house that evening with thoughts of supper on his mind, he was surprised to see three mounted riders out front. The riders were wearing military uniforms . . . and the uniforms were blue.

"What's this about?" He hurried, not bothering to take the team to the barn, but going directly to the house. His ma and sister were standing on the porch, talking to the soldiers.

"Ma, what's going on?" he asked.

"Nothin' you have to be concerned about," Pearl replied. "They've come to try 'n take you into the army."

"Wouldn't you like to serve your country, boy?" asked the soldier who had three stripes on his sleeve.

"His father and his older brother are already serving," Pearl said. "Kirby is only fourteen years old. Is the government drafting fourteen-year-olds now?

"Beggin' your pardon, ma'am, but he sure don't look like no fourteen-year-old."

"Can you read, Sergeant?" Pearl asked.

"Yes, I can read."

"I got his name wrote in the Bible, along with his sister's and older brother's names. That tells when they was born. If you can read and cipher, you can figure out for yourself how old he is. Do you want to see the Bible?"

"How would I know you didn't just put down when he was born so's to keep him from gettin' took into the army?" the sergeant asked. "Is that true, boy? Are you only fourteen?"

Kirby looked the soldier in the eye. "You ain't callin' my ma a liar, are you, mister? 'Cause I don't think I'd take too kindly to that."

"Feisty, ain't he?" the sergeant said to the two soldiers with them. They laughed.

"All right, boy. We'll take your ma's word for it. But if this war's still goin' on when you come of age, you need to think about your duty and come join up with us. Come on, men, we're gettin' nothin' done here."

Kirby watched the men ride away.

"You didn't tell 'em Pa and Luke had joined up with the Gray, did you, Ma?"

Pearl shook her head. "I thought it would be best not to. Supper will be ready soon."

"I'll be in soon as I put the mules away."

Supper was pork chops, poke salad, and corn bread. As Janey had predicted, Kirby ate heartily.

The little town of Lamar, Missouri, was sleeping when Angus Shardeen approached it on the July morning. He held his hand up to stop the thirty-six men riding with him.

"What do we hit first, Angus?" Billy Bartell, Angus's second in command, asked.

"Start by burnin' the houses," Shardeen said. "That'll get ever'one drawn out to put out the fires and save the citizens, then we'll be able to ride on into town without much opposition, I'm thinkin'."

Bartell stood in his stirrups, then looked back toward the other riders. "All right men, get them torches lit!" he shouted.

A match was struck to light one torch, then it was used to pass the light on down until twenty torches were aflame.

"Let's go, men! Burn the town!" Shardeen shouted.

The group rode into town at a gallop. As they encountered the first houses, they tossed the torches toward them. Citizens ran out into the street and were shot down without regard to age or sex. By the time Shardeen's men reached the middle of town, at least eight houses were burning and sixteen men, women, and children had been shot down.

The Jayhawkers stopped in front of the town's only hotel.

"Bartell," Shardeen ordered. "Take five men down to the marshal's office and kill anyone you find there."

"What if somebody's in jail?"

"Kill them, too," Shardeen ordered. "Tompkins, find the newspaper editor and bring him to me."

One hour later, ten women and girls were being held in one of the Lamar Hotel rooms. Shardeen was in the dining room, enjoying the breakfast he had forced the cook to prepare for him. He looked at the emergency broadsheet he had forced the newspaper to print.

PEOPLE OF LAMAR

YOUR TOWN HAS BEEN CAPTURED BY THE SHARDEEN RAIDERS. TEN OF YOUR WOMEN ARE BEING HELD PRIS-ONER. THE TOWN IS BEING CHARGED A RANSOM OF FIVE THOUSAND DOLLARS FOR THEIR RELEASE. IF THE MONEY HAS NOT BEEN COLLECTED BY THREE O'CLOCK THIS AFTERNOON, THE WOMEN WILL BE KILLED.

BY ORDER OF COLONEL ANGUS SHARDEEN,
COMMANDING OFFICER

"Yes," Shardeen said after reading the paper. He smiled and handed it back. "This is exactly what I want. Now, print enough copies so everyone in town will be sure to see it."

"Don't hurt the women, please," the newspaper editor begged.

"If you do your job, and if the town responds, none of the women will be killed."

"Bartell?" Shardeen said after the editor left.

"Yeah?"

"Which one of the women is the best lookin' one?"

"Well, the best lookin' one would be the mayor's daughter. But you almost couldn't call her a woman, seein' as I don't think she's much over fourteen or fifteen."

"Then she's woman enough. I'm goin' upstairs to find me a room. Bring 'er to me."

"All right if I take 'er after you get 'er broke in?"

"Fine with me."

One hour later, Brenda Tadlock, fourteen-year-old daughter of the mayor of Lamar, lay dead in the alley behind the hotel. Bartell never got his chance at her. Brenda had jumped out of the window as soon as Shardeen left her alone in the room.

News of the Shardeen raid on Lamar spread throughout southwest Missouri. Small communities held meetings to discuss the possible organization of a militia to defend themselves should such an attack occur against their town.

"What good would a militia do?" Tom Byrd asked in Galena. "Most of the fightin' age men are already gone. The rest of us is on farms outside of town. Why, by the time you got us mobilized, it would be too late."

"Tom's right," another said.

After an hour of discussion, it was finally decided that raising a city militia would not be possible. The meeting disbanded without any action.

Kirby had come to town, hoping that some sort of militia would be formed, because he was sure that they would take him. He was disappointed with the results of the meeting.

Janey had come with him and, as the meeting was being conducted, had gone to Bloomberg's Mercantile to buy some jars for canning. She was surprised to see Belle Robb there. It was the first time she had ever seen the woman anywhere but riding in her carriage. Looking around to make certain that she wasn't being observed, Janey mustered up the courage to approach the notorious madam. "Hello, Miss Robb."

Belle glanced up, obviously surprised at being addressed by a local citizen. When she saw that it was a young and very beautiful girl who had spoken, and not one of the matriarchs of the town, she smiled. "Hello, dear. Can I help you with something?"

"No, I just wanted to say hello."

"How nice of you."

"Also, I was wondering how . . . I mean, suppose someone wanted to do what you do, how would—" Janey stopped in mid-sentence. "Uh, never mind. I have no right to bother you."

"What is it, exactly, that you think I do, dear?"

"I don't know, exactly, what you do," Janey admitted. "All I know is that you are the most beautiful woman I have ever seen. And you seem to be rich."

Belle laughed. "Oh, believe me, I am rich, Miss . . . what is your name?"

"Janey. Janey . . ." She started to tell her last name but at the last minute thought better of it. "Just Janey."

"Well, 'just Janey,' not everyone can do what I do."

"I suppose not. I'm sure that someone would have to be very beautiful."

"Don't you worry about that. You are certainly beautiful enough. But it takes more than beauty. It takes someone who has the ability to put aside what others may think or say about her. Do you think you could do that?"

"I . . . I don't know. I've never actually thought about it."

"But you are thinking about it now?"

"Maybe."

"Why?"

"The farm," Janey said with a dismissive wave of her hand. "You don't know what it's like. It's nothing but work and drudgery from dawn to dusk. And the thought of marrying a farmer and living the rest of my life that way is almost more than I can take."

"You're wrong, honey. I know exactly what it's like. I was raised on a farm near New Madrid, Missouri. Not a large plantation with slaves to do our every bidding, mind you, but a small pig farm. I couldn't wait to get out of there."

"Then you *do* understand," Janey said with a broad smile.

"Oh, yes. I understand all right. How old are you, Janey?"

"I'm . . . uh . . . eighteen."

Belle smiled. "How old are you, really?"

"Seventeen," Janey lied.

"I'll tell you what. Wait a year. When you're eighteen, come visit me and we'll have a long talk."

"A talk about what?"

"Why, Janey, we'll talk about anything you want to talk about," Belle said.

"All right, and thanks. I'm sorry I bothered you."

"Oh, honey, you have been nothing but nice to me. How could that possibly be a bother?"

Later, as Janey was loading her purchases into the buckboard, a man approached her. She thought he might be the most handsome man she had ever met. His dark hair was perfectly combed, he had a neatly trimmed moustache, and he was wearing a dark green jacket with mustard-colored pants which were tucked down into highly polished boots. The vest was white, and a pearl pin was stuck in the red ascot at his throat.

"May I be of assistance, Janey?"

"Thank you, I— How do you know my name?"

"I heard you give your name to Belle."

"You . . . were listening to our conversation? Sir, you should have made your presence known."

"I feared that to do so might cause you some embarrassment. Please forgive me if I erred."

"What is your name?"

"Paul Garner at your service." He lifted his finger to his eyebrow.

"Mr. Garner . . ."

"Please, it is Paul."

"Paul, how is that you aren't away at war?"

Garner laughed. "You do get right to the point, don't you?"

"My pa, my brother, so many of the county men are at war. I was just wondering why you weren't, is all."

"Do you believe in this war, Janey?"

"I've never given any thought to whether I believe in it or not."

"Well, I *don't* believe in it. I don't believe in the concept of holding men and women as slaves. I don't own any myself, nor have I ever, and I won't fight a war so those who do own slaves can keep them.

"On the other hand, I think if some states want to break away and go out on their own, they certainly should have the right to do so. I won't fight for an army that would force a state to belong to a union to which it no longer wishes to belong.

"So, as you see, Janey, I see nothing noble or uplifting about either belligerent party in this war. Were I to go, I would have no idea which side to support. Therefore, I have made the conscious choice to remain neutral."

"I've never heard anyone talk like you do," Janey said.

"You mean in my observation of the futility of the war?"

"No. Yes, but I mean, I've never heard anyone use pretty words the way you do. Not even my teacher talked like that. That is, when I had a teacher. She's gone now. Besides, it's been a long time since I was a schoolgirl. Are you an educated man, Paul?"

"Yes. I attended school at Westminster College in Fulton," Paul said.

"What do you do for a living?"

"I'm a peddler."

"A peddler? You mean like Mr. Gray, who goes about in a wagon selling pots, pans, notions, and the like?"

"Not exactly. I sell money."

"Money? How do you sell money?"

"I deal in investments. People invest in me and I make money for them. When I make money for them, I also make money for myself."

"I've never heard of such a thing."

"It can be quite lucrative," Paul said with a broad smile.

She tried not to smile back. "I must get back home," Janey said.

Again, Paul touched his eyebrow. "It has been a most pleasant few minutes, Janey. I do hope we see each other again."

They did see each other again, several times, at first meeting "by chance" in town, until finally, Garner took the bold step of going to the farm where Janey introduced him to her mother and brother.

"I don't like him," Kirby said after a few visits.

"He seems like a nice enough young man," Pearl said.

"I can't help but feel like he has somethin' up his sleeve. Ma, he has to be twenty-three or -four, or somethin' like that. And Janey's only sixteen. What's he doin' hangin' around her? Don't you think she's too young for him?"

"Kirby, you know that Janey ain't none like you or Luke. Ever since she was a little girl, she's been more like a feral cat than a tame kitten. Your pa and I have worried a lot about that girl, wonderin' what is going to become of her. It could be that this feller, Paul Garner, is just what Janey needs. And I warn't but seventeen when I was married."

"I hope so, Ma. But I don't mind tellin' you, he seems

a bit uppity to me. I'll keep quiet about it, though. Who am I to tell Janey who she should or shouldn't like?"

"I would appreciate you doin' that," Pearl said.

Frequent and nourishing rains throughout the long summer ensured a bumper crop and, as Fred Matthews had suggested, it was a sellers' market when Kirby took his harvest in to peddle. He was paid $2,088, which was the biggest single year, ever, for the little farm.

"What are you plannin' on doin' with that two thousand dollars you made from selling your crops?" Paul Garner asked during one of his frequent visits.

"What makes you think I made two thousand dollars?" Kirby asked, obviously irritated by the question.

"Why, Janey told me."

"She had no business telling you."

"Janey and I have no secrets between us," Garner said.

"Yeah, well this ain't just between you 'n Janey. This is the whole family, and as far as I'm concerned, you got no business knowin' anything about it."

"I can understand your concern, but my interest is more than mere curiosity. The reason I asked, is because if you will trust me, I can double your money for you in no time."

"How?"

"As I explained to your sister, I deal in money. My profession is to invest money in certain mathematical probabilities, doing so in such a way as to maximize the return."

"Sounds to me like you're usin' big words to say that you are a gamblin' man."

Garner laughed out loud. "Yes, in any investment transaction there is a degree of risk, so, I suppose you could call it gambling. But the degree of risk is inversely proportional to the skill with which the transaction is handled."

"Garner, you can use all the big words you want, I'll not be trusting you with money that I broke my back for most a year to earn. Except for what it takes my ma, my sister, 'n me to live on, I'm puttin' the rest of the money away so that when Pa comes back home, we'll have a good stake to start with."

"Have you not read the Bible?" Garner asked. "Are you not aware of the parable of the talents?"

"I don't know what you are talking about."

"In the Book of Matthew, it tells of a wealthy master who left money with three of his servants. Two of his servants invested the money so they could give even more of it to the master when he returned. But the third buried the money he was given, and when the master returned, that servant gave him only what had been left with him. 'You wicked, lazy servant! You should have put my money on deposit with the bankers, so that when I returned I would have received it back with interest.' "Is that how you want to face your father when he returns, not with an increase, but only with what he left?"

"That don't apply to me," Kirby said. "Pa didn't leave me any money. He left me only a team of mules and forty acres of rock and dirt. I wasn't given the money I'm holdin' for him. I earned it."

"Yes, and you are to be commended for it," Garner said. "I only wanted to help, is all. Of course, it is your money and you should do with it as you wish."

* * *

"You were rude to Paul," Janey said to Kirby later that evening after Garner left.

"I wasn't rude. I was honest with him. He has no business bein' concerned with how much money we have, and you had no business tellin' him."

"Why not?"

"Janey, I'm going to have to agree with your brother on this," Pearl said. "Your pa always said it's best that not ever'one knows our business."

"I'm sorry," Janey said. "I didn't mean nothin' by it. I was just bragging on you, Kirby. I'm real proud of what you have done."

"I'm just askin' you not to share all our business with him. Sometimes it's good to keep secrets."

The expression on Kirby's face reminded Janey that he had kept a secret for her, and she understood exactly what he was saying. "All right, Kirby. I won't say anything else about it. Please don't be mad at me."

Kirby smiled, and kissed his sister on the cheek. "I'm not mad at you, Janey. I just want you to be careful, that's all."

After their initial meeting in Bloomberg's Mercantile, Janey had become more bold, frequently visiting Belle in her place of business. On one of her visits, one of the customers—Belle referred to them as "guests"—mistook Janey for one of the girls who worked there.

"She is not on the line," Belle said. "And I'll expect you to honor the code that we all follow here. Just as the visits of my guests are kept secret, so too shall the presence of my friend be kept secret. If I ever hear anything spoken about her, I will hold you responsible, and the consequences will be grave."

Belle's admonition to her clients had been heeded, and men that Janey recognized—married men and officials of the town—were confident that knowledge of their visits would not go beyond Belle's establishment. Janey was equally confident that her secret was safe, and she and Belle's clients developed a symbiotic relationship.

"It's called a rubber," Belle said, showing it to Janey.

She had asked how it was that the girls who worked for her didn't get pregnant.

"After it is used, it must be washed very thoroughly to make certain that nothing is left in it. Then it should be lubricated and put it back into its box."

"And that will keep me, uh, I mean the girl from getting—?"

Belle looked at Janey knowingly. She nodded. "Yes. It will. I've made every man I've ever been with use it before I will let him lie with me, and I've never gotten pregnant. You are asking about this for yourself, aren't you?"

"Yes," Janey replied rather sheepishly.

"Paul Garner?"

"Yes. I've been lucky so far but every time, I'm frightened as to what would happen if I got pregnant. How would I face my Ma and Pa?"

"It's probably smart of you to have him wear this."

"What will I say to him to make him use it?"

"All you have to do is ask him. He has used it before. Many times, I suspect. I see no reason why he wouldn't use it with you."

"He has?"

Belle put her hand on Janey's shoulder. "Honey, you didn't think you were getting a virgin, did you?"

"No. No, I guess not."

CHAPTER 5

April 1863

The day was unseasonably warm. Kirby was walking behind the plow being pulled by the two mules, Ange and Rhoda, opening the ground to plant this year's corn. He was at the far end of a row when he heard a scream coming from the house. He didn't know if the scream came from his mother or his sister, but it didn't matter. It was a scream of absolute terror. He dropped the reins and started for the house on a dead run.

He heard another scream and saw smoke curling up into the sky. Reaching the fence, he saw at least a dozen men carrying hams and sides of bacon, taken from the smokehouse before it had been set afire.

Jayhawkers!

Janey was on the ground naked. Her clothes had been torn off.

"Spread 'er legs out, boys. I'm goin' to have me a little of this." The raider was a big ugly man with only half of one ear.

"Get away from her!" Pearl attacked the man.

Their leader was standing off to one side, watching it all. He had red hair, a red beard, and a scar that started at the corner of his mouth, then zigzagged like a lightning bolt up the side of his face, ending with a deformed eye. The horse next to him had a dark blue saddle blanket. In a corner was the silver eagle insignia of a colonel outlined in gold.

Kirby knew the man was Angus Shardeen!

"What the hell, Bartell? Can't you handle a young girl and an old woman?" Shardeen asked with a demonic laugh. He raised his gun and shot Kirby's mother in the chest. She flew backwards as if being yanked violently by an invisible rope, then fell and was dead before she even hit the ground.

"Ma!" Kirby shouted as he ran toward her fallen form. Before he reached her, Shardeen brought the butt of his gun down on Kirby's head, and he went down as well.

Kirby came to lying on the ground. For a long moment, he tried to understand what he was doing there. He turned his head, saw his mother lying nearby, and knew that she was dead. In that moment, he remembered what happened.

"I see you aren't dead." The words came from his sister, and they were spoken in a flat and totally unemotional tone of voice.

Looking toward her, Kirby saw that she was sitting on the front porch. She was dressed, and there was a bag sitting beside her.

"Janey." He sat up and felt a sharp pain in the back of his head. Reaching up, he felt blood.

"I didn't know if you was dead or alive," Janey said.

"I reckon I'm alive. How are you?"

"What do you mean, how am I? You know how I am. You seen me lyin' on the ground, bein' used by all of them."

Kirby was surprised to see that, rather than crying uncontrollably, she seemed to express only anger. He was oddly proud of her for showing such gumption.

"I'm sorry I didn't get here in time to stop them." Gingerly, Kirby stood up.

"What could you have done? If you woulda got here any earlier, you'd more 'n like be lyin' there dead, like Ma."

Kirby walked slowly to the porch and sat on the step. "Janey, let's don't tell Pa how Ma died. He don't need to know that while he was off fightin' in the war 'n all, that Shardeen's Raiders come here and killed her. Let's tell him that she died peacefully in her sleep. I think he'll takc it somewhat easier, that way."

Janey shrugged. "You can tell him anythin' you want. I won't be here."

"What do you mean, you won't be here?"

"Paul's been tryin' to get me to run off with 'im. The only reason I ain't done so before now is because of Ma. But what with she bein' dead 'n all, I don't see nothin' to keep me here any longer."

"You can't go, Janey. You're my sister. With Ma gone, I need to look after you."

"Yeah, and you did such a good job of it, didn't you?" Janey asked sarcastically.

"I—" Kirby hung his head. "I'm sorry. You're right. I didn't do such a good job of it, did I?"

"It wasn't your fault. Like I said, there wasn't nothin' you coulda done, anyhow."

"But what will I tell Pa when he comes back and finds you're gone?"

"Tell him anything. Tell him I ran off with a peddler."

"Will you at least stay here till I get Ma buried?" Kirby asked.

"Where you goin' to bury her?"

"Up on the hill, I reckon," Kirby said, pointing. "She always liked it up there. She'd go up there to watch the sunsets."

"All right. You go dig her grave, and I'll get her changed into her best dress. I wouldn't want to see her buried in that old work dress."

"Thanks."

"Soon as she's buried, I'm leavin'. I'd like you to drive me into town, but if you don't, I'll walk. 'Cause believe me, brother, I am leaving."

It took Kirby the better part of an hour to dig the grave, but he threw himself into the work to keep from being overwhelmed by grief. He tried to hold back the tears that welled up in his eyes. His father would not have cried. Kirby would not, either. Still, he could not get the horrific image out of his mind of his mother being slaughtered. The woman had given him life, had loved him and his brother and sister with all her heart.

Halfway through the digging, Janey came up to stand beside him. She was still in a state of shock, Kirby knew.

"I got her nice dress on her, but I was thinkin' that if we don't have a box to put her in, the dress will get all messed up when you start throwin' the dirt back into the hole."

"I was thinkin' about that as well, and I got it all figured out," Kirby said.

"What are you goin' to do?"

"The trough we put the hay in to feed the mules is big enough for her. I'll put her in that, then I'll find somethin' to close off the top. It won't be nothin' fancy, but it'll make a passable coffin."

Janey nodded. "Yes. Yes, it will. But, once we get Ma in it, how will we get it up here? I think it'll be too heavy, even for the both of us to handle."

"Soon as I get her into it, I'll hook Ange up to it and let him pull her uphill."

"That's a good idea."

Kirby saw tears in Janey's eyes.

Forty-five minutes later, the feeding-trough-cum-coffin, its top closed with a door from the tack room, had been dragged up the hill, lowered in the grave, and covered.

"All right. Let's go," Janey said.

Kirby raised a hand. "Hold on a moment. Don't you think we ought to say a few words?"

"What for? There ain't neither one of us preachers."

"No, but she was our ma. Seems to me, the least we could do is say a few words over her grave."

'You're right. I'm sorry. Go ahead. Say somethin'."

Kirby took off the hat he'd been wearing to protect him from the sun and held it in front of him as he looked down at the grave. "You was a good ma. You done what you could with us, and I appreciate it, an' loved you for it. I know that I didn't tell you that I loved you as much as I should have, but I never was much for speakin' a lot of words. I reckon I just thought that you always knew.

"Listen, Ma. I ain't goin' to tell Pa how it is that you died. I mean, gettin' killed 'n all. I don't figure it's somethin' he needs to know right away. The time's goin' to come when you 'n him will be together again an' I reckon if you want to, you can tell 'im then, how it was that you died."

Kirby quit speaking, and after a moment of silence, he glanced across the grave at Janey. Tears were rolling down her face.

"You goin' to say somethin'?"

Janey nodded. "Ma, I don't know as I'll ever have any children. I know that I don't want to . . . 'cause I could never be as good a ma as you was. I know I was always a big disappointment to you, and I reckon that while you'll be lookin' down on me, I'll be even more of a disappointment. But, all I can say about that is that I'm sorry." Janey grew quiet then.

Kirby waited for a moment before he spoke again. "That was real good, Janey. I know Ma heard you."

"Will you take me into town now?"

Kirby nodded. "Yeah, I'll take you to town."

It was as if Janey had dropped off the face of the earth. Kirby never heard another word from her, and when he checked on Paul Garner, he learned that he was gone, too. He didn't want to ask around town about his sister, figuring it was nobody else's business that he had lost track of her.

With his mother dead and his sister gone, Kirby was all alone. That didn't actually bother him all that much. On the contrary, he learned to appreciate the solitude.

As he was sitting out on the front porch one day, wondering if he should get a dog, he heard the sound of galloping horses. His first thought was to hide, but he decided not to. It was his farm, and he'd be damned if he would be run off his own property.

Twelve mounted men followed a rider carrying a dark blue flag—the Kansas state flag. Kirby had seen it when the Jayhawkers killed his ma. The riders didn't stop, but continued on at a full gallop.

As it turned out, they were being pursued. No more than fifteen minutes later, another group came riding through, carrying a black flag with a blood red cross. Kirby knew they were part of Bloody Bill Anderson's group.

They stopped when they saw Kirby standing on his front porch. Three of the riders rode toward him. One was wearing a hat with a long, sweeping feather, one was in buckskins, and the third was a young rider who couldn't have been more than a year older than Kirby.

"Boy, did you see a bunch of riders comin' this way?" Anderson asked.

"Fifteen, maybe twenty minutes ago. Headin' west, they were," Kirby replied.

"Jayhawkers?"

"That's what I figure."

"Where's your pa?"

"He's away fightin'. Him 'n my brother."

"Which side is he fightin' for?"

"They's fightin' for the Gray. Same as you."

"What about your ma?"

"She was killed by Angus Shardeen."

"You're runnin' this place all by yourself, are you?"

"Yeah."

"That's quite a responsibility for a boy no older 'n you," said the one in buckskins.

Kirby stood tall. "I'm old enough."

Anderson chuckled. "He's got you there, Gleason."

"I reckon he does, seein' as he's doin' it. Tell me, boy, is it all right if we water our horses, here?"

"Sure. Go right ahead."

Anderson and Gleason went back to water their horses, but the young man who had ridden up with him, hung back. He spoke for the first time. "What's your name?"

"Jensen. Kirby Jensen."

"You got a gun, Jensen?"

"I got a shotgun."

"That ain't good enough. You need a gun you can tote." The young man had two pistols, one in a holster, and a second stuck down in his belt. He pulled the gun from his belt, and tossed it down to Kirby. Then, reaching into his pocket, he grabbed an extra cylinder and tossed it down to him, as well.

"The gun and the cylinder are already loaded. When it comes time for you to have more ammunition, it takes a .36 caliber. You think you can remember that?"

Kirby held out the pistol to examine it. The initials *JJ* were carved into the handle.

"I reckon I can remember that. You're givin' me this pistol, are you?"

"I am."

"These initials, *JJ*. What do they stand for?"

"They stand for my name. Jesse James."

"Dingus, get on back over here 'n get your horse

watered. We ain't goin' to spend the night here," another man called, only slightly older than Jesse.

"Dingus?" Kirby asked.

"That's my brother, Frank. He took to callin' me that when we was kids, and it sort of stuck."

With a nod of his head, Jesse James rode over to the nearby stream to water his horse.

Kirby watched them ride off. He looked at the pistol for a moment longer, then he aimed it at a nearby tree and pulled the trigger. The pistol boomed, he felt the recoil, and he saw a chip of bark fly away. He had hit his target.

When Janey left Missouri with Paul Garner, she thought she knew him. She found out quickly that she knew virtually nothing about him. The investments and the financial risks he spoke of were nothing but wagers. Paul Garner was a gambler . . . a card shark.

"This"—he smiled a huge smile, holding up the two thousand dollars Janey had given him to invest—"is going to make us very rich."

"Not just us," Janey replied. "As soon as we can, I want to replace that money. Kirby doesn't know I took it. He doesn't even know that I knew where he had hidden it."

She'd also expected Garner to marry her, but it hadn't happened.

"You'll be a lot more valuable to me if we aren't married," Garner had said.

"What does that mean?"

"Well, just think about it, Janey. If you are my wife, nobody is going to want to flirt with you. But if you aren't married, why every drover, driver, clerk, and soldier will think you are fair game, and they'll all believe they have a chance to crawl into bed with you. And that's going to make us a lot of money."

"Paul! Are you telling me that you want me to be a prostitute for you?"

"No, you don't understand. You won't have to lie with any man. In fact, I don't want you to." Garner had reached out to put his fingers on her cheek. "You're my woman, and I don't want to share you with anyone else. I just want you to make the others *think* you are available."

Garner gave her lessons on how to act as a distraction. She would wait for his signal and then, at an opportune time, approach a table, making certain that the player Garner had picked out would be paying more attention to her than to the game at hand.

The dresses she wore were cut so low that they left little to the imagination and though she had made friends with some of the bar girls, she wasn't one of them. At first, the other girls were a little resentful, but when they learned that she wasn't in competition with them in any way, they actually welcomed her presence. Having one more, very seductively dressed girl in the saloon increased the business traffic for all of them. They also learned that she had her own reason for being there, dressed as she was.

Neither Janey nor the others knew that Garner wasn't using her just to prevent a man from playing his best game. He was using her as a diversion in order to allow him to cheat his mark. The best plans often went awry, however. Despite Janey's most seductive attire and actions, the two thousand dollar poke they had was steadily diminishing.

"I thought you said you could double the money!" Janey had cried, concerned at how fast the money was dwindling. "We've got less than a thousand dollars left! I have to get this money back. Don't you understand? I stole it from my own father and brothers!"

Garner had been unconcerned. "Relax. In any game of chance, you are going to have your ups and downs. The secret to success is not to panic. We'll recover this sooner than you think. Then we can go on to make some real money."

At the moment, Janey was sitting at a table in the back of the Red Bull Saloon, playing a game of solitaire.

A bar girl named Callie approached the table. "Janey, would you be a dear and take this beer to that man sitting by the piano? He just ordered it, but I have to go upstairs for a while."

"Sure, I'll take it to him," Janey replied. Folding up the deck of cards she took the beer to the man Callie had pointed out.

"I was hoping you'd stop by to see me sometime," the man said. "You aren't like the other girls. You don't seem to get around to all the men."

"I don't work here," Janey replied. "I just come here as a customer, the same as you."

"Really? Well that's—"

"You cheatin' son of a—" someone shouted, followed by the sound of a gunshot.

Janey looked toward the table where Garner was playing cards and saw him sitting in his chair with a pained expression on his face. His hands were clasped across his chest and blood was spilling through his fingers.

"Paul!" she shouted, rushing across the room to him.

"Where were you?" Garner asked accusingly. "I gave you the sign and you weren't there. Now I've been—"

He was unable to finish his sentence.

Kirby bought several boxes of .36 caliber cartridges. He didn't have a holster, so he carried the pistol Jesse James had given him stuck into his waistband. With no holster, he wasn't able to practice drawing, but he was able to practice shooting. He quickly became exceptionally adept in the use of a pistol.

He had always been good with a rifle and a shotgun, and had proven that skill as a hunter almost from the time he was five. However, he had no basis of comparison as far as shooting a pistol was concerned. He knew only that he was consistently hitting anything he shot at.

Not long after an afternoon of target practice, he heard the approach of a group of riders, and quickly climbed up into the loft of the barn. He would stay out of sight, but if he was discovered and their intention was hostile, he was determined to shoot as many as he could before they got him.

When he saw that they were carrying a Confederate flag, he called out to them, then climbed down.

"Where is everyone else?" the leader of the group asked.

"There ain't nobody else."

"You're here all alone?"

"My ma was killed by Jayhawkers, my sister run away to I don't know where, and my pa and brother are off fighting in the war."

"For which side?"

Kirby pointed to the flag. "That's the flag they're fightin' for."

The leader nodded. "If your ma was killed by Jayhawkers, that's who I would expect them to be fighting for. The name is Asa Briggs."

Kirby nodded. "I've heard of you, Mr. Briggs, and I thought this might be you."

"I see you've got a pistol. What were you planning on doing with it?"

"If you had been Jayhawkers, I figured to shoot as many as I could before you got me."

Briggs chuckled. "Did you now? Can you shoot?"

"Yes sir."

"How well can you shoot?"

Kirby shrugged. "I don't know. Pretty good, I reckon."

"You want to show me?"

"All right."

Kirby picked up a pecan and handed it to him.

"That's a pretty small target. You sure you don't want to pick something a little larger?"

"No, this is big enough. Put it on that fence post over there."

"Boy, that's got to be more 'n a hundred feet," Briggs said. "You sure you don't want it a little closer?"

"No, put it there."

The other riders realized what was going on, and all conversation and watering stopped as they turned to watch the shooting demonstration.

"I got a dollar says he misses," someone said.

When nobody took the bet, Briggs spoke up. "I'll take the bet." He put the pecan on the post Kirby had pointed out to him.

Kirby raised the pistol to eye level, aimed, and pulled the trigger. Pieces of the pecan flew off the post.

The riders gasped and shouted in disbelief.

"Damn," Briggs said, a wide smile spreading across his face. "Damn! Who taught you to shoot? I ain't never seen nothin' like that."

"I just sort of taught myself," Kirby said, pleased by the accolades.

"Tell me, boy. Do you want to stay here and break dirt, and maybe get burned out again? Or would you like to go after Shardeen and take a little revenge?"

"I can't leave my mules."

"All right."

"But I'm pretty sure Mr. Byrd will look after them for me."

"Then grab your mules, and let's go."

Paul Garner had been caught cheating, so every cent he had on him—five hundred and seventeen dollars—was divided evenly among all the men who had been playing with him at the time he was killed. That represented the rest of the money Janey had brought to their partnership, which meant she was left virtually penniless . . . except for Garner's pearl stick pin and gold money clip, which she took.

She was forced to leave Ft. Worth but had money enough to go only as far as Dallas.

She tried for a little while to earn an honest living, working in a boardinghouse, but the treatment was brutal, and the pay was barely enough to keep body and soul together. Then one day she saw a woman driving a surrey. The woman was attractive, well dressed, and heavily made up. She didn't recognize the woman, but she did recognize the woman's profession.

"They call her Chicago Sue," explained one of the other women who worked at the boardinghouse. "They say she's a"—in her early fifties, the speaker was clearly embarrassed by the subject of the conversation, and she lowered her voice before completing her sentence—"an immoral woman. But I think she is somebody that immoral girls work for. She's very brazen, the way she promenades around town in her fancy dresses and her surrey. None of the other girls do that."

"Where does she live? Do you know?"

"Somewhere on Griffin Street, I think. They call it the Palace Princess Emporium, and it's the biggest and gaudiest house on the block."

That evening, just before dark, Janey put on one of the dresses she had worn when she was a *distraction* for Garner, and went to the Palace Princess Emporium. She knocked on the door.

Chicago Sue answered it. "Who are you?"

"I'm someone who is going to make you a lot of money," Janey said.

Chicago Sue looked at her and chuckled. "Honey, you just might at that. Come on in."

Janey followed Chicago Sue into her house, through an attractive foyer with a Turkish carpet, and into a drawing room. The walls were covered with a deep crimson wallpaper and the furniture was painted white with a rich gilding of gold that complemented the damask-patterned blue area rugs. The divan and the chairs were shades of greens and blues.

The women sat across from each other and Chicago Sue asked, "Now, dear, where have you worked before?"

Janey started to say that she had worked for Belle Robb but decided against it. She wouldn't be able to answer any questions if Chicago Sue started asking questions about the business. Taking a deep breath, Janey said, "I've never worked anywhere before. At least, not in a place like this."

Chicago Sue frowned. "Oh? And when you say, a place like this, what do you mean?"

"A place this elegant."

The frown left Chicago Sue's face, replaced by a smile. "How sweet of you. Yes, it is elegant, isn't it?"

"Very elegant."

"Have you ever worked as a paid woman before?"

"No."

"Then what brings you to me? It isn't as if you have the usual hard-time story. Not dressed as you are."

"I had a friend who was in the business. I spent some time with her."

"But you didn't go on the line for her? Why not? You obviously have nothing against the concept, or you wouldn't be here."

"I-I guess I just wasn't ready yet."

"But you are now?"

"Yes."

"Please tell me that you aren't a virgin."

"I'm not a virgin."

"Thank God we can get that out of the way then. What is your name?"

"My name is Janey Jensen."

Chicago Sue shook her head. "No, it isn't."

"Of course it is. I know my own name."

"You know it, and now I know it. But I'd strongly advise against using your real name in a business like this. No one does." She smiled. "You don't really think my name is Chicago Sue, do you? It isn't Sue, and hell, I've never even been to Chicago."

Janey laughed. "I didn't think that was your real name."

"Do you want to choose your own name? Or shall I give you a name to use?"

"You give me a name."

"All right." Chicago Sue crossed one arm across her chest and lifted the other to grasp her chin as she studied Janey. "Yes," she finally said. "Yes, it will be perfect for you."

"What will be perfect?"

"Your new name. I've always liked the name Lil. Your new name will be Lil." She shook her head slightly. "No, not just Lil. It will be Fancy Lil."

"Fancy Lil." Janey smiled broadly. "I like it."

"Have you eaten anything?" Chicago Sue asked.

"I had lunch," Janie said.

"Not dinner?"

"No."

"I haven't eaten, either. Come with me. Mrs. Peabody has probably already gone to bed but I'm sure I can rustle us up something."

"Thank you."

"Do you take coffee or tea?"

"Coffee normally, but it seems a little late for that."

Chicago Sue chuckled. "Oh, honey, if you plan to work here, your days and nights will be backward. My girls are just getting started. And a good strong cup of coffee will keep you going."

"All right, coffee then," Janey said.

"Where did you come from?" Sue asked as they walked to the kitchen.

"Fort Worth."

"Nobody comes from Fort Worth. You were somewhere else first. Where is that?"

"Missouri," Janey said without being more specific.

"Something brought you to me, didn't it? I mean, I don't think you grew up thinking that one day you might want to be a soiled dove."

"Soiled dove?"

"It's a rather genteel way we have of referring to ourselves. Other words are so harsh."

"No, I can't say as I grew up wanting to be a soiled dove."

"I wouldn't think so. Are you running from the law or a man?"

"I would say it is more of a situation that I'm running from."

"Are you with child?"

"No."

"That's good. In our business, babies can really complicate things." Chicago Sue took down two cups, then picked up the coffeepot.

"Do you take cream or sugar?"

"I drink it black."

"Smart move," Chicago Sue said as she poured the coffee.

CHAPTER 6

One thing about being with Briggs raiders was that Kirby didn't have to spend all his time with them. The Ghost Riders would take part in an operation or two, then they would disband and he would actually go back home for weeks at a time.

According to Briggs, doing it that way made it less likely that the Yankees would be able to catch up with them.

Late spring, 1864

Kirby returned to Galena, his first time in town in over a month. As he always did when returning home, he checked at the post office, not really expecting to get any mail. To his surprise, he *did* get a letter, but it wasn't from his father, and it was addressed to Mrs. Pearl Jensen. Kirby opened the letter before he even left the post office.

Dear Mrs. Jensen.
It is with much regret that I tell you that your son, Luke Jensen, was killed in battle on Wilderness Creek

*in Northern Virginia. We didn't find the body, but
believe that the Yankees found him on the battlefield
and buried him.*

> *Sincerely,*
> *Colonel Edward Willis*
> *12th Georgia, Commanding*

Kirby folded the letter up and put it in his pocket,
wondering if his pa knew about it. Perhaps not, since
the last word he had received from his pa said that he
and Luke had been separated.

Back outside, Kirby climbed onto Ange's back.
When he was riding with Briggs, he was mounted on a
horse, but the horse didn't belong to him.

Briggs had offered to give him one of the Yankee
horses, but pointed out that it might be dangerous. "If
the Yankee soldiers come through and find you
mounted on one of their horses, they'll hang you for
being a bushwhacker. If not for that, for horse stealing. On the other hand, if they see you ridin' a mule,
they won't give you a second thought."

Briggs had been right. More than once Kirby had
encountered Yankee soldiers, but to the soldiers, he
was nothing more than a farm boy, riding a mule.

Two events occurred in Missouri that had some
bearing on the fate of the war within the state. The first
was on October 26 when Yankees located Bloody Bill
Anderson just outside Glasgow. Though greatly outnumbered, Anderson and his men charged the Union
forces, killing five or six of them before encountering
heavy fire. Only Anderson and Elmer Gleason contin-

ued the attack, Gleason riding side by side with his leader. The others retreated.

Anderson was hit by a bullet behind his ear and killed instantly. Gleason immediately turned and joined the others in retreat. Four other guerrillas were also killed in the attack, but the rest of the men were able to escape.

The second significant event occurred when General Sterling Price was defeated by General James Blunt's Union cavalry in the battle of Newtonia. Price and his entire corps withdrew, effectively ending any real Confederate presence in Missouri. No longer were any regular Confederate troops in Missouri, but sporadic guerrilla operations continued.

Archie Clement led what had been Bloody Bill's guerrillas for a little while after Anderson's death, but the group splintered by mid-November, and most of the men joined Quantrill, though many, realizing that the war was lost, gave up the battle.

Elmer Gleason was the only man of Anderson's original group to join Asa Briggs. Shortly after he joined Briggs' group, he recognized Kirby by the gun he was carrying. "You're the boy Jesse give one of his guns to, ain't you? It was right after your ma was killed, as I recall."

"I'm the one," Kirby said. "I remember you. You're the one who wondered if I was old enough to run the farm."

"You've got a good memory." Gleason was at least fifteen years older, but he and Kirby became very good friends.

Briggs continued to operate as he always had, uniting his group for a particular undertaking, then having them break up and return to their homes. That ruse worked so well that the participation of most members was unknown, even to their nearest neighbors. From time to time, the men would encounter each other in town or on the road but would make no show of recognition.

The Union Army had no idea who was and who wasn't a member of the group, giving credence to the sobriquet "Ghost Riders."

Kirby's biggest disappointment during his time with Briggs was that they had not encountered Angus Shardeen. They came close once, arriving at a farm just in time to save a farmer and his wife.

Shardeen had been through an hour earlier, robbing the smoke house of the cured hams and bacon. In a macabre joke, he had tied a noose around the woman's neck and thrown the rope over a beam protruding from the hayloft of the barn. He placed her on her husband's shoulders so that she would live only as long as he could stand there supporting her.

The farmer was at the point of exhaustion when the Ghost Riders arrived.

"Kirby! Get up there and cut her down!" Asa Briggs ordered, and Kirby stood on his saddle and pulled himself up into the hayloft. He cut the rope just as her husband collapsed.

They stayed with the couple until both had recovered from the ordeal, spending the night in the barn.

"I'm going to kill him," Kirby told Elmer.

"Yeah, we would all like to get our hands on him before this war ends."

"No, not *like* to kill him. I am *going* to kill him," Kirby said. "I'm going to hunt him down, no matter where he is and no matter how long it takes. I don't care whether the war is still going or whether the war has ended. I am going to dedicate myself to finding him. And when I find him, I'm going to kill him."

January 1865

Briggs' Ghost Riders who had not taken part in the battle for Newtonia found themselves in position to, in Briggs' words, "hit the Yankees a lick." They were going to rob the payroll being transported to the Baxter Springs post.

"The best way to hurt 'em is to take their money," Briggs said. "And that's just what we're agoin' to do."

To that end, the Ghost Riders were waiting in a cornfield alongside the Columbus Road in Cherokee County. It was very cold.

Kirby shivered in the early morning chill.

"Damn. Why couldn't we wait and do this in the summer time?" Elmer Gleason complained.

"I don't know," Kirby said. "Do you think it might be because the payroll is comin' today and not this summer?"

"There you go, gettin' all practical on me," Elmer teased.

"Asa! The coach is acomin'!" one of the others called.

"All right. Get ready."

Kirby crept up to the edge of the cornfield, then lay down where he would have a good view of the road. He could hear the rumble and squeak of the approaching coach, as well as the drum of hoofbeats, not only from the team, but also from the eight men who were riding as escort.

Briggs pulled his pistol. "I'm goin' to shoot one of the coach horses. After that, all hell's goin' to break loose, so get ready."

The coach and outriders were close enough that Kirby could hear the driver's whistles and shouts to the team. He didn't like the idea of shooting an innocent horse but knew that in order for the plan to succeed, it would have to be done.

Briggs fired, and the first, off-side horse stumbled and went down, bringing the coach to an immediate halt.

Within the opening seconds, at least four of the Union soldiers were down. Others tried to return fire, but were unable to find a target. They simply fired wildly into the cornfield.

"Let's get outta here!" one of the soldiers shouted, and the others fled at a gallop.

The Ghost Riders cheered, then ran out onto the road and yelled after the retreating soldiers with cat calls and jeers.

The coach driver had been unarmed and had not taken part in the brief battle. He was still sitting on the high seat with his hands in the air.

"Throw down that strong box," Briggs called.

"What for?" the driver replied. "There ain't nothin' in it."

"What do you mean, there ain't nothin' in it? You went to pick up the payroll, didn't you?"

"Yeah, that's what we went to do all right. But the money wasn't there."

"I don't believe you," Briggs said.

"I'll throw down the strong box 'n let you see for yourself."

"All right. Do it."

The driver reached down between his legs.

Briggs pointed his gun and called out, "No, hold it. Climb down here. I'll get the strong box myself."

Nodding, and obviously frightened, the driver climbed down from the high seat.

Briggs climbed up, retrieved the strong box, then tossed it down onto the road. "Open it up."

"Kirby, you're the best shot among us," Elmer said. "Think you can shoot the lock off?"

Kirby nodded, pulled his pistol, and fired. The bullet cut the hasp.

Elmer opened the lid and looked inside. "It's empty."

"I'll be damned." Briggs jumped down from the coach and ordered, "Cut the team loose and let the horses go."

The driver, who still had his hands raised, protested. "No need for that. All I need to do is cut the dead horse free, then I can go on."

"You can go on, but it's goin' to be afoot," Briggs said. "Now, cut the team loose, unless you want to see 'em burn to death when I set fire to the coach."

"No, I wouldn't want to see no more of the horses killed." The driver set about the task Briggs had set for him.

Half an hour later, with the driver and horses gone, the dozen Ghost Riders stood near the burning coach, enjoying the heat it was putting out.

"Boys," Briggs said. "I reckon this war is all but over.

I aim to give it up. You're all free to go wherever you want." He pointed to the coach. "I had planned for this to be the last operation anyway, but I hoped we'd have some Yankee money to divide before we broke up. I'm sorry it didn't work out."

"Hell, Asa, you don't mind if some of us go ahead 'n try 'n get some of that Yankee money, do you?" Elmer asked.

"I don't mind at all, but you're on your own. I'm out of it."

"What are you going to do?" Kirby asked.

"I'm goin' to Texas," Briggs said. "You want to come along?"

"Now, why would he want to do that when he can come with me 'n get some of that Yankee money?" Elmer asked.

Kirby shook his head. "I appreciate the invite from both of you and would be honored to join either one of you, but I reckon my pa will be coming back sometime soon now. I wouldn't want him to come home 'n find nobody waitin' there for him."

"How do you know your pa is still alive?" Elmer asked.

"Truth is, Elmer, I don't know. But if he is, I aim to be there waitin' for him. Most especially since there ain't goin' to be no one else waitin' there for 'im."

Elmer nodded. "I can see that." He stuck his hand out. "Don't know as we'll ever run acrossed each other again, but, don't let nobody never call you boy no more. You're a man, Kirby, and you done proved it more 'n oncet."

* * *

Returning to the farm, the first thing Kirby did was dig up the lidded Mason jar he had buried near the corner of the outhouse. It contained the two thousand dollars he'd received from the crops that first year. If his pa came back, he would give him the money. If he didn't come back, Kirby would have that money to start out on his own.

The stench around the outhouse was pretty intense, but it was for precisely that reason he had chosen to bury the money there. He figured nobody would think someone would choose such a place to bury money, and it was unlikely anyone would make any exploratory digs there.

It took only a few minutes to get to the jar, and with a smile, he reached down to retrieve it. The smile faded when he saw that the money was gone, replaced by a note.

Kirby,
   I took the money to invest with Paul Garner. I figure half of it is mine anyway, and I'll pay you back your half, with interest.

Janey

"Janey! You sorry-assed hellcat!" Kirby shouted at the top of his voice. He threw the jar against the side of the outhouse and watched it shatter.

By June, six months after Kirby made his last ride with the Ghost Riders, the war had been over and done for better than two months. If his father was coming home, he should be along any time.

Kirby had made the conscious decision not to tell his father about his own experiences during the war. His father had been with the regular army. Kirby wasn't sure how he would take to the idea of his son having been a Bushwhacker. He remembered his father's reaction when Luke had said he wanted to join up with George Clark, who was what his pa had said he was—a murderer and an outlaw. Briggs was an irregular, but he had not killed any innocents, nor burned any private homes or farms. Nevertheless, Kirby decided he would keep his participation in such activity to himself.

The very way Briggs had operated during the war, allowing the men to spend a lot of time at home, would help keep his secret. Tom Byrd knew of Kirby's frequent absences because he kept the mules while Kirby was gone. Kirby had told him that he was earning money by delivering messages and, as far as he knew, Byrd still believed that.

Kirby wondered what his pa would say when he learned his daughter had run off? He wondered, also, if he knew his oldest boy was dead?

Kirby was entertaining all these thoughts as he was busy plowing. Because of his guerrilla activity, he had not put in any crops in the previous two years. He didn't think he needed to; after all, there was no need for him to support anyone but himself. And he'd taken comfort from knowing that he had two thousand dollars set aside for when his pa returned.

Or at least, he thought he did.

As he thought about finding the money gone with only Janey's note in the bottle, he got angry again.

Like his mother had said, Janey always was a little wild, but he never would have thought she was a thief. What bothered him more than the thought of her taking the money was her giving it to Paul Garner. It would have been bad enough had she kept it for herself. At least she was family. But to have given it to Paul Garner? That was almost more than Kirby could take.

He would like to run into Garner again, some day. Not as much as he wanted to run into Angus Shardeen, but he would like to encounter him some day, whether Janey was still with him or not.

"Where the hell are you now, Janey?" Kirby asked aloud. "Are you still with that sorry buzzard?"

The plow hit a rock and jolted Kirby out of his musing and back to his surroundings, popping his teeth together and wrenching his arms. "Damn, Ange. Didn't you see that rock?"

Kirby unhooked the plow, running the lines through the eyes of the single tree, and left the plow sitting in the middle of the field. He was late getting the crops in, but no later than anyone else in the hollows and valleys of that part of Missouri. The rains had come and stayed, making fieldwork impossible. But he wanted to get something up before his pa returned. He didn't want his pa to think that he was a wastrel.

Folding and shortening the traces, Kirby jumped onto Ange's back and kicked the mule into movement. He plodded down the turn row on the east side of the field when dust from the road caught his eye. It was one rider, pulling up to the house leading a saddled but riderless horse, a bay.

Wondering who it might be, Kirby touched the

smooth butt of the Navy .36, which he now wore in a holster. As Ange plodded closer to the house, Kirby smiled when he made out the figure in the front yard.

It was his pa.

Kirby slid off the mule and walked over to his father.

"Boy," Emmett Jensen said, looking at his son, "I swear you've grown two feet."

"You've been gone for four years, Pa. Someone my age grows a lot in four years." Kirby wanted to throw his arms around his pa, but didn't. His pa didn't hold with a lot of touching between men. He stuck out his hand and Emmett shook it.

"Strong, too," Emmett commented.

"Thank you. Plowin' will do that for you."

"I expect it will. Crops is late, Kirby."

"Yes, sir. Rains come and stayed."

"I wasn't faulting you, boy." Emmett let his eyes sweep the land. He coughed, a dry hacking. "I seen a cross on the hill overlooking the creek. Would that be your ma?"

"Yes, sir."

"When did she pass?"

"Spring, three years ago," Kirby said, remembering Shardeen's raid and thinking with a twinge of regret, that all the time he had been with Briggs, they had never encountered Shardeen.

"She go hard?"

She was shot down in front of her kids. Was that hard enough? He wanted to share that with his father, and maybe he would someday. There was no need to burden him with that now.

"No, sir, it wasn't hard at all. She went in her sleep. I found her the next morning when I took her coffee and grits."

"Good coffee is scarce. What did you do with the coffee?"

"I drank it," Kirby replied.

"Right nice service?"

She's buried in a feeding trough, covered by a door. Only ones here were Janey and me, and I had to talk Janey into staying until I said a few words. Kirby did not vocalize his thoughts. "Real good service. Folks come from all over to see her off."

Emmett cleared his throat and coughed. "Well, I think I'll go up to the hill and sit with your ma for a while. You put up the horses and rub them down. We'll talk over supper. I assume we got somethin' to eat in the house, don't we?"

"We got some greens. I shot 'n cleaned a squirrel no more 'n a couple hours ago. Was plannin' on fryin' it up. I'll make us some cornbread."

"Sounds good to me." Emmett's eyes flicked over the Navy .36 Colt his son was wearing in a holster. If the sight surprised him, he said nothing about it.

"Pa?"

The father looked at his son.

"I'm glad you're back."

What his pa did then couldn't have astonished Kirby any more, if he had suddenly started dancing. Stepping forward, Emmett put his arms around his son and held him. "I'm glad to be back."

Emmett turned and walked up the hill as Kirby tended to the horses.

* * *

The cross had been handmade, probably by Kirby, Emmett decided. If so, he had done a good job. The particulars were put on the cross with white paint, the words neatly printed.

PEARL VIRGINIA JENSEN
Wife of Emmett Jensen
Oct 13, 1824–April 23, 1862

Emmett wondered why Kirby hadn't mentioned that she was also a mother, but perhaps he felt he wouldn't have room to get it all onto the cross.

He took off his hat and stared down at the grave. Except for the cross, nothing indicated that anyone was buried there. The earth in front of the cross looked no different from the rest of the hill.

"Pearl, I wish I could've been here for you. I don't think this country has ever done anything more foolish than the killin' spree we just come through. I was a part of it when I shoulda been here.

"I don't reckon I need to tell you Luke got hisself killed in this war. An' the reason I don't reckon I need to tell you is, because more 'n likely, you 'n him is together right now." Despite the solemnity of the moment, Emmett smiled. "I hope the first thing you done for 'im when you seen 'im was make him some cornbread so's he could crumble it up in his milk. Lord knows, that boy did like his cornbread 'n milk.

"About Kirby 'n Janey. I didn't do right by them, neither, leavin' 'em here to look after themselves." Emmett looked around the farm. "But truth to tell, I ain't seen hide nor hair of Janey yet. Could be she's fixin' supper, but seein' as how Kirby said he would do it, I think it's more 'n likely that she's gone.

"And speakin' of bein' gone, I ain't told the boy yet, but I plan for me 'n him to get on out of here. Too many memories here. Even the good ones is painful, what with you gone 'n all. It troubles me some to be goin' off 'n leavin' you, but I know that you ain't really here now. You're up in heaven, an' the day'll come when I'll join you. So, I reckon this is the last time I'll be visitin' you like this. I need to get on in with the boy now. We've got some palaverin' to do." Emmett put his hat back on, turned, and walked down the hill.

Over greens, fried squirrel, and corn bread, the father and son ate and talked through the years that they had lost and gained. A few moments of uncomfortable silence came between them occasionally as they adjusted to the time and place, and the fact that their positions had changed.

No change had occurred in the actual relationship; they were still father and son. But Emmett had left a boy; he came home to a man.

"We done our best," Emmett said. "Can't nobody say we didn't. And there ain't nobody got nothin' to be ashamed of."

Kirby hadn't asked him anything about the war, not knowing if he should. He didn't know if his pa wanted to talk about it. But when his pa started talking, Kirby just listened.

"I thought it wrong for the Yankees to burn folks' homes like they done. But it was war, and terrible things happen in war. I didn't know there was that many Yankees in the whole world." Emmett began coughing, a deep, racking cough. It lasted for several seconds before he continued.

"Sometimes when they would come at us, why, we would mow them down like takin' a sickle to wheat. But the Blue bellies just kept on acomin'. You got to give 'em credit for courage. They saw their friends goin' down all around 'em, but they kept on acomin'. Shoot one and five more would take his place."

Emmett was quiet for a moment, and Kirby thought he was finished, but his pa continued. "They weren't near 'bout the riflemen we was, nor the riders neither, but they whupped us fair and square and now it's time to put all that behind us and get on with livin'."

"Yes, sir. That's what I was thinkin'."

Emmett sopped a piece of cornbread through the juice of his greens, and chewed for a time before he spoke again. "You know your brother Luke is dead, don't you?"

"Yes, sir. I didn't know if you knew it or not. I got a letter from a fella named Colonel Willis. He said Luke was killed last year in a place called The Wilderness. Fighting with Lee, wasn't he?"

Emmett nodded, but he was quiet for a moment.

Luke had always been Pa's favorite, or so Kirby had felt.

"We wasn't together, you know. I think I sent your ma a letter tellin' her that we wasn't together no more."

"Yes, sir."

"About the letters." Emmett coughed again. "I know I didn't send many, but it was hard tryin' to find some way to get the mail to go out. How was we to send 'em?

The Yankees wouldn't allow any mail to pass through their lines, and they made a point of interrupting our mail as much as they could. I didn't much cotton to the idea of some Yankee reading one of my letters, so I didn't hardly write none at all.

"But, as for Luke gettin' killed, I prob'ly don't know much more 'n you do. From time to time, messengers would get through between our armies. From what I heard, he was tryin' to get back to The Wilderness. Leastwise, that's what I was told."

"Yes, sir."

"I don't see no sign of your sister Janey, and you ain't brought up her name. What are you holdin' back, Kirby?"

It was the moment Kirby had been dreading.

"She's run off, ain't she?"

"She run off with some fella, Pa. Right after Ma died."

"What kind of feller was he?"

"He was a gambler, I'd say."

"Smooth talker, I'd wager."

"Yes, sir."

"What did his hands look like?"

"Soft."

"You're right. More 'n likely was a gambler. You say this was after your ma died?"

"Yes sir."

"Prob'ly just as good. If she had run off before your ma died, it woulda more 'n likely help kill her." Emmett said it flatly, shaking his head, then rose from the table.

"I've ridden a far piece these last few weeks 'cause I

wanted to get home. I was hopin' I would be comin' home to Pearl, but what is past is past 'n there's no point in chewin' on it. Now I'm home, and I'm tired. Reckon you are too, son. We'll get some sleep, then we'll have us a talk in the morning. I got a plan." He covered his mouth and coughed.

Breakfast was meager the next morning—grits and coffee that was mostly chicory, along with a piece of leftover cornbread. Kirby knew that his pa was working up to say something, and he was anxious to hear what it was, but he waited.

Finally, washing down the last piece of bread with the last swallow of coffee, Emmett began to speak. "I spent some time talkin' to your ma last night, 'n I'm goin' to tell you what I told her. I don't think it's good to stay here, boy. Too many memories and the land's got too many rocks to farm. You got 'ny money left from four years of farmin' since I been gone? I figure crops prob'ly brought in a fair price, bein' as so many farmers was off fightin' in the war."

Kirby wanted to tell his pa about the two thousand dollars he had been saving, the money that Janey took, but he held his tongue about that. "I . . . uh, ain't got no money at all."

"Ah, don't fret over it. Farmin' is a hard way to make a livin', and truth to tell, I'm proud of you just for supportin' yourself while I was gone.

"We'll sell the mules and milk cows and buy a couple o' good pack horses. The mules is getting too old for where we're goin'. Problem is, they may be too old to even sell. If we can't sell 'em, I'd hate to have to put 'em down."

"We ain't goin' to put Ange and Rhoda down, Pa," Kirby said resolutely. "If that's what it takes for us to go, you just go on without me an' I'll stay here with the mules."

Kirby's response irritated Emmett, but only for a moment, then inexplicably, he smiled. "You got grit, boy. You ain't just growed in body. All right. We'll find somethin' to do with the mules."

"I don't know if Mr. Byrd will buy 'em, but he'd take 'em, and look after 'em. He likes 'em, and the mules like him."

The expression on Emmett's face indicated surprise and curiosity. "How do you know that?"

Kirby wasn't ready to tell his pa just yet about going out with Asa Briggs and leaving the mules with Tom Byrd.

"He, uh, told me one time that if I ever wanted to get rid of the mules that he would take them." That wasn't a complete lie. Byrd had said once that, as often as Kirby brought the team over, he may as well leave them with him.

"All right. We'll leave 'em with Tom," Emmett said. "What day is this, anyway?

"It's Wednesday, Pa."

"How far you been from this holler?"

Kirby thought about his experiences with the Ghost Riders. He had been as far north as Liberty and Glasgow, Missouri, west into Kansas, east to Clark's Mill, Missouri, and south to Cane Hill, Arkansas. He felt bad about deceiving his pa, but again, that wasn't information he was ready to share just yet. "A good piece, Pa. I been to Springfield."

"Then it's about time you got out to see more of this country." Emmett stuffed his pipe and lit it, then pushed his rawhide-bottomed chair back and looked at his son.

"You got somethin' in mind, don't you, Pa?"

"Toward the end of the war, Kirby, some Texicans and some mountain men joined up with us. Them mountain men had been all the way to the Pacific Ocean, but they talked a lot about a place the Shoshone Indians call Idee ho, or somethin' like that.

"I'd like to see it. Texas too, and some of the rest of the country between here and there, and maybe get all the way out to the Pacific Ocean." Emmett coughed again.

"I seen the Atlantic Ocean, and I tell you boy, you never seen so much water. If I was to see the Pacific Ocean, too, why that would mean I been all the way across this country from east to west. You just got no idea how big this country is. But the West is where all the people seems to be headed now, so I figure we'll just head on out that way, too."

"Pa? How will we know when we get to where it is we're going?"

"We'll know."

"You got any regrets, Kirby? Leaving this place, I mean."

"Hard work, not always enough food, Jayhawks, Yankees, cold winters, and some bad memories," Kirby replied. "If that's regrets, I'm happy to leave them behind."

Emmett's reply was unusually soft. "You was just a

boy when I pulled out with the Grays. I reckon I done you, your sister 'n your ma a disservice, like half a million other men done their loved ones. I didn't leave you no time for youthful foolishness, no time to be a young boy. You had to be a man at an awful young age, and I don't know if I can make up for that, but I aim to try. From now on, son, it'll be you and me."

CHAPTER 7

The Jensens pulled out the following Sunday morning just as the sun was touching the eastern rim of the Ozark Mountains of Missouri. Kirby rode the bay, sitting on a worn-out McClellan saddle, which wasn't the most comfortable saddle ever invented. Emmett had bought it from a down on his luck Confederate soldier trying to get back to Louisiana.

They left the cool valleys and hills of Missouri, with rushing creeks and shade trees, and rode into a hot Kansas summer. The pair rode slowly, the pack horses trailing from lead ropes. The father and son had no deadline to meet and no particular place to go.

They passed a small sign that read BAXTER SPRINGS 2 MILES.

"Boy, what do you say we stop in this little town ahead?"

"Why?"

"Why not? It's been a hot ride and a beer might taste pretty good about now, don't you think?"

Kirby shrugged. "I don't know. I've never drunk a beer."

"You haven't?" Emmett laughed. "I guess not. You were just a boy when I left. Well, as far as I'm concerned, you're a man now, so if you want a beer, this is as good a time and place to start as any."

Baxter Springs was one of the places Kirby had visited when he was riding with Asa Briggs. They had crossed into Kansas looking for Shardeen but didn't find him. By chance, they ran into Quantrill heading south on the Texas Road on his way to winter in Texas. A short time before the two groups met, he had happened upon and killed two Union teamsters who were from a post called Baxter Springs.

Briggs and Quantrill decided to join their bands together for an attack on the post. They encountered Union soldiers, most of whom were black, and chased them back to the earth and log fort.

There, the Rebels attacked, but the garrison, with the help of a howitzer, managed to fight them off. Quantrill decided to move on the post from a different direction, and chanced upon a small Union detachment escorting Major General James G. Blunt and wagons transporting his personal items from his former headquarters in the Department of the Frontier at Fort Scott to his new one at Fort Smith. During the engagement, nearly all of the Union soldiers were killed, though General Blunt and a few mounted men managed to escape.

As a result, what had started as a battle became known as the Baxter Springs Massacre. Neither Briggs, nor any of his men had participated in that part of the fight, but the word *massacre* had been applied to the entire campaign, which by, implication, included Kirby.

Although he had been but one of many who had participated in the fight, he was a little hesitant about going into the settlement again. He took a deep breath, thinking. It had happened almost two years ago. He could be reasonably certain that he wouldn't be recognized as one of the guerrillas who had been there that day.

Kirby nodded his agreement and they approached the little settlement which had grown up around the fort. A small building built of rip-sawed unpainted boards had already weathered gray. The roof sagged, the building leaned, and an extension was obviously newer than the rest of the building. The sign out front read:

Murphy's
BEER WHISKEY EATS

Kirby and his pa tied their horses and pack animals off at the hitching rail, then stepped inside. The interior light was dim, filtered as it was through the dirty windows. Beams of light projected through the cracks between the boards, the shining beams alive with hanging dust motes.

The bar, such as it was, consisted of a few boards stretched between barrels. In a white apron and a low-crowned hat, the bartender was wiping glasses and putting them on a shelf behind the bar. Above the glasses, another shelf sported a row of whiskey bottles. A barrel of beer was just to the side.

Four tables with chairs made up the seating, one of them occupied by three men.

"This is a saloon, ain't it, Pa?"

"Not the fanciest I've ever seen, but yes, it's a saloon."

The two stepped up to the bar.

"We'll each have a beer," Emmett ordered, putting a dime down on the plank bar. He started coughing again, a deep and ragged cough.

"That's some cough you got there, mister."

"It's the dust," Emmett said.

The bartender didn't respond, but filled two mugs and set them before Emmett and Kirby. The two took the mugs over to a table and sat down.

"Drink up, boy," Emmett said, holding his mug out across the table toward Kirby.

Kirby took a swallow. It wasn't the best thing he had ever tasted, but on the day of a long, hot ride, it tasted good enough.

"Ha!" Emmett said, slapping his hand on the table. "I was there when you took your first step, I was there when you spoke your first word, and now I'm here for your first beer. It tastes better when it's cold."

"Hey!" called one of the three men sitting at the other table. "Them pants you're wearin' . . . they're Rebel pants, ain't they?"

"They're just trousers," Emmett replied.

"But they're Rebel pants."

"If you don't like my pants, mister, don't look at 'em."

From under the table, the man brought his hand up holding a pistol, pointing it toward Emmett. "Take 'em off. We don't allow Rebels . . . or Rebel pants here."

"I've no intention of takin' 'em off."

"Do you know who I am? My name is Tim Shardeen.

I reckon that name means somethin' to you, don't it, Reb?"

Emmett shook his head. "It don't mean a damn thing to me."

"It woulda meant somethin' if we had ever met durin' the war. The outfit I rode with was called Shardeen's Raiders. Angus Shardeen is my brother. That mean anythin' to you now?"

"Only that you was a bunch of murderin' Jayhawkers."

Tim grinned. "Then you know I ain't kiddin' when I tell you that if you don't take off them Rebel pants, I'll shoot you dead 'n take 'em off you myself."

"Let it go, Tim. What are you wantin' to get involved in this for? Hell, him 'n the boy ain't doin' nothin' but drinkin' a beer," one of the others at the table pointed out.

"I don't like Rebs."

"The war's over," said the third man at the table.

"Not for him, it ain't. I'm goin' to count to three 'n if he ain't took off them pants by the time I get to three, I'm goin' to shoot him dead. One—"

A loud boom interrupted the count, and Tim dropped his pistol and grabbed a bloody wound in his wrist. Everyone looked from Tim to Kirby, who was holding a smoking pistol, having drawn it quietly and unobserved.

"Damn! You shot me!" Tim shouted.

"Yeah, I did," Kirby replied.

A pressure bandage was quickly applied to the wound.

"How . . . how the hell did you make a shot like that?" Tim asked through clenched teeth.

Kirby shrugged. "It was an accident."

"An accident?"

"I was tryin' to kill you."

One of Tim's drinking buddies stood up. "We'd better get 'im to Doc Strafford before he bleeds to death."

Still gripping his wrist, Tim headed to the door with his friends.

"Mister?" Kirby called to him.

Tim Shardeen turned with a frown on his face. "Don't waste your time apologizin' to me."

"Oh, I ain't apologizin'. I want you to take a message to your brother for me."

"What would that message be?"

"My name is Kirby Jensen. I want you to tell your brother that if I ever run into him, I plan to kill 'im."

"Ha! You're goin' to kill my brother, are you? How old are you, boy?"

"How old do you have to be to kill a man?" Kirby pointed his pistol at Tim Shardeen again.

"No, no! Don't shoot!"

"You will deliver that message for me, won't you?"

"Yeah, yeah. I'll deliver it."

"Thank you. I appreciate that."

The three men left the saloon.

A few minutes later, Emmett and Kirby rode on, a little wary at first, but the farther away from the town they got, the less concerned they were. By the time they made camp, they were more than thirty miles west of Baxter Springs.

"Are you good enough with that handgun to get us a squirrel for our supper?" Emmett asked.

"I reckon I am, if I see one."

"What about that one?" Emmett asked, pointing to a squirrel halfway up a tree about a hundred feet away.

Kirby pulled his pistol, raised it to eye level, aimed, and fired. The squirrel fell to the ground and he hurried over to retrieve it.

"You clean the squirrel. I'll gather some wood and get us a fire goin'," Emmett said.

Half an hour later, the spitted squirrel was roasting over the fire, coffee was boiling, and the Jensens were sitting nearby.

Emmett looked at Kirby pointedly. "What happened back in the saloon . . . when you shot the gun out of that feller's hand? That warn't no accident, was it?"

"No."

"I didn't think it was." Emmett nodded toward the gun. "I been aimin' to ask you about that pistol. I know you didn't have it when I left home. How did you come by it? And how did you learn to shoot like that?"

"A bunch of Jayhawkers come through the farm one night, headin' back to Kansas like the devil was chasing them, 'n that was just about right 'cause about half an hour later Bloody Bill Anderson and his boys come ridin' up. They stopped to rest and water the horses.

"Turned out this young fellow was with them. He couldn't have been no more 'n a year or so older 'n me. He seen me there alone with nothin' but a shotgun, so he give me this Navy gun and an extra cylinder."

"That seemed like a right nice thing for him to do," Emmett replied.

"Yes, sir. I thought it was. He was nice . . . and soft-spoken, too."

"You seen him since?"

Kirby looked straight ahead. "No, sir."

In fact, he had seen him several times since then, on those occasions when the Ghost Riders and Quantrill's Raiders happened to join up for an operation. He felt bad about lying to his father, but he justified it by telling himself that the day would come when he'd tell everything.

"You thank him proper, did you?"

"Yes, sir."

"Did he tell you his name?"

"He told me. He said it was James. Jesse James. His brother Frank was with the bunch, too. Frank was somewhat older 'n Jesse."

"All right. That tells me how you got the gun. But it don't say nothin' 'bout how come it is you can shoot so well."

Kirby looked at his pa and grinned. "I practiced a lot."

"You musta spent a lot of money for bullets."

"Yes, sir, I reckon I did."

"Well, then, I can see why you didn't have no money left from the farmin', seein' as you spent it all on bullets for practicin'. As things is turnin' out, what with where we're goin' 'n all, bein' able to shoot is goin' to be a lot more important than knowin' how to plow a straight row."

"Yes, sir."

"Tell me about Angus Shardeen."

"Pa, you know about him. He's the one that burned the Gimlin farm, remember?"

Emmett frowned. "That's why you said you wanted to kill 'im?"

"That's not the only reason. He also come through on a raid and kilt Kenny Prosser 'n his ma and his little brother. Kenny was a good friend of mine, if you 'member. 'N he also kilt Merlin Lewis 'n his family."

Kirby was telling the truth. Those two county families had been killed by Angus Shardeen.

"All right. You do know that takin' a blood oath like that, which is pretty much what you just done in tellin' a man that you aim to kill his brother, is puttin' quite a load on your shoulders."

"Yes, sir."

"How fast can you get the gun out of the holster?"

"I don't know," Kirby admitted. "It ain't anythin' I've ever had to do." Being able to shoot straight had been not only a help but a necessity when he was riding the Bushwhacker trail, but a quick draw wasn't.

"If you set yourself the job of findin' someone and killin' 'im, especially someone like Angus Shardeen, bein' able to pull the gun out fast is somethin' that might come in pretty handy, don't you think? It's called a quick draw."

"A quick draw," Kirby repeated.

"Yeah. Stand up there and do a quick draw for me. Let me see what you can do."

Kirby stood up, then made a grab for his pistol. It was awkward and the draw was slow.

Emmett laughed. "Looks like we've got some work to do. You've already showed that you can shoot straight. Now you need to learn how to draw."

"You think I can learn?"

"I don't have no doubt. You have sort of a natural-born smoothness about you, so I have a feelin' you're goin' to learn pretty fast how to do a quick draw. With that and accurate shootin', I've no doubt but that you'll wind up bein' a man to be reckoned with."

"Why would I have to be reckoned with?"

"Because where we're goin', you're goin' to have to live by laws that aren't necessarily wrote down anywhere. But just 'cause they ain't wrote down, don't mean they ain't laws that need to be followed."

"What kind of laws are you talkin' about?"

Emmett had another bout of coughing before he responded. "I'm talkin' bout the laws of decency and good sense. Don't take what ain't yours, don't cheat at cards—for that matter, don't cheat at nothin' else, either—don't call a man a liar if he ain't, and don't be afraid to call him one if he is. And if you do, you have to be prepared to back it up."

"Back it up with a gun, you mean?"

"Yes. Where we're goin', the time is more 'n likely goin' to come when no matter how much you try and avoid it, you'll wind up gettin' pushed into a corner. When that happens, you won't have no choice but to try and defend yourself. If the one who done the evil is faster and better with a gun than the one that got the evil done to him, the wrong man might die."

"I see what you mean."

"I hope you do see what I mean, Kirby, because I'm going to teach you how to make a quick draw."

"Can you do a fast draw, Pa?"

"Fair to middlin'."

"How did you learn?"

Emmett leaned back against a big rock, thinking about what he wanted to say. "Remember me tellin' you 'bout those boys from Texas? They taught me all the skills a person needs, and I can pass those skills on to you. But it takes more than skills. It takes a natural ability like what I was tellin' you about. I've seen you move all your life, Kirby, and you got a natural way of doin' it. Things has always come easy to you, easier than it ever did to your brother. Easier than it ever did to me, easier than it has to anyone else I've ever knowed or even seen. With a little practice, you'll not only be a lot faster 'n me, few—if any—in the country will be able to stand up to you. But that'll come with a sense of responsibility."

"What kind of responsibility?"

"The responsibility to use your gun only when it's right, only to defend yourself or the innocent. Can I count on you to do that?"

"Yes, Pa."

"You promise me?"

"I promise."

"I know you will, son. I only asked you to make the promise so's it'll be somethin' you'll always keep in your mind." Emmett had another coughing spell.

"Pa, you told the bartender that it was the dust makin' you cough. Only, there ain't no dust here now. Besides which, you been acoughin' a lot ever' since you got back from the war. Why is it you're coughin' so much? You ain't got what they call the consumption, do you?"

"Where did you hear about consumption?"

"Miss Margrabe said her pa died of the consumption."

"I ain't got the consumption. Now, are you ready for your first lesson?"

"Yes sir, I reckon I am."

"Good. But before I teach you the fast draw, I'm going to have to teach you to shoot."

Kirby chuckled. "Pa, I've already showed you that I can shoot."

"You have, huh?" Emmett pointed to a thumb-sized protrusion from the branch of a nearby cottonwood tree. "Take a shot at that little branch for me."

Kirby raised the pistol to eye-level and fired. His bullet snapped the branch and he turned to his father with a satisfied smile on his face. "I told you I could shoot."

"You aimed, didn't you?"

"Of course I did."

"Why?"

"Why? Because I wanted to hit what I was shootin' at. That's why."

Emmett gave instructions. "Shoot at it again, but don't aim this time."

"What do you mean, don't aim? I don't understand. How am I going to hit it, if I don't aim?"

"You are going to think the bullet onto your target."

"*What?*"

"Let me show you what I'm talking about." Emmett pulled his own pistol and shot at the part of the branch that was left. He didn't raise the pistol to eye level and aim, he just pulled the trigger and another piece of the branch was shot away.

Kirby's jaw dropped. "How did you do that without aiming?"

"I told you. I just thought the bullet onto the target."

"I don't understand what that means."

"Here's the thing," Emmett said as he put his pistol back in the holster. "There's no sense in drawing really fast if you have to stop and aim. You have to draw, aim, and shoot all at the same time. In order to do that, you have to think the bullet onto the target. Now, you try it."

Kirby pulled the pistol and automatically started to raise it. He stopped himself, then held the gun out in front of his body and fired. He missed.

Emmett stood up. "Here, let me help you out. Turn yourself at an angle, sort of caddy corner, so that you aren't facing the target." He positioned Kirby accordingly. "Now, don't turn your body, but look at the target by turning your head back toward it."

Kirby responded.

"Bring the pistol up to eye level and aim at the target, just as you did before, but don't shoot."

Kirby did.

"Good. Close your eyes and lower your pistol so that it is pointing straight down."

Kirby did as instructed.

"Now, with your eyes closed, aim at it again."

Kirby opened his eyes and looked at his pa. "What do you mean, aim at it again? How am I going to do that if my eyes are closed?"

"Just listen to me, boy. Close your eyes and with them still closed, bring your arm back up, thinking about where the target is. When you think you have it lined up, tell me."

Kirby closed his eyes and brought his arm up until he thought he was aligned with the target.

"Pull the trigger, but don't open your eyes."

Kirby pulled the trigger.

"Now, open your eyes and look."

He did that and saw a white chip had been taken out of the limb, just below the small branch he had been shooting at. It was a miss, but it was a very close miss.

"I almost hit it!" he said excitedly.

"That was pretty good. Now, spread your feet apart about the width of your shoulders. Keep your legs straight, but not stiff. Think you can do that?"

Kirby tried it a few times, then looked at Emmett. "Yes, I can do it."

"What are you going to do with your other arm?" Emmett asked.

Kirby looked down. "I don't know. I hadn't thought about it."

"Good."

"Good?"

"It's good that you hadn't thought about it. As far as you're concerned, the other arm isn't even there.

"Put your pistol back in the holster, then look at your target by turning your head and eyes slightly without moving from the neck down. When you know exactly where the target is, pull the pistol from the holster, but don't raise the gun to eye level. Shoot it as soon as your arm comes level."

Anxious, Kirby asked, "Should I try a quick draw?"

"No. That comes later. First learn to shoot, then learn to draw. Now, pull the gun and shoot it."

Kirby pulled the pistol and fired as soon as it came level. He had no idea where the bullet went.

Fancy Lil was easily the most beautiful dove in the covey of doves Chicago Sue employed at the Palace

Princess Emporium. She had managed to avoid the dissipation so prevalent among the others. While most would lay with anywhere from three to five men a night, Fancy Lil rarely shared her bed. The others charged from two dollars to five dollars, depending on the girl and the length of the visit. It cost fifty dollars to visit Fancy Lil for a short while, and one hundred and fifty dollars to spend the night with her.

Her room, in keeping with her station as Chicago Sue's most expensive girl, was attractively furnished with lace curtains on the window and a floral carpet on the floor. The furniture was made of English oak and the headboard featured elaborate carvings.

Her clientele was of a considerably higher caliber than the average visitor to the place. She entertained wealthy cattlemen, high ranking officers who'd been in the Confederate military, and politicians, including a couple Texas state senators.

Her most frequent visitor, and the one she actually enjoyed being with, was a big man, a Confederate veteran who stood six feet seven inches tall, and weighed 330 pounds. He had given only his first name, Ben.

The well-appointed room was redolent with the scent of sex. She and Ben were lying together, naked skin against naked skin.

Though it had become a little more than routine for Janey—an act without feeling, emotionally or physically—it wasn't like that with Ben. With him, she had experienced every sensation.

Their times together were passion-filled, but she also felt a relaxed shared possessiveness between them that she had never felt with anyone else, not even Paul Garner.

She put her head on Ben's shoulder, and he wrapped

his arm around her, cupping her breast in his hand. It wasn't sexual. It was comfortable.

"What is your name?" she asked. "I know there has to be more to it than just Ben."

"Some folks call me Big Ben."

Janey chuckled. "*Big* Ben? Yes, I can see that. But am I to believe that's all there is to it?"

"Am I to believe there is no more to your name than Fancy Lil?"

"I can't give my real name," Janey said.

"Why not?"

"Because girls in my . . . profession . . . never give their real names."

Big Ben smiled. "And men like me, who visit girls like you, never give our real names."

"You are a wealthy man, aren't you, Ben?"

"Why do you say that?"

"Because it costs a lot of money to visit me . . . and lately, you have been visiting me more than all my other gentlemen callers combined."

"I enjoy visiting you."

"But you can get the same thing from other girls for a lot less money."

Big Ben shook his head. "No, I can't. Lil, I would have thought that, by now, you understood. It isn't just the time we're in bed together. It's more than that. With you . . . with us . . . it's just . . . more. I thought . . . that is, I hoped . . . that it was a little more for you, as well."

Janey felt her eyes well with tears, and she leaned up to kiss him on his cheek, feeling the stubble of a day's growth of beard. "My name is Janey. Janey Garner."

She'd decided to expose herself to him, but she chose to use Garner's last name, rather than Jensen. She didn't want to bring any more shame to the Jensen name than she already had. Assuming, that is, that there were any Jensens left alive.

Big Ben turned to smile at her. "Conyers. Benjamin R. Conyers."

CHAPTER 8

Millions of soldiers who had worn the blue and the gray had laid down their arms and picked up where they had left off. Families split by the war were reunited. Friendships were renewed, crops were put in, men and women were married, children were born.

But it was not so for all men. For some, the wounds had cut too deeply and the price had been too dear. Families, fortunes, and dreams were consumed in flames and drowned in blood. So it was for Kirby and Emmett. They had only each other, along with their guns and their courage.

After leaving Baxter Springs, they headed west for a bit, then turned south through Indian Territory, heading for Texas.

"Do you think we need to be wary of the Indians, Pa?"

"No need. All the Indians here is civilized. They got their own towns, their own laws. Most even like white men. Lots of 'em even fought 'n the war. It's farther out West that we got to be wary of 'em. Out there, I hear tell that Indians is notional folks. The same bands that would leave you alone today might try to kill you tomorrow."

"Why?"

"I can't say. It's hard for the average white man to understand the Indians' way of life. But I'm sure there are white men livin' in the mountains, prob'ly been there thirty or forty years or more, who can understand them better 'n whites can now, them bein' gone so long from civilization 'n all."

Every night as they camped, Kirby would practice shooting, though he limited his practice to no more than three shots each day. They were a long way from any chance of buying new bullets.

On the seventh day, he fired three shots, *thinking* his bullets into the targets all three times. "Did you see that, Pa?"

"Can you do it again?"

Kirby repeated his performance, again hitting his targets with all three bullets.

"All right. Instead of shooting one at a time, I want you to fire three times, one shot right on top of another, and hit these three targets." Emmett put pine cones on three rocks, the two farthest rocks separated by at least ten yards. He came back to stand beside Kirby.

"Now?" Kirby asked.

"Not yet. I'm going to add something to it." Emmett took a mess skillet from his pack and put it on the ground in front of him, then he picked up a rock. "When I say, 'now,' I want you to start shooting. At the same time, I'll drop this rock, and I want to hear all three shots before the rock hits the skillet. Do you think you can do that?"

"I can get all three shots off, yes sir."

"And hit all three targets," Emmett said.

"I don't know, Pa. That's askin' quite a lot."

"Wrong answer. Do you think you can do that?"

Kirby smiled. "Yes, sir."

Emmett returned the smile. "That's my boy. Now!" he shouted without further notice.

Using his left hand to fan the hammer, Kirby fired three shots so close that it sounded like one. Then *clank*—the rock hit the skillet. All three targets had been hit.

"You didn't give me any warning," Kirby complained.

"I didn't, did I? Well, you don't always get a warning. I think the time has come to teach you the quick draw. And this won't be costin' us any bullets at all."

"I'm ready," Kirby said with a broad smile.

"All right. Empty your pistol before we begin. I wouldn't want the damn thing to go off accidental while you're tryin' to learn."

Kirby pulled his pistol, poked all the shells out of the cylinder, and stuck it back down into the holster.

"Now, look down at the shank of your holster. That's the part that's attached to the belt. It should have a little kink in it, so that it causes the butt of the pistol to stick out just a little. You can adjust it, but we may have to make a little modification later on, so that the pistol sticks out far enough all the time so there won't be anything to get in the way of your draw."

Kirby made a few adjustments to the shank and finally, after examining it closely, Emmett announced that it was ready and continued with his instructions. "Let your arm hang down completely limp and natural along your side. Don't crook the elbow . . . don't stiffen your arm. Don't do nothin' but just let it hang there."

Kirby did as he was instructed.

"Now, without drawing the gun, bend your arm at the elbow until your hand has come up level with the ground. Stick out your trigger finger. Where is it pointing?"

"It's pointing in the same direction as my arm," Kirby said.

"All right, now what I want you to do is, move the gun belt until the gun is exactly under your hand. The butt of the pistol should be poking out away from your body just a little. That was why we adjusted the shank a while ago. Remember?"

Kirby adjusted the holster as directed, and Emmett inspected the position of the gun.

"Yes," he said, smiling. "Just like that. And the holster should be at the same angle as your arm was a while ago when you lifted it. Do that."

Kirby repositioned the holster.

"Move your hips forward real slow and bring your shoulders back, grabbing the gun as your hips and shoulders move. But don't grab it with your whole hand. Curl your middle finger, ring finger, and little finger around the butt of the gun. If you've got your holster positioned right, that will put the gun in your hand before you even start to draw it."

Kirby reacted to the directions, and as Emmett had pointed out, his hand fell naturally to the butt of the pistol. He smiled at the result. "Pa, my hand went right where you said it would."

"Good. That's very good. Keep your holster there, and do it that way every time, so that when the gun comes out of the holster, it will just naturally be pointed in the right direction. Now, when you make the draw, make sure you bring the barrel up level, 'cause if you don't, you'll shoot low ever' time."

Kirby nodded, indicating that he understood the instructions.

"All right. Good. Now, it's time to cock the gun as you draw it. What you want to do is, pull your thumb across the hammer to cock the gun at the same time you are drawing. The thumb should be moving the hammer back all the while you are bringing the gun up. You got that?"

"Yes, Pa. I got it."

Emmett chuckled. "So you say. We'll just see if you listened to anything I said. I want you to draw the gun just the way I told you. But I want you to draw it real slow, so I can see it, and make sure you're doing everything the right way. Go ahead and draw it now."

Kirby made the draw, doing it slowly and exactly as he had been instructed. Emmett smiled.

"How did you like that?" Kirby asked.

"Don't go getting all smug on me now," Emmett said.

"I did it perfectly."

"How do you know you did?"

"Because, if I hadn't done it perfectly, you wouldn't have called me smug," Kirby said with a pleased smile.

"Right. Now . . . pick out something to shoot at and draw as fast as you can."

Kirby frowned. "I don't have any bullets in the gun."

"You don't need any bullets right now. All you need to do is what I told you. Now, I want you to pick out a target."

"What about that leaf there?"

"What leaf? There are hundreds of leaves. How do I

know you won't just shoot, then claim the leaf you hit is the one you wanted to hit?"

Kirby walked over to a nearby tree and put his finger on one of the leaves. "This one."

"All right. Draw your pistol as fast as you can and shoot at it."

Still confused, Kirby asked, "How can I shoot if I don't have any bullets?"

"Just do what I tell you, Kirby. If I want questions, I'll ask for them."

Kirby returned to his original position, drew his pistol, thumbed back the hammer, and pulled the trigger. The hammer fell on an empty chamber.

"Did you hit the leaf?" Emmett asked.

Kirby started to ask his father again how he could hit the leaf if he had no bullets in his gun but checked the question and smiled instead. "Yeah, I hit the leaf."

"Good. Now, put some bullets in your gun and do it again."

Kirby loaded the pistol and put it in his holster. He got ready to make his draw—

"Wait." Emmett stopped him. He picked up the rock.

"You're goin' to drop the rock on the skillet again?" Kirby asked.

"No. This time you're goin' to drop the rock. What I want you to do is hold it out in front of you. When I tell you to, drop the rock, draw your pistol, and shoot at that leaf."

Kirby held the rock out in front of him, shoulder high.

"Now!" Emmett shouted.

Kirby dropped the rock, drew his pistol, and fired. Not until after the gun fired, was there the clank of the rock hitting the skillet. The leaf, cut from the tree, fluttered down. Kirby looked over at Emmett and smiled.

"Not bad," Emmett said.

"Not bad? What do you mean, *not bad?*"

"You had your hand shoulder high. I want you to be able to do that when your hand is no higher than this." Emmett demonstrated, holding his hand lower than Kirby's waist.

"Nobody can do that." Kirby shook his head.

"You can," Emmett said. "And better."

"If you think so," Kirby said.

"No, Kirby, it's not what I think. It's what *you* think. Actually, it's not what you think, it's what you *know*. You have to *know* that you can do this."

Kirby picked up the rock and held it just below his waist. Then, with a confident grin, he moved the rock even lower. Taking a deep breath, he dropped the rock, drew the pistol, and fired . . . before the rock clanked against the skillet. And he hit the target.

As Kirby bedded down that night next to glowing embers of the fire that had cooked their supper, he let his mind pass over events that had brought him and his father near the Cherokee town of Tahlequah in the Indian Territory. He had grown up thinking he would be a farmer like his father. Once he and Luke had even discussed buying acreage just across Shoal Creek from the family farm. If they bought 40 acres apiece, they could farm all the land jointly . . . 120 acres, which would make it one of the biggest farms in Stone County. And because all the land had access to a year-round supply of water, it could be the best farm in the county.

But none of that was to be. His mother was dead. Luke was dead. Janey had run off, who knows where, and his pa had come back from the war no longer interested in farming. If Kirby was truthful with himself, he was no longer interested in it, either.

How strange life was that it could start out in one direction, then make a turn in a completely different direction.

Emmett had another bad coughing spell in his sleep.

Kirby sat up and looked over toward him. "Pa?"

Emmett coughed again. "I'm all right, son. I've just got a cough I can't shake, is all. Go back to sleep."

Kirby lay back down. He hadn't been asleep so there was no *going back to sleep*, but as he lay there, his eyelids began to grow heavy, and finally sleep pushed away all the thoughts tumbling through his mind.

Over the next several days Kirby continued to practice. His draw became so fast that it was a blur, too fast for the eye to follow. His shooting was deadly accurate, as well.

Emmett, having handled guns all his life, was a very good shooter. As he watched, he realized that Kirby was exceptionally good—already better than his pa. Emmett smiled, proud.

He had once been the city marshal of a small town in Missouri, and had found it necessary, in defense of his own life, to kill two men during his tenure in office. God alone knew how many more men he had killed during the war.

Emmett was glad that the boy could handle himself. He had not told Kirby everything—that he would have gone West whether Pearl was dead or alive, and whether or not Kirby had come with him; that his journey was not one of pure impulse; that he had given his word to Mosby that if it took him forever, he would find and kill the men who had murdered Luke and stolen the gold he was carrying to the Confederate government in Georgia.

In this, he was like his son. Kirby had taken his own oath to kill someone. Ideally, they would be together when they encountered the men they were after.

Crossing into Texas, they came across a few stage stops and trading posts along the way but didn't ride into any towns until they reached Dallas.

Emmett looked around. "This is it, boy. Dallas, Texas."

"Wow, this is purt' nigh as large as Springfield," Kirby said, taking it all in.

The main street was cut with wheel ruts and hoof marks, and covered with enough horse apples to permeate the air with strong odor. A busy town, it was filled with buckboards, surreys, carriages, and wagons, as well as riders on horseback. Boardwalks ran the entire length of each block and were filled with the citizens of the town, many of them women who walked around holding handkerchiefs to their nose to blot out the smell.

"We might want to stop here, first," Emmett said, pointing to a gun store. "I expect you're about out of ammunition, ain't you?"

"I could sure use some more," Kirby replied.

Tying their four horses off, the two men went inside.

A clerk sitting behind the counter in a wooden chair

leaning against the wall was the only person in the store. He stood up when they entered. "Yes, sir, can I help you?"

"I need some thirty-six caliber shells," Kirby said.

"Very good sir. How many do you need?"

"I'd say about two hundred."

The clerk whistled. "Two hundred? My, that's a lot of ammunition. I do hope you aren't planning on restarting the war." He laughed at his own joke.

"Got no intention of doin' that," Kirby said. "But travelin' like we are, you don't always find a place where you can get it."

"I understand." The man took four boxes from a case, then opened one of the boxes. "As you can see there are fifty bullets in each little box. Four times fifty is two hundred."

"Open all four boxes," Emmett said.

"Do you really think that is necessary?"

"Open all four boxes," Emmett said again.

The man started to put one of the boxes back in the case, but Emmett reached out to grab his wrist. "What's wrong with that box?"

"To tell the truth, it felt a little light to me, so I . . ."

Before he could finish his statement, Emmett opened the box. It was only about half full. "A little light, you said?"

"Yes. You did notice that I was putting it back," the clerk said self-righteously. He put four boxes on the counter and opened them. "Two dollars."

Satisfied that the boxes were full, Kirby paid for the ammunition, and he and Emmett went back outside.

"How'd you know he was plannin' to cheat me, Pa?"

Emmett put his finger alongside his nose. "I smelled it."

"You smelled it?" Kirby asked incredulously.

"You don't actually smell it," Emmett explained. "It's just something that you say when you have a feelin' that somethin' ain't quite right. And I had a feelin' that somethin' wasn't quite right."

"How do you learn to have them feelin's?"

"It's not somethin' you learn. It's somethin' that just sort of comes to you as you get older. I expect it'll come over you, too, eventually."

Looking around, they spotted the Lone Star Hotel.

"What do you say we spend the night in a bed instead of on the ground?" Emmett asked.

"Sounds good to me," Kirby agreed.

After checking into the hotel and boarding their horses, they walked up the wide, sunbaked street, hurrying from the shade of one building to the next, taking every opportunity to get out of the sun. After walking a few blocks, they were drenched with sweat, and the cool interior of the Yellow Dog Saloon beckoned them.

Pushing their way through the bat wing doors, they stepped inside and stood in the dark for a moment or two until their eyes adjusted to the dim light. Unlike the rather coarse establishment in Baxter Springs, this place was rather elegant. Made of burnished mahogany, the bar had a highly polished brass foot rail. Crisp, clean white towels hung from hooks on the customers' side of the bar, spaced every four feet. A mirror behind the bar was flanked on each side by a small statue of a nude woman set back in a special niche. A row of whiskey bottles sat in front of the mirror, reflected in the glass so that the row of bottles seemed to be two deep. A bartender with pomaded black hair and a waxed handlebar moustache stood behind the bar. A towel was draped across his shoulders, and his arms were folded across his chest.

"Is the beer cool?" Emmett asked.

"It's cooler than horse piss," he said in a matter-of-fact voice.

Emmett chuckled. "Good enough. We'll have a couple."

The bartender drew the beers and set them in front of Kirby and Emmett.

Kirby picked up the beer and took a drink.

"What do you think?" Emmett asked. "Is the second one better?"

"Yes, sir. It's a lot better."

"It's good to be able to enjoy a beer now 'n again but, what with you just startin' out to drink, I need to tell you to be careful about drinkin'."

"Careful? What do you mean? Why do I have to be careful?"

"I say that 'cause some folks start to likin' their liquor too much, 'n the next thing they know, 'bout the only important things in their life is the next drink 'n where it's comin' from. I sure don't want to see that happen to you."

"I don't neither. I promise you, I will take care." Kirby turned to look around the place. Nearly every table was occupied.

One of the tables was near enough to where they were standing that Emmett could quite easily listen in on the conversation that was taking place between three men.

"Her name is Lil. Fancy Lil," one of the men was saying. "She works down at the Palace Princess Emporium."

"That ain't her real name, is it, Doc?"

"I'm sure that Fancy is not a part of her sobriquet, though Lil might be. Young ladies who find themselves in such occupations, however, rarely use their real names."

"She must be somethin'," said the man in a blue shirt. "I heard that iffen you want to choose her, it's goin' to cost you a hunnert dollars. Maybe even more."

The man with a bushy mustache shook his head. "There ain't no woman worth a hunnert dollars."

"Oh, believe me, this young lady is," replied the one called Doc.

Bushy Mustache couldn't believe it. "Doc, don't tell me you spend a hunnert dollars on her."

"I have not, but only because I don't have a hundred dollars to spare. But if I did, I would do so without a moment's hesitation."

"The Palace Princess Emporium. That's Chicago Sue's place, ain't it?" Blue Shirt asked.

"Yes."

"Yeah, well, mayhaps that's why I ain't never seen this here Fancy Lil that you're talking about. I ain't never been to Chicago Sue's establishment. They ain't any of them at Chicago Sue's place that's cheap."

"Oh, I wouldn't complain. Those at the Palace Princess Emporium are different," Doc said.

"What do you mean, *different?* They's same as saloon girls, ain't they?"

"No, they are ladies that entertain."

"Does it cost money to be entertained?" Bushy Mustache wanted to know.

"Yes."

Blue Shirt wasn't convinced. "And, does that entertainment include sleepin' with 'em?"

"Yes."

Blue Shirt crossed his arms. "If a woman will go to bed with you for money, she's same as a saloon girl, no matter how much it costs."

"I'm sure that as dissipation takes its toll, some of the young ladies who work there will slip down the scale until you can rightly throw them in with saloon girls, but not now. And you certainly can't say that for Fancy Lil. Anyone who can command one hundred dollars for her services is certainly more than a common saloon girl."

Bushy Mustache didn't believe it. "This Fancy Lil must be some kind of woman."

"She is," Doc replied. "Perhaps Christopher Marlowe expressed it best."

"Christopher Marlowe? Hmm, I don't think I know him."

"That wouldn't be likely, since he died almost two hundred years ago," Doc said.

Bushy Mustache was more confused than ever. "What? Then how could he say anything about Fancy Lil?"

"He was actually speaking of Helen of Troy, but it could have been Fancy Lil." Doc cleared his throat, then, in dramatic fashion, said the words, *Was this the face that launch'd a thousand ships . . . And burnt the topless towers of Ilium? . . . Sweet Helen, make me immortal with a kiss.*"

His table mates were stunned.

Bushy Mustache grinned. "Doc, you're the smartest man I've ever knowed. You must be. Hell, I don't understand half of what you say."

"I have established the idea that this lady, Fancy Lil, is a person of rare beauty, haven't I?"

"Oh, yeah, you've done that all right. Only I'll never

get to see her. A hunnert dollars? I ain't never had that much money at one time in my whole life."

"It doesn't cost a hundred dollars just to see her. For five dollars, you can visit the parlor of the Palace Princess Emporium, enjoy food, drink, and conversation with beautiful women and a convivial atmosphere," Doc pointed out.

"Five dollars? But that don't get you no woman, does it?"

"Only in friendly conversation."

Blue Shirt looked at Bushy Mustache. "Will Fancy Lil be there?"

"She often is, when she isn't otherwise engaged."

"You mean with someone?"

"Yes."

"Hmmph. If it cost one hunnert dollars to be with her, I can't imagine she's with someone all that much."

"She is very selective," Doc replied.

Kirby had been listening intently to the conversation. He turned to Emmett, who was staring into his glass. "You know what, Pa? I'd like to see this woman they're talkin' about."

"Why?"

"You heard what Doc said. That she is the most beautiful woman he had ever seen. Wouldn't you like to see such a woman?"

"Boy, what do you know about such things? Have you ever been to such a place?" Emmett's question was pointed, but not challenging.

Kirby had never been, but he had seen one . . . once.

It had been pointed out by Elmer Gleason. He couldn't share that information with his father, though, without sharing that he had ridden with Asa Briggs.

"No, sir, I ain't never been to one. But I know what one is. Some of the other boys in school was talkin' 'bout 'em one day." That was true. The subject had come up, but none of the boys who'd been discussing it knew exactly what went on there.

"Yeah, I reckon there are some things you can learn at school that ain't really all that good."

Kirby chuckled. "I never heard that till I was in the seventh grade. And remember, I wanted to quit soon as I finished the fifth grade."

Emmett chuckled, then took another drink. "Well now, ain't you glad I made you stay?"

At that moment, the back door opened and a tall, broad-shouldered, bearded man wearing a badge stepped through the door and looked around. For a long moment, he scrutinized Kirby and Emmett, obviously aware that they were new in town, then continued his perusal of the room until he saw a man who caught his attention.

"You," he said, pointing. "We got a telegram sayin' you was comin' to Dallas. I didn't think you was actually that dumb, Cox."

The man stood up slowly, then turned to face the lawman. "Yeah? Why shouldn't I come to Dallas? Am I supposed to be afraid of some piss-ant deputy?"

The situation had the look of an impending gunfight. The others at the table stood up and moved out of the way. All other conversation within the saloon ceased.

"Unbuckle your gun belt," the lawman said, making a motion with the gun he was holding. "And do it slow and easy, so's I don't get the idea you're tryin' anything."

Cox shook his head no. "I don't think so, Deputy. I think me an' you's goin' to have to settle this thing, right here and right now."

Kirby had heard stories about deadly gunfights between men, but not in all the time he had been riding with Briggs had he ever seen one. The shooting he had experienced was from a distance, and it was always one group of men against another group. He had never seen a one-on-one confrontation.

"Are you crazy, Cox?" the deputy asked. "I've already got you covered."

"Do you now?" Cox asked with a mysterious smile on his face.

Kirby was watching intently, wondering why the man called Cox didn't seem to be worrying about the gun that was pointing toward him. When he saw a man standing up in the corner, aiming his pistol at the lawman, he shouted, "Deputy, look out! There's a gun behind you!"

The man in the corner turned the pistol toward the Jensens.

Kirby acted instinctively. Dropping his beer, he pulled his pistol and fired just as the man in the corner pulled the trigger on his own gun. The would-be assailant's bullet hit the mirror behind the bar, and it fell with a crash, leaving nothing but a few jagged shards hanging in place to reflect twisting images of the dramatic scene.

Just like in all of his practicing, Kirby's bullet had gone true . . . only his target had been a man . . . who dropped his weapon and grabbed his neck. His eyes rolled up in his head and he fell backward.

The two gunshots had riveted everyone's attention to that exchange. Cox took the opportunity to go for his own gun. Suddenly, the saloon was filled with the roar of another gunshot as he fired at the deputy, whose attention had also been diverted by the gunplay between Kirby and the man in the corner. Cox's bullet struck the deputy in the back of the head.

Making a fatal mistake, Cox swung his pistol toward Kirby.

Emmett's bullet caught Cox in the center of his chest, and he went down. He sat on the floor, leaning back against the table, his gun lying on the floor beside him. "Who . . . who the hell are you?" he asked, gasping out the question. "What did you get involved for?"

"It seemed the thing to do," Emmett said.

One more gasp, and Cox was dead.

CHAPTER 9

"What's goin' on in here?" asked a loud authoritative voice. "Who's doin' all the shootin'?"

Holding smoking guns, Kirby and his pa turned toward the sound of the voice to see a man standing just inside the open door. With the brightness of the light behind him, he could be seen in silhouette only.

"Get out of the light," Emmett said, his voice a low growl.

"You don't tell me what to do, I—"

Click. Emmett pulled the hammer back and his pistol made a deadly metallic sound as the sear engaged the cylinder. "I said get out of the light," he repeated.

The figure moved out of the light. Kirby and Emmett could see that he was wearing a badge and put their pistols away.

"Marshal, I'm glad you come," said one of the men who had been sitting with Cox. "These here fellas just killed your deputy. Then they killed Haggart, 'n Cox, too, 'n they done it all in cold blood."

"That ain't true," Emmett said.

"Julius McCoy wasn't just my deputy, he was also my friend and my sister's husband. I think you two had better come down to the jail with me till I get to the bottom of this."

Although Kirby had already holstered his pistol, it suddenly appeared in his hand again, the draw so fast that it caught everyone in the saloon by surprise. He didn't shoot at the end of his draw. "I don't think we want to do that, Marshal. If you want to get to the bottom of this, you can find out what happened by askin' these people right here. I'm sure some of 'em must be honest."

Emmett had his gun out, as well, and was covering everyone else in the saloon.

"All right," the marshal said. "Let me hear what you have to say."

"I didn't have anything to do with killing your deputy, but I did kill that one." Kirby pointed to the man lying back in the corner.

"What did you shoot him for?" the marshal asked.

"He had a gun pointed at your deputy's back and was about to shoot him."

"Who killed the other two?"

"I killed that one," Emmett admitted, pointing toward Cox's body. "Unfortunately, not before he killed your deputy."

The marshal looked around until he noticed the man who had been speaking so eloquently about a woman named Fancy Lil. "Doc Dunaway, did you see what happened here?"

"I did indeed." Dr. Dunaway pointed to Kirby and Emmett. "These two men are telling the truth, Marshal. Deputy McCoy was trying to arrest Cox, when that unfortunate gentleman"—he pointed to the body lying back in the far corner—"declared his intention of interrupting the operation by pointing a pistol at McCoy. He was about to shoot, but the boy shouted a warning. At that, he turned his weapon toward those two and fired. The broken mirror behind the bar should be all the evidence you need to validate that. It was a misguided move of the part of the would-be assassin, because the young man drew his pistol and returned fire. It was quite a long shot, too.

"While all that was in progress, Cox killed the deputy when McCoy wasn't payin' attention and then he swung his gun around toward these two. By then, the older gentleman had his own pistol out. He shot Cox. If I am asked to testify in court, I will say, emphatically, that he had every right to do so."

"That's true. Ever'thing Doc said is true. That's the feller that's lyin'." Blue Shirt pointed to the man who had been sitting at the table with Cox—the one who had accused Kirby and Emmett of killing all three men.

"I, uh, just told what I thought I seen," the man said nervously.

Dr. Dunaway's testimony opened the floodgate. Nearly everyone else in the saloon began telling their own stories of the incident, and though there were a few slight variations in the telling, one theme was consistent throughout—all but one of the shootings were entirely justified.

The marshal let out a big sigh and waved his hand dismissively. "I reckon you two can put them guns away. What with ever'one in here tellin' the same story, there won't be no need in arrestin' you. But you might want to come down to my office tomorrow, anyway."

"Why would we want to do that?" Emmett asked.

"Because there's a five-hundred-dollar reward out for Cox, and I expect you'll be wantin' to stick around long enough to collect it." The marshal looked over toward the other dead man. "I don't know nothin' about him, but there may be paper on him as well."

Emmett nodded. "I reckon that's reason enough to stay around for a couple days."

"What's your name?" the marshal asked.

"I'm Emmett Jensen. This is my son, Kirby."

"I don't think I've ever heard the names before. Are you new in town?"

"We just arrived today," Emmett said.

"Just passing through, are you?"

"Sort of. Actually, I'm looking for some friends of mine. Wiley Potter, Keith Stratton, and Josh Richards. Perhaps you have run across them."

The marshal shook his head. "Nope. 'Fraid I've never heard of 'em."

"What about Angus Shardeen?" Kirby asked.

The marshal's eyes narrowed. "Would he be a friend as well?"

Kirby shook his head. "Not hardly. I've got a score to settle with him."

"Apparently a lot of people do. He's took to doin' the same he was doin' durin' the war, only now he ain't got the war as an excuse. He's a thief and a murderer."

"Is he anywhere nearby?"

"Not that I know of."

"Boy, you got quite an appetite on you, you know that?" Emmett's comment was made over supper that night at the Rustic Rock restaurant.

Kirby was eating a steak that was so large he needed a second plate for his potatoes and green beans. He had also asked for an extra serving of rolls. "Can you blame me? We ain't had nothin' but squirrel and rabbit and such for near two months. I just figured when I get a chance to eat like this, well, maybe I should."

"I don't reckon I can argue with that. By the way, Kirby, I been wantin' to say somethin' to you. The way you handled yourself today, even the way you handled yourself back in Baxter, was somethin' special. I'm just real proud of you."

"It wasn't all that much," Kirby said, embarrassed by his pa's accolades.

"Don't sell yourself short. I've been in more battles than I can count and I've seen many men get so scared that they could barely breathe when the shootin' starts."

Kirby took a bite of potatoes and nodded. "Sounds like a reasonable thing to do."

"Yes. But you've been in two shootin' scrapes, and you didn't get panicked either time."

"Didn't seem like the time for it," Kirby said.

"Still, I want you to know that I'm proud of you."

"Pa, who are these men you mentioned, Casey, Potter, Stratton, and Richards? I've never heard you mention those names before."

"Why do you ask?"

"I'm just wonderin' is all. You told the marshal they was your friends, but if they are, how come you haven't mentioned them before now?"

The response to Kirby's question was a long silence, then the silence was broken, not by Emmett's answer, but by another coughing attack. Not until the coughing fit stopped, did Emmett speak. "Why are you so interested?"

Kirby put his finger alongside his nose as his father had done back in the gun shop. "Because there's somethin' not quite right here. I can smell it."

Emmett nodded. "You're gettin' a little smarter after all. You're right. They aren't friends at all. What Angus Shardeen is to you, those men are to me. If and when I find 'em, I plan to kill 'em."

"What did they do?"

"They stole some gold that belonged to the Confederate government, and they killed a lot of good men while they was stealing it."

"Pa, the war's over. There ain't no Confederate government no more, which to my thinkin' means there ain't no Confederate gold no more."

"That's true. But it ain't the gold I'm concerned with, Kirby. It's the men they killed while they was comin' by it. One of 'em was your brother."

Kirby got a surprised expression on his face. "Are you sure, Pa? The letter I got from Colonel Willis said that Luke was killed in battle on Wilderness Creek."

"That's what the report said. But what really happened was that Casey, Potter, Stratton, and Richards shot 'im."

"Colonel Willis said Luke's body wasn't found. He thought that maybe the Yankees found him and buried him."

"I went up to Wilderness Creek lookin' for his body, but I never found it, so it could be that the Yankees did find him and bury him. It's for sure that the men who killed him didn't take the time to give him a proper burial."

"Pa, you're sure that's what happened? That he was shot by those men you mentioned?"

'Yes. I am very sure." Emmett spoke with such absolute authority, that Kirby felt no need to question it any further.

"Do you think those men might be here in Texas?"

"They could be. They might also be in New Mexico, or Colorado, or Idaho."

"Like you said, Pa, this is an awful big country. How do you plan to find them in such wide open spaces? They could be anywhere between here and the Pacific Ocean."

"I told you they stole Confederate gold. They stole a lot of it, Kirby, enough to make all of 'em rich as Croesus. Men with that much money can't hide. They're goin' to be spendin' a lot of it, and that's goin' to get them noticed. All I have to do is live long enough to find 'em."

Kirby chuckled. "Well, that'll be fifty, sixty years. I reckon we'll find 'em all right."

"Maybe not." The tone of Emmett's voice was flat and absolute.

"What are you talkin' about, Pa? What do you mean, maybe not?"

"I mean that, in all likelihood, I don't have that long left to live."

Kirby put his fork down and looked at his pa. "The cough?"

"Yeah, but the cough is the result, not the cause." As if on cue, Emmett coughed again, then he continued with his story. "I caught a ball in the lung, Kirby. Not a lot of men survived a wound like that, and I don't mind tellin' you that it laid me flat on my back for weeks. It got all festered up on me. Then lung fever hit the other lung.

"Maybe, just maybe, if I stayed in a dry climate, I might make it, according to the doctors. But they didn't sound hopeful. They also said that I should rest, and I shouldn't exert myself too much. But I can't do that. I swore I would find those men, and I aim to do it.'

"That's why you wanted me to learn the fast draw, and how to shoot without aiming, isn't it?"

"Sort of," Emmett admitted. "If you are with me when I find 'em, you're goin' to just naturally get drawed into it. So, I wanted you to be able to take care of yourself. What happened tonight tells me I'm not going to have to worry."

"Pa . . . we'll find 'em. And if you don't live long enough to find all of 'em, I will. I promise you that. I owe it to you . . . and to Luke."

Emmett reached across the table and squeezed his son's hand. "I knew I could count on you."

"You think they've got dessert in this place?" Kirby asked as he took the last bite of steak, then pushed the plate to one side.

"Lord, boy. You mean you still have room for dessert?"

"Well, not a whole lot of dessert. Just enough to finish out the meal."

"What kind of dessert would you want?"

"Maybe a couple pieces of apple pie, with a slab of cheese melted on top." Kirby smiled. "We can afford it, Pa. We'll be gettin' the reward money tomorrow, don't forget."

Emmett chuckled and shook his head. "You're right. Travelin' around the way we're doin', we won't always have an opportunity to buy pie. I reckon I'll have a piece with you."

"As long as you get your own so I don't have to share," Kirby replied with a smile.

At that same moment, Dr. Tom Dunaway was standing at the buffet in the parlor of the Palace Princess Emporium, perusing the viand that was laid out for the guests—a glistening ham, a roast beef, and fried or baked chicken. In addition, mashed potatoes, baked sweet potatoes, black-eyed peas, fried and boiled okra, baked loaves of bread, rolls, biscuits, and corn bread were spread out on the long table.

Filling his plate, Dr. Dunaway found an overstuffed chair near the fireplace, which had no fire because it was summer. He began to enjoy the food.

"My goodness, Tom," Janey said. "From the looks of your plate, one would think that you hadn't eaten in a month of Sundays."

"What can I say, Lil? I come to the Palace because the food here is better than can be found at any restaurant in town."

"Oh, my. Now you have hurt my feelings. I thought you came here to enjoy my company. But now I learn it is only the food that brings you to the Palace."

"*Au contraire, mon cheri*," Dr. Dunaway said. "It is the lovely *Mademoiselle* Lil that brings me here. *Je viens à vous prélasser dans votre beauté.*"

When it was obvious that Janey had no idea what he had just said, he translated it for her. "I come to bask in your beauty."

"Oh, what a nice thing for you to say, and to say it in such pretty words."

"Yes, French is a beautiful language." Dr. Dunaway nodded toward the plate he was holding. "The food is really a secondary reason." He took a bite of roast beef, then smiled. "But I must admit that it is a strong, secondary reason."

Janey laughed.

"Say, Doc," one of the other guests called out. "Is it true that you were in the Yellow Dog when the shootin' took place this afternoon?"

"Yes, I was there. And I testified to Marshal Wallace that the shooting, at least in two of the cases, was justified."

"McComb seen it, too, 'n he said one of them wasn't no more 'n sixteen or seventeen, and that he was really fast."

"He may have been a little older than that, but not much, I would wager," Dr. Dunaway replied. "And McComb is right, I don't believe I've ever seen anyone extract their weapon with more speed than that young man did."

The parlor was relatively crowded at the moment. Some of the men were waiting for their particular choice in girls; some had already been with a woman and hadn't left yet, while others, like Dr. Dunaway, were just visiting.

Chicago Sue had established her policy that a man could pay five dollars to visit and eat. That was very expensive for a meal that could be had for no more than a dollar at any other restaurant in town, but the food wasn't the only attraction. The five dollars allowed them to fill their plates from the buffet, and also to visit with the women who weren't currently engaged. However, their interaction with the women could go no further than visiting. If they wished to advance the temporary relationship with one of the young ladies, they were charged an additional fee.

Fancy Lil was one of the principal attractions of the parlor because she was an entertaining conversationalist . . . and the men liked being around someone as beautiful as she was. Her presence also provided the catalyst that some might need to engage one of the other girls for a more intimate visit.

"Fancy Lil," Dr. Dunaway said, holding out a wine goblet. "Would you pour me a little more wine?"

"Of course. I would be glad to," Janey replied with a practiced smile. "Red or white?"

"Red wine, of course. White wine is for women and sodomites. It isn't for real men."

Janey smiled. "Well then, by all means, it shall be red wine."

"Say, Doc, what did that feller say the gunmen's names was?" one of the other guests asked.

"I wouldn't call them gunmen," Dr. Dunaway replied. "After all, the word *gunman* has such a negative connotation."

"What would you call them, then?"

"I would call them gentlemen, who, by circumstances not of their own making, were challenged by unexpected events. And they met that challenge, quite admirably."

Janey approached Dr. Dunaway with a bottle of red wine.

"All right, *gentlemen* then. What was their names?"

Janey started to pour the wine.

"Jensen, I think. It was a father and son. Emmett and Kirby Jensen. They were—"

With a gasp, Janey poured wine onto Dr. Dunaway's trousers.

"Lil, watch what you're doing!"

"I'm . . . I'm sorry." She handed Dr. Dunaway the wine bottle, then turned and ran quickly from the parlor.

"Wait, you don't have to run away! I know it was just an accident!"

The other guest frowned. "What did you say to her, Doc?"

"Nothing that would make her run away like that. I don't know what that was all about."

Chicago Sue had never seen Janey act in such a way, so she excused herself and hurried to Janey's room. "Lil?" she called, knocking lightly on the door. She heard nothing from the other side of the door. "Lil, it's me, Sue. Please open the door, dear."

Janey opened the door, then turned and walked back into her room.

Sue followed her inside, then closed the door behind her. "What's wrong, Janey?" she asked, using her real name. "Did Dr. Dunaway do or say something to upset you? If so, I'll make certain that he leaves tonight, and I won't let him come back until you get an apology and a guarantee that he won't do it again."

"No, no, he didn't do anything wrong. It's nothing like that," Janey said, waving her hand.

"Then what is it? What has upset you? Something has, and that's for sure."

"It's them. They are in Dallas. Oh, Sue, they've come for me. I know they have."

"Who? Who has come for you? Janey, are you in trouble with the law?"

"No."

"Then I don't understand. Who has come for you?"

"My father and my brother. I know they have come to take me back to Missouri. Oh, Sue, what can I do? I'll never go back to Missouri. I can't go back!"

"Are they downstairs now? If so, I'll go talk to them."

"No! They aren't downstairs. I'm sure that they don't know that I'm working here. At least not yet."

"Then, how do you know they are here?"

"Did you hear about the shooting in the Yellow Dog Saloon today?"

"Yes, everyone has heard about it. That's all anyone is talking about."

"That was them. The two men all the people are talking about . . . are my father and brother."

"How do you know?"

"Dr. Dunaway said that the shooters' names were Emmett and Kirby Jensen. That can't be a mere coincidence."

"Jensen? I thought your last name was Garner."

Janey sighed. "My last name is Jensen. I left Missouri with a man named Paul Garner, and even though we never got married, I took his name."

"Where is Paul Garner now? Perhaps he is the one who told your family where to find you."

"He's dead. He was caught cheating in a card game and was shot."

"Janey, if you don't want to go back with your father and your brother, there is no need for you to do so.

You are certainly old enough to make up your own mind about such things."

"There's more to it than that."

"Oh?"

"Pa was away in the war and Kirby was running the farm all by himself. He did it from the time he was thirteen. And he did a real good job with it, too. He supported my ma and me. He was saving all the money he made to give to Pa when he came home from the war. Two thousand dollars. He hid the money—"

"And you took it." Sue's comment was more matter-of-fact than accusing.

"Yes. Paul talked me into doing it. He told me that he was an investor, and that if I gave him the two thousand dollars he could double it. I didn't really intend to steal it. I thought I would be able to pay the money back, with interest, before Kirby missed it. I even left a note in the empty jar when I took the money, promising to pay it back."

"But Paul didn't double the money, did he?"

"No, he lost it all. Or almost all. He still had some of the money left when he was shot, but the other card players—the ones who had been cheated by him—took the money and divided it."

"Would you like me to talk to your father and brother?"

"No! Please, no! They can't know that I'm in Dallas! And they especially can't know that I'm a . . . that I'm . . . here," she said, taking in her room with a wave of her hand.

Sue reached out to put her hand on Janey's shoulder. "Honey, you aren't the first girl to run away from home, and you aren't the first girl who took money from her family to finance her escape. And you aren't the first girl who ever wound up on the line." She smiled. "But you are the most beautiful of all the girls I have ever known in such a situation."

Janey smiled through her tears.

"Why don't you let me check around a bit? I won't mention you, and I'll see what I can find out. It may be that they are here for an entirely different reason. You didn't let anyone back in Missouri know you were coming to Dallas, did you?"

"No."

"Then, how could they possibly know you are here? I'm sure the fact that they are in Dallas is just a coincidence."

"They must not know about me, Sue," Janey said. "Please, don't say anything that would get them even suspicious."

"I promise, I'll say nothing about you."

Emmett and Kirby were having breakfast in the dining room of the Lone Star Hotel the next morning when Kirby saw a very attractive woman come into the dining room. She spoke briefly to the maître d', who pointed to their table.

Kirby leaned forward and whispered, "Pa, there's a real pretty woman comin' toward our table. I wonder if it's Fancy Lil."

"Who?"

"You know, the woman Doc and them were talkin' about yesterday. The one they said was so pretty."

Emmett chuckled. "What would make Fancy Lil, or any woman for that matter, come to our table?"

"I don't know, but here she comes."

"I'm sure you are just—" Emmett stopped in mid-sentence when it became evident that the woman actually was coming toward them. "Stand up."

"What for?"

"It's what a gentleman does when a lady approaches him . . . if he is sitting." Emmett stood up.

Following his father's example, Kirby stood as well.

"You would be the Jensens?" the woman asked. "Father and son, I believe." She smiled broadly.

"Yes, ma'am," Emmett replied. "What can we do for you?"

"Oh, you have already done it."

"I beg your pardon?"

"I understand that you killed Emerson Cox, yesterday."

"Yes, ma'am. It wasn't by intention. It was something that—"

"From what I hear, you had no choice. It was either kill him or be killed by him."

"Yes, ma'am. Something like that. Oh, would you join us, Miss . . ."

"Sue. Everyone just calls me Sue. Yes, I would have a cup of coffee with you, if you don't mind being seen with me."

"I don't understand. Why should we mind being seen with you?"

"I told you my name is Sue, but I'm better known as Chicago Sue." The woman smiled again. "That isn't my real name, of course. But women in my profession rarely give their real names."

"Oh." Emmett blushed just a little.

"So you can see why you might not want to embarrass yourself by being seen with me. If you wish to withdraw your invitation to sit with you, I will understand and think no ill of you because of it."

"Don't be silly, Miss Sue. The invitation stands." Emmett held the chair as Sue sat at the table, then he raised his hand to signal for a waiter.

"Yes, sir?" the waiter asked, arriving at the table. The expression on his face as he saw Sue indicated that he knew who she was and that he didn't approve of her being there.

"Coffee for the lady."

"Sir, as you are new in town, perhaps you don't know who she is. Are you sure . . ."

"That I want coffee for the lady? Yes, I'm quite sure. Please bring it."

"Yes, sir."

"I'm sorry. I shouldn't have come," Sue said.

"Don't be silly. You are welcome at our table. But I am curious. Why did you come?"

"The man you shot, Mr. Cox, beat up one of the young ladies in my employ recently. I had him arrested, and he swore that he would extract revenge. I can't be sure that is the only reason he returned to Dallas, but neither can I discount it. At any rate, thanks to you, I no longer have to be afraid of him."

"Does Fancy Lil work for you?" Kirby asked impatiently.

Sue gasped. "What? What do you know about Fancy Lil?"

"We know nothing about her," Emmett replied quickly. He smiled and shook his head. "I don't know what got into him for even asking such a thing."

"I know she is beautiful," Kirby said. "I heard someone in the saloon yesterday say that her face was so beautiful it would launch a thousand ships. I don't know what that means, but she must be some kind of beautiful for a man to say a crazy thing like that."

"Yes, Lil is a beautiful young woman, but then all my girls are . . . or they wouldn't be working for me."

Kirby smiled. "I'd sure like to see what she looks like."

"No, you wouldn't," Emmett said resolutely. "And we don't have time for such things."

"Anyway, it wouldn't be possible for you to see her now," Sue said. "She's away on a trip. I'm not sure when she'll be back."

"They asked about me?" Janey frowned.

"Not about you. The young one . . ."

"My brother."

"He asked about Fancy Lil. And he only asked because he heard someone talking about you in the Yellow Dog. Apparently, someone said that you were so beautiful that your face would launch a thousand ships." Sue laughed. "Now, who do you think would say such a thing?"

"Sounds like Dr. Dunaway."

"Of course, it's Dr. Dunaway. Apparently your brother was fascinated by the idea, and wanted to see someone whose face could do such a thing."

"What did you tell them?"

"I told them that you were away on a trip."

Janey twisted her hands in her lap. "Oh, Sue, what if they come here and see me?"

"I don't think they will. Your father strikes me as a bit of a prude."

Despite her concern, Janey laughed. "Yes, he is a prude."

"Do you really think your father would come to a place like this?"

"No, I don't think he would. But Kirby might."

CHAPTER 10

"**I** may not be here the next time you come," Janey said.

"What?" Big Ben raised himself up on one elbow and looked down at her lying beside him.

The cover came up only to her waist, leaving the rest of her bare body revealed to him. A bar of light slipped in around the edge of the drawn shade, falling upon her right breast and making it gleam in the light.

Ben frowned. "What do you mean you might not be here? Where would you be?"

"I don't know."

"Janey, that doesn't make sense." Since she'd told him her real name, he insisted on using it when they were together. "I mean, how can you say you aren't going to be here, but not have any idea where you will be?"

"It's just that I can't stay here any longer. I can't take the chance. They might find me."

"You can't take a chance on who finding you? Janey,

are you in trouble with the law? If you are, I can afford a lawyer. Hell, I can afford an entire army of lawyers. I don't care what you did. I know I can get you out of it."

"No, it isn't that. I'm not in trouble with the law. It's my pa and my brother that I'm afraid of."

"Why are you afraid of them?"

"Ben, do you really think I want them to know that I wound up doing what I do?"

"I don't think of you in that way."

"Of course you do. How else can you think of me?"

"I can think of you as my wife."

Janey sat up in bed and looked at Ben with a surprised expression on her face. "What?" her voice was so weak that she could barely be heard.

"I said you could be my wife."

Marshal Wallace found the Jensens in the hotel dining room. "If you two will come down to the bank, I'll see to it that you get your reward money. As it turns out, in addition to the five-hundred-dollar reward for Emerson Cox, there was another two hundred dollars bein' offered for Clarence Haggart. So the total comes to seven hundred dollars. That's a pretty good sum of money."

"Yes, sir, it is," Emmett said. "I wouldn't have killed the man for the money, but neither I nor my boy had any choice in the matter. What's done is done, and I have no regrets at taking the money."

Ben Conyers parked the surrey in front of the bank, and set the brake. "Wait here, I've got some business in the bank, but it'll only take a couple minutes," he said with a smile. "Then we'll go out to Live Oaks Ranch."

"Where is Live Oaks?" Janey asked.

"It's just north of Fort Worth. One hundred and twenty thousand acres of the finest land in Texas. You're going to love it there."

"I know that I will." She watched Ben tie off the team, then walk into the bank.

One hundred and twenty thousand acres, he had said. She remembered making the vow never to be the wife of a farmer, but when she'd made that vow she was thinking about the forty acres she had lived on with her family.

The family that she no longer had.

As she was sitting in the carriage she saw the marshal approaching. She knew that, technically, Chicago Sue was violating a city ordinance by running a house of "entertainment," but she knew, too, that the ordinance was aimed at the rowdy, bawdy houses, more than it was at the Palace Princess Emporium, which actually passed itself off as a private club. Fights, stabbings, and even occasional shootings occurred in the bawdy houses. Such a thing had never occurred at the Palace Princess Emporium, and because of that, neither the marshal, nor any of his deputies, had ever made an official visit.

The marshal stopped at the corner and looked back as if waiting for someone. Appearing from behind the building, two other men joined him.

Recognition dawned and Janey drew a quick, alarmed breath. Her pa and brother were headed right past the surrey! No way they would not see her! She looked around in panic. What could she do?

"Marshal Wallace?" someone shouted.

Marshal Wallace held out his hand to stop her pa and her brother, then he turned his attention to the man who had called out to him. So did Emmett and Kirby.

At that moment, Ben came out of the bank, smiling up at Janey. "We're all set."

"Ben, it's them!" Janey hissed.

"What? It's who? What are you talking about?"

"Those two men down there with Marshal Wallace. That's my pa and my brother."

"Have they seen you yet?"

"No."

"Come back into the bank with me until they're gone. No, wait, they might be going to the bank." Looking around, he saw the Elite Dress Shoppe and smiled. "Come." He pulled her from the surrey. "We'll go into the dress shop. It's for sure and certain they won't be going there."

He lifted her down, then put himself between her and the men. "Stay in front of me and keep your head down."

Although it was only a few steps from the surrey to the dress shop, Janey held her breath and clenched her fists, waiting to hear her name called. She breathed a sigh of relief when they went inside.

"Yes, can I help you?" a female clerk asked.

"Do you have any ready-made dresses? Not everyday work dresses, mind you. I want something fine and beautiful, for a beautiful lady."

"Indeed we do, sir," the clerk replied.

"Good, then help her find something, would you? And you can take your time."

In the bank, the chief teller counted out seven hundred dollars and handed the money to Emmett. Emmett turned and gave half the money to Kirby.

"That is a great deal of money to be carrying with you," the bank president said. "I would be very happy to open an account for you."

Emmett nodded. "Thank you, but we won't be staying in town long enough to have an account. We'll be moving on today."

"I don't know where you are bound, but if you are looking for a good place to settle down, you won't find any place any better than Dallas."

"I'm sure Dallas is a nice town. But my son and I have itchy feet. I've seen the Atlantic Ocean. Now I have a hankering to see the Pacific."

The bank president didn't understand. "Why? Once you've seen one ocean, you've seen them all."

"The boy hasn't seen either ocean," Emmett said.

As his pa and the banker were talking, Kirby saw a newspaper lying on a table in the middle of the bank, and he walked over to glance at it.

MISSOURI BUSHWHACKER
TO BE TRIED IN SALCEDO
Elmer Gleason Rode with
Bloody Bill Anderson

Elmer Gleason, who is one of the most malevolent men ever to come out of the late war, has been captured in Salcedo. It is said that when he rode with Quantrill and Bloody Bill Anderson he kept a string of ears severed from the heads of his victims, be they man, woman, or child.

Although those who followed their conscience to fight for the South have been paroled, the villains who rode with Quantrill and Bloody Bill Anderson can never be forgiven. The trespasses of such men are so great that only He, who is the final arbitrator of the transgressions of those who have made their temporary journey upon this mortal coil, will be able to grant them final remission and absolution of their sins.

Trial for Elmer Gleason will commence on the 28th instant.

"Pa?" Kirby asked when they left the bank a few minutes later. "How long would it take for us to get to Salcedo?"

"I don't know. I don't know where Salcedo is or how far it is from here. Why do you ask?"

"We need to go there."

"We need to go to Salcedo? Why?"

"A friend of mine is in trouble there."

Emmett frowned impatiently. "What friend? And how come you're just now tellin' me this?"

"I didn't know about it until just now. I saw it in the paper while we was in the bank. We need to be there by the twenty-eighth of this month."

"You saw in the paper that you have a friend in trouble in Salcedo, and we have to be there by the twenty-eighth? What happens if we don't get there by the twenty-eighth?"

"It's more 'n likely, Elmer will get hung."

"All right. Who is Elmer?"

Kirby figured it was now or never. "Pa, there's somethin' me 'n you need to talk about."

"I'm sure there is." Emmett waited . . . impatiently.

"Well, I reckon it's about as good a time as any to tell you." Kirby took a deep breath. "Pa, the fella I killed yesterday . . . wasn't the first man I ever killed. I've been in some battles, quite a few of 'em, only there wasn't none of 'em big battles like the kind you fought."

Without expanding on his own role in the battles, he told of riding with Asa Briggs and being in fights at such places as Clark's Mill, Hartville, Pilot Knob, Glasgow, Lexington, and Newtonia.

"I was at Baxter Springs, too," Kirby said. "That's why I was a little hesitant about us goin' there. I was afraid someone might recognize me."

Emmett was shocked. "Boy, answer me, and I want you to tell me the truth. Did you burn any private houses or kill any innocent people?"

"No, Pa, we didn't. I will say that the Ghost Riders, that's what those of us who rode with Briggs called ourselves, from time to time joined up with Quantrill for some of the battles. And I've heard of some of the things he done, but Briggs was real particular about not killin' innocent people. And none of that ever happened on those few times Asa Briggs teamed up with Quantrill. Fact is, I don't think I woulda stayed with him if he had done anything like that."

"What you just told me has something to do with your friend Elmer?"

"Yes, sir. His name is Elmer Gleason, 'n he rode some with Quantrill and some with Bloody Bill Anderson. Then, toward the end, he rode with Asa Briggs, 'n that's when he become my friend. But now they got him on trial at Salcedo, on account of he rode with Quantrill and Anderson."

Emmett gave it some thought. "You say you want to go to Salcedo. What do you plan to do?"

"I'm not sure. But if we can figure out how to do it, I'd like to rescue him."

"It would mean violatin' the law."

"That might be true, Pa. But there's also such a thing as honor, ain't there? Seems to me, if I didn't try to save my friend, that would violate my honor."

Emmett looked at Kirby for a long moment, then nodded and put his hand on his son's shoulder. "You're right. There is such a thing as honor. But, I've got a feelin' you ain't told me ever'thing."

'No, sir. I reckon I ain't."

"Is it about your ma and your sister?"

"Yes, sir. You asked me why I wanted to kill Angus Shardeen, and what I told you about him killin' Kenny 'n his family and Merlin 'n his family is true, but that ain't the all of it. Ma didn't die in her sleep like I told you. She was killed by the Jayhawkers. Angus Shardeen is the one that shot her."

"Him in particular? Or one of his men?"

"It was him in particular, Pa, 'cause I seen him do it. I didn't have no gun or nothin', so there wasn't nothin' I could do. The only reason I joined up with Asa Briggs was 'cause I wanted to go after Shardeen. I wanted to find him and kill him. But we never found him. That's why I say that if I find him, I'm goin' to kill 'im."

"Seems reasonable to me," Emmett said. "We'll just add his name to the list of Potter, Stratton, Casey, and Richards."

"Oh, and Pa, about the funeral for Ma? I lied to you about that, too. I told you that folks come from all over, but the truth is that the only funeral was the one that me 'n Janey give her. It was Janey that dressed her in her best dress, and I'm the one that dug the grave. Janey cleaned out the feedin' trough, the one that was used for the milk cows, and that's what we put Ma in. I'm sorry we didn't have somethin' a lot more fine for her."

Emmett nodded. "You know, I have a feelin' that your ma probably appreciated that a lot more 'n she would have if a whole lot of folks had showed up for it."

"Yes, sir. I kinda hope that's the way it is."

"What about Janey? Did she actually run off like you said?"

"Yes, sir, she did. But I can't hardly blame her. The same men that killed Ma used Janey, Pa. They used her bad. She left home right after we buried Ma."

"With the gamblin' fella?"

Kirby nodded. "Yes, sir."

"When you started tellin' the story, I thought it might be somethin' like that. I reckon now I don't hold it ag'in her so much that she left as I did. I reckon she felt like she had a good enough reason."

She might have had a good reason to leave, but she didn't have a good reason to take all their money with her, Kirby thought, but he didn't share that with his pa.

"I wonder where she is now?" Emmett asked. "I wonder if she is alive?"

* * *

"Oh, it's beautiful!" Janey was looking at herself in the mirror at the dress shop as she tried on one of the dresses.

Ben sat in a nearby chair. "Would you like it?"

"Oh, Ben, no. I mean yes, of course I like it. But I can't let you buy this for me."

"Why not? It isn't like I can't afford it."

"That's not the point."

"Of course it's the point. You like it, and I like seeing it on you." He looked at the clerk. "We'll take it."

"Wonderful. I'll just go get the ledger book and the cash box."

"They're gone," Ben said quietly after the clerk left.

Janey turned toward him. "How do you know?"

"I saw them leave the bank and walk down to the Lone Star Hotel. As soon as I pay the clerk, we'll leave town in the opposite direction."

"Oh, Ben, are you sure it will be safe? I don't know what I would do if they actually saw me."

"How long has it been since either of them saw you?"

"It's been four years since Pa last saw me, and three years since Kirby saw me."

"What were you wearing, then?"

"What? I don't know. Some sort of plain cotton dress, I think."

"Nothing like this," he said, taking in the dress she was wearing with a wave of his hand.

Janey looked down at the beautiful dress. "No, nothing like this."

Ben saw a hat with a veil, and he smiled and picked it up. "Put this on when we leave. The way you look now, you could bump right into them, and I doubt that either of them would recognize you."

Janey chuckled. "I think you might be right."

Kirby and Emmett rode into Waco on the twenty-seventh and went straight to the livery stable.

"What can I do for you gentlemen?" the liveryman asked, meeting them as they dismounted.

"We need to board our horses," Emmett said. "Is there a place we can leave our things from the pack animals?"

"Yes, sir. We got individual tack rooms you can rent for fifteen cents a night. For an extra nickel, you can rent a lock."

"Good, that's what we'll do."

"You goin' to be here long?"

"We'll be ridin' out tomorrow, but I plan to leave the two pack horses here for a while. Not sure exactly how long."

"Your horses will be a quarter apiece. That includes hay. Thirty cents if you want 'em to have oats."

"We'll want the oats," Emmett said. "How far is Salcedo from here?"

"It's about ten miles. Just follow the railroad south, and you can't miss it. Headin' that way, are you?"

"I thought we might take a look."

"It ain't that pleasant a town to visit if you want to know the truth of it. They's a bunch of Yankee soldiers down there right now reconstructin' us, 'n they've plumb took over the town. The mayor and the city marshal got no say at all. They got a Yankee captain that runs the town 'n a Yankee judge that makes the laws. The people o' the town ain't got nothin' to say about it."

"I thank you for the information."

"But you plannin' on goin' anyway, ain't you?"

"Yeah," Emmett answered. "We'll take the two saddle mounts tomorrow. Here's sixty cents for them."

"What about the pack horses?"

"I'd like to sell 'em, if you know anyone that might be interested."

The liveryman stroked his chin and examined the two pack horses. "I might be. How much would you be askin' for 'em?"

"Fifty dollars apiece."

"I need to make a little money from 'em. I'll give you thirty dollars."

They settled on forty dollars apiece.

The liveryman gave Emmett the money. "I'll look after 'em real good until I sell 'em. Good luck in Salcedo."

Emmett nodded. "Thanks."

"What do you have in mind for tomorrow?" Emmett asked Kirby in their hotel room that night.

"I don't know, exactly, Pa. Maybe I could testify for him or somethin'."

"What would you say?"

"I'd say that I rode with him when I was with the Ghost Riders, and I never saw him do anything bad."

"I doubt that will help."

"Prob'ly not. But, Pa, he's a friend. I can't just turn my back on a friend now, can I?"

"No," Emmett said. "You're right to try and do what you can for a friend."

* * *

Emmett and Kirby followed the railroad south from Waco until they came to Salcedo, identified by a sign attached to the end of the depot, a small, red-painted, wooden building. Posted alongside the track was another sign.

CAUTION TO BRAKEMEN
NO SIDE CLEARANCE AHEAD

As they passed the depot they saw another sign that listed the passenger schedule.

NORTHBOUND TRAINS
11 AM 5 PM 11 PM
SOUTHBOUND TRAINS
9 AM 2 PM 9 PM

Leaving the track they had followed from Waco, they rode on into town where they passed a hangman's gallows in the middle of the street. They stopped to read a sign that had been nailed to the gallows.

AT TEN O'CLOCK TOMORROW MORNING
ELMER GLEASON
THE BUSHWHACKER BUTCHER
WILL BE HANGED
ON THESE GALLOWS

"You boys here for the hangin', are you?" asked a toothless old man.

"Have we missed the trial?" Kirby asked. "The paper said the trial was today."

"No, you ain't missed it. They'll be holdin' the trial at one o'clock today."

"I don't understand. This sign says Elmer will be hung tomorrow morning. How can they say that if he hasn't been found guilty."

"Oh, they'll find him guilty all right. They ain't no gettin' around that. You called him Elmer. He a friend o' yours, is he?"

"Elmer is what the name on the sign says, isn't it?" Emmett asked, speaking quickly before his son could reply.

The old-timer nodded. "Yeah, that's what the sign says, all right."

"Then that's why we called him Elmer. Where's the trial to be held?" Emmett asked.

"Onliest place it can be held." The old man pointed toward the largest building in town. "Right down there in the Scalded Cat Saloon. But iffen you're wantin' a drink, you'd best get it before one o'clock, 'cause that Yankee that's been appointed judge won't let Clyde sell any liquor while the trial is goin' on."

"Thank you for the information," Emmett said.

"Sorry 'bout your friend." The old man waved a hand as the two rode farther into town.

They passed the jail. Two armed soldiers were standing out front.

"Pa, do you think they'd let us see Elmer?"

"I don't know. But we won't know unless we try."

Dismounting, the two tied off their horses, then started across the street toward the jail.

One of the soldiers stepped out in front of them. "Where do you think you're goin'?"

"We want to talk to the prisoner," Kirby said.

"Why?"

"That would be between us and the prisoner," Emmett replied.

"Yeah? Well it don't matter what it's about, 'cause you ain't goin' to see 'im."

"Take their guns and let 'em see 'im," said the other soldier, a sergeant. "He'll be dead by a little after three today, anyway, so what's it goin' to hurt?"

"All right, Sarge. If you say so," the private said. "You boys give me your guns, 'n you can go on in."

Emmett and Kirby surrendered their pistols, then stepped into the office. Four men were playing cards around a desk, two civilians wearing badges and two soldiers. One of the soldiers had captain's bars on his shoulder board.

One of the men wearing a badge looked up. "What can I do for you?"

Kirby spoke first. "Marshal, the sergeant out front took our weapons and told us we could visit with the prisoner."

"Yeah? Why do you want to visit with him?"

"We're looking for someone and he might be able to tell us where to find him," Emmett said.

The marshal was quiet for a moment, then he nodded. "All right. Go ahead, but I'll tell you right now, he ain't much of a talker. We've been tryin' to get him to tell us if there's any more of Quantrill or Anderson's men down here, but he ain't told us nothin'."

"You goin' to talk all day or are you goin' to play cards?" one of the others asked. "I've got a good hand here, one that's goin' to get me back even."

"Go on over there and talk to him, if you want," the marshal said, pointing to the single cell at the back of the room.

Kirby walked to the cell. Elmer Gleason was lying

on his bunk with his hands laced behind his head, staring up at the ceiling.

"Hi, Elmer," Kirby said.

"Damn, I thought that sounded like your voice." Elmer sat up and threw his legs over the side of his bunk. "What are you doing here?"

"I came to see you.

"Well, that was damn fine of you."

Kirby motioned to his pa. "Elmer, this is my pa."

Elmer walked over to stick his hand through the bars. "It's good to meet the boy's pa after all this time. He's always spoke high of you, but I'm sure you know that."

"He's a good boy," Emmett replied.

"Elmer, how'd you wind up here in jail?" Kirby asked.

"I got drunk."

"Drunk? They put you in jail for bein' drunk?"

"Not exactly just for bein' drunk. What happened was, I was just passin' through town 'n I stopped in at the Scalded Cat for a couple o' drinks. Well, it was a lot of drinks, 'n I got drunk 'n wound up tellin' that I rode with Quantrill. I figured, this bein' a Southern town, there wouldn't be no problem with it. Turned out they was a lot of Yankee soldiers in the saloon alistenin' to me, 'n the next thing I knew, I was arrested and brought here."

"Why would they arrest you for that? There's no paper out on any of the men who rode with Quantrill, is there?" Emmett asked.

"Not that I know of, except maybe Archie Clement," Elmer said. "But I don't think that matters. They want me, and they've got me."

"All right. You've visited with the prisoner long enough," the marshal said. "We've got to get him ready for the trial."

"We'll be at your trial," Kirby said.

"I appreciate it. And it was real nice of you two to drop by."

CHAPTER 11

"Hear ye, hear ye, hear ye! This here trial is about to commence, the honorable Daniel Gilmore, presidin'," the bailiff shouted.

The judge stepped up from the back of the saloon and took his seat behind a table being used as the judge's bench. He adjusted the glasses on the end of his nose, then cleared his throat. "Would the bailiff please bring the accused before the bench?"

The bailiff, who was leaning against the side wall, spit a quid of tobacco into the brass spittoon, then walked over to the table where Elmer was sitting. "Get up, you," he growled. "Present yourself before the judge."

Elmer approached the bench.

"Elmer Gleason, the charge against you is that you rode for that butchering, thieving, raping bushwhacker Quantrill," the judge said. "How do you plead?"

"Quantrill never raped nobody," Elmer said. "It was only them Jayhawkers that ever done any rapin', 'n they done plenty of it, I can tell you."

"You aren't here to make a speech. I'm going to ask you again, how do you plead?"

Keith Davenport, the attorney appointed to represent Elmer, stood up behind the table he'd shared with his defendant. "Your Honor, if it please the court."

"You got somethin' to say to this court, Mr. Davenport?" the judge asked.

"Yes, Your Honor. Quantrill conducted all of his operations in Kansas and Missouri."

"What does that have to do with anything?"

"Well, Your Honor, we are in Texas. Even if Mr. Gleason is guilty of murder and looting, it didn't happen in this state. Either Kansas or Missouri is the state that should be trying this case. We don't have jurisdiction to try it here."

"Your Honor, if I may?" the prosecutor spoke up quickly. "Everybody knows that Quantrill spent a winter right here in Texas. That's all we need to give this court standing."

The judge nodded. "Your point is well taken, Mr. Taylor."

"But Your Honor, these were his own people. Even if he was here, you know that neither Quantrill, nor by extension, my client, would have done any murdering or thieving while they were here."

"None that we know of, Your Honor," Taylor countered. "But that doesn't matter anyway. We're trying this defendant for being one of Quantrill's riders, not for any specific act of murder or robbery he may have done. Therefore, the fact that Quantrill was once in Texas, and that this defendant was with him, is all that is required to put this case under your jurisdiction."

The judge slapped his gavel on the bench again.

"You are right, Mr. Prosecutor. Mr. Davenport, your motion for dismissal is denied. This case shall proceed."

"Very well, Your Honor."

"How do you plead?" the judge asked again.

Before Elmer got a word out, his attorney spoke. "Your Honor, my client pleads guilty and throws himself upon the mercy of the court."

"What? Wait a minute!" Elmer shouted. "Judge, I ain't pleadin' guilty to nothin'!"

"You have already confessed your guilt, Mr. Gleason," the judge replied.

"The hell I have. That was my lawyer that just done that. It warn't me."

"I'm not talking about your lawyer's plea. I'm talking about your own declaration of guilt. Did you, or did you not, confess before several assembled men in the Scalded Cat Saloon, that you rode with Quantrill?"

"I wouldn't put it that it was a confession," Elmer said. "It was mostly just me drinkin' 'n tellin' war stories."

"In the telling of those stories, did you say you rode with Quantrill?" the judge asked again.

"I ain't confessin' to nothin'," Elmer said.

"Very well," the judge said. "Clerk, change Mr. Gleason's plea from guilty to not guilty."

"Your Honor, may I have a moment with my client?" Davenport asked.

"You may."

Elmer returned to the table and sat down.

Davenport spoke quietly. "Mr. Gleason, I think you are making a big mistake here. If you plead guilty, the judge might show some mercy in his final decision. On the other, if this goes to trial, and you're found guilty, you'll get none."

"So what if I am found guilty? What's he goin' to do to me, tell me I can't vote or somethin'? Hell, I ain't never voted for nobody nohow. I ain't got no truck with politicians."

"Do you really not know? No, how could you? You have been in jail all this time."

"What is it I don't know?"

"Mr. Gleason, I'm afraid that a gallows has already been constructed. You are scheduled to be hanged at nine o'clock tomorrow morning."

"What? How the hell can they already say I'm goin' to be hung, when I ain't even been tried yet?"

"That's the point I'm trying to make. Don't you understand? This trial is totally immaterial. The judge has already made up his mind to find you guilty. Your only hope is to plead guilty and beg for mercy."

"The hell I will. I ain't beggin' that Yankee judge for nothin'."

"Very well, Mr. Gleason. But don't say I didn't warn you." Davenport looked back toward the bench. "Your honor, the conference with my client is concluded."

"Have you reconsidered your plea, Mr. Gleason?" the judge asked.

"No, I ain't. I said I was not guilty 'n that's what I'm standin' by."

"So you say, and so it shall be. Mr. Prosecutor, are you prepared to make your case?" the judge asked.

"I am, Your Honor."

"You may call your first witness."

"You men over there," the prosecutor said, pointing to three men sitting in the front row. All three were wearing the uniform of the US Army. "You are my witnesses. Stand up and hold up your right hand."

The men did as they were instructed, and the clerk swore them in.

"Now," the prosecutor said. "Did any of you hear this man say that he had ridden for Quantrill?"

The witnesses answered in the affirmative.

"We all heard him say that," added the only sergeant within the group.

The prosecutor turned back toward the judge. "Well, there you go, Your Honor. All three of these men have just sworn that they heard the defendant admit to being one of Quantrill's riders during the war."

"Mr. Davenport, do you wish to question any of these men?" Judge Gilmore asked.

"Yes, Your Honor. You, Sergeant"—Davenport pointed to the soldier who was wearing three stripes on his sleeves—"what, exactly, did you hear my client say?"

"He said that he rode with Quantrill 'n Bloody Bill Anderson, 'n that him 'n others that rode with 'em kilt a bunch of Yankee ba— Aw, Judge, I don't want to say what he called 'em. Not where women might hear."

"I think we can figure it out. He said that?" Judge Gilmore asked.

The sergeant nodded. "Yes, sir. That's what he said."

"You may continue your cross, Mr. Davenport."

Davenport asked the witness, "Did he say, specifically, that he had killed civilians?"

"Like I told you, all he said was that he had kilt a bunch of Yankee . . . you know."

"Sergeant, did you take part in any battles in the late war?" Davenport asked.

"Yes, sir."

"And did you kill anyone?"

The sergeant smiled. "Oh, I reckon I musta kilt me at least five or six of the Secesh sons of bit—" He halted in mid-word, then corrected himself. "Uh, that is, I figure I kilt five or six of the enemy soldiers."

"Five or six, by your own count?"

"Yeah."

"Sergeant, do you consider yourself a murderer?"

"What? No, it was war. If you kill someone in a war, that ain't murder."

"If you kill someone in a war, it isn't murder. Is that what you are saying?"

"You're damn right that's what I'm sayin'."

Davenport looked pointedly at Elmer. "That's good to hear. No further questions."

"Redirect, Mr. Taylor?" the judge asked.

"Sergeant, did you kill any civilians during the war?" Taylor asked.

"No, sir. Ever'one I kilt was a soldier."

"Thank you. I'm through with this witness."

"Does defense wish to call any witnesses?"

"Your Honor, I have no—" Davenport started, but he was interrupted.

The entire court was surprised when Kirby suddenly stood up and shouted, "Me, Your Honor!"

Angrily, the judge rapped his gavel on the table. "Order in the court! Here, what do you mean by interrupting my court in such a way?"

"I'd like to be a witness on behalf of the defendant."

"Do you know anything about this, Counselor?" the judge asked Davenport.

"No, sir."

"Do you have anything that would qualify you to bear witness to this case?" the judge asked Kirby.

"I do, Your Honor."

"Get to the bottom of this, Mr. Davenport," the judge ordered.

The defense attorney walked to where Kirby was still standing. "Young man, do you know the defendant?"

"Yes, sir, I know him."

The marshal waved his hand. "Your Honor, this man came to visit the prisoner in the jail last night."

"Why didn't you say anything about it?" Judge Gilmore asked.

"I didn't say nothin' 'cause I didn't have no idea he was goin' to want to be a witness. He never told me anythin' about that last night. He and another man just visited with the prisoner, is all."

The judge looked at the gallery. "Is the other man who was with him, present in this court?"

"Yes, sir. He's sittin' right there beside him." The marshal pointed toward Emmett.

"Is it your wish to be a witness as well?" Judge Gilmore asked.

"No, sir. I never met the man before last night," Emmett replied. "I couldn't say one way or the other whether or not he's guilty."

"You." Gilmore pointed toward Kirby. "Who are you, and what information do you have that you think might be pertinent to this case?"

"My name is Kirby Jensen, Your Honor. And, during the war, I rode with the defendant."

Several gasps of surprise came from those who were present to watch the trial.

The judge rapped his gavel. "Are you telling the court that you rode with Quantrill?"

"I rode with Quantrill, Bloody Bill Anderson, and Asa Briggs," Kirby replied.

"Bailiff, swear this man in," the judge ordered.

The bailiff signaled for Kirby to come forward, then he held forth a Bible. "Do you swear to tell the truth, the whole truth, and nothing but the truth, so help you God?"

"I do."

"Now, Mr. Jensen, I ask you again," Judge Gilmore said. "And this time you are under oath. Did you ride with Quantrill, Anderson, Briggs, and this man, Elmer Gleason?"

Kirby knew that he hadn't ridden with Quantrill or Anderson in the scope of the question as was being posed by the judge. But at times a merging of the guerrilla groups had occurred, and from that perspective, he could, truthfully, answer the question in the affirmative. "I did, Your Honor."

"Marshal Ferrell, take this man's gun, and place him under arrest."

"I'm not wearin' a gun," Kirby said.

"Make certain," the judge said.

The marshal checked him closely. "He's tellin' the truth, Judge. He ain't got no gun."

"Very well. He may testify as a witness, but he is also a defendant. This has become a double trial. Mr. Jensen is being tried along with Mr. Gleason, and any verdict reached for one, shall apply to both. Put him at the defendant's table alongside Gleason."

"Yes, sir," the marshal said.

"Mr. Davenport, you may present your case now," the judge said.

"I call my first witness, Mister—" Davenport looked directly at Kirby. "Excuse me, what did you say your name was?"

"Jensen. Kirby Jensen."

"Would you take the stand, Mr. Jensen?"

As Kirby sat in the witness chair, the judge looked over toward him. "I would remind the witness that you are already sworn in."

"Yes, sir," Kirby replied.

"Mr. Jensen, you have stated that you rode with the Southern guerrillas."

"Yes, sir."

"How old are you?"

"I'm seventeen."

"Seventeen? Isn't that a little young? How old were you when you began riding with the guerrillas?"

"I was fifteen."

"And you have ridden, specifically, with Mr. Gleason?"

"Yes, sir."

"Did you ever see Mr. Gleason kill an innocent civilian, or a woman, or a child?"

"No, sir, I never did."

"Thank you. Your witness, counselor."

Taylor stood up. "Have you ever killed anyone, Jensen?"

"Yes, sir."

"No further questions."

"The witness is dismissed."

Kirby started, "Your Honor, the only ones I ever killed—"

Rap! The judge cut him short with the sharp rap of his gavel. "I said you are dismissed."

"Your Honor, redirect?" Davenport called quickly.

Judge Gilmore sighed audibly. "Very well, Counselor, you may redirect."

Davenport stood in front of Kirby. "You were about to make a statement. You may make it now."

"I was just goin' to say that the only men I've ever killed were trying to kill me," Kirby said.

"Have you ever killed any women or children?"

"No, sir."

"Thank you. No further questions."

"Marshal Ferrell, return this man to the defendant's table," the judge ordered.

The marshal stepped up to Kirby and walked him to the defense table.

"Mr. Davenport, will Mr. Gleason take the stand in his own defense?"

"You're damn right I will," Elmer said.

Davenport sighed. It was obvious that he would have rather his client not take the stand.

"Can I say somethin' before you start askin' questions?" Elmer asked.

"You may."

Elmer pointed to Kirby. "Kirby warn't nothin' but a boy when I first seen 'im. Hell, he ain't more 'n a boy now. But boy or not, he's a good man. I never seen him do nothin' wrong. Even comin' here, he come to help me 'cause he read about it in the paper. That's the kind of person he is. He coulda just kept on agoin', 'n none of you woulda ever even heerd of 'im. So I'm askin' you now, whatever happens to me, I want you to leave the boy out of it. Like I said, he never done nothin' wrong." Elmer nodded at Davenport. "All right, you can ask your questions now."

"Mr. Gleason, why did you ride with such men as Quantrill and Anderson?" Davenport asked.

"We was at war," Elmer said. "And I felt like it was the right thing to do."

"Did you gain personally from riding with the guerrillas? By that, I mean did you enrich yourself by looting and pillaging?"

"I'm not sure what pillagin' means. But if you're askin' did I ever keep any of the money we took from time to time, the answer is no."

"In your mind, would you say that the only reason you participated in the war was from a sense of duty to your state?"

"Yes. I was just a soldier doin' my duty," Elmer said. "I know they was lots of men that rode for the Blue who done just as bad, and some of 'em done worse 'n we did. I ain't holdin' that against 'em, now that all the fightin' is over. It was a war, 'n I reckon they was thinkin' it was their duty, just like them of us that rode with Quantrill or Anderson. But they ain't none of them looked on as criminals like we are, 'n there ain't nothin' right about that. Nothin' at all."

"Thank you, Mr. Gleason. I have no further questions, Your Honor."

"Cross, Mr. Taylor?"

Taylor stood up, then walked over to stand in front of Elmer. He folded his arms across his chest, leaned forward, and stared directly at Elmer. "You were just a soldier doing your duty, you say?" he asked sarcastically.

"Yes, sir. That's what I done, all right. I done my duty."

"Tell me, Mr. Gleason, would you consider the burning and sacking, and the murder of civilians in the town of Lawrence, Kansas, as just doing your duty? You do recall that, don't you?"

Elmer didn't respond.

"Were you present when Quantrill attacked Lawrence?"

Elmer still didn't answer.

Taylor turned to the judge. "Your Honor, I request you order the defendant to answer the question."

The judge nodded. "The defendant will answer the question."

"Were you present on that day, Mr. Gleason?" the prosecutor asked again.

"Yes, sir, I was there," Elmer replied, the words so quiet that they could barely be heard.

"Speak up please. Loudly enough so that everyone can hear you. Were you present for the sacking of Lawrence, Kansas?"

"Yes!" Elmer said loudly.

"Old men and young boys were rounded up and murdered. Houses and businesses were burned," Taylor said. "Is that duty, Mr. Gleason?"

"It was war. I ain't proud of it, but it was war."

"Your Honor, I am finished with this man," Taylor said.

"Redirect, Mr. Davenport?" the judge asked.

"No, Your Honor."

"Then defense may make a closing argument."

"Your Honor, Marshal Ferrell is a Texan. But he's the only person of authority who is a Texan. I know that you and the appointed mayor and the prosecutor, and just about everyone else with any power in this town, in this state, and throughout the South, are Yankees, sent here for reconstruction.

"But if you would just look out into the gallery you'll see men and women who were born and raised here. They are good people, Your Honor, Southerners by birth, and, during the late unpleasantness, they were Southerners by loyalty. If you ask them to pass judgment against these men, simply because they fought for what they believed in, they're goin' to tell you that Mr. Gleason 'n the boy sittin' there beside him, were no more than soldiers doing their duty in a war that, by its very existence, pitted friend against friend, brother against brother, and in some cases, father against son. Because of that, the war was particularly brutal. It's going to take several generations before all hard feelings go away. As you have come to live among us, I ask that you pass judgment on this matter with some feeling for the sensitivities of those who, by appointment and not by election, you now represent."

The gallery broke into cheers and applause.

Judge Gilmore was surprised by the spontaneous reaction of the gallery and, angrily, he banged his gavel until they were quiet.

"You forget, Mr. Davenport, that the state of Texas is in subjugation to the laws of the United States. I do not give a whit about the laws or the sensitivities of the people of Texas. I am here to perform the duty for which I was appointed." He looked over toward the jury. "You gentlemen of the jury. Do you go along with these folks in the gallery? Do you think these men who rode with Quantrill were nothing more than soldiers doing their duty?"

The men of the jury looked at each other, spoke quietly among themselves, then one of them spoke out. "Yes, sir, Your Honor. That's exactly what we think."

"Are you telling me that if I asked this jury for a verdict right now, it would be not guilty?"

"Yes, sir. We've spoke about it, 'n we've already come to a verdict. The verdict is they ain't neither one of 'em guilty."

Again, everyone cheered. Kirby, Elmer, and Davenport smiled broadly.

Judge Gilmore pounded his gavel on the makeshift bench until the gallery was quiet. "Your celebration is premature. I have not called for a verdict, nor shall I call for a verdict. This jury is dismissed," the judge said angrily.

Davenport objected. "Your Honor, if you empanel another jury, and hold this trial again, you are going to get the same result. No jury of this man's peers is going to find him guilty for doing his duty."

"You don't understand, Mr. Davenport," the judge said with an evil grin. "I have no intention of calling another jury. I will make the decision myself."

"What?" Davenport bellowed. "Your Honor, you can't do that! That's not legal."

"I can and I will. I find both defendants guilty as charged. You are free, Mr. Davenport, to appeal my decision, but in all candor I must tell you that an appeal would be nothing but a waste of time, for the sentence will have been long carried out before any decision can be made on the appeal. Elmer Gleason and—" He glanced toward the prosecutor. What's the boy's name?"

"Jensen, Your Honor. Kirby Jensen," Taylor said.

"Elmer Gleason and Kirby Jensen, please present yourselves before my bench while I administer the sentence."

"Your Honor, we beg for mercy," Davenport said quickly.

"No, we don't, by God!" Elmer said sharply. He glanced over at Kirby. "I don't know about the boy. I'll let him make his own decision."

"I'll not be beggin' for mercy," Kirby said.

Judge Gilmore took off his glasses and began polishing them. He put them back on, hooking them carefully over his ears. He looked at the two defendants standing before him and cleared his throat. "Elmer Gleason and . . ." Again he paused.

"Kirby Jensen," Taylor added quietly.

"Elmer Gleason and Kirby Jensen, you have been tried before me and have been found guilty of the crime of riding with the butcher Quantrill, and aiding and abetting in the atrocities of murder, arson, and robbery that he visited upon innocent people. It is the sentence of this court that you be taken from this courthouse and put in jail where you will spend your last night on this mortal coil. At ten o'clock of the morrow, you will be taken to the gallows already constructed, and there, both of you will be suspended by your necks until you are dead."

"No!" someone in the court shouted. "You can't hang them, you Yankee crook! They ain't guilty of nothin' but bein' soldiers!"

"Marshal" the judge said. "Arrest the man who just made that outburst, and hold him in contempt of court!"

Marshal Ferrell stood and looked out over the gallery. "Arrest which man, Judge? I didn't see who it was."

To a man, every person in the courtroom was quiet.

"Who was it?" the judge asked. "Who made that outburst?"

There was no response to his inquiry.

"All right, all right!" the judge said. "You Rebels think you are putting one over on me, do you? But we'll see who has the last laugh tomorrow when these men are legally executed. Court is adjourned." He rapped the gavel once more.

The judge, the bailiff, and the prosecutor left the saloon by the back door.

"Damn, Marshal Ferrell, you ain't really goin' to hang 'em, are you?" someone called.

"You heard the judge. He give me the order. There ain't nothin' I can do about it."

"Kirby, what 'n hell did you do that for?" Elmer asked after the two men were taken back to the cell.

"I wanted to do what I could to help."

Elmer shook his head. "Well, you didn't have to go so far. Damn, boy, just showin' up woulda been enough. But what you done is got yourself caught up into the same mess I'm in."

To Elmer's surprise, Kirby flashed a big smile. "Yeah, I did, didn't I?"

Elmer frowned at him. "Boy, have you gone daft on me? Ain't you got no idea as to what's goin' to happen?"

"I know exactly what's going to happen," Kirby said. "That's why I got myself put in here."

"You got yourself put in here? Of a pure purpose?"

Kirby nodded. "Of a pure purpose."

CHAPTER 12

At that same moment, Emmett was at the livery, looking at a horse advertised for sale.

"He's a real good ridin' horse," the liveryman said. "It was rode by one of the officers in John Bell Hood's Division. Iffen you know'd anything about Hood, you know he had only the best horses."

"Yes, I know all about General Hood," Emmett replied. Hood, though an aggressive and effective officer for most of the war, had gotten many of his men slaughtered in an ill-advised frontal attack at Franklin, but Emmett didn't mention it.

"Do you have a saddle for sale as well?"

"I do, sir. I do indeed."

"Saddle him up, then ride him around the corral for me. I'd like to see him work, if you don't mind," Emmett said.

"Yes, sir. I would be happy to."

A few minutes later, the horse was saddled, and the liveryman rode him in compliance with Emmett's request. During the ride, Emmett observed the horse closely, listening to the rhythm of the gait and checking for equal striding in distance and time on the ground. He watched how the horse held his head and observed the footfalls to see if the animal showed any indication of sore feet. The horse passed his rather thorough examination.

Satisfied, Emmett said, "I'll take him. Please have this horse, and the two that I am now boarding with you, saddled and ready for me to pick up by seven o'clock this evening."

"Yes, sir. They'll be ready for you." The liveryman was happy to have made the sale.

"In the meantime, I need to rent a horse and a buckboard for a couple hours."

"All right. I'll get that ready for you right now."

A few minutes later, Emmett drove the buckboard from the livery down to the depot where he examined the rather high growth of weeds along the track. He decided they were in just the right place as they stretched just far enough to be perfect for his purpose.

Checking the time, he saw that it was just before five o'clock, which meant a train would be arriving shortly. He walked onto the depot platform and waited until the northbound train arrived. The arrivals and departures of the trains in the small railroad town of Salcedo caused much excitement and were always well attended. Emmett aroused no attention as he stood in the crowd, watching the disembarking and boarding passengers. Pulling his watch from his pocket again, he timed exactly how long the train stood in the station before it departed.

Four minutes and thirty-five seconds after the train arrived, it was on its way again. That was good. If the train's stay was much shorter, he wouldn't have time to do what he planned to do. Staying any longer would increase the possibility of being discovered.

He would time the nine o'clock train as well, then do an average of the two times, but for now, he had another stop to make.

Returning to the buckboard parked with several others, surreys, and wagons, he drove to the opposite end of town to Sikes' Hardware Store. A small bell attached to the door rang as he pushed it open and entered the store. "What is the longest chain you have?" he asked the clerk who'd hustled over to see what he needed.

"They are all the same length, twenty feet. But it doesn't really matter. You can make the chain as long as you need it to be," the clerk replied. He picked up the end of one of the chains and showed it to Emmett. "There are hooks on each end, so all you have to do is connect them together. How long a chain do you need?"

"I'm going to snake some sunken logs out of the Colorado River, so I'm thinkin' I'm goin' to be needin' at least a hunnert and fifty feet."

"That won't be any problem. I can give you eight, twenty foot lengths. It's going to cost you forty dollars, though. Do you think those sunken logs are worth forty dollars?"

"I know some people up North who'll buy 'em. The lumber from 'em makes real shiny floors."

Emmett made the purchase, then loaded the chains onto the buckboard.

Shortly after nine o'clock, Emmett worked alongside the track in the dark. The train that just left had been in the station for six minutes and ten seconds. He could hear a dog barking. From somewhere a bit more distant, a baby began to cry. The most prominent sounds, however, came from the Scalded Cat Saloon—the tinkling of a piano, the shriek of a woman, followed by the loud guffaw of several men. From the corral of the freight wagon company, came the bray of a mule.

A cat came walking up, looking at him curiously, its eyes shining in the dark.

Emmett looked back into the weeds, but could see no evidence of the work he had just done. So far, not one person had seen him and that was very good. He didn't need to be arousing any suspicions.

Once his work was finished, he walked back to the jail and went inside.

One man, a soldier, was sitting at the desk. He looked up from the game of solitaire he was playing. "If you're lookin' for the marshal, he ain't here. Him and the deputy is out makin' the rounds." He wasn't one of the three witnesses at the trial, nor had he been there when Emmett and Kirby had come to see Elmer.

"I'm not here to see him. I'm here to see my son."

"Your son?"

"Kirby Jensen, one of your prisoners, is my son," Emmett said. "I'd like to visit him."

The soldier examined one of the stacks of cards, then turned up a card and seeing that he could use it, applied it to another stack.

"That's cheatin' you know."

"Yeah, but I ain't cheatin' no one but myself. Leave your gun here 'n go on back. Seein' as he's goin' to get his neck stretched tomorrow, I don't see no reason why you can't tell him good-bye."

"Thanks."

Emmett lay his gun on the desk, then stepped into the back. Elmer was sitting on one of the bunks, and Kirby was on the other. They looked up as Emmett approached the cell.

"Hi, Pa," Kirby said easily.

"Kirby, Elmer, I've got somethin' I'm goin' to need you to do. First of all, make certain that you are awake at eleven o'clock tonight."

"Hell, there ain't goin' to be no problem with that," Elmer said. "If this here is to be my last night on earth, I sure don't plan to be awastin' it by sleepin'."

Emmett chuckled. "This won't be your last night."

"You've got it all worked out?" Kirby asked. "Is it just the way we planned?"

"Yes."

"We'll be ready."

At a quarter till eleven that night, Emmett took the three saddled horses to the back of the apothecary, two buildings down the alley from the jail. From there, he walked out to the track, hoisted one end of the chain he had stretched out along the track two hours earlier, and pulled it over to the back of the jail.

He looked in through the barred window. "Kirby?"

"Yeah, Pa. We're here."

Emmett poked the chain in through the bars. "Take this, wrap it around all four bars, then pass it back out to me."

Kirby did as Emmett instructed, and taking the end his son had given him, Emmett connected the hook through one of the links. "Now, when you hear the train whistle, get over there to the corner, as far away from the wall as you can."

"All right."

With the chain wrapped around the bars, Emmett hurried back to the depot and waited.

He could hear the train before he could see it, first the whistle, then the chugging sound. As it came around the bend, about a quarter mile down the track, he could see the light, the sheltered gas flame set in a polished reflector to cast a beam before the engine. It was little over a minute before the engine reached him, so heavy that the ground shook as it rolled by. Steam was gushing from the drive cylinders and glowing coals were falling from the firebox. The engineer, with a pipe clenched tightly between his teeth, was leaning out of the open window of the cab, staring straight ahead.

After the engine came the tender, the express car, the baggage car, then the four passenger cars, lit from inside. The train squealed and screeched to a stop. It was still, but it wasn't silent as overheated journals snapped and popped, the water in the boiler bubbled, and escaping steam made a quiet hiss.

Grabbing the end of the chain and bending low, Emmett stayed in the shadows as he hurried up to the rear of the train. There, he wrapped the chain through the coupling, connecting it back on itself. That done, he ran back to the apothecary and, untying the horses, held the three sets of reins in his hand and waited.

The engineer gave two short toots on the whistle, and a gush of steam spewed forth as he opened the throttle.

Emmett watched the chain lift from the ground and grow taut He heard the loud crashing sound as half of the back wall of the jail was pulled down and hurried up the alley with the three horses. "Let's go!" he called, as he saw Kirby and Elmer climbing out through the hole.

"Hey! What's going on back here!" the soldier shouted, coming from the front. Seeing the two men escaping through the collapsed wall, he pulled his gun and fired, but Kirby and Elmer were already out of harm's way.

"Here's your gun." Emmett handed Kirby's pistol and gun belt to him.

"And here's your horse." Emmett handed Elmer a set of reins.

The three men galloped down the alley, onto the main road, and out of town.

"Did you steal this horse?" Elmer asked the next morning. "The reason I ask is, do I need to be worryin' 'bout someone hangin' me for horse stealin'?"

"Here's the bill of sale," Emmett said. "I've already signed it over to you."

Elmer shook his head. "I ain't got no money to pay you for it. Fact is, I ain't got no money at all."

"Here." Emmett gave him fifty dollars in cash.

"No, sir." Elmer shook his head, pushing the money away. "I didn't say that hopin' for some money."

"I know you didn't, Elmer. But the way I look at it, it's my way of sayin' thanks for lookin' after my boy while I was gone."

"It warn't exactly that way. When we was ridin' together, he was lookin' out for me half the time 'n I was lookin' out for him the other half the time."

"All right. Then this is for the times you was lookin' out for him."

Reluctantly, Elmer took the money. "You've kept me from gettin' hung, you've given me a horse, 'n you give me some money. I don't know what to say. Like as not, we ain't never goin' to run into each other again. I don't know how I'm ever goin' to be able to pay you back."

"Then don't try," Emmett said.

Elmer nodded, then got mounted. "I do have a piece of information you might be interested in. I heerd where Shardeen is."

"What?" Kirby asked excitedly. "Where?"

"I only heerd where he is. I cain't say for sure 'cause I didn't see him for my ownself. And I don't know if he's still there or not. But, last I heard, he was in Dorena."

"Pa?"

Emmett nodded. "All right. We'll go to Dorena."

Emmett and Kirby surveyed the town as they rode in. Kirby had seen many small towns like this since he left Missouri. At this point in his life he didn't realize it, but he would see many hundreds more in the years to come.

Dorena wasn't that unlike Salcedo, except there was no railroad. The single street was faced by false-fronted shanties, a few sod buildings, and even a handful of tents, straggling along for nearly a quarter mile. Just as abruptly as the town started, it quit, and nothing but open road and empty prairie existed ahead.

The street was baked hard as a rock from the summer heat. The sun was still yellow and hot in early September. In the winter and spring, the street would be a muddy mire, worked by the horses' hooves and mixed with their droppings so that it became a stinking, sucking, pool of ooze.

The biggest and grandest structure in town was a building with a sign stretching across the front that read EL CABALLO Y EL TORO CANTINA. It also had a picture of a beer mug on one end of the sign and a liquor bottle on the other. Across the street from the building, they saw a man leaning up against the post that was supporting the roof of a leather store.

"Tell me, mister," Emmett said, pointing to the building. "Would that be a saloon?"

"It's a cantina," the man said. "That's Mex for a saloon."

"What does the name mean?"

"The horse and the bull."

"Thanks."

They rode over to the cantina, dismounted, and tied their horses off at a hitching rail. The shadows gave an illusion of coolness inside, but it was an illusion only. The dozen and a half drinking customers had to keep their bandanas handy to wipe the sweat from their faces.

Over the last few months, Emmett had taught Kirby how to enter a saloon. "We're lookin' for men we aim to kill," Emmett had explained. "As time goes on 'n more and more people find out what we are about, we're likely to have men looking for us as well, for one reason or another. So you need to know how to enter a saloon, and it needs to become a habit with you so's that you do it without even thinkin' about it."

Following the lesson his pa taught him, Kirby was on the alert as they stepped inside. He and Emmett surveyed the place with such calmness that the average person would think it no more than a glance of idle curiosity. In reality, it was a very thorough appraisal of the room. They checked out who was armed, what type of weapons they were carrying, and if they were wearing their guns in the way that showed they knew how to use them.

Less than half of the drinkers were even wearing guns, though there was a man standing at the other end of the bar who was armed. His gun was in a holster that was kicked-out in the way that indicated he might know how to use it.

The walls of the saloon were decorated with game heads and pictures, including one of a reclining nude woman. Some marksman had improved the painting by putting a single bullet hole in a most appropriate place.

Several large jars of boiled eggs and pickled pigs' feet sat on the bar. A stairway led to an upstairs section at the back. Kirby could see rooms opening off the second-floor landing as he watched a heavily painted saloon girl take a cowboy up the stairs with her.

The upstairs area didn't extend all the way to the front of the building, which meant that the main room of the saloon was big, with exposed rafters below the high, peaked ceiling. Nearly a dozen tables were full of drinking customers.

The piano player wore a small, round, derby hat and kept his sleeves up with garters. He was pounding away at the piano, though the music was practically lost amidst the noise of a dozen or more conversations.

"What'll it be, gents?" the barkeep asked as he moved down toward them. He wiped up a spill with a wet, smelly rag before draping the rag over his shoulder.

"A couple beers," Emmett said.

"That'll be ten cents," the bartender said as he put

two mugs on the bar before them. Emmett slid a dime across to him.

A bar girl sidled up to Kirby. She was heavily painted and showed the dissipation of her profession. "Oh, honey, you are a sweet one, you are."

He was embarrassed by her attention. It wasn't the first time he had ever been in a saloon, but it was the first time he had ever actually been approached by one of the bar girls.

"Whoa, Becky," said a man at one of the tables. "You sure you know what you're doin' there? You don't want to be robbin' the cradle, do you? Seems to me like you'd be better off goin' after the old one."

Several customers laughed.

"Yeah," one of the others said. "The old one looks like he ain't had a woman in near twenty years, and the young 'un there, why, I bet he ain't never had no woman."

"Would you like a drink?" Kirby asked Becky.

"A drink? Well, yes, honey, I think I would like a drink."

Kirby turned to the bartender. "Sir, would you give the lady whatever it is she would like to drink?"

The bartender took a bottle from beneath the bar and poured it into a short glass. "That'll be a quarter."

"Kirby, it would appear that your lady friend has expensive taste," Emmett said with a smile as Kirby put a quarter on the bar.

Becky picked the glass up and tossed the drink down in one gulp. Then, smiling, she put her hand on Kirby's shoulder. "Why don't you come upstairs with me, honey, and let me make a man out of you?" she suggested.

Kirby had no idea how old she was, but he was sure that she was older than Miss Margrabe would be.

Wherever Miss Margrabe was.

"No, thank you, ma'am," Kirby said. "I bought you a drink because you were being nice to me. But, I don't want to do anything else."

"Now, just a minute here, boy." The man at the other end of the bar stood up straight. "I think you just insulted my woman."

"I'm sorry, ma'am, if I insulted you," Kirby said.

"Honey, you didn't insult me." Becky turned her head back toward the man who had spoken. "And Streeter, I ain't your woman."

"Sure you are," Streeter replied with an evil grin. "You're anybody's woman that pays you. I've paid you, so that makes you my woman."

"Well you ain't payin' me now."

"Are you sassin' me, woman? 'Cause I ain't goin' to stand for no sassin'."

Becky put her hands on her hips. "I'm not sassin' you. I just told you that I'm not your woman, and I'm not."

"I say you're sassin' me, 'n if you don't apologize to me right now, why I might just have to knock some manners into you."

"I'm sorry," Becky said, showing genuine fright.

"You're sorry all right. You are sorry, washed up, and ought to be glad that anyone at all would talk to you."

"Mr. Streeter, why don't you leave the lady alone?" Kirby said. "She told you she's sorry."

"What?" Streeter nearly shouted the word in surprise that the young boy would talk to him like that. "What did you just say to me?"

"I asked you politely to leave the lady alone."

"First of all, she ain't no lady. But I reckon you're too dumb to know the difference." Streeter's tone of voice had gotten very challenging. With such a sharp edge to it, all other conversation in the bar had stopped. Everyone watched to see what was going to happen next.

"Miss Becky, I'd be real pleased if you would have another drink with me." Kirby put another quarter on the bar.

"Boy, you're beginnin' to put a burr under my saddle, you know that? But I'm goin' to let it pass for now. Because you're new in town, maybe you don't know who I am."

"The lady called you Streeter, so I reckon that's your name."

"That's it. Emile Streeter. I reckon you've heard of Emile Streeter."

Kirby shook his head. "No, sir, I can't say as I have."

"Tell 'im who I am, Jake," Streeter said to the bartender.

"Mr. Streeter, why don't you leave him alone. He's just a boy."

"He's a boy with a smart mouth, and he needs to be taught a lesson," Streeter said. "Tell 'im who I am."

"Young man, Mr. Streeter is a man of some notoriety in these parts. He is quite good with a gun." Jake pointed to the nude painting. "You might have noticed the bullet hole between the young lady's legs. Streeter put it there."

"You shoot paintings, do you?" Kirby asked. "Do they ever shoot back?"

"Boy, I've had about enough of you!" Streeter said.

Kirby smiled at the man. "Mr. Streeter, it looks like

me 'n you got off on the wrong foot. If I've put a burr under your saddle, I apologize. Bartender, I would like to buy a drink for Mr. Streeter."

"Uh-uh," Streeter said, shaking his head slowly. "This has come too far for you to back out now."

"Streeter, for God's sake, leave him alone. Can't you see he's tryin' to apologize?" the bartender said as he put another whiskey in front of Streeter.

"You stay out of this, Jake, or I'll be settlin' with you after I'm finished with the boy here."

"Streeter, that's enough! What has gotten into you? Leave the boy alone!" Becky turned to Kirby. "Honey, I'm sorry I come up to you like I did. Believe me, I would have never done so, if I had had any idea that this fool was going to carry on like this."

"Well now, boy, ever'one seems awful worried about you, so I tell you what. If you'll get down on your knees and ask me, please, not to shoot you, this can all be over. Otherwise, me 'n you's goin' to have us a little dance." Streeter laughed, a high-pitched, insane sound. "Me 'n you's goin' to dance. I like that."

"Please do it," Becky begged. "He'll kill you."

"Don't worry. He's not going to kill me," Kirby said, his voice flat and amazingly calm.

"You don't understand," Becky said desperately.

Kirby had had just about enough. "No. Streeter doesn't understand. And one of the things he doesn't understand is that I'm not a boy."

"Hey you, old man," Streeter called to Emmett.

For the entire interplay between Streeter and Kirby, Emmett had done nothing but sip his beer and watch, almost dispassionately. He looked Streeter in the eye. "Are you talking to me?"

"Yeah. Looks like me 'n this boy is about to have us that little dance we was talkin' about. And you're in the way."

"I'm not in the way." Emmett coughed.

"What do you mean, you're not in the way? You're standin' right there behind the boy, ain't you?"

"I suppose I am, but it doesn't matter. You heard what he said. He's not a boy. And you won't get a shot off."

"What? What do you mean I won't get a shot off, you old fool?"

"Kirby?" Emmett said.

"Yes, Pa?"

"Pa? You mean this is your boy?" Streeter asked, laughing.

Emmett didn't move. "This bragging fool seems to be pretty proud of what he done to that painting. But it looks to me like there's room for a couple additions."

Kirby glanced up at the painting of the nude woman and smiled. "Yes, sir. I know what you mean."

"Why don't you finish the job he started?"

In a flash, Kirby pulled his pistol, fired twice, and put the pistol back in its holster. Both breasts in the painting had been punched through by perfectly placed bullet holes.

"What the hell?" someone gasped. "I didn't even see him draw!"

"That's impossible!" another said. "There cain't nobody shoot that good and that fast!"

"Now, Streeter—I believe that's what you told me your name was—shall we get this over with?" Kirby asked.

Eyes wide and mouth open, Streeter reached out

with a shaking hand, picked up the glass of whiskey still on the bar, and drained it. He put the empty glass down, then turned to look at Kirby.

Kirby smiled at him, but absolutely nothing young nor innocent was in the smile. It was old as time and as dangerous as the open mouth of a hissing rattlesnake.

"I . . . uh . . . I," Streeter stammered. Glancing at the others in the room, his face mirroring his absolute fear, he held an empty hand out toward Kirby. "Don't shoot. Don't shoot." He started toward the door.

"Come back, Streeter. Next time you want to show off!" Becky called to him, and everyone in the saloon laughed.

Streeter pulled his hat down more firmly on his head and pushed through the swinging batwing doors without so much as a look back.

"Lord almighty! I ain't never seen nothin' like that!" someone said.

"I wouldn't be surprised if Streeter don't never come back here," another said.

"If he don't never come back, it'll be the town's gain, and we owe this young fella a vote of thanks." Jake drew two more mugs of beer and set them on the bar. "These are on the house. What brings you two to town?"

Kirby turned back to the bar. "I'm looking for Angus Shardeen."

The smile left the bartender's face. It wasn't only the expression that changed. The tone of his voice changed, as well. "A friend of yours, is he?"

Kirby shook his head. "Believe me, Angus Shardeen is no friend."

Jake relaxed, and the smile returned. "Good. If he

was your friend, I'd be thinkin' a lot less of you than I am now."

"Where is he?"

"Nobody knows. He kilt a young cowboy about a month ago, then he skedaddled out of here."

"Most likely, he went back up to Kansas," Becky said. "I believe that's where he come from."

"Yes ma'am. That is where he came from," Kirby said.

"Why are you lookin' for him, if I might ask?" Jake inquired.

"He killed my ma," Kirby replied.

Jake nodded. "I reckon I can see why you're lookin' for him then. How long do you plan to stay in town?"

Emmett answered the question. "Long enough to finish this beer."

Kirby and his father left Texas and rode north through Indian Territory, following the Washita River. Changing colors, it snaked out across the gently undulating prairie before them—shining gold in the setting sun, sometimes white where it broke over rocks, at other times shimmering a deep blue-green in the swirling eddies and trapped pools, and sometimes running red with clay silt.

Late in the afternoon, a rabbit hopped up and bounded down the trail ahead of him.

"There's supper," Emmett said.

Kirby drew his pistol and fired. A puff of fur and spray of blood flew up as the rabbit made a head-first somersault, then lay perfectly still.

They stopped for the day and made camp under a

growth of cottonwoods. Emmett started a fire while Kirby skinned and cleaned the rabbit, then skewered it on a green willow branch and suspended it over the fire between two forked limbs.

Except for Emmett's occasional coughing, they were quiet, staring at the cooking rabbit.

Finally, Kirby broke the silence. "Pa, it's been five days, 'n you ain't said nothin' about what happened back there in Dorena with that Streeter fella."

"No, I reckon I haven't," Emmett replied.

"How come you ain't said nothin'?"

Emmett coughed again before he answered. "I thought you were handlin' things pretty well."

"I figured you musta thought that, else you woulda been tellin' me what I shoulda done."

"Kirby, I'm not goin' to be here forever. Fact is, I ain't goin' to be here much longer at all, 'n you're goin' to be on your own. A fella with a skill like yours, word's goin' to get around. When that happens, people will be comin' for you, wantin' to try you out to make a name for killing Kirby Jensen."

"How can that be, Pa? There ain't anybody even knows my name."

"They will know your name, and soon. I pretty much gave you your head back there because you need to know how to handle yourself. And like I said, you did pretty well."

"I woulda killed him if it hadn't been for you comin' up with a way that let me avoid it," Kirby said.

Emmett coughed again, then reached out to turn the skewer, allowing another side of the rabbit to face the fire. The aroma of the cooking meat permeated the campsite.

"I reckon you might have," Emmett said. "And truth to tell, you woulda been justified. But, anytime you can find a way to do what needs to be done without killin', it's best."

"Yeah, I can see that. I'm glad you come up with the idea about shootin' holes in the woman's . . . you know."

Emmett laughed.

"Pa, that woman . . . Becky. She wanted me to go upstairs with her."

"Yes, I heard her ask."

"I thought about it."

"Did you?"

"What would you have said if I had done it?"

"I wouldn'ta said nothin' at all. They's some things so private that nobody else can tell you one way or the other what to do. Why didn't you go upstairs with her?"

"I ain't never been with a woman before," Kirby said. "Leastwise, I ain't never been with a woman in . . . that . . . way . . . the way she wanted to be. I sorta figure that if you're goin' to do somethin' like that with a woman, then maybe it ought to mean somethin'."

"That's a good way of lookin' at it. Rabbit's done." Emmett lifted the golden brown piece of meat off the fire, seasoned it with their dwindling supply of salt, then lay it on a flat rock and split it right down the middle, head to tail. He gave half of it to Kirby.

Kirby began eating, pulling the meat away with his teeth even when it was almost too hot to hold.

After his supper, he stirred the fire, then lay down alongside it, using his saddle as a pillow. He stared into the coals, watching the red sparks ride a heated column of air high up into the night sky. Still glowing red and orange, they joined the jewel-like scattering of stars.

"Pa?"

"Yes, son?"

"Just so you know, when I find Shardeen, I won't be lookin' for a way to avoid it, no more 'n I reckon you'll be lookin' for a way not to kill them men you're after."

"I wouldn't expect you to," Emmett said.

CHAPTER 13

Three months of dusty cow towns and wide open spaces proved fruitless. The Jensens had not found Shardeen, nor had they located any of the men Emmett was looking for. At the moment, they were in the middle of nowhere, with no particular place to go. Well, it wasn't actually *nowhere*. They knew they were somewhere in Kansas. Or at least, they *thought* they were in Kansas.

It was a cold and very gray day.

"Pa, what's the date?"

"I don't rightly know," Emmett admitted. "Late October, early November, maybe?"

"It's got to be later than that. I don't think it would be this cold unless it was at least December."

"Could be that you're right," Emmett agreed. "You know what I'm thinkin'?"

"What's that?"

"I'm thinkin' that the next town we see, we might want to put in for the winter."

Kirby frowned. "You got 'ny idea where that next town might be?"

"Not the slightest. But that fella we run into a couple days ago said the Arkansas River was in front of us, and it can't be more 'n a day's ride away. Once we get to the river, all we'll have to do is follow it. It's goin' to eventually take us to a town."

"All right," Kirby agreed. "Let's find the river."

During the night, snow began to fall. It came down softly, silently. It was quite a surprise when Kirby awoke the next morning to find himself almost completely buried in snow. He looked around for his father but didn't see him.

"Pa?" Kirby called. "Pa? Where are you?"

"Hrmmph!" Emmett grunted and suddenly sat up from under a blanket of snow. The white stuff was in his hair, his eyebrows, and hanging from his beard.

Kirby laughed.

"What's so funny?"

"You look like a snowman."

Emmett looked around. "We had quite a snowfall, didn't we?"

"Yes, sir, I would say that we did."

"Have you checked on the horses?"

"No, sir. Seemed like the first thing I should check on was you."

Emmett chuckled and nodded. "Good idea. Let's find the horses."

Both men stood, stomped and shook the snow from themselves, and dug through the snow to find their saddles. They walked to where the horses stood, knee deep in snow. They looked cold and miserable.

"Wow, these are going to feel awfully cold to the

horses when we put them on," Kirby said as he held up the saddle, still dripping with snow.

Emmett laughed. "It's going to be just as cold on our butts."

Kirby laughed as well. "Yeah, I hadn't thought about that."

Big Ben Conyers' ranch, Live Oaks, lay just north of Ft. Worth. The gently rolling grassland and scores of year-round streams and creeks made it ideal for cattle ranching. Two dozen cowboys were part-time employees, and another two dozen were full-time employees. Those who weren't married lived in a couple long, low, bunkhouses, white with red roofs. The married couples lived in small houses adjacent to the bunkhouses, all of them painted green with red roofs. A cookhouse large enough to feed all the single men, a barn, a machine shed, a granary, and a large stable were also on the property.

The most dominating feature of the ranch was what the cowboys called "The Big House." A stucco-sided example of Spanish Colonial Revival, it had an arcaded portico on the southeast corner, stained-glass windows, and an elaborate arched entryway.

In the parlor, Ben watched as Janey decorated the Christmas tree, adding gaily colored pine cones to the red and green ribbon laced all through it. The many small candles would be lit once all the decorations were in place.

"I do believe that is the prettiest Christmas tree I have ever seen," Ben said.

Janey turned toward him. "It's easy for me to say

that. This is the first Christmas tree I've ever seen, anywhere."

"Well then, I'm glad that your first tree is so fine. It'll be even prettier when all the gifts are under it."

"Ben, please, no gifts for me," Janey said.

"What do you mean, no gifts for you? Of course there will be gifts for you. Why, what is Christmas without the presents?"

"But, I have no present for you."

"You know what I want from you. It would be the most wonderful present I can imagine."

Janey didn't respond.

"Marry me, Janey. I couldn't ask for a greater present than to have you as my bride."

"Ben, I can't."

"Why can't you? You aren't already married, are you?"

"No, I'm not married. But you know why I can't. You are a very important man here. Maybe if we lived somewhere else . . . someplace where there is less a chance that I would be recognized, I could consider it. But you know, without a doubt, that there are people who know who I am . . . and what I am . . . was. If word would get around, it would be terribly embarrassing. I couldn't do that to you."

"Some may recognize you, that is true. But how would they recognize you unless they, too, had visited the Palace Princess Emporium? If that was the case, it would be just as embarrassing to them as it would be to me. At any rate, I assure you, Janey, nobody will ever dare say anything about it to my face, nor would they even take a chance on me learning that they had spoken of it behind my back."

"But what if they do? What would you do? Would you kill them?"

"If I had to."

"That's what I'm afraid of."

Ben walked over to Janey and pulled her to him in an embrace. "I don't want you to ever be afraid of anything. As long as you are with me, you don't have to be. If you don't want to get married yet, I'll just enjoy whatever part of you, you are willing to share. I love you, Janey. I don't care about your background."

"Oh, Ben, why couldn't I have met you before?" Janey asked, her eyes welling with tears.

"Nothing that happened before now matters. Only *now* matters, and we are together now. So we'll just enjoy what we have, and we'll see where it leads. If I'm the luckiest man in the world, it will lead to matrimony."

As Janey lay in bed that night, she thought of their conversation. Ben had told her that he didn't want her to ever be afraid of anything, but she was afraid. She was pregnant. Ben had accepted the idea that it was his baby, but she couldn't be certain. She wasn't sure exactly how long she had been pregnant, but she had been with at least two other men a few days before she had left Dallas with Ben.

That had been in August. If the baby was born any later than April, she would know that it was Ben's. If it was born in April, or earlier, it might not be.

January 1866

Emmett and Kirby were wintering in Delphi, Kansas, a small town on the Arkansas River near the border of

Kansas and the territory of Colorado. Although they still had most of the bounty money that had been paid for Cox and Haggart, they opted to take jobs through the winter to preserve what money they had.

Emmett worked for the company that operated the ferry across the river, while Kirby had agreed to become a deputy for City Marshal Darrell Wright.

"We don't have much call for lawin' here," Marshal Wright told him when he was hired. "About all we ever have to do is pick up a drunk now 'n then. Most of the time, the onliest reason we pick 'em up is 'cause they sometimes pass out on the street. In the winter time, they could likely freeze if we didn't bring 'em in."

It was the cold that worried Kirby the most—not for himself, but for his pa, who was exposed to the weather on the ferry boat. He tried to get his father to quit. "It's not costin' us all that much to live. I'm makin' enough as a deputy to pay the boardin'house . . . and the boardin'house is feedin' us. With your lung 'n all, it can't be good for you to be out in the cold all the time."

"I ain't so damn feeble that my own son has to take care of me," Emmett said. "The work ain't hard, 'n I can wrap up in a buffalo robe that keeps me warm. You don't be worryin' about me."

"I just wish you'd quit, is all."

"And do what? Sit around with my thumb up my ass all the time?"

Kirby laughed out loud. "Well, I don't guess I'd want to see you doin' that, exactly."

"I would damn sure hope not. Now, you do your work 'n I'll do mine, if you'll just let me be."

"All right, Pa. But if it gets too much for you, remember, it ain't somethin' you have to do."

* * *

The boardinghouse where they stayed was the Homestead House, owned and run by Mrs. Pauline Foley, an attractive widow in her mid-forties.

"I made biscuits this morning, Emmett," she said when Emmett and Kirby came down for breakfast. "I know how you like to sop them through sour cream and sugar."

"You're too kind to me, Mrs. Foley."

"Oh please, won't you call me Pauline?"

"I would be honored to, Pauline. I just don't want to be too forward."

"You could never be too forward," she said, smiling as she poured coffee into Emmett's cup.

As they left the boardinghouse to go to their respective jobs, Kirby smiled at his father. "Pa, I think Mrs. Foley likes you."

"She's a business woman. She's just being nice to her customers, that's all."

"Uh-huh. But she's nicer to you than she is to Mrs. Simmons or Mr. Clark."

"Boy, you know what your problem is?"

"What?"

"You see too many things that aren't there."

"She likes you, Pa. You know she does," Kirby said with a broad smile.

Emmett sighed. "She might, but I'm not encouragin' it. We'll be leavin' here, come spring. I don't want to do anythin' that might cause her some hurt. She's a good and decent woman, and she don't fit in with my plans. You do understand that, don't you, boy?"

Kirby nodded. "Yeah Pa, I do."

"Then please, don't do or say anything to her that might give her the wrong idea."

"I won't, Pa."

"I'll see you at supper."

Kirby nodded. "Try 'n stay warm out there on the water today."

One of the advantages of working as a deputy was Kirby's access to WANTED posters. He had mixed feelings about those he had seen on Angus Shardeen. On the one hand, he was glad that Shardeen was being regarded as a wanted outlaw . . . and not a hero as was James Henry Lane. On the other hand, because Shardeen was a wanted man with a price on his head, it was quite possible that someone else might find and kill him before Kirby had the satisfaction of doing so.

As he was looking through the WANTED posters, he was surprised to see his and his father's name, not on a reward poster, but on a document that rescinded their wanted status.

> Notice is hereby given that the Wanted status of Elmer Gleason, Emmett Jensen, and Kirby Jensen has been withdrawn. Reason for revocation: an appeal filed on their behalf by Keith Davenport has been granted, and Daniel Gilmore has been removed from the federal bench due to malfeasance.

Kirby smiled as he read the document, and he gave a silent thanks for the honesty and integrity of the lawyer who, even though he would probably never see his clients again, had done the right thing.

On an early spring day, Kirby was in the bank to deposit a county check for the sheriff's office when his landlady came in with two men. "Hello, Mrs. Foley."

As soon as he spoke to her, he saw that the expression on her face was one of terror. He also saw the reason for her terror. Both men who had come into the bank were armed, and one of them had his gun stuck into her back.

"This is a holdup!" shouted one of the two men.

"Here, what are you doing?" the bank teller called. "You let that woman go!"

"We will, soon as you fill this bag with money." The second armed man stepped up to the teller's cage, passing a cloth bag over the counter.

With shaking hands, the teller began taking money from his drawer, and sticking it into the cloth bag.

"Hurry up!" the robber urged.

"There's no need for you to hurry, Mr. Montgomery," Kirby said easily. "These two men are under arrest. I'm going to ask you to let Mrs. Foley go . . . now."

"What did you say?"

"You may have noticed the star on my jacket. I'm the deputy marshal here, and I'm putting both of you under arrest."

The outlaws laughed.

"Are you tryin' to be funny, mister?" one asked.

"No, I'm quite serious."

"You may have a deputy's star, but you ain't got no sense. Maybe you're too dumb to notice, but you don't have a gun in your hand, and we do."

"That's true," Kirby agreed. "But you're pointing your gun at Mrs. Foley, and your friend is pointing his gun at the bank teller. Neither one of you are pointing your guns toward me. And that's where you have made your mistake."

The one holding his gun to Mrs. Foley glanced at his partner. "Can you believe this guy?"

"I'm going to ask you one more time to let Mrs. Foley go," Kirby said, his voice quiet and calm as it was the first time he'd addressed them.

"What the hell! Let's just shoot him and get it over with!" The one holding Mrs. Foley seemed to be the leader.

Kirby was watching both men very carefully. The instant the man holding Mrs. Foley moved his pistol, Kirby drew and fired twice, one on top of the other. Both would-be bank robbers went down, each of them with a bullet in his forehead, dead before realizing they were in danger.

Shocked by the sudden and unexpected turn of events, the scream that Mrs. Foley tried to make died in her throat. By the time she looked toward Kirby, he had already returned his pistol to his holster. The bank teller, with an expression of utter shock on his face, was still holding the half-filled bag of money.

"You can put the money back in the drawer now, Mr. Montgomery," Kirby said. "Oh, and the sheriff would like to deposit this county check."

The two bank robbers were identified as Frank Morris and Seth Crandall, former Jayhawkers. Within a week, word of Kirby Jensen's unbelievable performance had traveled up and down the Arkansas River and beyond.

Some declared the story fanciful since only two eyewitnesses could claim that they had seen it happen. It didn't seem possible that anyone could have actually done what was being told.

"I'm proud of you, son," Emmett said. "You are already getting a taste of what I told you was going to happen. You are beginning to build a name for yourself. I do believe there's goin' to come the time when ever'one in the West knows who you are."

"I'm not sure that's somethin' I want, Pa," Kirby said.

"I'm not goin' to lie to you. It's goin' to be a burden. But as long as you use this skill and talent for the good, you'll go to bed ever' night with a clear conscience."

Had Kirby known how close he was to Angus Shardeen, he would have turned in his badge and gone after him. The raiding Jayhawker was camped less than fifteen miles west of Delphi, just across the line in Colorado.

"Both of them?" Shardeen replied after being told about what had happened in the bank in Delphi. "Morris and Crandall were both killed?"

"Yes," Bartell said. "By that same kid that shot Tim in the hand."

"Why didn't you do somethin'?" Shardeen asked.

"I was outside with the horses. When I heard the shootin' 'n Frank 'n Seth didn't come out, I figured it was best I not give myself away. I just went across the street into the saloon. That's when I heard what happened."

"He said he was comin' for you, Angus," Tim said.

"One man? And a kid at that?"

"Yeah, but he ain't like any other kid I've ever heard of. Frank 'n Seth both had their guns already drawed when they went into the bank," Bartell said. "Jensen shot 'em both."

"A tiny bank in a one-horse town, 'n Morris and Crandall get themselves kilt. Next time I'll send better men."

Rebecca Jean Conyers was born on April 15, 1866. The date of her birth did not preclude Ben being her father, but neither did it absolutely establish that he was. She had red hair, and Ben was quick to point out that his mother's sister had been redheaded.

Janey promised that she would marry him but asked for a little time to recover from the birth.

On the day that Becca was three months old, Janey was standing in the nursery holding her.

"Do you want me to give the baby a bath?" asked Juanita Gomez, the nanny Ben had hired to look after the baby.

"Not yet," Janey said. "Juanita, I'm going to be gone for a while. I want you to look after Becca while I'm gone."

"El bebé hermoso que yo velo," Juanita said. Then she repeated it in English. "The beautiful baby, I will watch."

"I know you will. Oh, would you have Mr. McNally to bring the surrey around? I'm ready to leave."

"*Sí, Señora.*" Juanita knew that Janey and Ben weren't married, but she called her Señora anyway.

Janey waited until Juanita was gone, then she kissed the baby again. Her eyes shining brightly, Becca smiled up at Janey.

"Good-bye, my sweet child. I know you don't understand now, and you may never understand. But what I'm doing is best for you and for your father. I'll never see you again, but I swear to you, I'll never forget you."

Janey put the baby in her crib, then raised up with tears streaming down her cheeks.

When Ben returned later in the day, he went into Rebecca's room, picked her up, and kissed her on the forehead. "If you aren't the most beautiful baby in the entire state of Texas, I'll eat my hat. Without salt," he added with a laugh. He put her back in her crib and looked over toward the nanny. "Juanita, where is Janey?"

"She said she will be gone for *unos pocos días.*"

"She's going to be gone for a few days? Where did she go? Did she say?"

"No, Señor."

"That's damn odd," Ben said.

Puzzled by Janey's strange and unexpected disappearance, Ben went into the parlor. On the fireplace mantel was an envelope that bore his name.

Even more puzzled and a little worried, he hurried over to retrieve the envelope, then tore it open to read it:

Dear Ben,
    Please forgive me, but I cannot stay here. I am
afraid that to do so can do nothing but cause you

*embarrassment and pain. I'm leaving Becca with
you. You have enough love and means to give her a
wonderful life. I have nothing to offer her but my love,
and on the day she learns of my past, my love won't be
enough. Then, I will be an embarrassment to her, as
well, and I don't think I'd be able to bear that. Tell her
that I died, for it would be much better if she grows up
believing that.*

*I do love you, Ben, but it is a love that cannot be.
If you love me, I beg of you, make no effort to find me.
Instead, give all your love to our daughter.*

Janey

Ben went back into the nursery and picked up the
baby again. He took her into the library, locked the
door behind him, and walked over to sit in the big
leather chair. There, the six-foot-four, 330-pound man
held his baby close to him and wept.

The days had grown warmer and it was time to move
on. Emmett and Kirby said good-bye to the friends they
had made in Delphi.

"I wish you would stay," Pauline said. "You wouldn't
have to work on the ferry boat anymore. You could
help me run the boardinghouse."

Emmett took her hands in his, raised them to his
lips, and kissed them. "Pauline, you are a very sweet
woman. My son and I were lucky to have met you, and
are very grateful for the way you made us feel so welcome. But we can't stay here. We have to go on."

"But why, Emmett?"

"I'm not sure I can answer that. At least, not in the way you could understand."

"Is it because you are dying?"

"What?"

"I've heard that kind of cough before, Emmett. I don't know how much longer you have, but I know I could make you happy in what time you do have left."

"Pauline, you don't know how much I want to do this. But I have sworn to do something, and I must do it. If I stayed here, I wouldn't actually be with you, not really. The part of me that needs to do this thing would take over my heart and soul, and I would have nothing left. You are too good a woman to have to live with that."

With tears in her eyes, Pauline nodded. "I'll always remember you, Emmett. And I'll keep you in my prayers."

"I'm blessed to have met someone like you. It's just too bad that we didn't meet under different circumstances."

"Pa, would you have stayed there?" Kirby asked as they rode out of town. "I mean if you wasn't lookin' for them men, and I wasn't lookin' for Shardeen. Would you have stayed with Mrs. Foley?"

"I don't know, Kirby. I might have," Emmett admitted. "She's a very good woman, and a man can't ask for more than to have a very good woman." He was quiet for a while, then added, "Your ma was a very good woman, too, and I didn't do right by her. I had no business goin' off to war. I was old enough that I didn't really have to go. If I had been home when the Jayhawkers came through—"

"You'd more 'n likely be dead now," Kirby said, interrupting him in mid-sentence. "There were too many of 'em, Pa."

"Maybe. But about Pauline. She deserves a man who will stay with her, and look after her. You 'n I both know that I can't do that. Not with this lung fever I got."

"Maybe when we get farther west and into dry country, it'll get better like the doc said," Kirby suggested.

"Maybe," Emmett said, but there was very little conviction in his voice.

CHAPTER 14

They rode west and north for several days across seemingly endless plains of tall grass with no sign of human habitation, then they came across a pile of rocks that had not been arranged by nature.

"Pa, look," Kirby said, pointing to the rocks.

They pulled up.

"Some of the mountain men I met told me about them," Emmett said. "That's what I been looking for."

"What's it here for?"

"It's a sign telling travelers that this here is the Santa Fe Trail. North and west of here will be Fort Larned, and north of that will be Pawnee Rock."

"Pawnee Rock? What's that, Pa?"

"Pawnee Rock would be a landmark, Pilgrim." The voice came from behind them.

Turning toward the one who had spoken, Kirby saw, without a doubt, the dirtiest man he had ever seen. The man was dressed entirely in buckskin, from the moccasins on his feet to his wide-brimmed leather hat.

A white, tobacco-stained beard covered his face. His nose was red and his eyes twinkled with mischief. He was mounted on a spotted pony and had two pack animals with him.

"Ain't no pilgrim, old-timer," Emmett said, low menace in his tone.

"Reckon you're right, at that."

"Where did you come from?" Emmett asked.

"I been watching you two pilgrims from that ravine yonder," he said with a jerk of his head. "You don't know much about traveling in Injun country, do you? It's best to stay off the ridges. You two been standin' out like a third titty." The old mountain man shifted his gaze to Kirby. "What are you staring at, boy?"

The boy leaned forward in his saddle. "Be darned if I rightly know."

The old man laughed. "You got sand to your bottom, all right." He looked at Emmett. "He your'n?"

"My son."

"I'll trade you for 'im," he said, the old eyes sparkling. "Injuns will pay right smart for a strong boy like this 'n."

"My son is not for trade, old-timer."

"Tell you what. I won't call you pilgrim, you don't call me old-timer. Deal?"

Emmett smiled and nodded. "Deal."

"You don't know where you are, do you?"

"Yeah, I know."

"Do you now? And just where would that be?"

"We're somewhere west of the state of Missouri, and east of the Pacific Ocean."

The old man chuckled. "In other words, you're lost as a lizard."

"If you got no particular place to go, you ain't never lost," Emmett said.

Again, the old man laughed. "Well now, you do have a point there. You got names?"

"I'm Emmett. This is my son, Kirby."

"Folks call me Preacher."

"You're a preacher?" Kirby asked, surprised at the response.

"Didn't say I was a preacher. I said that's my handle. That's what folks call me."

Kirby laughed out loud.

"What you laughin' at, boy?"

"I'm laughin' at your name."

"Don't scoff. It ain't nice to scoff at a man's name. If I wasn't a gentle type man, I might let the hairs on my neck get stiff."

"Preacher can't be your real name."

"Well, no, you right about that, but I been called Preacher for so long, that I've near 'bout forgot my Christian name. So, Preacher it'll be. That or nothin'."

"Well, it was nice talkin' with you, but I reckon we'll be goin' on now, Preacher," Emmett said. "Maybe we'll see you again."

Preacher's eyes shifted to the northwest, then narrowed, his lips tightening in a weird smile. "Yep. I reckon you will."

Emmett turned his horse and pointed its nose west-northwest. Kirby reluctantly followed. He would have liked to stay and talk with the old man.

When they were out of earshot, Kirby said, "Pa, that old man was so dirty he smelled."

"He's a mountain man, some away from home base, I'm figuring. More 'n likely trying to get back. Cantankerous old boys, they are. Some of them mean as snakes. I think they get together once a year and bathe."

"But you said you soldiered with some mountain men."

"I did, but they didn't stay that long. They had to get back to the high lonesome."

"Where is the high lonesome?"

"It's more of a condition, than a place. Men like Preacher stay up in the high country for years. Don't do nothing but trap and such. They won't see another human being for a year or more, and not a white man more 'n once ever' two years or so. All they've got is their horses and guns and the whistling wind and the silence of the mountains. They're all alone, and it does something to them. They get notional, funny acting."

"You mean they go crazy?"

"In a way, I'm thinking. I don't know much about them. Nobody does, I don't reckon. But I think maybe that most of the folks who would go off 'n live like that, don't like people all that much to begin with. They crave the lawlessness of open space.

"The mountain men I was with, now, they were some different. They told me about that old man's kind. They're very brave men, son, don't ever doubt that. Probably the bravest in the world. They got to be to live like they do."

Kirby looked behind them. "Pa? That old man is following us, and he's shucked his rifle out of its boot."

Preacher galloped up to the pair, his rifle in his hand. "Don't get nervous. I ain't the one you need to be afeared of, but I do believe we fixin' to get ambushed."

"Ambushed by who?" Emmett asked.

"Kiowa would be my thinkin'. But they could be Pawnee. My eyes ain't as sharp as they once was. But I seen one of 'em stick his head up out of a wash over yonder. He's young or he wouldn't have done that. But that don't mean that the others with him is young."

"How many?"

"Don't know. In this country, one is too many. Do know this—we better be agettin'. If memory serves me, right over yonder, over that ridge, they's a little crick behind the stand of cottonwoods, with a old Buffalo waller in front of it." He looked up, stood up in his stirrups, and cocked his shaggy head. "Here they come, boys. Get agoin'."

Even as he was speaking, the old man slapped Kirby's bay on the rump, and they were galloping off. With the mountain man taking the lead, the three of them rode for the ridge. Cresting the ridge, the riders slid down the incline and galloped into the timber, down into the wallow. Whoops and cries of the Indians were close behind him.

Preacher might well have been past his good years, but the mountain man leaped off his spotted pony, rifle in hand, and was in position and firing as quickly as Emmett and Kirby. Preacher had a Sharps .52. It fired a paper cartridge, but was deadly up to 700 yards or more.

Kirby looked up in time to see a brave fly off his pony, a crimson gash on his naked chest. The Indian hit the ground and didn't move.

Emmett got a buck in the sights, led him on his fast running pony, then fired the Spencer in his hands. The buck was knocked off his pony, bounced once on the ground, then leaped to his feet, dodging for cover.

He didn't make it. Preacher shot him in the side and lifted him off his feet, dropping him dead.

Emmett fired six more rounds in a thunderous barrage of black smoke, and the Indians scattered to cover, disappearing behind a ridge, horses and all.

"Scared 'em off," Preacher said. "They ain't used to repeaters. All they know is single shots. Let me get something out of my pack, 'n I'll show you a thing or two."

He went to one of his pack animals, which, along with the other horses, was standing just inside the tree line. He untied one of the side packs and let it fall to the ground, then pulled out the most beautiful rifle Kirby had ever seen.

"Damn!" Emmett said. "The Blue bellies had some of those toward the end of the war. But I never could get my hands on one."

Preacher smiled and pulled another Henry repeating rifle from the pack. Unpredictable as mountain men were, he tossed the second Henry to Emmett, along with a sack of cartridges.

"Now we be friends." Preacher laughed, exposing tobacco-stained stubs of teeth.

"I'll pay you for this," Emmett said running his hands over the sleek barrel.

"What for? I didn't pay nothin' for either one of 'em," Preacher replied. "I won both of 'em in some shootin'. Besides, somebody's got to look out for the two of you. You're liable to wander around out here and get hurt. It appears to be, you don't neither of you know tip from tat 'bout staying alive in Injun country."

"You may be right," Emmett admitted. He loaded the Henry. "So I thank you kindly."

Preacher looked at Kirby. "Boy, you plannin' on gettin' into this fight? Wait a minute, maybe I better ask you, can you shoot? Iffen you cain't shoot, better stay out of it. Don't want to worry none 'bout you maybe shootin' one of us."

Proud of his son, Emmett answered. "He can shoot. Kirby, pick up the Spencer."

"Better do it quick. Here they come," Preacher said.

"How do you know that, Preacher?" Kirby asked. "I don't see anything."

"Wind just shifted, and I smelled 'em. They close, so get ready."

Kirby wondered how the old man could smell anything over the fumes from his own body.

Emmett, a veteran of four years of continuous war, could not believe an enemy could slip up on him in open daylight. At the sound of Preacher jacking back the hammer of his Henry .44, Emmett saw a big painted up buck almost on top of him. Suddenly, the open meadow was filled with screaming, charging Indians. Emmett brought the buck down with a slug through the chest, flinging the Indian backward, the yelling abruptly cut off in his throat.

The area changed from the peacefulness of summer quiet, to a screaming, gun-smoke-filled hell.

Kirby jerked his gaze to the small creek in front of them. He had seen movement on the right side of the stream. For what seemed an eternity, he watched the young brave, a boy about his own age, leap and thrash through the water. Then he pulled back the hammer of the Spencer, aimed at the brave, and pulled the trigger.

Kirby heard a wild screaming and spun around. His

father was locked in hand-to-hand combat with two knife wielding braves. Too close to use the rifle, Kirby jerked the pistol from the holster and fired in one smooth motion. He hit one of the braves in the head, just as his father buried his Arkansas toothpick to the hilt in the chest of the other.

Then as abruptly as they came, the Indians were gone. Two braves lay dead in front of Preacher, two more lay dead in the shallow ravine. The boy Kirby had shot was facedown in the creek, arms outstretched, the waters a deep crimson, the body slowly floating downstream.

A thin finger of smoke lifted from the barrel of the Navy .36 Kirby held in his hand.

Preacher smiled and spat tobacco juice. "You're some swift with that hogleg. Yep. Smoke will suit you just fine so. So Smoke it'll be."

"Sir?" Kirby asked.

"Smoke," the old man repeated. "That'll be your name from now on. That's what I aim to call you. Smoke."

Preacher took another .36 Navy Colt from one of the dead Indians, then tossed it to Kirby. "I seen the way you handled that pistol. Ain't never seen no one your age that good with a handgun, and not sure that I've seen anyone full growed who was any better. Now you got yourself two guns."

From another Indian, Preacher took a long-bladed knife in a beaded sheath and handed that to him, as well. "Any man worth his salt out here needs hisself a good knife, too. Most especial someone who calls hisself Smoke."

"I don't call myself Smoke."

"You will."

"Why should I?"

"All famous men needs 'em a moniker, a name other 'n the one they was borned with. I've knowed some right famous men in my day, and Smoke sounds good to me."

"But I ain't famous."

"You're goin' to be, Smoke. Ain't no doubt in my mind. No doubt at all. You're goin' to be a famous man someday, the kind of man folks writes books about."

"I doubt that," Kirby said, but already he was beginning to think of himself as Smoke. He smiled. Yes, he liked that name.

Kirby and Emmett were shocked at what happened next. Preacher scalped the Indians they had killed.

"Good God, man, what are you doing?" Emmett asked.

"What's it look like I'm a' doin'? I'm takin' hair. I know a tradin' post that'll pay a dollar a scalp for ever'one I bring in. I won't do this with a Ute or a Crow. I've lived with them for too long. But I pure dee can't abide a Kiowa or a Pawnee." Carrying the scalps with him, Preacher started back toward the horses. "What we need to do is get out of here now . . . put as much distance between us and the Injuns as we can." He put the scalps into a buckskin bag that hung from one of the pack animals.

"Won't those stink?" Kirby asked.

"They do get ripe," Preacher replied as he mounted his pony.

The three men left the site of the battle at a gallop. Holding the gallop for several miles, they then walked their horses, then galloped them again, then walked them again, so that by late afternoon, Emmett believed they may have ridden as far as thirty miles. They made a quick camp by a creek.

"Get a fire goin'," Preacher said. "I'll get us some grub."

"I'll go hunting if you want," Kirby offered.

"'Preciate the offer, Smoke, but you'd more 'n likely have to shoot our food. Don't know who might be lurkin' around here listenin', so whatever game we take tonight has to be took quiet."

"I guess Smoke's my new name," Kirby said after the old man left the camp afoot. While there was still light, he carefully cleaned and oiled the Navy Colt taken from the dead Indian.

Emmett looked at him. "What do you think about that?"

"You know what? I kinda like it."

They ate an early supper, then doused the fire, carefully checking for any live coals that might touch off a prairie fire, something as feared as any Indian attack, for a racing fire could outrun a galloping horse. They moved on, riding for an hour before pulling into a small stand of timber to make camp for the night.

Preacher spread out his blankets, used his saddle for a pillow, and promptly closed his eyes.

"I'll stand the first watch, *Smoke*," Emmett said, grinning at Kirby. "Then I'll wake Preacher for the second, and you can take the last watch, from two until daylight. Best you go on to sleep now until you're needed."

"All right, Pa."

Just as Kirby was drifting off to sleep, Emmett said, "If you don't like that nickname, son, we can change it."

"It's all right, Pa," the boy murmured, warmed by

the wool of the blanket. "Pa? You know what? I kind of like Preacher."

"So do I," Emmett replied.

"That makes both of you good judges of character," the mountain man spoke from his blankets. "Now why don't you two quit all that jawin', 'n let an old man get some rest?"

"Night, Pa, Preacher."

"Night, Smoke," they both replied.

Preacher rolled the boy out of his blankets at two in the morning, into the summer coolness of the plains. The night was hung with the brilliance of a million stars.

"Stay sharp, now, Smoke," Preacher cautioned. "Injuns don't usually attack at night 'cause they think it's bad medicine for them. A brave gets killed at night, his spirit wanders forever, don't never get to the hereafter in peace. But Injuns is notional kind of folk, 'n not all tribes believe the same. Never can tell what they're goin' to do. More 'n likely, if they're out there, they'll hit us at first light, but you don't never know for sure." He rolled over into his blankets and was soon snoring.

The boy poured himself a cup of scalding hot coffee, strong enough to support a horseshoe, then replaced the pot on the rock grate. The fire was fueled by buffalo chips, hot and smokeless, and it couldn't be seen from ten feet away. Preacher had given him a holster for his second weapon and a wide belt from his seemingly never empty packs. Smoke adjusted it so that he was wearing a brace of pistols.

He had no way of knowing—with what had happened in Salcedo and especially in Delphi—that he had already taken the first steps toward creating a legend that would endure as long as writers would write of the West. Men would fear and respect him, women would desire him, children would play games imitating the man called Smoke. Songs would be written and sung about him in the Indian's villages and in the white man's cities.

On this pleasant night, Smoke—he was already thinking of himself as Smoke—was still some time away from being a living legend. He was just a young man in the middle of a vast open plain watching for savage Indians. He almost dozed off, caught himself, and jerked back awake. He bent forward for another cup of coffee, rubbing his sleepy eyes.

That movement saved his life.

A quivering arrow drove into the tree where, just a second before, he had been resting. Had he not leaned forward *at that precise moment*, the arrow would have driven through his chest.

Smoke drew first the right-hand Colt, then the left-hand gun, his motions almost liquid in their smoothness. The twin Colts were in the hands of one of the few men to whom guns were but an extension of the body. Two Pawnee braves went down under the first two shots. He shifted position. The muzzle flashes were like lightning, and the gunshots like thunder as the Colts roared. Two more bucks were cut down by the .36 caliber balls.

The night, filled with acrid smelling gun smoke, was silent except for the fading sounds of ponies racing away. The Indians wanted no more of that camp. They had lost too many braves.

"I ain't never seen nothing like this!" Preacher explained, walking around the dead and dying Indians. "I knowed Jim Bridger, Kit Carson, Broken Hand Fitzpatrick, uncle Dick Watt, 'n as many as a hunnert other salty old boys, but I ain't never seen nothing to top this here show you just put on. I tell you what, Smoke, you may be a youngster in years, but you'll damn sure do to ride to the river with."

Smoke did not yet know it, but that was the highest compliment a mountain man could ever give to another man.

"Thank you," Smoke said to Preacher as he reloaded the empty cylinders.

July 1867

Early morning, and though most self-respecting roosters had announced the fact long ago, half-a-dozen cocks were still trying to stake a claim on the day. The sun had been up for quite a while but the disc was still hidden by the mountains in the east. The light had already turned from red to white and here and there were signs that Westport Landing was starting another day

A pump creaked as a housewife began pumping water for her daily chores and somewhere a carpenter was hammering. Janey was awakened by the sounds of commerce. She could scarcely believe that she was living in Kansas, given the hard feelings between Kansas and Missouri during the recent war. But she was in the place that was sometimes called the City of Kansas and sometimes called Kansas City, though it wouldn't acquire that name for a few years to come. It was known as Westport Landing, Kansas.

Getting up, she poured a basin of water and washed her face and hands. She stood by the open window and looked out on the town. She had been there for almost a year. Her baby would be fifteen months old, and she wondered if Becca was speaking. Did Becca know she had a mother? Did she wonder about her mother?

Scarcely a day went by without Janey thinking about Rebecca. Sometimes she considered going back—when she thought she couldn't stand being away any longer—begging Ben for forgiveness and spending time with her daughter. But she never followed through on it. Maybe after the first few weeks, maybe even after the first couple of months, she could have done so. But it was far too late for that.

Westport Landing was considerably more unruly than anyplace she had been. The customers of the house where she worked were rugged men who were more at home in the saddle than in a parlor. Some were hell-raisers when they came to town. Often they let off steam by shooting their guns, if not at each other in some spontaneous fight, then at any target that might catch their fancy.

The most troublesome of all the visitors to the place was a man named Cole Brennen. Twice in the last month, he had abused the woman he was with, and Maggie had told him he wasn't welcome anymore.

As expected, he didn't take that too kindly. He was a member of the city council and threatened Maggie with closure if she ever tried to deny him services.

Maggie Mouchette owned and operated the Pretty Girl and Happy Cowboy House. Janey did not occupy quite as elite a position as she had at the Palace Princess Emporium, but she and Maggie had become very good friends over the past year. As a result, Janey operated as Maggie's second in charge.

As Janey looked outside, a couple freight wagons rolled slowly through the street. The boardwalks were full of people, and a game of horseshoes was being played between two of the buildings on the opposite side of the street.

There was a knock on her door. "Abbigail? Are you ready for some breakfast?" Maggie called.

"Sure, I'll be right down."

Janey had gotten rid of the name Fancy Lil, because just as she didn't want her father or brother to track down Janey Jensen, neither did she want Ben Conyers to find Fancy Lil. She didn't really think there was much chance of him finding her, though. Westport Landing was quite a ways from Dallas.

Most of the citizens of the town had eaten breakfast quite some time ago but, as Maggie said, "The town people have their schedule, we have ours."

The other girls were already sitting at the table when Janey came down. Penelope was holding a cat in her lap.

"Penelope, why do you bring that dirty old cat in here?" one of the girls asked.

"Hortense isn't a dirty cat. He cleans himself all the time," Penelope said. "Don't you, Hortense?"

"That's another thing. If it's a tomcat, why do you call him Hortense?"

"Because I like the name."

"You are a strange person."

An older woman wearing a black dress and a white pinafore came in. "Ladies, breakfast is served."

The days passed leisurely for Maggie's girls. Some napped, some played cards, and some read. Normally

Janey was one who enjoyed reading, but she had agreed to go to town with Maggie. When any of the girls went to town, they wore no makeup of any kind and plain dresses, which made them appear no different from any of the other women of the town.

Despite the fact that they purposely dressed down, all the girls were known on sight. When they went somewhere, they were generally shunned, not only by the "good" girls of the town, but quite often by the same men who frequently came calling on them at night.

Not everyone shunned them. One who was always nice to them was Elmer Gleason. He had arrived in town at about the same time Janey did. She heard, once, that he had ridden with Asa Briggs during the war, and though she was not aware that her own brother had ridden with him, she knew that many young men from the county had. It was quite possible that if Elmer Gleason ever learned her real name that he would know who she was. But he would never connect Abbigail Fontaine "from New Orleans" to Janey Jensen.

Elmer was a shotgun guard for the Westport-Landing-to-Wichita stage line, so he was often gone. When he was in town though, he was a frequent guest of the Pretty Girl and Happy Cowboy House, and had even been with Janey a few times.

His visits with her were limited though. Her time didn't cost as much here as it did back in Dallas, but she was still the most expensive girl on the line. As he once said, "In the dark, they all look alike."

Elmer was in the hardware store when Janey and Maggie stepped inside. When he saw them, he smiled, and touched the brim of his hat. Janey smiled back at him. Unfortunately, Elmer wasn't the only one in the store. Cole Brennen was there as well.

"Mr. Deckert," Brennen said to the proprietor of the hardware store. "You do know what these two women are, don't you?"

"As far as I'm concerned, they are customers," Deckert said. "The young women from Miss Mouchette's establishment stop by here from time to time, and they have always been good customers."

"Yes, well, they may not be good customers much longer. I intend to introduce a city ordinance which will close that den of iniquity, once and for all."

"Then where will you go, Brennen?" Elmer asked.

"What? Why you insolent cur! I'll sue you for libel and slander."

"I don't know what them fancy words mean," Elmer said. "But if you're tryin' to say you ain't never before been to Miss Mouchette's place, then I'm callin' you a liar, 'cause I've seen you there."

Brennen wheezed and gasped for breath, then angrily spun around and stomped out of the building.

Maggie laughed. "Elmer, next time you come to my place, I'll set you up for a free drink."

"Just a free drink?" Elmer asked.

"And a visit with one of the girls," Maggie added.

"That's more like it. All right, missy, I'll be by tonight."

CHAPTER 15

Elmer did show up that night, and he had his drink—whiskey—then claimed Penelope for his free visit.

But he wasn't the only one who showed up. Cole Brennen also arrived with another man that neither Janey nor Maggie recognized.

"This here is Marvin Lewis with the Westport Landing City Marshal's office. I've brought him with me to be a witness to what's goin' on here. However, if you treat us right, why, nothin' will happen to you, 'n you can go on doing business just like you always have."

"You are a pathetic excuse of a man, Brennen," Maggie said.

Brennen's malevolent smile stretched the skin tight across his face, giving his head the appearance of a skull. "I may be. But it seems to me like you got no choice but to be nice to us."

By midnight, all the visitors were gone except for Elmer, who had opted to spend the night with Penelope, and Cole Brennen, who was in one of the downstairs rooms with a girl named Louise. Even Marvin Lewis, who had come with Brennen, was gone.

Janey and Maggie were alone in the parlor, sitting in front of the fireplace, drinking a glass of wine.

"I don't usually pry into the past lives of my girls," Maggie said. "Almost all of them have a story as to why they got into this business. Some of them share it and some don't. Before I ask you to share your story, I'll tell you mine.

"I'm the daughter of a preacher man. I married the son of a very rich Boston banker, but he treated me like dirt, so I left him. No divorce. I just left him. Because of who he was, I had to leave Boston." She smiled. "But I took ten thousand dollars with me when I left. That's how I was able to buy this house and start my business here."

Janey thought of the two thousand dollars she had taken from Kirby, but before she responded, they heard a blood-curdling scream coming from Louise's room.

"What is going on in there?" Maggie asked, jumping up quickly, with an expression of anger and concern on her face. "Louise, what is it? What's happening?"

Maggie ran to Louise's room with Janey close behind her. She opened the door and they saw Brennen, his naked body shining gold in the light of the lamp. He was holding a bloody knife in his hand. Louise had her hand across a bloody cheek.

"He cut me!" Louise cried.

Maggie picked up a vase and held it over her head as she approached Brennen. "Get out of here!" she shouted angrily. "Get out of here now! And don't you ever come back!"

Brennen suddenly thrust his hand forward, burying the knife up to its hilt in Maggie's chest. With an expression of pain and shock on her face, Maggie stepped back from him.

"You've killed her!" Janey screamed.

Brennen turned to face her. He was nearly covered in blood, and the reflected flame in his eyes could have been the fires of hell. The smile was demonic, and he held the knife out toward her. "You're next," he said in a low hiss.

Janey backed away from him, stumbling into the chair where Brennen had put his clothes. She stuck her hand back to keep from falling and felt his pistol!

Instantly and instinctively, she pulled the pistol out of its holster and brought it around, firing just as Brennen lunged for her. The bullet hit him in the chest. The impact knocked him back against the fireplace, and he slid down to the hearth, leaving a smear of blood on the bricks behind him.

Elmer Gleason raced into the room with a gun in his hand. He didn't have to ask what happened. In one all-encompassing look, he took it in. "Girl, throw what clothes together as fast as you can. We're getting out of here."

"I had no choice!" Janey said. "He killed Maggie and he was coming after me."

"That's true," Louise said. "Abbigail didn't have any choice!"

"I believe you, Louise," Elmer said. "I believe both of you. But this feller is on the city council, 'n the man who come here earlier is a deputy marshal. They ain't nobody goin' to believe you. That's why we got to get out of here now."

"Elmer, no. If you run with me, they'll be after you, too."

"I need to get out of here, anyway," Elmer said. "I made a few rides with a feller over in Missouri called Jesse James. So I expect my welcome here is goin' to be wore out pretty quick."

Smoke and Emmett were about to partake in an event that would be one of the last of its kind. It was called Rendezvous, a gathering of the breed of men civilization sometimes raised a dubious head toward and pushed the mountain men into history. The smoke of scores of campfires could be seen from some distance away. As Smoke and his father drew closer, they became aware of the sounds of Rendezvous and the aromas of roasting meat from the many cooking fires.

In the early days of trapping, before the war and the Western migration, Rendezvous would be the biggest city between the Pacific Ocean and St. Louis. Those days were over. The mountain men that remained were, for the most part, advanced in years, heading for the sunset of their lives. They had spent their youth, their best years, and the midpoint of their lives, in elements where one careless move could result in either sudden death or slow torture from hostiles.

Mountain men were not easily impressed, but those gathered were standing and watching as Smoke and his father rode slowly into the ruins of the old post, rifles across their saddles. Preacher had already spread the word about the boy called Smoke.

As did many boys of that hard era, he looked older than his years. His face was deeply tanned. His shoulders and arms were lean, but hard with muscle.

"I don't know. He don't look all that much to me," an aging mountain man said to a friend.

"Neither did Kit Carson if you recall," his friend replied. "Hell, he warn't but four inches over five feet, but he were one hell of a man."

"The boy is faster than a snake, Preacher says."

The mountain man cocked his eye at his friend. "Yeah, but don't forget, Preacher has been known to spin a tall tale ever' now and then, when he thinks it might be a mite more interestin' than tellin' the truth."

"Yeah, but not this time, I wager. Look at this kid. He's got a mean look to his eyes."

Smoke and Emmett sat their horses and stared. Neither had ever seen anything like the colorful assemblage. The men, all of whom were over sixty years old, were dressed in wild, bright colors—buckskin breeches and shirts, beaded leggings, wide red, blue, or yellow sashes about their waists. Some were wearing cord trousers with silk shirts shining in a rainbow of colors. All were beaded and booted and bearded. Some held long muzzle-loading Kentucky rifles. A few had lever-action repeating rifles. Many were decorated with colorfully dyed rawhide strings dangling from the barrel, the shot and powder bags decorated with beads.

It would not be the last, but nearly the last great gathering of the magnificent breed of men called mountain men.

When Emmett and Smoke spotted Preacher, they couldn't believe their eyes. They sat their horses and stared.

He was clean and his beard was well trimmed. He wore new buckskins, new leggings, and a red sash around his waist. His eyes sparkled with a light they had never seen. "Howdy," he called. "Y'all light and sit, boys."

"I don't believe it," Emmett said. "His face is clean."

"There's water to wash in over there," Preacher said, pointing. "Good strong soap, too. But you'd best dump what's in the barrel and refill it. It's got fleas in it along with the ticks."

Elmer took Janey to the one-room cabin where he lived, just on the edge of town. It had been the middle of the night when they left the Pretty Girl and Happy Cowboy House. Nobody had seen him sneak her into his place.

She stayed in the cabin for two weeks, not daring to show herself outside. The wisdom of that decision was borne out when Elmer brought a newspaper by a couple days later.

Murder So Foul

Cole Brennen, a sterling citizen and member of the city council, was murdered on the 19th instant. Brennen and Deputy Marshal Marvin Lewis were investigating a residence on the suspicion that activity of an illicit nature might be taking place there. It had been reported that the owner of the house, Maggie Mouchette, was running, not a boarding house for young women as her city license stated, but a bawdy house.

Deputy Lewis reports that, upon confirming that such was true, Brennen informed them that he would be reporting the true nature of the business to the authorities. That was when two of the occupants of the house attacked him. Although Brennen was able to subdue Miss Mouchette, the other woman, Abbigail Fontaine, managed to secure a pistol and shot at him. The ball, thus energized, struck Brennen in the chest, taking terrible effect.

Abbigail Fontaine has since disappeared, and authorities have asked that anyone who can give information as to her location should provide such to Marshal Kilgore.

"Lewis wasn't even there," Janey said after she read the story. "But Penelope was. Why didn't they ask her what happened?"

"I'm sure she did tell them what happened, but bein' as she is what she is, why it's most likely they didn't pay her no never mind," Elmer said.

"Elmer, what am I going to do? I can't stay here in your cabin forever."

"How'd you like to go West?"

"Go West?"

"They's a riverboat leavin' first thing in the mornin', headin' up the Missouri toward a place called Montana. I figure to get us on it."

"How am I going to get to the boat without being seen?"

"You let me worry about that."

When Elmer returned to the cabin that night, he showed Janey the tickets for the riverboat *Cora Two*.

"You're Mrs. John Smith. I'm John Smith. I figured maybe we should go up river as husband and wife. Folks that's lookin' for you, won't be lookin' for you to be travelin' with a husband. Most especial since we'll be usin' names that ain't our'n."

"And John Smith is so original," Janey said.

"Yeah, I thought it was pretty good my ownself. It was the first name I come up with," Elmer said, failing to catch the sarcasm in Janey's voice.

Janey smiled. Who was she to criticize this man who had made all the arrangements to get her away? And, she was pretty sure that once she was away from West-port Landing, she would be safe. The authorities would be looking for a woman named Abbigail Fontaine from New Orleans. She had never given her real last name to anyone, not even to Maggie, nor had she ever shared with anyone that she had come from Missouri, by way of Texas.

It was after dark when they left Elmer's house, and they reached the river without arousing any suspicion. The *Cora Two* was tied up at the landing, a long, white, stern wheeler with three decks and a pilot house. Two chimneys sprouted from just aft of the pilot house.

Once they were aboard, Janey stepped out onto the hurricane deck, which was between the boiler deck and the Texas deck and looked out over the town of West-port Landing. It was quiet and dark, and she could hear a dog barking way off in the distance. The city was so peaceful at that hour of the night. The loudest sounds were the gentle lapping of the river against the hull and the creaking of the boat at its hawsers as it pulled at the current while at anchor.

She walked forward and stood against the railing to look out over the bow. Down on the boiler deck she could see neat stacks of cargo, ricks of firewood, and the men, women, and even children, who held steerage tickets. They would be making the journey on that deck. They had no bunks, and would have to bed down wherever they could find room, unprotected against the weather.

A cool breeze came up and Janey shivered, then hugged herself. She thought of the river they would be following, stretched out before them for many miles. It was, she decided, a metaphor, not only bridging the distance she must travel, but reaching into her future as well. What did lie before her?

Smoke stood in front of the trading post at dawn. His pa was mounted; he wasn't.

"You do understand my ridin' off alone, don't you, boy? I wouldn't be leavin' you, but I've seen you when you was up against it, 'n you come through just fine. You can handle them guns better 'n anyone I ever saw, so I ain't worried none 'bout you bein' able to take care of yourself. But there's some things you're goin' to need to learn 'bout livin' out here. I cain't think of nobody more able to teach you them things than Preacher. Problem is, it's goin' to take you some time to learn all you need to learn, 'n me 'n you know that I don't have that much time left. So, I aim to leave you here to get your learnin' while I go out lookin' for them men that kilt your brother. You got 'ny problem with that?"

"I reckon not," Smoke replied quietly. "I know you're doin' what you feel you got to do."

"You're a good boy, Kirby. No, you're a good man. I know that when you was growin' up, you might sometimes thought I was favorin' Luke. I warn't. It was just that he was older and a mite easier for me to understand. But there ain't no man ever lived, who had himself a son he was more proud of than I am of you. I'm glad the Good Lord give us this time to be together, so's I could find that out.

"Bye, Kirby." Emmett smiled. "I mean, bye, Smoke. That'll be your name from now on."

He turned and rode away. He had taken only a little of the money with him, leaving the rest with Smoke. He rode for some distance, then stopped, turned his horse, and waved at his son. Then he was gone, dipping out of sight, over the rise of a small hill.

Smoke knew, at that moment, that he would never see his father again and tried to swallow the knot that was in his throat.

For the entire time of their good-bye, Preacher had sat on the porch of the trading post, watching, saying nothing.

Smoke turned away from the road and looked up at the man who was to become his mentor. "He won't be back."

Preacher spat a stream of tobacco off the porch and onto the dusty ground. "Some things, Smoke, a man's just got to do before his time on earth slips away. Your pa has things to do. If you're wantin' to cry, I want you to know that there ain't no shame in it."

Smoke squared his shoulders. "I'm a man. I lived alone, I worked the land, and I paid the taxes all by myself. And I haven't cried since Ma died."

"Ain't nobody ever goin' to question whether or

not you're a man, Smoke. You're as much a man as anyone I've ever knowed."

Smoke put his foot on the steps. "Let's get outfitted." He climbed the steps and entered the trading post. He bought a new Henry repeating rifle, one hundred rounds of .44 caliber ammunition for it, and an extra cylinder for his left hand .36, then they rode out.

Preacher told him he knew of a friendly band of Indians up north of the post. He'd see to it that Smoke got himself a pair of moccasins and leggings and a buckskin jacket, fancy beaded.

"I ain't got that kind of money to waste, Preacher."

"Ain't going to cost you nothing. I know the lady who will make them for you."

"She must like you pretty well."

Preacher smiled. "She's my daughter."

On board the *Cora Two*, a long, deep throated blast blew from the boat's horn, then the captain stepped out of the pilot house. Lifting a megaphone to his lips, he called forward to the main deck bow. "Lead man!"

"Lead man, aye!" an unseen voice called back from the front of the boat.

"Sound the bottom!"

"Aye, Cap'n!"

"We must be in shallow water," Elmer said.

Janey walked up to the front of the boat. The soundings had been taken frequently during the long journey upriver, and she was familiar with the routine.

"By the mark two!" the lead man called. To make certain that his call was heard in the pilot house, it was repeated by someone up on the Texas Deck.

The lead man continued to call his soundings,

which were then echoed, both calls intoned so melod-
ically that it was almost as if the men were singing.
Janey had actually grown to appreciate them, and enjoyed listening to the calls as they played against the
rhythmic slap of the paddlewheel in the water.

During the trip upriver the boat had to proceed
very cautiously because of shallow water. Three times
they had encountered sandbars with the water so shallow that it was necessary to "grasshopper" over them
with long heavy spars carried vertically on derricks
near the bow. The ends of the spars were dropped to
the bottom, tops slanted forward, and with block,
tackle, cable, and capstan, lifted and pushed the boat
forward as if on crutches while the paddle wheel
thrashed furiously. After each splash down, the spars
were reset for the next "hop," until the boat was free.

At the moment, they seemed to be proceeding upriver at a steady, brisk pace.

Seventy-one days after the *Cora Two* left Westport
Landing, Janey stood on the hurricane deck and
watched the bluffs slide by on the south bank as the
boat worked its way up the Missouri River to Ft. Benton.

Elmer came over to stand beside her. "Well, our
long journey is nearly over. The cap'n told me we'd
reach Fort Benton today."

"Elmer, I can't thank you enough for helping me
out the way you did. I mean, you gave up your job and
everything."

Elmer chuckled. "Ridin' shotgun on a stagecoach ain't
that much of a job. It was about time I was movin' on."

The *Cora Two* beat its way against the current as it

approached around a wide, sweeping bend. Smoke was pouring from the twin chimneys and the engine steam-pipe was booming as loudly as if the town were under a cannonading. With the engine clattering and the paddle wheel slapping at the water, it approached the Ft. Benton landing.

"Deck men, fore and aft, stand by to throw out the lines!" the captain called.

"Aye, Cap'n, standing by!" the first mate called back as two men rushed to the front of the boat and stood side by side, holding the ropes.

At the last minute, the engine was reversed, and the paddle started whirling in the opposite direction, causing the water to froth at the action. The reversing paddle wheel held the speed of the boat until the movement through the water was but a slow, gentle glide up to the dock. Waiting stevedores stood ready to receive the lines.

"Heave out your lines!" the first mate shouted, and both ropes were tossed ashore. One of the men on the boat deck walked his rope back to the stern where he wrapped it securely around a stanchion. The men ashore pulled on the lines—fore and aft—so that the boat was pulled sideways until it was snug up against the dock.

"Well, missy, we're here," Elmer said. "You got 'ny ideas as to what you might do next?"

Janey smiled. "Don't worry about me, Elmer. For the next few years, at least for as long as I can keep my looks, I'll always be able to make a living."

Elmer laughed out loud. "I reckon you will."

* * *

Janey checked into the Grand Mountain Hotel. Once she was in her room she went through her dresses and selected one that left little to the imagination. Donning the dress, she got out her powders and paints, and with an artistry developed over the last few years, she transformed her face, combining subtle eye shadows with bold lashes and mascara. A crimson smear across her lips completed the transformation, and when she walked through the lobby of the hotel a short while later, not one person would have connected her with the woman who had registered as Fannie Webber.

Exiting the hotel, Janey made her way to the largest and grandest saloon in town, the Gold Strike. She went inside, strode up to the bar, and ordered a drink.

"What kind of drink?" the bartender asked.

"I expect, if I'm going to be drinking with men all day, you'd better give me something that doesn't make me drunk." Janey fixed him with a penetrating stare.

"Uh . . . drinking with men?" the bartender asked.

The well-dressed man sitting at a table close to the bar got up and walked over to stand beside her. "Henry, I do believe this young lady is applying for a job."

"I might be," Janey replied, turning her charm toward the man. "If so, who should I see?"

"That would be me. The name is Andrew McGhee. And you would be?"

Janey thought for a moment, wondering if she should use the same name she used when she checked into the hotel. "The name I use will depend upon whether or not I can get a room here in the saloon."

McGhee laughed out loud. "For you, my finest room."

Janie's smile broadened, and she stuck out her hand. "It's nice to meet you, Andrew. My name is Fannie Webber."

CHAPTER 16

July 1869

It had been two years since Emmett rode off on his own, and Smoke had not heard anything from him since. He wasn't surprised by that, given that Emmett had written only two letters the whole time he was away fighting the war.

Nothing of the boy was left. Smoke was a man, fully grown and hard in body, face, and eyes. The bay he had ridden west hadn't survived the first year after Emmett left. The horse had fallen on the ice and broken his leg. Smoke had had to put him down, but Preacher found another horse for him, a large, mean-tempered Appaloosa. The Indian had sold him cheap, because he hadn't been able to break him.

Strangely, not only to the Indian who sold him, but to other Indians who knew the animal, the horse seemed to bond immediately with Smoke. He was a stallion, and he was mean, his eyes warning any knowledgeable person away. In addition to its distinctive markings—the

mottled hide, vertically striped hooves, and pale eyes—
the Appaloosa had a perfectly shaped numeral seven
between his eyes. And that became his name—Seven.

"Smoke, I've done learned you about as much as I
know how to learn anyone," Preacher said one summer morning. "There ain't no doubt in my mind, but
that you could light in the middle of the mountains
some'ers and live as good as me or any other mountain man I ever knowed could.

"But truth to tell, the time of the mountain man is
gone. There warn't even no Rendezvous this year, 'n I
don't know if they'll ever be another 'n. Just be glad
you got to see one of 'em when you did."

"I am glad," Smoke said. "If I live to be as old a man
as you are, I'll still remember gettin' to go to that Rendezvous."

"Whoa, now! Are you tellin' me that's all you're
goin' to remember? That you ain't goin' to 'member
nothin' else I learned you in all this time?"

Smoke laughed. "I reckon I'll be rememberin' that,
as well."

Shortly after that conversation an old mountain
man rode into their camp. "You just as ugly as I remembered, Preacher," he said in the form of greeting.

"I didn't think you was even still alive, Grizzly,"
Preacher said. "I heard you got et up by a pack o' wolves.
No, wait. That ain't right. Now that I think on it, they said
you was so old and dried up that the wolves didn't want
nothin' to do with you."

Smoke had already learned that mountain men insulted each other whenever possible. It was their way
of showing affection.

"Can I talk in front of the boy?" Grizzly asked.

"Anythin' you can tell me, you can say in front of him," Preacher replied.

Smoke poured himself a cup of coffee and waited.

"A man rode into the Hole about two months ago. All shot up, he was. And 'sides that, he had a bad cough."

"Is he still alive?" Smoke blurted.

The old man turned cold eyes toward him. "Don't ever interrupt a man when he's palaverin'. 'Tain't polite. One thing about Indians, they know manners. They know to allow a man to speak his piece without interrupting."

"Sorry," Smoke said.

"Accepted. No, he's dead. Strange man. Dug his own grave. Come the time, I buried him. He's planted on that their little plain at the base of the high peak east side of the canyon. Zenobia Peak, it's called. You remember it, Preacher?"

Preacher nodded.

The old mountain man reached inside his war bag and pulled out a heavy sack and tossed it to Smoke. "This would be your'n, I reckon. It's from your pa, a right smart amount of gold." Again, he dipped into the war bag and pulled out a rawhide-wrapped flat object. "And this is a piece of paper with words on it. Names, your pa said, of the men who put lead in him. He said you'd know what to do, but for me to tell you, don't do nothing rash."

His business done, the old man rose to his feet. "I done what I give my word I'd do. Now I'll be goin' on."

Smoke had purposely held off reading the letter until he found his pa's grave. When he did find it, he used a rock to chisel his pa's name onto it.

EMMETT JENSEN
BORN 1815 DIED 1869

He wasn't sure that 1815 was correct, but he figured it was close enough, especially since he was the only relative left who would ever see it, or even care about it. He wasn't counting Janey.

With the words chiseled onto the stone, Smoke moved it over to the mound of earth that was the gravesite. The stone was big and hard to move, and he was glad. That meant it would be too heavy for any vandals to mess with it for no reason other than to make mischief.

Not until the tombstone was put into position, did Smoke turn his attention to the letter. He opened it and read it by the fading light.

Son,

    I found some of the men who killed your brother Luke and stoled the gold that belonged to the Gray. They was more of them than I first thought. I killed two of them but they got lead in me and I had to hightail it out. Ackerman is the man Luke thought was his best friend, and the one that betrade him. He got away.

    Came here, but not going to make it. Son, you don't owe nothin' to the cause of the Gray. So don't get it in your mind you do.

    I got word that your sis Janey left that gambler. Don't know where she is now, but I wouldn't fret much about her. She is mine, but I think she is trash. Don't know what she got that bad streek from.

    I'm gettin' tared and seein is hard. I love you Smoke.

Pa

"You're goin' out after 'em now, ain't you." Preacher said. "The fella that kilt your ma, and the ones that kilt your brother and your pa." It was more a statement than a question.

"Yeah, I am," Smoke said.

"Like I said when your pa left, they's some things a man just has to do."

Over the next couple months, Smoke's justice was thorough and extreme.

Two names he learned about belonged to men who had been complicit in shooting his brother, stealing the Confederate gold, and ultimately killing his pa. Ted Casey was the fourth man who'd stolen the Confederacy gold with Stratton, Richards, and Potter—the men Emmett had set out to find and kill. Ackerman had ridden with Quantrill. Smoke didn't know Ackerman's first name, but he'd learned from someone he met that the Confederate deserter owned a ranch just outside Canon City, Colorado.

"Sounds like all them boys done right good for themselves," Preacher said. "They all come out here and commenced ranchin'."

"They started ranchin' on the gold they stole from the South after shootin' my brother," Smoke said sourly.

Casey's place—TC Ranch—was close by so they headed there first. The shootout was deadly, with the ranch hands putting up quite a fight before they were killed. Casey wasn't among those killed at the ranch, but Smoke found him, then hung him in front of a sheriff and scores of people from the nearby town. Nobody made any real effort to stop him.

"Now," Smoke said. "I'm goin' to Canon City."

"*We're* goin', you mean," Preacher said.

"All right, we're goin' to Canon City."

"Oreodelphia," Preacher said.

"What?"

"That's what they wanted to name it. Oreodelphia, but there couldn't nobody hardly even say it, let alone spell it, so they wound up callin' it Canon City."

Smoke frowned, thinking that was more information than he needed to know at the moment. "Do you know how to get there?"

"I know."

"Then why are we standing here jawboning?"

"Boy, you got to learn patience, you know that?"

"What is his name?" Ackerman asked.

"Smoke."

"Smoke? Somebody named Smoke killed Casey and all his hands?"

"His last name is Jensen. I was told that would mean somethin' to you."

Ackerman smiled. "Luke had a brother 'n a sister he used to talk about some. His sister was named Janey. Accordin' to Luke, she was a real good looker. She must be somethin' by now. His brother was named Kirby. I ain't never heard of anyone named Smoke Jensen."

"Well, from what I've heard, he's Emmett Jensen's son."

"Damn," Ackerman said. "Then it has to be the one Luke said was Kirby. Smoke must just be the name he's took for some reason. And he's comin' here, you say?"

"That's what I've been told."

"All right. We'll just take care of 'im when he gets here. Once we kill him, there won't be nobody left but the sister. An' she ain't likely to go out after nobody."

For two days, Smoke and Preacher waited and relaxed in Canon City, making a special effort to keep out of trouble. Smoke bathed twice behind the barbershop, and Preacher told him if he didn't stop that, he was going to come down with some dreadful illness.

The mountain man and the gunfighter were civil to the men and polite to the ladies. Some of the ladies batted their eyes and swished their bustled fannies as they passed by Smoke, but he paid them no attention.

"You boys are sure taking your time buying supplies," the sheriff noted on the second day.

"We like to think things through before buying," Preacher told him. "Smoke here is a right cautious man when it comes to partin' with the greenback. You might even call him tight."

The sheriff didn't find that amusing. "You boys wouldn't be waiting for Ackerman to make a move, would you?"

"Ackerman?" Smoke looked at the sheriff. "What is an Ackerman?"

The sheriff's smile was grim. "What do you boys do for a living? I have a law on the books about vagrants."

"I'm retired," Preacher told him. "Enjoying the sunset of my years, I am. Smoke here, he runs a string of horses."

"Would you like to buy a horse?" Smoke asked. "I've got some really nice ones, and bein' as you are with the law, I can give you a real good deal."

"I ought to run you both out of this town."

"Why?" Smoke asked. "On what charge? We haven't caused you any trouble."

"Yet." The sheriff's back was stiff with anger as he walked away. The man knew a set up when he saw one.

But his feelings were mixed. Ackerman and his bunch of rowdies were all troublemakers, and he owed them nothing. He swung no wide political loop in this country, and there were persistent rumors that Ackerman had been a thief and a murderer during the war, as well as a deserter. The sheriff could not abide a coward.

He sighed. If he was right in reading the young man called Smoke, Ackerman's future looked very bleak.

A hard ridden horse hammered the street into dust. A cowhand from the Bar X slid to a halt in front of the sheriff's office. "Ackerman and his bunch is ridin' in, Sheriff," the cowhand said, still panting from his ride. "They're huntin' bear. He told me to tell you he's going to kill this kid called Smoke and anyone else that gets in his way."

The sheriff's smile grudgingly filled with admiration. The kid's patience had paid off. Ackerman had made his boast and his threat, which meant that anything the kid did now could only be called self-defense.

The sheriff thanked the cowboy and told him to hunt a hole to hide in. He crossed the street and told his deputy to clear the street from the apothecary to the blacksmith shop.

In five minutes, the main street resembled a ghost town. A yellow dog was the only living thing that had not cleared out. Behind curtains, closed doors, and shuttered windows, men and women watched and waited, anticipating the roar of gunfire from the street.

At the edge of town, Ackerman, a bull of a man with small, mean eyes, stopped for a moment. With a small wave, he started the five cowhands with him down the street, riding slowly, six abreast.

Standing on the porch of the hotel with Smoke, Preacher stuffed his mouth full of chewing tobacco, then they walked out into the street to face the six men.

"I've come for you, kid," said the big man in the center of the riders.

"Oh? Who are you?" Smoke asked.

"You know who I am, kid. I'm Ackerman."

"Ah yes!" Smoke said. "I do know that. You're the man who was supposed to be my brother's best friend, but you helped kill him by shooting him in the back. Then you stole the gold he was guarding."

Inside the hotel, pressed against the wall, the desk clerk listened intently, his mouth open in anticipation of gunfire.

"You're a liar. I didn't shoot your brother. That was Potter and his bunch."

"You stood by and watched it. Then you stole the gold."

"It was war, kid."

"But you were on the same side," Smoke said. "That not only makes you a killer, it makes you a traitor and a coward."

"I'll kill you for saying that!"

"You'll burn in hell a long time before I'm dead," Smoke told him.

Ackerman grabbed for his pistol.

The street exploded in gunfire and black powder

fumes. Horses screamed and bucked in fear. One rider was thrown to the dust by his lunging Mustang.

Smoke took the men on the left, Preacher the men on the right. The battle lasted no more than ten or twelve seconds. When the noise and the gun smoke cleared, five men lay in the street, two of them dead. Two more would die from their wounds. The one shot in the side would live. Ackerman had been shot three times—once in the belly, once in the chest, and one ball had taken him in the side of the face as the muzzle of the .36 had lifted him with each blast. Dead, he still sat in his saddle. The big man finally leaned to one side and toppled from his horse, one booted foot hanging up in the stirrup. The horse shied, then began walking down the dusty street, dragging Ackerman and leaving a bloody trail on the ground behind him.

The excited clerk ran out the door. "I heard it all! You were right, Mr. Smoke. Yes, sir. Right all the way." He looked at Smoke. "Why, you've been wounded, sir."

A slug had nicked the young man on the cheek, another had punched a hole in the fleshy part of his left arm, high up. Both were minor wounds.

Preacher had been grazed on the leg. He spat into the street. "Damn near swallowed my terbacky."

"I never saw a draw that fast," a man spoke from the storefront. "It was a blur."

The sheriff and the deputy came out of the jail, walking down the bloody, dusty street. Both were carrying Greeners, double-barreled, twelve-gauge shotguns.

"Right down the street," the sheriff said, pointing,

"is the doctor's office. Get yourselves patched up and then get out of town. You have one hour."

"Sheriff, it was a fair fight," the desk clerk said. "I seen it."

The sheriff never took his eyes off Smoke. "One hour," he repeated.

"We'll be gone." Smoke wiped a smear of blood from his cheek.

Townspeople began hauling the bodies off. The local photographer set up his cumbersome equipment and began popping flash powder, sealing the gruesome scene for posterity. He also took a picture of Smoke.

The editor of the paper walked up to stand by the sheriff. He watched the old man and the young gun hand walk down the street. He truly had seen it all. The old man had killed one man and wounded another. The young man had killed four. "What's the young man's name?"

"His name is Smoke Jensen. But if you ask me, he's the devil."

"Your pa would be pleased," Preacher said as they rode out of town within the hour assigned by the sheriff. "Do you plan to get the other men he was looking for?"

"Yes, I do. But I'm going after Shardeen first."

"Before you start out, I want you to come to Denver with me. I've got a fella there I'd like for you to meet."

"Somebody who can help me find Shardeen?"

"You might say that," Preacher replied, without being any more specific.

* * *

It took them three days to get to Denver.

Preacher led Smoke to a low-lying building made of white limestone. A United States flag flew from the flagpole out front, and as they started into the building, Smoke saw a sign chiseled above the doorway. UNITED STATES FEDERAL OFFICE BUILDING.

"What are we going in here for?"

"You're askin' questions again. Didn't I tell you a long time ago that when words is goin' outta your mouth, nothin' can be comin' in your ears? You learn quicker if you're just quiet and pay attention," Preacher said.

Smoke smiled. "Have you always been such a cantankerous old fart?"

"Pretty much," Preacher said.

Both men were wearing buckskins, and both were a little more gamey than the average citizen of Denver. When Swayne Hodge, the office clerk, looked up and saw the two men coming in, he became a little agitated. "Gentlemen, gentlemen, are you lost?"

"Pilgrim, I been out here more 'n fifty years 'n I ain't never been lost but one time. I cain't say as I was all that lost then, since it didn't take me more 'n a month to find my way back to the trail."

"But you *do* know that this is a federal office building, don't you?"

"I didn't exactly figure it to be a house of ill repute," Preacher said.

"Oh, my," Hodge said, clearly discomforted by the vulgarity.

"Preacher! What are you doing here?" Another voice spoke openly and without reservation.

"Excuse me, Marshal Holloway, do you actually

know these, uh, gentlemen?" Hodge asked, stumbling over the word *gentlemen.*

"I don't know both of them," the marshal said. "But I certainly know the older gentleman. Preacher, come into my office and introduce me to your young friend."

Hodge remained standing, watching with his mouth agape as Uriah B. Holloway, United States Marshal for the Colorado District, holding his commission by U.S. Senate confirmation since April 10, 1866, led the two unwashed men into his office.

"Have a seat, men," Marshal Holloway offered.

"Thank ye, kindly, Uriah." Preacher held his hand out toward Smoke. "This here is Smoke Jensen."

Holloway frowned. "Smoke? His name is Smoke?"

"It's as much Smoke as my name is Preacher."

The marshal chuckled. "All right, Preacher, I'll go along with that. Smoke, it is good to meet you."

"Marshal," Smoke replied, taking the lawman's extended hand.

"Now, what can I do for you?"

"Have you ever heard of a man named Angus Shardeen?" Preacher asked.

Holloway's eyes narrowed. "Yes, I've heard of him. What about him?"

"First, let me ask what you know about him," Preacher replied.

"He has federal and state arrest warrants out on him," Holloway replied. "He's wanted for murder, robbery, arson, and probably half a dozen other things."

"Do you have any idea where he might be now?"

Holloway shook his head. "I can't say as I do. I do know, however, that he has some bad men with him."

"An army?" Smoke asked.

"You might say that. Angus Shardeen was a colonel in the Union Army during the war . . . though there are some who dispute that. He was actually a Jayhawker, operating at the head of a gang of guerrillas, supposedly riding in support of Union troops. But his tactics were so brutal, and quite frankly, so self-enriching, that if he ever did actually hold a commission, it was probably withdrawn.

"Since the end of the war, he has continued the guerrilla operations using many of the same men, only it is without regard to any cause, other than his own."

"Bein' as you are a U.S. Marshal, would you have the authority to go after 'im, no matter where he is?" Preacher asked.

Holloway nodded. "I would."

"And say there was somebody who was a Deputy U.S. Marshal, say it was someone that you appointed. Would that fella also be able to go after Shardeen, no matter where he might be?"

"Yes, he would. Tell me, Preacher, why are you asking me all these questions? Do you know where Shardeen is?"

"I don't have 'ny idee where he is, but if you was to appoint Smoke as one of your deputies, he'll find 'im for you."

Holloway looked over at Smoke. "Do you have an idea as to where Shardeen might be?"

"No, sir."

"Then what makes you think you'll be able to find him, when I haven't."

"Marshal, you bein' the law for this whole territory, I would expect that you have a lot more things to do than just look for Angus Shardeen, don't you?"

"Well, yes, as a matter of fact, I do."

"I don't and I intend to find him," Smoke replied with grit.

"And you want me to appoint you deputy so that you can?"

"No, sir."

"No?" Holloway looked over at Preacher in surprise. "Look here, isn't this what you just asked me to do?"

"I mean no, sir, I don't want you to appoint me deputy so I can find him," Smoke said. "I intend to find 'im, whether I'm appointed as your deputy or not."

"You did hear me tell you that Shardeen was riding at the head of his own army, didn't you?"

"Yes, sir, I heard you say that."

"Well, here's the thing, Mr. Jensen. I don't have funding for another deputy."

Preacher spoke up. "Look here, Uriah. Sometimes when you form a posse to go after someone, don't you appoint them men in the posse as Deputy U.S. Marshals?"

"Yes, I do. But I don't pay them."

"You don't have to pay me," Smoke said.

"Let me get this straight. You are willing to be an unpaid deputy in order to go out, single-handed, to find Angus Shardeen, even though you know there are at least half a dozen with him?"

Smoke nodded. "Yes, sir."

"You will have to function alone. I don't have enough men to assign anybody to one specific task."

"That's all right."

Marshal Holloway looked over at Preacher again. "Preacher, you go along with this?"

"I do."

"All right, Smoke Jensen, raise your right hand."

Smoke did as he was directed.

"Now, repeat after me. I Smoke Jensen . . ."

"I Smoke Jensen . . ." He continued with the oath as administered by Marshal Holloway. "Do solemnly swear that I will faithfully execute all lawful precepts, directed to the Marshal of the United States for the District of Colorado, under the authority of the United States, and true returns make, in all things well and truly. And without malice or partiality, perform the duties of Deputy Marshal for the District of Colorado during my continuance in said office, so help me God."

That done, Holloway reached out to shake Smoke's hand. "Congratulations, Smoke. You are now a Deputy U.S. Marshal. That gives you full authority to arrest any fugitive, anywhere within the borders of the United States. That includes all states and territories." Holloway smiled. "But you won't be paid."

"I understand."

"But even though you won't be paid, you still intend to bring him in."

"No."

"I beg your pardon? I thought that was the whole reason for appointing you a Deputy U.S. Marshal."

"I won't be bringing him in," Smoke said cryptically.

Shortly afterward, Smoke took his hunt for Angus Shardeen public. He had a letter printed in newspapers all over Kansas, Colorado, Idaho, and Wyoming.

To the murderer and bandit, Angus Shardeen.

You killed many women, children, and old men during the war. You have continued your murdering and killing since the war, having abandoned all pretense of patriotism, and are doing so for selfish reasons.

During your murderous spree, one of the women you killed was my mother, Pearl Jensen. I watched you do this, then you clubbed me down and left me for dead. You should have checked me more closely Shardeen, for I was not dead, and now I am coming for you.

I'm coming for you for my mother and for the families of all the innocents you have killed, and I am doing this, not for revenge, but for justice. That is because as an official Deputy United States Marshal, I have the power of the law on my side.

Smoke Jensen.

"Who in the hell does this arrogant deputy marshal think he is?" Shardeen demanded angrily, after he read the letter in the newspaper.

"He tells us right there who he is," Bartell said. "He is Smoke Jensen."

"Is that name supposed to mean anything to me?"

"From what I've heard, he may be the fastest gun there is," Bartell replied. "And they say he can shoot the eye out of a squirrel from a hundred yards away."

"*They* say? Who says?" Shardeen demanded.

"People who have seen him shoot. He could give us trouble."

"How much trouble can he be if he is dead? I want him dead," Shardeen said. "And I'm willing to pay well for it."

CHAPTER 17

March 1870

In the six months since Smoke had pinned on the star of Deputy U.S. Marshal, he had been wandering around, sometimes chasing a lead, sometimes going from town to town with no particular lead but merely "casting his net," as Preacher described his travels. And like fishermen who cast their nets into to the sea, his net came up empty many more times than it provided results.

Even as he rode on, he remembered what he'd learned two months ago in the small town of Sage Creek, Wyoming.

A bartender nervously handed him a piece of paper. "I don't know if you know anything about this, and I want you to know I ain't havin' nothin' to do with it. By that, I mean I ain't handin' these things out to nobody, even though somebody give me near a hunnert of 'em 'n tole me to pass 'em out to any cowboy who might want to make a little money.

"What is it?" Smoke asked, wondering what the mysterious piece of paper might be. He opened it to read.

> Five Hundred Dollars
> Will Be Paid By
> Angus Shardeen
> To Anyone Who Kills
> Smoke Jensen

Smoke chuckled.

"If you don't mind my sayin' so, Mr. Jensen, that seems like an odd reaction from someone seein' his name on a flyer that's offerin' five hunnert dollars for his bein' kilt."

"I suppose so. But to me it means that I've finally got his attention. And it isn't as if these are something that's been put out by the law." Smoke folded the paper over.

"Yeah, but to an awful lot of bounty hunters it don't make no difference who is payin' the reward, long as there is one," the bartender said.

Smoke nodded. "I guess you have a point there."

Smoke stopped on a ridge just above the road leading into the town of Commerce, Idaho. The cold gray sky was spitting snow, though it wasn't falling heavily. He tried to take a drink of water from his canteen, but it was frozen. He wasn't thirsty enough to start a fire to melt it.

He watched a stagecoach a few minutes as it started down from the pass, making its way into the town. Then, corking the canteen, he put it away, hunkered down inside his buffalo coat, slapped his legs against the side of his horse, and sloped down the long ridge. Although he was actually farther away from town than the coach, he would beat it there because he was going by a more direct route.

He stopped beside a small sign just on the edge of town.

COMMERCE

POPULATION 125
A Growing Community

The weathered board and faded letters indicated that it had been there for some time, most likely erected when optimism for the town's future was still prevalent. Smoke doubted there were that many residents in the town, and he was positive the town had no future.

He continued on into town, checking the corners and rooftops of buildings, doorways, and kiosks ... any place that might provide concealment for a would-be shooter. His pa had taught him to be cautious. Preacher had suggested that the better he became known, the more cautious he should be. The actual procedure as to when, where, and how to look out for snipers and those who would ambush him was something he had developed by experience and common sense.

A moment later, he pulled up in front of the saloon, dismounted, and made a cautious entrance inside. Taking off his hat, he brushed away the snow, then removed his heavy coat and hung it on a stop that protruded from the wall.

He examined the saloon for a moment. Two potbellied stoves blazed away with such intensity that they were gleaming red. The heat was disproportional with an area that was too hot close to the stoves ... and too cold far away, but with a wide comfort zone in between. Most of the bar was within that comfort zone, and Smoke stepped up to it.

"What'll it be?" the bartender asked.

"A beer and maybe a little information," Smoke replied.

"The beer I can supply. Not sure about the information, but you can try."

Smoke waited until the beer mug was put in front of him before he asked, "Does the name Angus Shardeen mean anything to you?"

"I know who he is. I expect just about ever'one in the West knows who he is."

"But do you know where he is?"

"I don't have any idea where he is, 'n I'm not sure I'd tell you where if I knew."

"Why not?"

"If you're plannin' on joinin' up with him, far as I'm concerned, he has enough dregs with him already. And anyone who is plannin' on joinin' up with him is a lowlife."

"And if I'm not plannin' on joinin' him?"

"Then I got two reasons not to tell you nothin'. Number one, I don't want to give you information that could get you kilt. And number two, I don't want it gettin' back to Shardeen that I'm tellin' folks how to find him."

At the opposite end of the bar stood a man wearing a slouch hat above a weather-lined face. Hanging low in a quick-draw holster on the right side of a bullet-studded belt was a silver-plated Colt .44, its grip inlaid with mother-of-pearl.

He had been listening to the conversation and watching Smoke in the mirror. When he'd heard enough, he tossed his drink down and wiped the back of his hand across his mouth. Then he turned to look at Smoke. "Hey, you."

Smoke did not turn.

"I'm talkin' to you, boy."

Smoke looked at him and raised his beer in salute. "Good afternoon." He knew from the tone of the man's voice that it wasn't going to be a simple exchange of pleasantries.

"You're lookin' for Angus Shardeen, are you?"

"I am."

"And would your name be Smoke Jensen?"

"I am."

"You do know, don't you, Mr. Smoke Jensen, Mr. famous . . . gunfighter"—he set the last word apart from the rest of the sentence and said it with a sneer—"that there's reward money out for you."

"How would you know that?" Smoke asked.

"I know that because I'm a bounty hunter, 'n it's my business to know."

"Well, I hate to disappoint you, Bounty Hunter," Smoke said. "But you don't want me. That dodger isn't official. I'm not wanted by the law."

The bounty hunter laughed a harsh and dismissive laugh. "Hell, mister, that don't matter none to me. A reward is a reward, 'n I don't really give a damn who pays it."

"What's your name?"

An evil smile spread across the bounty hunter's face. "The name would be Blackwell. Sledge Blackwell."

Smoke gave a short nod in acknowledgment. "Well, Mr. Blackwell, I would suggest that you not try to collect this particular reward."

"Don't try?" Blackwell replied.

The saloon had grown deathly still as the patrons sat quietly, nervously, and yet titillated by the life and death drama that had suddenly begun to unfold in front of them.

He turned to address the others. "You'd like for me not to try and collect the reward. Is that what you're saying? I suppose you would rather I just walk away, wouldn't you?"

Smoke put the beer down with a tired sigh and turned to face his tormentor. "It would be better for both of us if you would. But you're not going to do that, are you?"

"I can't. Why, this is how I make my livin', boy. I'm sure you've heard of Sledge Blackwell."

"Yeah, I've heard of you." In truth, Smoke had never heard of Blackwell.

"Yeah? What have you heard?" Blackwell asked, the smile on his face broadening.

"I've heard that you are a used-up old man who shoots people in the back because you don't have the guts to face them down."

Smoke's response had just the effect he wanted it to have. The smile on Blackwell's face turned to an angry snarl. "Draw, Jensen!" he shouted, going for his own gun even before he issued the challenge.

Blackwell was fast and had proved his mettle in many gunfights, but midway through his draw, he realized that he had made a big mistake. The arrogant confidence in his eyes was replaced by fear, then acceptance of the fact that he was about to be killed.

The two pistols discharged almost simultaneously, but Smoke had been able to bring his gun to bear and his bullet plunged into Blackwell's chest, while the bounty hunter didn't even get his gun high enough to avoid punching a hole in the floor.

Looking down at himself, Blackwell put his hand over his wound, then pulled it away and examined the blood that had pooled in his palm. When he looked back at Smoke, an almost whimsical smile appeared on his face. "Damn, you're fast. I ain't never seen any-one that . . ." His sentence ended with a cough, then he fell back against the bar, making an attempt to grab onto the bar to keep himself erect. His arm moved across the top of the bar, sweeping away both drinks. His shot glass and Smoke's beer mug wound up on the floor. The slouch hat fell from his head into the half-filled spittoon. The eye-burning, acrid smoke of two discharges hung in a gray-blue cloud just below the ceiling.

Smoke turned back to the bar. "Looks like I'm going to need another beer."

"Yes, sir, another beer, and this one is on the house," the bartender said, holding a new mug under the spigot of the beer barrel.

Behind Smoke, the silence was broken as everyone discussed what they had just seen. He was only halfway through his beer when the town marshal and two of his deputies arrived.

"What happened here?" the marshal asked.

The question wasn't directed to anyone in particular, so everyone started answering at once, availing themselves of the first opportunity to tell a story they would be telling for the rest of their lives.

"Hold it, hold it!" The marshal put up his hands. "Don't everyone talk at once." He looked over toward the bartender. "Ed, did you see what happened?"

"It's this way, Marshal Moore. Blackwell tried to brace this man."

The marshal looked at Smoke. "Blackwell braced you?" the marshal asked.

"Yes."

"Blackwell's a bounty hunter. If he braced you, he must've thought you've got a wanted flyer out on you. Do you, mister?"

Smoke started to reach for his shirt pocket.

"What are you doing?" Marshal Moore demanded anxiously.

"Take it easy, Marshal," Smoke replied. "You asked if I had paper out on me, and I'm about to show it to you."

"You mean to say that you are a wanted man, and you not only admit it, but you are going to prove it?"

Smoke smiled. "Yeah, you might say something like that." He pulled a folded up piece of paper from his pocket and handed it to the marshal.

The marshal unfolded the paper, read it, then looked up at Smoke. "You're Smoke Jensen?"

"Yes, sir."

Moore folded the paper and handed it back. "Did Blackwell realize this wasn't a real reward poster?"

"Oh, it's real all right, Marshal. It's just isn't a reward that was put out by the law."

"Evidently, Blackwell didn't care who put out the reward."

"That's right, Marshal," the bartender said. "Why, Blackwell stood right here and said as much."

"I've heard of you, Jensen. But I'm curious as to what brought you to our town?"

Smoke showed the marshal his Deputy U.S. Marshal badge. "I'm looking for Angus Shardeen."

"Alone?"

"Yes. Do you know where he is?"

"I'm sorry. I don't have the slightest idea."

"That's too bad. I was hoping you might have some idea."

"Look Jensen, with all the men Shardeen has around him, I hope you're just trying to locate him, and don't have any intention of bringing him in by yourself."

"I have no intention of bringing him in," Smoke said, repeating what he had told Marshal Holloway.

"That's being smart," Marshal Moore said, not understanding the intent of Smoke's reply.

Three hundred miles north of Commerce, the town of Fort Benton sat alongside the completely iced-over Missouri River. Elmer Gleason stopped by the Gold Strike Saloon to see Janey. He had taken a job as deputy city marshal and though he did drop by to see her fairly often, he had never become one of her more intimate customers. For one thing, he couldn't afford her. She was considerably more expensive than any other girl who worked the saloon. But the real reason was more complex than that.

"It's just that I sort of look at you as my sister, Abbigail," Elmer told her as they shared a table, using the name by which he had first known her. "I ain't never had me no sister, but if I did, I sure wouldn't be takin' her to bed."

Janey laughed. "No, I wouldn't think so."

"You got 'ny brothers?"

The smile left Janey's face, and Elmer held up his hand. "Never mind. Hell, I know better 'n to ask a question like that. Forget that I asked."

"No, it's all right," Janey said. "I think I will tell you. It might be nice having a friend who knows something about me. Otherwise, being this far from home, with a name that isn't mine, and with nobody who really knows me, it becomes almost like I don't exist. Do you know what I mean?"

Elmer smiled. "I'm not sure that I do. That kind of talk is sort of hard for me to get aholt of."

"It means I want somebody to know me, to really know who I am. And I'd like for that somebody to be you. That is, if you don't mind listenin' to my story.

Elmer nodded. "I think I'd be plumb honored if you'd tell me."

"To begin with, yes, I do have a brother. I had two brothers, but one of them was killed in the war. And of course, my name isn't really Fannie Webber, nor is it Abbigail Fontaine. My real name is Jane. Janey, my family always called me. Janey Jensen."

Elmer was surprised. "Jensen?"

"Yes. My father is Emmett, and my brother is—"

"Kirby," Elmer said. It wasn't a question, rather a statement of fact.

Janey gasped and put her hand to her mouth. "How long have you known?"

"I didn't know. Not till right now when you told me. But it turns out that I do know your brother. Me 'n him rode together with the Ghost Riders durin' the war."

"I didn't know Kirby had gone off to war. It must've been after I left."

"He was a good man to ride with, one you could count on when things got a little testy. Me 'n him was great friends. He 'n your pa even saved my life oncet."

"My pa? You also know my pa?"

"I met 'im."

Janey reached across the table and put her hand on Elmer's arm. "Elmer, please, you must swear to me that you will never tell them about me. Don't tell them where I am. Don't even tell them that you know me."

"They are good people, Abbi . . . uh, Janey. Why not tell them?"

"Do you have to ask? You're right. They are good people. But you know me for what I am. Do you really think I could compare the life I have lived with the lives they have lived?"

"Janey, you being what you are don't make you a bad person. Fact is, you're one of the best women I've ever knowed."

"Please, Elmer, if you care anything at all for me, you'll never tell them about me."

"All right. Prob'ly don't matter, anyhow. I don't expect to ever see either one of 'em again. One of the reasons I come by today was to tell you good-bye."

"Good-bye? What do mean, good-bye? Where are you goin'?"

"I've always had me a hankerin' to go sailin' acrossed the ocean so's I could see me some of the rest of the world."

"Will you write me?"

"I ain't never been much for writin'," Elmer said. "Anyhow, I don't even know how I'd go about sendin' you a letter from Australia or Siam or China, or some such place. Besides, you more 'n likely won't be here much longer, anyhow. You damn near got as much of a wanderin' around itch as I do."

Janey smiled. "I do at that. I reckon I'll leave soon as you're gone. There's bound to be some place that's warmer 'n Fort Benton."

"You got that right."

"I'm goin' to miss you, Elmer. If I never see you again, I'll keep your memory forever in my heart."

Elmer nodded and got a strange, almost yearning look in his eyes. "Abbi . . . I mean, Janey, that thought brings me more comfort than I can say."

The two hugged good-bye.

"Sally, dear, I'm so happy you decided to come to New York to visit your old aunt."

"Oh, I'd hardly call you old, Aunt Mildred." Sally Reynolds was sitting on the windowsill of the third floor of one of the Greek Revival row houses on the north side of Washington Square. The apartment belonged to her Aunt Mildred, and Sally had come to New York to spend a couple weeks with her. It was a cold and gray day in late March. The steely sunlight illuminated but did not warm the city. Spring had already begun, but the pedestrians walking on the sidewalk below wore heavy coats and scarves. From this elevation, they were a never-ending flow of black figures, rather like a stream of ants on the march.

She heard the distant rumble of an el train and the clatter of an omnibus, and wondered about so many people on the move. Who were they? Where were they going? What lay ahead of them?

What lay ahead for *her*?

Sally had already made the decision for her own future and had announced it to her family with great passion and intensity. She had recently graduated from Mary Woodson Normal College and was a qualified teacher. She was going West to teach school and to see some of the country she had only read about.

Sally's parents were completely opposed to the idea and had sent her to New York on a visit in the hope that she would, in her father's words, "come to her senses."

"Have you given any thought as to what you want for supper?" Aunt Mildred asked. "There are so many nice restaurants close by."

"Could we just have some scrambled eggs and stay home for supper?" Sally asked. "I've something I would like to speak with you about."

"Of course we can. But instead of scrambled eggs, suppose I make us an omelet? If you don't mind a little bragging, I will tell you that I make a wonderful omelet."

"That would be great," Sally replied with a smile.

A short while later, the two sat down at the kitchen table for supper.

"Oh," Sally said after her first bite. "It's not bragging if what you say is true. This really *is* a wonderful omelet."

"Why, thank you, dear. You said you had something you wanted to discuss with me. Would it be your idea about going West to teach school?"

"Oh!" Sally replied with a gasp. "How did you know that?"

"I got a letter from my brother telling me about it. He wants me to talk some sense into you."

"And are you going to try?"

"Yes."

"I see."

Mildred smiled and put her hand across the table. "I'm going to tell you to go where your heart tells you to go."

"What? Oh, Aunt Mildred, I thought . . . that is, I was afraid . . ."

"I know what you thought. You thought I was going to try and talk you out of it. May I share a secret with you?"

"Yes, of course!"

"There was a time when, more than anything else in the world, I wanted to move to San Francisco, to see what was on the other side of this country.

"I didn't go, because my older brother, your father, talked me out of it. I've wondered about that decision for my entire life. I know now that I should have gone. I don't want you to spend the rest of your life wondering. Go, Sally. Follow your heart while you are still young. If you find that you don't like it, you can always come back home, like the prodigal son, or in this case the prodigal daughter." Aunt Mildred chuckled.

"I'm going to do it," Sally said, a broad smile spreading across her face.

"Do you have any idea where you'll wind up?"

"I sent some letters out, and the only place that responded was a town called Bury, Idaho."

One month later, Elmer Gleason was standing on the waterfront in San Francisco. The ship *Pacific Dancer* was tied alongside the dock. The canvas was rolled tight against the yardarms and the lines hung loose, whistling in the breeze. The ship was taking on a cargo of buffalo hides, and it rocked gently in the waves that lapped ashore.

Elmer had just applied for a job as an able-bodied seaman.

"Have you ever sailed before?" the purser asked.

"Cain't say as I have, 'cause I ain't," Elmer said.

"Why should I sign you on, then? More 'n likely you'd wind up doin' nothin' more 'n spendin' all your time pukin' on the deck. The crew will have enough to do without cleanin' up your puke."

"Look, sonny. Sign me up or don't sign me up, I really don't give a damn which one you do. This here ain't the only ship tied up in the bay. If you don't take me on, I don't reckon it's goin' to be all that hard to find me one that will." Elmer turned and started to walk away.

"Wait," the purser called out to him. He chuckled. "It might be good to see you get seasick at that. Could be that it'll take you down a notch or two. Can you sign your name?"

Elmer wrote his name in bold, legible letters.

"Report to the First Mate."

"Who would that be?"

The purser pointed to the gangplank. "Go on aboard and stand there without doin' nothin' for a moment or two. The man that yells at you will be the first mate."

"Where's this ship bound?"

"You mean you signed on without even knowin' where the ship was goin'?"

"Yeah."

"Why would you do that?"

"Because I didn't really care where it was goin'."

"Then why do you care now?"

"'Cause now I'm actual on it," Elmer replied, starting toward the gangplank.

"China," the purser yelled at him. "We're goin' to China."

Elmer lifted his hand in recognition that he had

heard, but he didn't turn his head around. He had seen his share of Chinamen. Now, he supposed, he was about to see a whole bunch of them.

The man caught Janey's attention as soon as he got on the train. He was a handsome man, tall, with black hair, dark eyes, a fine nose, and a strong chin. The clothes he was wearing indicated that he must be a wealthy man. He was wearing fawn-colored riding breeches tucked into highly polished calf-high boots, a dark jacket held closed by one brass button, and a vest that matched his trousers, across which was strung a gold watch chain. At his neck he wore a maroon cravat.

He looked as if he might be every bit as wealthy as Big Ben Conyers, but something else about him Janey found even more intriguing. She knew instinctively that he was a man who had few compunctions and little concern about what others might think of him.

She got up from her seat and walked to the front of the car to take a drink of water from the water barrel. She gave him a very close look as she passed him by, then studied him over the brim of the dipper. When she walked back to her seat, she managed to lose her balance just as she drew even with him. "Oh, my!" she exclaimed as she fell into his lap. "Oh, dear. I'm so sorry."

She made an effort to get back on her feet, but she put her hand on the inside of his thigh, then slipped again, causing her hand to slide up his thigh. "Oh! I'm so clumsy. Please forgive me!"

"Nothing to forgive, my dear," the man said, smiling at her. "It can sometimes be difficult walking on a moving train."

"So I see."

"May I suggest that you sit next to me until you have quite recovered."

"Thank you, sir. You are such a gentleman. I don't know how to thank you, mister . . ."

"Richards. Josh Richards."

"I'm Janey Garner."

"It's good to meet you, Miss Garner."

"It's Mrs. Garner."

"Oh, I beg your pardon for the mistake."

Janey smiled. "I assume Mrs. is still appropriate. Poor Paul was killed in . . . a boating accident." She'd started to say, "in the war," but since the war was some five years past, she didn't want to appear old enough to be a war widow.

"Actually, and I do hope you don't think it too forward of me, I would prefer to be called Janey."

"Then Janey it shall be," Richards said.

"Where are you going, Mr. Richards?"

"Please, if I am to call you Janey, you must call me Josh."

"Very well, Josh. Where are you going?" She put her hand across her mouth. "Oh, please, you must forgive me. I have no business in inquiring about such a personal matter."

"No forgiveness in necessary. I don't mind at all telling you where I'm going. I am an owner of the PSR, which is an obscenely large ranch just outside the town of Bury, Idaho."

"Oh! What a coincidence! I, too, am going to Bury," Janey said, making the decision at that very instant. "I am sure that your wife is looking forward quite anxiously to your return."

"I suppose she would be if I had a wife. I'm not married, Janey."

"Well now, that is very nice to know."

CHAPTER 18

Smoke heard the high, keening sound of a steam-powered saw and knew that he was close to a town. If he had followed directions, the town was Buffington. At least, he hoped it was Buffington. A couple weeks ago a man had told him that Angus Shardeen had been seen in the town.

As he rode closer, he smelled meat cooking and bread baking. His stomach churned as those aromas reminded him of just how hungry he was.

Finally, he saw a church steeple through the trees, a tall spire, topped by a brass-plated cross that glistened in the high noon sun. He reached a road running parallel to the railroad tracks and moved onto it, following it the rest of the way into the settlement.

The town impressed him with its bustling activity. In addition to the working sawmill, he saw several other examples of commerce—freight wagons lumbering down the street, carpenters erecting a new building, a store clerk in a white apron sweeping the boardwalk in front of his place of employment. Well-maintained boardwalks ran the length of the town on either side of the street. At the end of each block, planks were laid across the road to allow pedestrians to cross to the other side without having to walk in the dirt or mud.

Smoke stopped his horse and waited patiently at one of the intersections while he watched a woman cross on the plank, daintily holding her skirt up above her ankles to keep the hem from getting soiled. She nodded her appreciation to him as she stepped up onto the boardwalk on the opposite side of the street.

Smoke clucked at Seven, and the Appaloosa stepped across the plank, then headed toward the livery, a little farther down. Smoke dismounted in front of it.

An old man got up from the barrel he had been sitting on and walked, with a limp, over to Smoke. "Boardin' your horse, mister?"

'Yes."

"How long will you be stayin'?" he asked.

"I'm not sure," Smoke said.

"It'll cost you fifteen cents a night."

"Does that include feeding him?"

"Hay, only. Oats'll cost you five cents extra."

Smoke gave the man a silver dollar. "I'll be back before this is worked off."

"Wes," the old man called, and a boy of about fourteen appeared from inside the barn.

"Yes, sir?"

"Take this man's horse."

"Wait a minute," Smoke said.

"Beg your pardon?"

"I need to let Seven know that you've got my permission to be around him. I'd better introduce you."

"Mister, I been handlin' horses since I was ten years

old," Wes said. "You don't need to introduce me to your horse."

Smoke smiled and stepped away. "All right, come get him."

The boy started toward the horse, and Seven lowered his head and bared his teeth.

Startled, the boy jumped back. "Uh, maybe you had better introduce us."

"Yeah, it might work out better that way," Smoke said with a smile. He put one hand on the side of the horse's face and the other hand on the boy's shoulder. "Seven, it's all right. This boy's name is Wes, and he's going to take good care of you while I'm gone."

Seven nodded his head, and Smoke reached out to take the boy's hand. He was about to put it on Seven's face, but Wes pulled back.

"It's all right," Smoke said. "Seven's going to treat you fine. Here, give him a couple pats."

Hesitantly, Wes allowed his hand to be put on Seven's face. Only when Seven moved his head against the hand, did the boy smile.

"There, now you and my horse are friends. Wes, I'd suggest that before anyone else handles him, you tell Seven it'll be all right."

"You mean he'll listen to me?"

"Sure he will. Like I said, you and Seven are friends now."

The smile broadened, spreading across Wes's face. "Yes, sir, I'll be sure 'n introduce the others to 'im!" he said proudly. "Come on, Seven. Like he said, me 'n you's friends now."

Smoke turned to the livery man. "The name of this town is Buffington, isn't it?"

"Yes, sir, it is." The man extended his hand. "I'm Tony Heckemeyer."

"Smoke Jensen." He examined Heckemeyer's face for any sign of recognition, but he gave none. "This seems like a nice, industrious town."

"Yes, sir. We like it."

Suddenly, several gunshots interrupted their conversation. Looking toward the opposite end of the street, Smoke saw two men backing out of a building.

"That's the bank! They're robbin' the bank!" Heckemeyer said.

A third man suddenly appeared from the alley that ran between the bank and the building next to it. He was mounted and leading two horses. Leaning down, he threw the reins to the two others. Once they mounted, all three began shooting up the town in order to keep people off the street.

Their efforts were effective, in that most people were scurrying to get out of the way. But Smoke saw a little girl not more than five or six years old standing at the edge of the street, obviously in the line of fire from the shooters. She was too frightened and too confused to move.

Dropping his saddlebags, Smoke ran out into the street toward her, scooped her up in his arms, and was about to carry her to safety, but it was too late. The three bank robbers were galloping down the street toward them.

He put the girl down, then stepped out between her and the gunmen. "Stay behind me and don't move!" he shouted at her.

Smoke's initial intention had been no more than to get the little girl to safety, but in so doing he had put himself in the path of the robbers' escape route.

Pulling his pistol, Smoke aimed at the closest rider and fired. Even as that robber was tumbling from his saddle, Smoke knocked a second rider from his horse. The two riderless horses galloped by.

The third robber, suddenly realizing that he was alone, reined in his own horse, tossed his gun down and threw both arms into the air. "No, no!" he shouted. "Don't shoot, don't shoot! I quit, I quit!"

With the surrender, nearly a dozen armed men of the town came running out into the street with their guns aimed at the one remaining robber.

"Get down from there, mister," one of the men shouted in an authoritative voice. His authority, Smoke saw, came from the badge he was wearing on his vest.

A woman came running into the street and picked up the little girl. "Oh, Frances, sweetheart! Are you all right!"

"Did any of the bullets hit her?" Smoke asked anxiously.

"No, no, I don't think so," the woman said. "I don't know how to thank you."

"Just seeing that she wasn't hurt is thanks enough for me," Smoke said.

"Take him to jail," the man with the badge said, referring to the robber who had given up. Two others responded to the order, prodding their prisoner along at gunpoint.

The man with the badge came back to speak to Smoke. He stuck out his hand. "I'm Sheriff Gwaltney. Mister, I want to thank you for what you done. You not only saved the little girl there, you probably saved several others by stoppin' those men before they could shoot up the whole town. Also, because of what you done we got the bank's money back. The whole town owes you for that."

"That was a real brave thing, you standin' out in the middle of the street like that," Heckemeyer said, coming over to join them.

"I didn't have much choice," Smoke said. "I sort of got caught out there."

"You coulda just stayed out of the way."

Smoke looked at the little girl, who was examining him closely with blue eyes that were open wide in wonder. He shook his head. "No, I couldn't."

Even as Smoke and the sheriff were speaking, a man wearing a long black coat came driving up in a wagon. He stopped the wagon between the two men Smoke had shot.

"Doolin, don't you go puttin' them fellas in any of your fancy coffins, thinkin' maybe that the county's goin' to pay for it," Sheriff Gwaltney said. "'Cause I'm tellin' you right now, we ain't agoin' to do it."

"I won't use nothin' but a couple plain pine boxes," Doolin replied.

"Why waste a box? Put both of 'em in the same box," another said, and those gathered laughed rather nervously at the macabre joke.

At that moment, Smoke couldn't help but think of the feeding trough he had used as the coffin to bury his mother.

Sheriff Gwaltney looked back at Smoke. "What's your name, mister?"

"Jensen. Smoke Jensen."

"Smoke Jensen?" Gwaltney replied as a look of recognition passed across his face. He stroked his chin. "Seems to me like I've heard that name before. Do you have any paper out on you?"

"Yeah, I do."

"What?"

As he had done with Marshal Moore, Smoke took out the WANTED poster that Angus Shardeen had circulated.

"Damn. That's purdee advertisin' for someone to murder you," Gwaltney said. "It takes someone evil and arrogant to do somethin' like that. Don't he know that somethin' like this will get the law after him?"

Smoke laughed.

"What's so funny?"

"The law is already after him. What would one more thing matter?"

Sheriff Gwaltney laughed. "I guess you're right. And, to tell you the truth, it wouldn't make no never mind to me whether the law had paper out on you or not. After stoppin' the bank robbery the way you done, you have certainly made some friends in this town. I don't know what brought you here, but I'm sure glad you showed up when you did."

"Mister Jensen, have you had your lunch yet?" asked the mother of the little girl.

"No, I haven't."

"My name's Kathy York. I would love to fix lunch for you."

"Well, I—uh . . ." Smoke stuttered his response.

Kathy chuckled. "It's not what you are thinking, Mr. Jensen." She pointed to a building directly across from them. "That's my café there, Dumplins. You come on over and have lunch, on me."

"Thanks," Smoke said.

* * *

298 _William W. Johnstone_

While Smoke was having his lunch, several of the townspeople stopped by his table to thank him for what he had done in saving little Frances York, and in stopping the bank robbery.

"Most ever'one in town's got money in that bank. Why, if them men had gotten away with it, there's several of us would've fallen on hard times, and that's for sure," one of the men said.

The accolades were growing so profuse that Smoke was beginning to feel self-conscious about it.

After lunch, Frances came over to Smoke's table, very carefully carrying a small plate. "This is Mama's blackberry cobbler."

Smoke smiled. "Well, thank you." He turned serious. "But I don't know. Is it any good?"

Frances nodded. "Oh, yes. It's very good."

"You know what? When I have something that is very good, like blackberry cobbler, I like to have someone else eat with me. Do you think your mama would let you have a plate of cobbler so you could eat with me?"

"Mama! He wants me to have some, too!" Frances called out happily, and a moment later she was sitting across the table from him as they ate the cobbler together.

Smoke got a sudden image of his sister when she was a little girl. Blackberry cobbler had been her favorite dessert, and he wondered if she still liked it. He wondered, too, where she was, and if he would ever see her again.

She had run away because she obviously wanted to be on her own. If that was really what she wanted, he had no intention of disturbing her.

* * *

Smoke walked back down to the sheriff's office.

"Mr. Jensen, what can I do for you?" the sheriff said, greeting him effusively.

"You asked me earlier what brought me here," Smoke said. "It didn't seem the right time or place to tell you then, but I'm looking for a man." Smoke turned his vest out, so the sheriff could see that he was a Deputy U.S. Marshal.

"A Deputy U.S. Marshal, are you? Well, now I can see how you were able to handle those two men so easily. Who are you looking for?"

"Angus Shardeen."

"Angus Shardeen? You mean the one that's put out the reward to have you killed?"

"Yes."

"Well then, with the two of you lookin' for each other, you're bound to meet up with him, don't you think?"

"No, there's a difference. He's not actually looking for me. All he's done is put out Wanted posters promising to reward anyone who can kill me. I'm actually looking for him."

"Do you have a posse with you? Or are you looking for him alone?"

"I have no one with me."

"That's quite a job for one man. I know Marshal Holloway. I can't imagine him sending one man out for Shardeen."

"He didn't send me out," Smoke said. "I volunteered."

"If you're tryin' to make a name for yourself, Jensen, you don't need to go so far as to try and tackle Shardeen all by yourself. Hell, you're already gettin' known around."

"It has nothing to do with making a name for myself," Smoke said. "Truth is, I'd just as soon not have a name. What's between Shardeen and me is personal."

"Yes, but there's the problem you see. It might be personal for you, but it won't be for him. Last I heard, he had at least six or seven men ridin' with him, and maybe even more than that. Here's the thing, most of 'em is the same ones that rode with him durin' the war."

"So I've heard. I also heard that he had been seen here in Buffington."

"That's true. He and his men passed through town one day a few weeks ago. They stocked up at the general store, then rode on. But like I said, there were quite a few of 'em. They didn't give us any trouble, so we didn't give them any trouble."

"You wouldn't have any idea as to where they might be now, would you?"

The sheriff shook his head. "No, I don't know. I'm just telling you that if you go after him alone, you may be takin' on a bigger bite than you can chew."

"You may be right, but I'm determined to find him. By the way, I don't think I saw a hotel when I came into town."

"The reason you didn't see one is because we don't have one. At least, not 'ny more. The one hotel we had burned down last month, and it ain't been built back. But if you're lookin' for a place to stay, you might check in at the Salt Lick Saloon. You can get a room there if they aren't all in use."

The Salt Lick was the most substantial-looking saloon in a row of saloons. A drunk was passed out on the steps in front of the place and Smoke had to step over him in order to go inside.

The chimneys of all the lanterns were soot-covered. Dingy light filtered through drifting smoke. The place smelled of sour whiskey, stale beer, and strong tobacco. The long bar on the left with a large mirror behind it was like everything else about the saloon—so dirty Smoke could scarcely see any images in it. What he could see was distorted by imperfections in the glass.

Eight or ten tables were nearly all occupied. A half-dozen or so bar girls were flitting about, pushing drinks. A few card games were in progress, but most of the patrons were just drinking and talking.

Smoke stepped up to the bar. The bartender was pouring the residue from abandoned whiskey glasses back into a bottle. He pulled a soggy cigar butt from one glass, laid the butt aside, then poured the whiskey back into the bottle without qualms.

One of the other men standing at the bar recognized Smoke. "Hey, you're the man that stopped the bank robbery, ain't you?"

"I was here when it happened," Smoke replied.

"Here? Hell, you was a lot more than just here. Sam, give this feller whatever it is he wants to drink. I'll pay for it."

"Thanks," Smoke said.

"What'll it be?" the bartender asked.

"A beer."

Sam drew a mug of beer, then set it before him.

"I'd also like a room."

"With or without."

That was confusing. "With or without what?"

The bartender looked up in surprise. "Are you kidding me, mister? With or without a woman."

"Without."

"All right. That'll be six bits."

"Six bits? Isn't that a little expensive?"

"If we left the room empty so the girls could use it for their customers, we could make three, maybe four times that," the bartender said. "But since the hotel got burnt down we sometimes take in people who just want a room so, we gotta charge six bits for it. Take it or leave it."

It had been a while since Smoke last slept in a bed, so even though he complained about having to pay seventy-five cents for a room, he considered it well worth it. "Here," he said, slapping the coins on the bar. "Tell your girls and their customers not to come into my room by mistake. If they do, they just might get shot."

"Mister, I don't know who the hell you are, but it ain't healthy to go around making threats you can't back up," the bartender growled. He picked up the silver and took it over to the money box, then reached for a key.

"Sam," someone called from the other end of the bar. "Come here."

The bartender went over to the customer, then leaned over as the customer whispered something in his ear. The bartender looked back toward Smoke, listened a moment longer, then nodded, and hurried back down the bar with the key.

"Mr. Jensen, you don't have to worry none about anyone disturbin' you tonight. I'll make sure you're left in peace."

"I appreciate that, Sam," Smoke replied.

One of the bar girls sidled over to Smoke. Dissipation had not yet taken its toll with her, and she was actually rather attractive. "I heard you say you didn't want to be disturbed tonight," she said as flirtatiously as she could. "I don't blame you. Once you find someone that you want to be with for the rest of the night, the last thing you'd want would be for someone to come bustin' in on you. My name is Gloria, and don't you worry, if you come to my room with me, I'll make certain we aren't disturbed."

Smoke smiled at her. "You know what, Gloria? You could almost tempt me to do just that. But I'm so tired that when I finally do get up there tonight, all I'm going to want to do is sleep."

"All right, honey," Gloria said. "But you don't know what you are missing."

"Oh, I've got a pretty good idea."

"We're losing a player here!" somebody called from one of the tables. "We need another man! Anybody want to get into the game?"

Suddenly Preacher's words came back to Smoke. *"You want to get the measure of any place, you get into a friendly card game in one of the local saloons. Men gets to palaverin' in a card game 'n if you keep your mouth shut, and just listen, why you'll learn more in an hour than you could by readin' a month o' newspapers."*

"I'd like to join you, if you don't mind a stranger playing with you," Smoke said.

"You be a stranger do you? Well, tell me, stranger, are you goin' to be playin' with American money?" asked one of the others at the table.

"Yes, but what difference would it make to you whether I'm playing with American money or not?

None of you will ever see it. I intend to win all the hands," Smoke teased.

"Ha! Come on in here, stranger, and sit at the table," another player said. "There ain't nothin' I like better 'n partin' an overconfident fool from his money. And anyone that thinks they're likely to not lose anythin' at all is just the kind of fool that is goin' to lose."

The others laughed, and Smoke joined them at the table. They noticed that he did not sit in a way that would compromise his ability to get to his gun quickly, if he had to.

The other players quickly learned that Smoke was the man who had stopped the bank robbery, and since all three of them had money in the bank, they were grateful to him.

One of the players was Robert Vaughan, owner and editor of the local newspaper. Seeing it as an opportunity to get a story, he began questioning Smoke rather extensively.

Smoke didn't mind the interrogation as it actually opened up avenues for conversation which allowed him to get information, as well as give it. "I understand that Angus Shardeen was in Buffington a while ago."

"He was here, all right," Vaughan said.

"I heard some folks say that it was him, but I don't know as that's true," Rick Adams replied as he picked up his cards.

"It's true, all right." Vaughan looked at the cards he'd been dealt.

"How do you know?" Smoke asked.

The conversation continued between Smoke and the newspaper editor as he answered, "I know because

I recognized two of them. Their leader had red hair, a red beard, and a scar that runs up the side of his face and looks like it damn near cuts his eye in two. That, my friends, could be no one but Angus Shardeen. I also recognized one of the others. He only has half an ear on the left side of his head. That could only be Billy Bartell."

"You wouldn't happen to know where they are holed up, would you?"

"I don't have any idea, but if I had to make an educated guess, I would say that they are holed up in the mountains where they can use the rocks and the draws as a fortress. That way they could stand off an army."

Smoke looked at his cards. "Has anyone actually ever gone into the mountains to try and find Shardeen and his men?"

"No, and they aren't likely to, either. At least, not anyone who has good sense. Why are you asking so many questions about Shardeen, anyway?"

Smoke chuckled. "I guess you could say I'm one of those people who doesn't have very good sense."

"I'll be damned! Are you planning to go after him?"

"Yes."

"I've heard about you, Smoke Jensen. They say you are quite skilled in the way you employ your pistol, in terms of speed with which you can extract your weapon and the deadly accuracy of your shooting. I also know that the reward being offered for Shardeen has reached a rather substantial amount. But no reward is worth getting yourself killed."

"The reward has nothing to do with it. I have a personal reason for going after Mr. Angus Shardeen."

For the remainder of the game, Smoke explained

his personal reasons for going after Shardeen, telling how he had witnessed his mother being murdered, and his sister violated.

"And after I take care of Shardeen I intend to deal with Mr. Billy Bartell. By the way, I raise the bet by five dollars," he added, pushing five more dollars into the pot.

"All I can do is wish you luck," Vaughan said. "And call your bet," he added with a triumphant smile.

When Smoke got up from the table somewhat later, he was down by twenty dollars. "Damn. Maybe I shouldn't have played with American money," he teased, and the others laughed.

After a supper of biscuits, bacon, and beans, which he ate at the saloon, he went up the backstairs to the room the bartender had rented him. Smoke poured water into the bowl, took off his shirt, washed, then turned the covers down and crawled into bed.

He was awakened in the middle of the night by a small clicking sound. Instantly, his hand went to the pistol hanging from the headboard. He slipped out of bed and walked barefoot across the carpet, then stood with his back to the wall just beside the door.

The *click* he had heard was the latch being unlocked. He watched the doorknob turn. Holding his pistol in his right hand, arm crooked at the elbow, and pistol pointing up, he eased back on the hammer, cocking it so slowly it made practically no sound as the sear engaged the cylinder.

The door opened, moving silently on the hinges. A little wedge of light spilled into the room from the hallway, the wedge growing wider as the door opened farther until finally it stretched from the open door all the way to the bed. Every muscle in Smoke's body tensed as he waited for the confrontation.

"Hello?" a woman's voice called quietly. "Is anyone in here?"

Who was this woman, and what was she doing here? With a sigh, Smoke's tension was relieved, and he eased the hammer back down as he lowered his pistol. "I'm here," he said from the darkness behind her.

"Oh!" the woman gasped, startled by the sound from an unexpected direction. She put her hand to her chest. "Don't do that! You could scare a body to death that way."

"You *should* be frightened."

"Who are you?"

"My name is Smoke Jensen. Who are you?"

"Smoke Jensen? You're the one who stopped the bank robbers, aren't you?"

"You didn't answer my question. Who are you, and what do you mean coming into my room in the middle of the night? I could've shot you."

"My name is Ida Jean, and this is my room."

"Ida Jean, is it? Well, Ida Jean, if this really is your room, why did you ask if anyone was in here?"

"Sometimes one of the other girls uses it to entertain one of their gentlemen friends. I didn't want to come bargin' in on something."

Smoke shook his head. "I'm all alone in here."

"You rented the room for the night, did you?"

"Yes."

"You know, you don't have to be all alone."

"Yeah, I do."

"Too bad," Ida Jean said. "All right. I'll go somewhere else."

"No," Smoke offered. "If this really is your room, I'll leave."

"Honey, there's no need for you to do that. I have somewhere else I can go. You don't. Good night . . . and sleep tight."

"Thanks," Smoke said.

Ida Jean left the room and Smoke closed and locked the door. He propped a chair under the doorknob. If the woman who just came in had a key, how many more keys were out there? he wondered.

As Smoke lay in the darkness, he thought about the woman and her offer. He had not yet been with a woman . . . in that way . . . and he sometimes wondered about it. He remembered his conversation with his pa.

"I ain't never been with a woman before. Leastwise, I ain't never been with a woman in . . . that . . . way. The way she wanted to be. And I sorta figure that if you're goin' to do somethin' like that with a woman, then maybe it ought to mean somethin'."

Smoke hadn't changed his mind.

CHAPTER 19

Smoke left the saloon the next morning and headed toward Dumplins for breakfast. He had just crossed the street when he heard a voice call out to him.

"Mr. Jensen, look out!" The warning was shouted by Wes, the boy from the stable.

Almost on top of the warning, Smoke felt a blow to the side of his head. He saw stars, but even as he was being hit, he was reacting to the warning so that, while it didn't prevent the attack, it did prevent him from being knocked down.

When his attacker swung at him a second time, Smoke was able to avoid him. With his fists up, he danced quickly out to the middle of the street, avoiding any more surprises from the shadows. It wasn't until then that he saw his attacker, a large man with heavy brows and a bulbous nose.

Smoke called out, "What are you doing? Why are you attacking me?"

"Mister," the man replied with a low growl, "you kilt my brother a few weeks ago."

Almost instantly, a crowd had gathered around Smoke and the man who had come at him from the shadows. It was still fairly early in the morning. He hadn't seen anyone on the street when he first came out of the saloon. Where had all these people come from? he wondered before calling out, "Who is your brother?"

"Damn. Have you kilt so many men that you can't even keep track? It was Sledge Blackwell."

"I'm sorry about your brother. I didn't have any choice. He drew against me."

"Yeah, well, bein' sorry don't do much for bringin' 'im back, does it?" Blackwell caught up with Smoke in the middle of the street.

"Ever'body knows that Sledge Blackwell wasn't worth a bucket of spit. Why's Bull fightin' for 'im?" someone asked.

"Because Bull ain't got good sense."

Blackwell threw a long wild swing at Smoke, but it was easy for Smoke to slip away from it, then counterpunch with a quick, slashing left to Blackwell's face. It was a well-delivered blow, one that would have dropped most men, but Blackwell barely showed the effects. He laughed a low evil laugh. "That the best you got?"

"Somebody ought to stop this," said a man on the boardwalk. "Bull is almost twice as big as Jensen. He's goin' to beat 'im to death."

"Yeah? Well, Smoke ain't no little man, and what he's got is all muscle. I'm goin' with him."

With an angry roar, Blackwell rushed Smoke again, and Smoke stepped aside, avoiding the rush. The big man slammed into a hitching rail, smashing through it as if it were kindling. He turned and faced Smoke again.

A hush fell over the crowd as they watched the two men, observing the fight with a great deal of interest, wanting to see if this young man could handle Blackwell.

Smoke and Blackwell circled around for a moment, holding their fists doubled in front of them, each trying to test the mettle of the other. Blackwell swung, a club-like swing which Smoke leaned away from. Smoke counterpunched and again he scored well, but again, Blackwell laughed it off.

Smoke hit Blackwell almost at will, and though the big man continued to shrug off the punches, the repeated blows were beginning to take effect. Blackwell's eyes began to puff up, and his lip had a nasty cut.

Smoke saw an opening and was set perfectly to deliver the blow. He sent a long, whistling right into Blackwell's nose and when he felt the nose go under his hand, he knew that he had broken it.

Blackwell's nose bled, the blood ran down across his teeth and chin. The big man continued to throw great swinging blows toward Smoke, but he was getting clumsier and more uncoordinated with each swing.

Growing exhausted from his ineffective efforts, Blackwell quit swinging and started with bull-like charges, all of which Smoke was able to easily avoid. As Blackwell rushed by with his head down, Smoke stepped to one side and sent a powerful right jab to Blackwell's neck, connecting with his Adam's apple. Grabbing his neck, Blackwell went down, gasping for breath.

Smoke stepped up to him and drew his fist back for the final blow, but he stopped when he saw the abject fear in Blackwell's eyes. "You are a lucky man. You came at me with your fists. If you had come after me with a gun, you'd be dead."

As Smoke walked away, he saw Wes standing close by. It was his warning that had enabled Smoke to duck, thus ameliorating Blackwell's first blow. "Thanks, Wes."

"I never thought you could whup him. He's a lot bigger 'n you are."

"Big doesn't always count," Smoke said.

"Yes, sir, I seen that. And I'm goin' to 'member it, too."

"How is Seven doing?"

Wes smiled. "He's a great horse, 'n he won't let anybody aroun' him unless I say it's all right."

"That's because he knows his friends." Smoke flipped a quarter to the boy. "Tell you what. Why don't you give him an extra rubdown today?"

"Yes, sir!" Wes replied enthusiastically.

Smoke stepped into Dumplins a few minutes later.

He was greeted warmly by Kathy. "I hope you like biscuits and gravy, because that's what I've made for breakfast this morning."

"My favorite," Smoke replied with a smile.

After breakfast, Smoke tried to pay for it, but Kathy refused his money.

Smoke shook his head. "No ma'am. You fed me last night. I don't intend you to lose money on me."

"I'm not losing money. Your breakfast has already been paid for."

"What? Who would do that?"

"Mr. Vaughan picked up your bill," Kathy said, pointing to the newspaper publisher.

Smoke walked over to him. "Mr. Vaughan, I want to thank you for buying my breakfast, but there was no need for you to do that."

"It was my pleasure, Smoke." Vaughan chuckled.

"Anyway, it isn't costing me anything. I paid for it with money that I won from you yesterday, so you might say that you are paying for it yourself."

"Well, then I don't feel so bad."

"By the way, do make it a point to read the *Delta Metro* today."

"*Delta Metro?*"

"That's my newspaper. The title comes from the delta formed by the confluence of Horse and Coffee creeks," Vaughan explained. "Not quite the Mississippi River Delta, I admit. But then, *metro* isn't any more appropriate than *delta*, so you might call it poetic license."

Later that same day, while sitting at a table in the back of the Salt Lick, Smoke saw his name in print for the very first time.

Smoke Jensen, Western Hero

Yesterday our fair town of Buffington rang with the sound of gunfire as three outlaws attempted to hold up the bank. They were stopped and economic disaster was prevented by the heroic and timely intervention of Smoke Jensen.

Like Leonidas at Thermopylae, Smoke stood his ground, defending a young child as he dispatched two of the would-be robbers and forced the third into an ignominious surrender.

It is said that Smoke Jensen is seeking that most perfidious of outlaws, Angus

Shardeen, with the intention of bringing him to justice. But Shardeen is a coward who surrounds himself with cowards, believing that there is bravery in numbers. This reporter has taken the measure of Smoke Jensen, and believes that he will find, and bring to justice, Angus Shardeen and his minions. Some may wish to compare Smoke Jensen with Don Quixote, dueling windmills. But I say that if it weren't for the Don Quixotes of the world, we would be overrun with windmills.

Smoke chose the corner, which not only put his back to the wall, but limited the access to him from either side. One of the bar girls approached him, and he recognized her as the one who had come into his room last night. "Hello, Ida Jean. You aren't planning on coming into my room again tonight, are you?"

"No. You made it pretty clear last night that you aren't really interested in that sort of thing."

"Just because I didn't want to share my bed with you, doesn't mean I won't have a drink with a pretty girl." He gave her some money and she walked back over to the bar to buy the drinks.

As he watched her, Smoke noticed a man standing at the far end of the bar staring at him. The man had only half an ear on the left side of his face, and he was glaring at Smoke. An old memory flashed back.

"Spread 'er legs out, boys, I'm goin' to have me a little of this," one of the men was saying. *He was a big ugly man with only half of one of his ears.*

*"Get away from her!" his ma said. She attacked the man.
"What the hell, Bartell, can't you handle a young girl
and an old woman?" Shardeen asked with a demonic laugh.*

The man at the bar was Billy Bartell, one of the men
he had seen at the farm that day, and one of the men,
it was said, who was still riding with Shardeen. Bartell
had no way of recognizing Smoke, but must have had
Smoke pointed out to him, because suddenly and without warning, Bartell reached for his pistol.

If Smoke had not recognized him, Bartell may have
had an insurmountable advantage. As it was, he did
have the advantage of drawing first, and his many
years on the outlaw trail had made him a formidable
man with a gun. He got his pistol out first, and for a
brief second Bartell actually thought he had won. He
smiled as he brought his pistol up.

It wasn't until then that Smoke drew and fired. The
bullet hit Bartell in the chest with the impact of a
hammer blow, and he was slammed back against the bar
before sliding down. He sat there, leaning back against
the bar, his gun hand empty and the unfired gun on the
floor beside him. He watched as Smoke approached
him.

"There ain't nobody that fast." Bartell coughed, a
body-shaking cough.

"Don't die yet, Bartell. I want you to know why I
killed you."

"I know you been alookin' for us. I reckon it's for
the reward."

"It isn't for the reward. It's for Janey."

"Janey?" Bartell got a puzzled look on his face. "Are
you crazy? I don't know nobody named Janey."

"I didn't say you knew her. But not knowing her didn't stop you from raping her when you and Shardeen raided my farm during the war."

"I raped a lot of women durin' the war. Some of 'em even liked it."

"She wasn't a woman. She was just a girl."

"How do you know it was me that done it?"

"Because I was there, and I saw you."

"You was there? You musta been just a kid then. How do you even know what you seen?"

Smoke's eyes glinted with retribution. "I know. Where is Angus Shardeen?"

Bartell coughed again, another body-racking cough, bringing up blood. "You know what? I think I am goin' to tell you where he's at. Only I ain't doin' you no favors, 'cause if you find 'im, he'll kill you."

"Where is he?"

"Rattlesnake Canyon." Bartell tried to laugh, but it turned into another blood-oozing cough. "Yeah, you go on out there . . . 'n after he kills you, me 'n you will be meetin' again . . . 'cause I'm goin' to be waitin' for you in hell."

There was a rattling sound deep in Bartell's throat, then his head fell to one side as his eyes, still open, glazed over.

Smoke called out, "Anybody know where Rattlesnake Canyon is?"

"It's about twenty miles west of here," one of the customers said.

"Thanks."

"Jensen, if that's really where he is, you might want to think twice 'bout goin' out there," the bartender said. "Shardeen has some bad men with 'im. You go out there alone, you'll just be committin' suicide."

"I thank you for your concern." Smoke started toward the door.

"You're goin' out there anyway, ain't you?" the man who had spoken to him earlier asked. "You're goin' out there, knowin' that in them rocks he may as well be in a fort, and knowin' how many men he's got with 'im."

Smoke stopped and turned around. "I've been after him for a long time. If he was on the moon, and there was some way I could get there, I would go after him."

"I know that area. Hell, if Shardeen is up there with his men, an army couldn't get him out of there."

"I won't be going with an army," Smoke said. "It'll just be me."

"All by yourself?"

"Yes. The problem with an army is that many men can't hide or keep quiet. Shardeen and his men would see an army comin', and they would be able get ready for them. But one man travelin' alone would more 'n likely be able slip around the rocks and through the crevices and such so as to be able to sneak up on them."

"Jensen, all I can say is, you got a lot more guts than you got brains."

Smoke left the saloon and went directly to the stable to get his horse.

Heckemeyer came over to talk to him as he was throwing the saddle over Seven. "I heered what you was plannin' on doin'. I mean, goin' after Shardeen 'n all."

"You aren't goin' to try and talk me out of it, are you, Mr. Heckemeyer? Because it won't do you any good. I'm goin'."

"I ain't goin' to try 'n talk you out of it. I just thought I might give you a little advice. When you get out there, they's two trails that go to the top," Heckemeyer said, speaking quietly. "You can stay mounted if you take the lower trail, but you'll have to leave your horse somewhere if you take the upper trail. The upper trail is a lot steeper and harder, but that's the one I'd take if I was you."

Smoke nodded as he tightened the cinch strap.

"Thing is . . . if you take the lower trail, you can be seen for a long way before you get there. You take the upper trail, you'll be on top long afore anyone has any idee that you're there."

"Thanks." Smoke handed Heckemeyer two dollar bills. "Give one of these to Wes. You keep the other one."

"Thank you," Heckemeyer said with a smile.

Smoke swung into the saddle, and with a nod, rode out through the open doors at the front of the stable.

Wes walked over then. "He won't be comin' back, will he?"

Heckemeyer gave Wes one of the two dollar bills. "More 'n likely, he won't even live to see the sun go down. 'N that's too bad. The world could use more men like him."

"He ain't goin' to get kilt," Wes said.

"What makes you so sure?"

"I just know."

Rattlesnake Canyon was unique in that it had so many perfectly formed arches that it almost looked as if they were man-made, rather than a work of nature.

The interior was so well concealed by rocks and ridge-lines that its entrance couldn't be seen unless some-one was specifically looking for it. Inside the canyon was a source of water, which made it an ideal place for an outlaw encampment.

After Smoke dismounted, he let Seven go, but not ground tethered. He was free to graze and water. Re-membering what Heckemeyer had told him about the two trails, Smoke took the upper one, staying close to the wall, and taking advantage of the many rocks and protrusions. He passed through apertures when possi-ble, rather than going around or over the long fingers. The climb up to the top of the promontory was easy enough at first with an inclining ledge that allowed him to walk upright. The higher he got, the more narrow the ledge became until finally the only way he could stay on the ledge was by holding on to whatever rocks and protrusions he could grab. Then the ledge disap-peared altogether, and at the very end of the climb, he had to go straight up, finding footholds and hand-holds where he could. Finally he reached the top.

From a concealed position, he saw several men sit-ting around a campfire about two hundred yards away. They were drinking coffee as casually as if they were in a downtown café, showing no concern about anyone approaching them, and why should they? There were five of them, and they were well fortified. Also, as Heckemeyer had promised, Smoke's approach had been totally unnoticed.

Smoke could see the men, but he couldn't approach them directly. Boulders and draws would provide them cover in any gunfight, but the two hundred yards be-tween him and them were wide open, with very few positions along the way where he might be able to take cover.

Lying on his stomach, Smoke used a looking glass to peruse the campsite. He was able to pick out Shardeen, the prominent scar on his face making him easy to spot. Smoke counted six more men and . . . no. As he studied the faces, he realized there were only five more men. The sixth person was a woman.

At first, he thought she was one of them, then he saw that her arms and legs were bound. Whoever the woman was, she was their prisoner!

Smoke gave some consideration to just shooting Shardeen. After all, the Jayhawker was the one he wanted. If he killed him, he could just leave the others behind, then go after Potter, Stratton, and Richards— the men his pa had been after.

Smoke put the looking glass in his pocket and jacked a round into the Henry, then aimed at Shardeen. His finger rested on the trigger, but he didn't shoot. He couldn't do it. He couldn't just shoot Shardeen and leave. He couldn't leave the woman at the mercy of the others. He was sure they would kill her.

With a sigh of frustration, Smoke kept the Henry cocked, then stood up and walked toward the encampment. For the first twenty-five yards or so, nobody noticed him. Nobody expected anyone to just walk in on them.

"When in the hell is Bartell comin' back? He's s'posed to bring me a bottle of whiskey," one of the men complained.

Smoke recognized him as Tim Shardeen, the man he and his father had encountered a few years ago, when they first started West.

"Hell, Tim. More 'n likely he's took your money and bought hisself a woman," one of the others replied, and they all laughed.

"He better not have done that."

"Bartell's not coming back," Smoke said, his voice startling those gathered around the campfire.

"What the hell?" Tim shouted. "Who the hell are you?"

"I'm the man who killed Bartell."

One of the other men, responding more quickly to the unexpected intrusion, pulled his pistol and fired. Smoke fired back, never lifting the rifle higher than his waist. The man with the pistol went down.

Smoke fired two more times, killing two others. The remaining three men ran behind cover, leaving only the woman exposed.

In the open as he was, Smoke was at a disadvantage. He ran quickly to a small rock that did little to provide cover for him. They began shooting at him, the bullets hitting the rocky ground all around him, whining as they ricocheted away.

A puff of gun smoke hung just over one of the distant boulders, indicating that someone was behind it. Smoke aimed at the corner of the boulder and waited.

A few seconds later, a man's head rose up, just far enough for the man to see where to shoot.

It was all the opening Smoke needed. He squeezed the trigger and watched a little spray of blood and brain detritus fly out from the bullet wound in the outlaw's head.

The shooting stilled. A long period of silence was finally broken by a man's shout. "Shardeen? Shardeen, you yellow belly! Don't you leave me here all alone!"

Was Shardeen really leaving? Or was it merely a ploy? Smoke wondered.

"Shardeen! Come back here, you low-assed chicken!"

After that last shout, Smoke heard the clatter of horseshoes on the rocky surface as a horse galloped away.

The man shouted more obscenities, the tone of his voice betraying his anger and fear.

"Mister, it looks like you've been deserted. There's only one of you left," Smoke called out from behind his scant rock.

"Who the hell are you?" the disembodied voice shouted.

"My name is Smoke Jensen. Who are you?"

"The name is Hanks."

"Hanks? That name doesn't mean anything to me. I didn't come for you, Hanks. I came for Shardeen."

"Yeah, well, you mighta come for Shardeen, but you have near 'bout kilt all of us."

"Come on out into the open, and let me see you," Smoke invited. "I think we can palaver a little, then both of us go on our way."

"I ain't acomin' out lessen you do."

"We can come out at the same time."

Hanks tried a bit of negotiating. "You said you didn't come for me?"

"That's right."

"Then why don't you just ride away?"

"I'm not leavin' the woman here."

"Why not? She ain't nothin' to you."

"I'm not leavin' her here," Smoke said again a bit stronger. "Now, if you want this to end, put your gun in your holster and come on out."

"I'll come out, but I ain't puttin' my gun away."

"All right. Come on. As long you aren't shooting."

"You said we'd come out at the same time," Hanks replied.

"I'll count to three."

Smoke counted. At three, he stepped cautiously out into the open.

A small man with a narrow face and a hook nose came out from behind the boulder across from Smoke, gun in hand, though the gun was pointing down.

Smoke stood up and walked toward him, still holding the rifle. "Do you have any idea where Shardeen might have gone?"

"Why should I tell you?"

"Why shouldn't you? He ran off, didn't he? You don't owe him anything."

Hanks was obstinate. "I don't owe you nothin' neither."

Smoke walked backwards to the woman, keeping his eyes on the outlaw.

Although out in the open during the entire exchange of gunfire, she hadn't been hit, but her eyes were wide open with fear. So far, she had not uttered a sound.

"Let me get you untied. Then we'll get you back home." Smoke put the rifle down and leaned over to untie the woman.

"Look out!" she shouted suddenly.

In one motion, Smoke drew and fired at Hanks, who was raising his pistol and thumbing back the hammer.

With a bullet in his chest, he stumbled back with a look of shock and pain on his face. He dropped his gun, then slapped both hands over the wound. "How did you—?" was as far as he got before tumbling over, dead.

"Chugwater, Wyoming," the woman said as Smoke untied her.

"That's where you live?"

"No. That's where Shardeen will be going."

"How do you know?"

"He has a woman there. Lulu Barton."

"You know this woman?"

"She's my sister."

Sally Reynolds' first day in Bury, Idaho, was nearly her last. Nobody had met her at the train, so leaving her luggage at the depot to be picked up later, she started down the boardwalk toward the address that was on the acceptance letter she held in her hand.

Suddenly, she heard and felt the concussion of something whizzing by her very fast. Concurrent with her hearing the report of a gunshot, a bullet crashed through one of the square panes of the big glass window next to her. Actually, it was two gunshots, one right on top of the other. She turned and looked out into the street. Two men faced each other with smoking guns in their hands. She stared at them in shock for a moment, then one of the two men fell to the dirt.

"Miss!" A very attractive and expensively dressed woman called out to her. "Get in here, off the street! Quickly!"

Sally didn't need a second invitation to hurry into the building, which turned out to be a dress shop.

"There's likely to be more shooting. Clay, the man

who was just shot, has a brother," the pretty woman said. "I expect Jeb will be coming out into the street shortly, wanting revenge."

"Heavens," Sally said. "Does this sort of thing go on often?"

"Fairly often."

True to the pretty lady's prediction a second man walked into the street, firing his pistol. The two men continued to shoot at each other until the second man, Sally assumed it was Jeb, went down. The first man put his gun back in the holster, then started toward a nearby saloon as several others rushed forward to congratulate him.

"It's over now," the pretty lady said.

"I must say, this was quite a dramatic welcome to Bury," Sally said.

"Just arrived?"

"Yes, by train a few minutes ago."

"Have you come to work at the Pink House?"

"The Pink House?"

The woman nodded. "For Miss Flora."

Sally shook her head. "I don't know who Miss Flora is." She smiled. "My name is Sally Reynolds, and I'm the new schoolteacher."

"A schoolteacher, are you? Well, Miss Reynolds, it's good to meet you. I'm Janey Garner." Janey remembered Miss Margrabe, and gave a passing wonder as to where she might be.

"Do you work at the Pink House? Whatever that is."

"No, I'm a business manager for PSR," Janey replied.

"PSR?"

"It's a ranch, the Potter, Stratton, and Richards. Only it's not just a ranch, it's a *huge* ranch."

"A lady ranch manager? That's most impressive. You must be as intelligent as you are beautiful."

Janey laughed and extended her hand. "Sally, I think you and I are going to wind up being very good friends."

CHAPTER 20

Smoke had been riding for more than six hours. Behind him, the darker color of hoof-churned earth stood out against the lighter, sunbaked ground. Before him, the desert stretched out in motionless waves, one right after another. As each wave was crested, another was exposed, and beyond that another still.

The only sounds were the jangle of the horse's bit and harness, the squeaking leather as he shifted his weight upon the saddle, and the dull thud of hoofbeats.

He had filled the canteen before he left Rattlesnake Canyon, but that was more than forty miles ago and he had come across no other water since then.

His tongue was swollen with thirst and the canteen was already down by a third, but he was allowing himself no more than one swallow of water per hour. He was also rationing the water for Seven by taking two mouthfuls, then spitting the water into his hat and holding the hat up for Seven to drink.

"I'm sorry, boy. This is all we have," he apologized,

feeling sorry for the horse. "I tell you what. I won't be riding you, anymore. We'll both walk the rest of the way," he promised.

Smoke had no idea how much farther he would have to go, but he was determined not to burden Seven any longer.

Just before dark, a scattering of adobe buildings rose from the desert floor, wavering in the shimmering heat waves. The buildings so matched the desert in color and texture that Smoke wasn't even sure the town was there. Gathering what strength he had remaining, he started toward it. He had no other choice. If it was real, he and Seven would live. If it was a mirage, they would probably die.

It took at least another hour to reach the town, but within thirty minutes he knew that the town was real. "It's real, Seven!" Smoke exclaimed, his voice hoarse from thirst. "It's a real town! A real town with water!"

At the edge of town he stopped to catch his breath and read the sign.

CHUGWATER, WYOMING
POP. 256
"Friendly People"

Smoke limped on into town and, seeing a pump in the town square, hurried toward it. He moved the handle a couple times and was rewarded by seeing a wide, cool stream of water pour from the pump mouth. Holding his hat under the pump, he filled his hat and let Seven drink. Seven finished that hatful and two more before Smoke allowed himself to drink. Putting his left hand in front of the spout, he caused the water to pool and, continuing to pump, drank deeply. Never, in his life, had anything tasted better to him.

With the killing thirst satisfied, Smoke stood up from the pump and patted Seven on his neck. "I'm sorry to have put you through that, Seven, but you were a good horse, and I'm proud of you."

Just down the street a door slammed, and an isinglass shade came down on the upstairs window. A sign creaked in the wind and flies buzzed loudly around a nearby pile of horse manure.

Smoke walked on down the street, leading Seven. He saw three saloons, sure that if Angus Shardeen was there, he would be in one of them.

But which one?

Smoke continued walking as he looked around. A horse in front of a saloon that identified itself as the Ace High caught his attention. Under the saddle was a distinctive saddle blanket—dark blue with a gold band around the outside edge. Nestled in the corner was the silver eagle insignia of a colonel.

He remembered seeing the very saddle blanket on one of the horses when his farm had been raided. He knew that would be Shardeen's horse. Whether he was really a colonel or not, he had passed himself off as such.

After examining the horse, Smoke started toward the saloon door.

A man stepped in front of him. "Where do you think you're goin'?"

The man blocking Smoke's way was thin and muscular, with a moustache that curved up at each end like the horns on a Texas steer. He was wearing a yellow duster, pulled back on one side to expose a Colt sheathed in a man's leg holster that was tied halfway down his leg. He had an angry, evil countenance, and looking directly at him was like staring into the eyes of an angry bull.

"Mister, you're in my way," Smoke said dryly.

"Would your name be Smoke Jensen?"

Smoke was surprised to hear himself addressed by name in a town that he had never visited.

"It is. Why? Do you have a particular interest in me?"

"Yeah, I've got an interest in you." The big man pulled his yellow duster to one side and Smoke saw a peace-officer's badge pinned to his shirt.

"I've got one of those, too." Smoke showed his own Deputy U.S. Marshal's badge. "And my badge out-ranks yours. Now, step out of the way. I've got business inside."

"Would that business have anything to do with Angus Shardeen?" the lawman asked.

"It would."

The lawman shook his head. "Uh-uh. Not here. Shardeen has been good to this town, so he has sanc-tuary in Chugwater."

"Mister, if I had to go to hell to get Shardeen, I would do it," Smoke said coldly. "As far as I'm con-cerned, he doesn't have sanctuary anywhere. Now, get out of my way."

The lawman went for his gun. He was exceptionally fast and his hand moved toward his Colt as quickly as a striking rattlesnake.

Smoke had not expected the lawman to draw on him and didn't even start for his gun until the man's gun was coming out. But if Smoke had been surprised by the lawman's sudden draw, the peace officer was undoubtedly surprised by the speed with which Smoke drew and fired.

The lawman staggered backward, crashing through the batwing doors, and backpedaling into the saloon, landing flat on his back, his unfired gun still in his hand.

Smoke bounded up the steps, onto the porch, then pushed through the batwing doors, following the lawman's body inside. A wisp of smoke curled up from the barrel of the pistol he still held in his hand.

"Mister, you just killed our marshal," said one of the men in the saloon.

"Yeah, I guess I did." Smoke slipped his pistol back into its holster.

"Damn. I never figured anyone would be good enough to beat Coyle."

"He drew first," Smoke said. "I didn't have any choice."

"Uh-huh. He drew first, but you still beat him. Is that what you want us to believe?"

"To tell the truth, I don't care whether any of you believe it or not," Smoke said. "I'm a Deputy United States Marshal, and I've come to arrest Angus Shardeen." He saw the nervous exchanges of glances among the customers in the saloon.

"What makes you think Shardeen is here?"

"His horse is out front." Smoke stood for a moment, studying the layout. To his left was the bar. In front of him were four tables; to the right, a potbellied stove, sitting in a box of sand. Because it was summer, the stove was cold, but the stale, acrid smell of last winter's smoke still hung in the air.

One man was behind the bar, three customers were

in front of it, and a heavily painted bar girl was standing at the far end of it. At least six more men sat at the
tables.

"I know he's here," Smoke said. "Now, where is he?"

No one answered.

Smoke drew his pistol from its holster. "I asked,
where is he?" When still no one answered, he pointed
his pistol toward the barkeep and pulled the hammer
back. A deadly double *click* sounded as the scar engaged the cylinder. "You want to die protecting a murderer like Shardeen?"

"I don't know where he is, mister," the barkeep answered nervously. "I don't pay no attention to what
folks come and go here."

"For God's sake, tell 'im, Gene!" the woman said.
"He's right, you know. A man like Shardeen ain't
worth dyin' for. Just—"

"Sue Ann, shut your mouth," the bartender ordered in sharp anger, cutting her off in mid-sentence.

"Mister, I think you had better be the one who keeps
quiet." Smoke lowered his pistol. "Go ahead, Sue Ann.
Where is he?"

She looked nervously toward the bartender.

"Don't be worrying about Gene. If that's all that's
keeping you from talking, I'll kill him for you right
now." Again, Smoke pointed his pistol toward the bartender.

"Tell 'im, Sue Ann!" Gene shouted nervously.
"Tell 'im!"

"He's up there," Sue Ann said, lifting her head toward the landing that looked out over the saloon floor.
"First room on the right. He went upstairs with Lulu."

"Thanks." With his pistol still cocked, and holding
it in his crooked arm, muzzle point up, Smoke started

up the stairs. He had just reached the top step when the bartender shouted a warning.

"Shardeen! Look out! Someone's comin' up for you!"

Surprised that anyone would actually shout a warning, Smoke turned to look back downstairs. Gene was standing at the bottom of the stairs with a double-barrel shotgun pointing up at him.

Smoke managed to jump behind the corner at the top of the stairs, just as Gene fired. The load of buckshot tore a large hole in the door to a room just behind him. Smoke fired back before Gene could get off a second shot. His bullet hit Gene in the forehead, and he dropped the shotgun, then fell heavily to the floor.

At almost the same moment, four shots sounded from inside one of the rooms. Dust and sawdust flew as the bullets punched holes through the door. Smoke flattened himself against the wall, clear of the door. A second later, he heard the sound of crashing window glass.

Smoke ran to the door, kicked it open, and dashed into the room. A naked woman on the bed screamed as he rushed by her to the broken window. He leaned through the shattered glass to look down to the ground below. If Shardeen had jumped through the window, Smoke should still be able to see him.

He wasn't there.

Intuitively, Smoke realized that someone was behind him and he turned, leaping to one side, just as Shardeen, with a broad, triumphant grin on his face, pulled the trigger. The bullet slammed into the wall behind where Smoke had been but a split second earlier.

Smoke fired back. As his bullet struck home, Shardeen's grin of triumph turned to a look of shock and pain.

Shardeen dropped his pistol, put his hands over the wound in his chest, then sank to his knees. He looked up at his shooter. "You must be Smoke Jensen."

"I am."

"Why? Why have you hounded me all these years? I don't even remember you."

"It doesn't matter. I remember you."

The old mountain man and the gunfighter rode slowly down the main street of Yampa, Colorado, drawing some attention. The sheriff and one of his deputies were among those watching the pair as they reined up in front of the saloon and dismounted.

The sheriff approached them. "Howdy, boys," he greeted.

"Sheriff," Smoke replied.

The lawman looked at the mountain man. "You're the one called Preacher?"

"That's what I'm called."

"And you are the gun hand called Smoke."

"That's what I'm called," Smoke replied, mimicking Preacher's response.

"You boys planning on staying long?"

Smoke turned his dark eyes on the sheriff and let them smolder for a few seconds. "Long enough to do what we plan to do."

"I've been hearing a lot about you, Smoke Jensen," the sheriff said speaking in low tones. "I've heard how you killed Sledge Blackwell, Billy Bartell, how you wiped Shardeen's band like some one man army, and how you went up to Chugwater, Wyoming, and killed Angus

Shardeen his ownself. I hope you ain't lookin' for anyone in this town. Yampa is a nice little place. I wouldn't want to see it turned into a battleground."

Smoke smiled at the sheriff. "You don't mind if we buy some supplies, have a few hot meals, and rest for a day or two, do you, Sheriff? Maybe take a hot bath?"

"Speak for yourself on that last part," Preacher said. "I had me a bath no more 'n a month ago. I don't hold with too much bathin'. It ain't healthy, keepin' your skin all exposed like that."

"Smoke, from ever'thing I've heard, you ain't never kilt nobody that didn't need killin'," the sheriff said. "I'm just sort of hopin' that nothin' like that happens here. If you'll give me your word on it, why, that'll be good enough for me."

"Sheriff, I'm not after anybody in this town. To be truthful with you, my pa is buried at the foot of Zenobia Peak, 'n all I got in mind is just visiting his grave and payin' my respects."

The sheriff nodded. "You got ever' right to do that. I'm sorry if I come off a bit cantankerous there, 'n I hope you don't take offense, but I feel like I owe it to the folks here 'bout to keep the peace as best I can."

"I understand. No offense taken," Smoke said.

"Also, I'm sorry 'bout your pa."

"I appreciate the sentiment," Smoke replied.

The sheriff wasn't the only one who had heard about Smoke single-handedly cleaning out the Angus Shardeen gang. By the time he and Preacher stepped into the saloon, word of their arrival had spread and, in the words of one of the saloon patrons, "Your money is no good here! Anybody that's got rid of a no-account polecat like Angus Shardeen and those scoundrels who rode with him has done a good service to ever'one between St. Louis and the Pacific Ocean."

"What will you have?" the bartender asked.

"Before we get started on the drinkin', don't you think maybe we should get us a bite or two to eat?" Preacher suggested.

"We got food," the bartender said. "Our food is as good as anything you'll get over to the City Pig Café."

"What do you have?"

"Beans cooked with ham, taters, and hot peppers, with a side of turnip greens, and cornbread."

"Sounds good enough," Smoke said.

"You got coffee?" Preacher asked. "I don't mean brown water. I mean real coffee."

"You like it strong, do you?" the bartender asked.

Smoke chuckled. "If it won't float a horseshoe, it's too weak."

"I'll see what I can do."

After the meal, Smoke and Preacher enjoyed a couple beers bought for them by the patrons of the saloon. They could have had as many as they wanted, without having to pay for any, but Smoke knew better than to ever allow himself to get drunk.

"Last thing you need is to be too drunk when some young scoundrel decides to make a name for hisself by shootin' you," Preacher had told him once.

It hadn't been necessary for Preacher to warn him. He had figured that out a long time ago.

* * *

In Bury, Idaho, Sally Reynolds was having lunch with Miss Flora. They were dining in Sally's house, because Flora didn't want to embarrass Sally by being seen in public with her.

"Nonsense," Sally said. "Why should I be embarrassed to be seen with you?"

"I'm a lady of the night, honey. I own the Pink House, and the girls who work there, work for me. I don't actually bed with men, but how do you think I got the money to buy the house in the first place?"

"I want to read something to you," Sally said. She stepped over to the buffet to pick up a Bible, turned to the selection she wanted, and began to read. "'And one of the Pharisees desired that he would eat with him. And he went into the Pharisee's house, and sat down to meat. And, behold, a woman in the city, which was a sinner, when she knew that Jesus sat at meat in the Pharisee's house, brought an alabaster box of ointment, and stood at his feet behind him weeping, and began to wash his feet with tears, and did wipe them with the hairs of her head, and kissed his feet, and anointed them with the ointment.

"'Now when the Pharisee which had bidden him saw it, he spake within himself, saying, This man, if he were a prophet, would have known who and what manner of woman this is that toucheth him: for she is a sinner.

"'And Jesus turned to the woman, and said unto Simon, Seest thou this woman? I entered into thine house, thou gavest me no water for my feet: but she hath washed my feet with tears, and wiped them with the hairs of her head. Thou gavest me no kiss: but this woman since the time I came in hath not ceased to kiss my feet. My head with oil thou didst not anoint: but this woman hath anointed my feet with ointment.

"'Wherefore I say unto thee, her sins, which are many, are forgiven; for she loved much: but to whom little is forgiven, the same loveth little.'"

Closing the Bible, Sally smiled at Miss Flora. "You are a *friend*, Flora."

"Janey said you were different from the others," Flora said. "She said you wouldn't judge her."

"You mean because she isn't just a business manager, she is also Josh Richards's mistress? No, I don't judge her at all. She was very nice to me the first day I arrived in town." Sally laughed. "She was more than nice. "I'm quite sure that she saved my life."

EPILOGUE

Smoke stood at the grave of his father, holding his hat in his hands. He was pleased to see that the markings he had chiseled in the rock-turned-tombstone were still quite legible. Preacher was standing some distance away, having told Smoke that he needed some private time with his pa.

"Pa, I've settled some accounts. I've killed Billy Bartell. He was the man that raped Janey, and in my way of thinking, is probably the one that sent her down the wrong trail. I don't know where she is now, and to be honest with you, I haven't been lookin' for her. I hope she's alive, and livin' well somewhere, but I figure that's none of my doin' anymore. I set things right for her, by killin' Bartell. What happens to her from now on is up to her.

"I'm happy to say, I also found and killed Angus Shardeen. I told you he's the one that killed Ma.

"I'd like to say that ever'thing is all settled now, but I can't say that just yet. I'm goin' after the ones that killed you and Luke. I killed Ted Casey already. He was one you didn't know about. I know the names of the others—Wiley Potter, Keith Stratton, and Josh Richards. I'm goin' to find 'em, Pa, and I'm goin' to make things right. I give you that promise."

Smoke stood there in silence for another moment, then put his hat on, and started back toward Preacher.

"Got things settled with your pa?" Preacher asked.

"Yeah."

"He was real proud of you, boy. Same as I am."

The lump in Smoke's throat wouldn't let him reply.

Turn the page for an exciting preview!

THE GREATEST WESTERN WRITERS
OF THE 21ST CENTURY

In one of the most shocking chapters in the Jensen family
saga, America's fearless frontier clan is about to take on an
enemy as cold and relentless as evil itself—a mad, sadistic
surgeon, skilled with knives, and his gang. They're
gunning for the Jensen Sugarloaf ranch to ravage Jensen
women and spill an ocean of Jensen blood . . .

When the Jensen boys decide to take a trip to
Smoke Jensen's ranch—leaving Sally, Pearle, and
Cal alone at the Sugarloaf—the family homestead
becomes an easy target for enemies, outlaws, and
one hell of a hardcase named Jonas Trask. A former
army doctor with a degree in cruelty, Trask and his
vicious band of followers descend on the nearby
town of Big Rock with a vengeance. First, he takes
out the sheriff. Then he kidnaps Sally Jensen. Now
he waits for the Jensen boys to return like lambs to
the slaughter. It doesn't take long for Matt,
Preacher, and Smoke to see that they're up against
a vicious maniac. What they can't figure out is why
this mad doctor Trask is doing this—or how they're
going to stop him. One thing is sure: the brothers
will perform the operation with surgical precision,
blazing guns, and not a shred of mercy . . .

USA TODAY AND *NEW YORK TIMES*
BESTSELLING AUTHORS
WILLIAM W. JOHNSTONE
with J. A. Johnstone

THE FAMILY JENSEN
BROTHERHOOD OF EVIL

On sale now, wherever Pinnacle Books are sold!

CHAPTER 1

Bitter cold rain sluiced down from gray, leaden skies, turning the single street of Espantosa, New Mexico Territory, into a muddy bog. It was the middle of the afternoon, but the thick overcast made it seem more like twilight.

No one was out and about except one man who muttered curses under his breath as he attempted to run up the street. The mud kept trying to suck the boots off his feet, so his run was more of a stumble.

Petey Tomlin was plumb miserable. He wore an old slicker, but it leaked in several places. Even if it hadn't, pounding rain always found a way to work itself inside a man's duds and make him wet and uncomfortable. In less than a block, Tomlin felt like he was soaked to the skin. Water ran in a steady stream from the brim of his battered old hat and made it difficult for him to see where he was going.

He kept his eyes on the yellow glow up ahead that marked the front windows of the Gilt-Edge Saloon.

That was his destination. He carried important news for the men who waited there.

Espantosa didn't have boardwalks along the two blocks of its business district. Most of the establishments opened directly onto the street. A few, like the Gilt-Edge, had covered porches, but that didn't help Tomlin stay out of the rain.

He could dry off and warm up later, he told himself, once he'd let Jack Shawcross know what he had seen at the livery stable down the street.

Shawcross had sent him to the stable to check on the horses, or so he'd claimed. Tomlin thought Shawcross had done it mostly to make him miserable. He got mean like that sometimes, especially when he'd been putting away the booze. He and the rest of the bunch had been in the Gilt-Edge all afternoon, drinking and playing cards and taking turns going upstairs with the saloon's lone bar girl.

Tomlin hadn't been up there with her yet. He was usually one of the last for anything good and the first for any unpleasant job like going out in the rain.

He would have to wait even longer for female companionship. He knew his boss would want to deal right away with what he'd discovered at the livery stable.

Maybe Shawcross would be feeling generous after that. He might even toss Tomlin an extra double eagle in appreciation for what he'd done.

He reached the steps leading up to the saloon's porch and climbed them, stomping to knock some of the mud off his boots, but the blasted stuff was just too thick and sticky.

At that time of year, the batwings were fastened back on either side of closed double doors. He grasped the right-hand doorknob, opened it, and stepped into the welcome warmth coming from a pot-bellied stove in the corner.

"Stop right there!" bellowed Ben Gormley, the craggy-faced bartender and the saloon's owner. "Don't come trackin' all that mud in here. Go outside and take them boots off."

The little outlaw ignored the man who stood behind the bar and scuttled across the room toward the round, baize-covered table where Jack Shawcross was playing poker with four members of the gang. Three more men were at the bar, nursing mugs of beer. The nine owlhoots were the only people in the Gilt-Edge's main room, other than the owner.

"Damn it!" Gormley said as he started out from behind the bar. "I told you—" He stopped instantly and shut up as Shawcross lifted a hand.

"Petey wouldn't be hurrying like that if he didn't have something important to tell us," the outlaw boss said.

"Sorry, Jack," Gormley muttered as he retreated behind the hardwood again.

The outlaws spent freely and generally behaved themselves in Espantosa, which they had adopted as their unofficial headquarters. Nobody wanted to get on their bad side—which, according to their reputation, was very bad indeed.

Tomlin took off his hat and tilted it so that water ran off and formed a puddle in the sawdust on the floor. The sawdust would soak it up, given time.

Shawcross turned his attention back to the cards in his hand but asked Tomlin, "How are the horses, Petey?" He snickered. "Staying dry?"

"I didn't check on 'em," Tomlin answered.

Shawcross frowned and looked at Tomlin coldly. "That's what I told you to do, wasn't it?"

"Yeah, but some fellas rode into the livery stable just before I got there. I saw 'em goin' in, and somethin' about one of 'em struck me as familiar. So I snuck up to the door and watched while they talked to ol' Ramon. I got a good look at 'em then, and I recognized one of them, just like I thought."

Shawcross slapped his cards on the table, facedown, and snapped, "Damn it. Spit it out already."

"It was Luke Jensen, Jack. I'm as sure of it as the day I was born."

CHAPTER 2

The name was loud in the saloon. Shawcross sat up straighter, as did the other men at the table. The three men drinking at the bar stiffened, set their drinks down, and turned around.

"You'd better not be trying to have a little sport with me, Petey." Shawcross's voice was soft, but it held a steel-edged quality that made a shiver go through Tomlin.

"I'd never do that, Jack." *Even though you might deserve it for all the times you've tormented me.* "It was Jensen, right enough. He didn't look exactly like he did in El Paso last year. He was a little skinny, like he'd been sick or something. But it was him, no doubt about it."

Shawcross turned his head and said to the men at the bar, "One of you go get Clancy." Then he got to his feet. The cards, the game, and the pile of greenbacks and coins in the middle of the table obviously were forgotten. He drew the heavy revolver from the holster at his hip, opened the cylinder, and took a cartridge from one of the loops on his shell belt. He thumbed it into the empty chamber and snapped the cylinder closed.

Around the table, the other men began doing likewise.

Shawcross pouched the iron and looked out the window at the falling rain. He was a lean, lantern-jawed man. His cheeks still bore the faint pockmarks of a childhood illness. His deep-set eyes burned with a fire that might be hate or insanity or both. "You said there were some other men with Jensen?"

Tomlin nodded. "Yeah, three more. A couple who looked younger than him, and one old-timer. I didn't recognize any of 'em."

"Doesn't matter. It's their bad luck to be here today. And to be friends with that bounty-hunter."

The man who had hurried upstairs in response to Shawcross's order reappeared with another outlaw following him. The second man was stocky and had a shaggy head of sandy hair, along with a ragged mustache of the same color. His hat was pushed to the back of his head, his gun belt was draped over his shoulder, and he was clumsily fastening his shirt buttons. His long red underwear was still visible through the gap.

"I don't understand what the dadblasted hurry is," he complained.

Shawcross called up the stairs. "Luke Jensen is in town, Clancy."

The shaggy-haired man stopped. His eyes widened for a second. "Why the all-fired hell didn't somebody say so? Let's go get him!"

"That's what we're doing." Shawcross turned back to Tomlin. "Did you happen to hear Jensen and his friends say where they were headed?"

"No, I hustled back here quick as I could in all that mud. Not many places in Espantosa they could go, though. The saloon here and the hotel are just about it. Shoot, they might still be at the livery stable. You know how that old Mex likes to talk."

Shawcross nodded slowly. "We'll find them. Grab your slickers, boys, and let's go."

The outlaws pulled on slickers, tugged down their hats, and stepped out onto the porch. From behind the bar, Gormley shook his head as he watched them go, as if he felt sorry for the man who was the object of their wrath and his unfortunate companions.

The mud made sucking sounds as the men walked along the street toward the livery stable in the next block. Both of the stable's big front doors were open, allowing lantern light to spill out into the street, but Shawcross and his men couldn't see into the building from where they were.

As they drew near the hotel, Shawcross said, "Neal, Wilson, check in there."

The two men hurried ahead, tracked mud into the hotel lobby, and returned to tell Shawcross that no strangers had arrived recently.

"And that slick-haired clerk was too scared not to be tellin' the truth, boss," one of them added.

Shawcross nodded. "They have to still be at the stable, then." He pointed to four of the men and went on. "You boys head around back and come in that way. The rest of us will take the front."

The four outlaws drifted off into the rain, quickly vanishing into the gloom. That left six men to tramp the rest of the way down the street to the stable.

Tomlin scrambled up next to Shawcross. "You reckon

Jensen will start shootin' as soon as he lays eyes on you, Jack?"

"He might. He probably heard that I swore to get him after he killed Trace last year."

Shawcross and Trace Bennett had been closer than brothers. Best friends and partners in leading the gang, they had been responsible for spreading outlawry across a wide swath of West Texas and New Mexico Territory.

The notorious bounty hunter Luke Jensen had trapped Bennett in a café in El Paso, gunning him down so that Trace had died in a welter of broken crockery, tangled in a checked tablecloth. Dying was bad enough; to do it in such undignified circumstances was an unforgivable insult.

Shawcross would have gone after Jensen then and there, as soon as he'd heard about what had happened, but a bunch of Rangers had ridden into town just then and the gang had to light a shuck to avoid being captured. By the time they'd made it back a couple weeks later, Jensen had already collected his blood money and was long gone.

Shawcross had insisted that he would cross trails with Luke Jensen again someday, and when he did, Jensen would die.

In the squalid little New Mexico settlement, it looked like that day had come.

"Clancy, Wilson, with me," Shawcross said softly. "You other three spread out a little as we go in. Wait for Jensen to start the ball. I want him to know who's gonna kill him and why he's fixing to die."

The others nodded in understanding. Usually, it

was best not to give an enemy any more chance than you had to, but the outlaws outnumbered Jensen and his pards more than two to one, and they would be caught in a crossfire, to boot. They wouldn't stand a chance.

As the outlaws moved into the broad, open doorway, they unfastened their slickers and swept them back so they could get to their guns in a hurry. The hard rain drummed on the roof, and the four men standing inside the stable, talking to old Ramon while the hostler tended to their horses, didn't seem to hear the newcomers enter.

Shawcross's nostrils flared as he took a deep breath at the sight of one of them. Tomlin was right. The tall man with the craggy, unhandsome but compelling face and curly dark hair was Luke Jensen, no doubt about that. He looked like he had lost some weight and his face was a little pale in the lantern light, but it was him.

A man a few years younger and a couple inches shorter than Jensen stood with him. He had sandy hair under a thumbed-back hat, and his shoulders seemed incredibly broad in the slicker he wore. The third man was a little taller than Luke, fair-haired, powerfully built, and younger still.

That left the grizzled, whip-thin old-timer who wore a buckskin shirt and an old, steeple-crowned hat that had seen much better days. Sitting next to him was a big, shaggy dog of some sort, looking miserable with its wet fur matted to its body. Somebody as ancient as the old man probably didn't represent any threat, but they would gun him down anyway.

There was no law in Espantosa to say they couldn't.

It was the dog who noticed them first. His big head swung toward them, and he bared his teeth in a snarl that suddenly made him look more wolf than dog.

That got the old man's attention. He turned to look and said in a voice cracked with years, "Looks like we got comp'ny, boys."

"Yeah," Jensen said, turning slowly to face Shawcross and the other outlaws. Recognition showed on his face. "Jack Shawcross. I didn't expect to run into you here."

"I'll just bet you didn't," Shawcross grated.

"You got some idea of settling the score for Trace Bennett?"

"You killed him!"

Jensen shrugged. "The reward posters said dead or alive. I took them at their word, especially when he drew on me first."

Quietly, the broad-shouldered man told old Ramon, "Drift on into the tack room, *tio*, and keep your head down."

Ramon swallowed hard, his Adam's apple bobbing. "*Sí, Señor Jensen.*"

Shawcross caught that and said quickly to Luke, "Jensen, eh? Your brother?"

A faint smile touched Luke's lips under his thin mustache. "That's right. This is my brother Smoke, and this is my other brother Matt. They call the old-timer Preacher."

As Petey Tomlin stood a couple yards to the right of Shawcross, Clancy, and Wilson, he felt his guts turn to water. Everybody had heard of Smoke Jensen, who was quite possibly the fastest, deadliest gunfighter in the entire West, and Matt Jensen's fame as a pistoleer was growing rapidly, too. And as for Preacher . . . well, that old man was a living legend, no two ways about it.

Tomlin wondered if he could turn around and run back out into the downpour before they killed him.

Too late. Jack Shawcross yelled a curse, and his hand stabbed toward the gun on his hip.

CHAPTER 3

Luke, Smoke, Matt, and Preacher hadn't been getting in any hurry to get back to Sugarloaf, Smoke's sprawling ranch in Colorado. They had been taking it easy as they rode through Arizona and New Mexico.

Luke knew that deliberate pace was mostly because of him. The other three had pulled him out of a bad spot. He'd been held captive for a good while under harsh conditions in an outlaw stronghold, and as a result he wasn't in the best of shape. None of the others wanted to push him too hard.

He appreciated their concern, but at the same time it annoyed him a little. He didn't want anybody feeling sorry for him.

He had already given some thought to going his own way and letting his three companions head back to Sugarloaf without him. He was grateful for what they'd done—they had saved his life, no doubt about that—but he had spent many years as a loner and even though he had been reunited with his family, that wasn't going to change.

As he stood in the livery stable that was pleasantly warm and smelled of horseflesh, straw, and manure and saw the outlaw named Jack Shawcross reach for his gun, Luke knew that if he and the others survived the next few seconds, it would be time for them to split up.

But first there was some killing to do.

He had already opened his slicker for a couple reasons. Doing so let his damp clothes air out and start drying. More important, he was in the habit of making it easy to reach for his guns.

His hands flashed across his body to twin ivory-handled Remingtons riding butt forward in cross-draw holsters. The long-barreled revolvers came out smoothly and spouted fire from their muzzles as he brought them level.

Both slugs plowed into the chest of Jack Shawcross, who had cleared leather but hadn't had time to raise his gun. He jerked the trigger as his muscles spasmed under the shock of Luke's bullets, but the slug smacked into the ground at his feet.

To Luke's right, Smoke's .45s roared. His lead hammered two more outlaws off their feet.

To the left, Matt and Preacher were about to deal with the remaining three gunmen. Matt had his Colt out, and Preacher had drawn the pair of revolvers he wore, his movements amazingly swift and supple for a man his age.

At that instant, however, shots blasted behind them and Preacher's hat flew off his head, plucked from its perch by a bullet that narrowly missed his skull.

Some of the gang had slipped around the stable and come in the back, Luke realized. They were still outnumbered and were caught in a crossfire. "Spread out!" he shouted as he triggered his Remingtons again and saw another man stagger from the bullet that ripped across his side.

Luke and Smoke went to the right, Matt, Preacher, and the big cur called Dog to the left. Smoke pressed his back against one of the thick beams that supported the hayloft. He fired in opposite directions, front and back, at the same time.

Luke ducked behind a grain bin and grimaced as a flying slug struck the bin's lid and sent splinters spraying against his cheek. He fired both Remingtons again at the outlaws who had come in the front doors and were scattering under the onslaught of Jensen bullets.

Matt dived off his feet and rolled against the gate of a stall. As he came to a stop on his belly, he fired up at an angle at one of the outlaws who had snuck in through the stable's back door. The slug caught the man under the chin, ranged up through his brain, and flipped him off his feet. He was dead when he hit the ground.

Preacher drifted into an empty stall and fired over its side wall. A gunman in the rear of the stable flew backward as if he'd been punched by a giant fist. Both of Preacher's bullets had found their mark. The man hit the back wall, bounced off of it, and reeled out through the open door. He collapsed in the rain, which made dark pink streaks run around him as it washed away the blood welling from his wounds.

At the same time, Dog leaped at one of the other men, who triggered a shot at the cur but hurried it and missed. He paid for that in a heartbeat as fangs tore into his neck and Dog's weight knocked him off his feet.

Matt gunned down another man with a well-placed shot, and another volley from Luke's Remingtons blew away a sizable chunk of an outlaw's head. The gun-thunder inside the stable had been deafeningly loud, but the echoes began to fade away as all the weapons fell silent.

All that was left were Dog's snarls as he finished mauling the man he had taken care of.

"Looks like they're all done for," Luke said into the eerie hush that followed the violence.

"Any of you fellas hurt?" Smoke asked.

"I'm fine," Matt said as he got to his feet and brushed straw and dirt off the front of his shirt.

"I ain't hurt," Preacher said angrily, "but one o' them scoundrels put a hole in my hat!"

"That hat's been to hell and back," Smoke said with a grin as he reloaded one of his Colts. "I don't reckon one more bullet hole is going to do that much more damage to it."

Preacher just snorted disgustedly as he picked up the headgear in question and clapped it down over his thinning gray hair.

"Hold on a minute," Matt said. "I count . . . nine of them. Six came in the front, and I would have sworn when they bushwhacked us from the back there were four more of them. That makes ten."

Luke nodded grimly. "So one of them got away."

"You want take a look for him?" Smoke asked.

Luke thought about it for a second. It was doubtful the lone surviving gang member posed much of a threat to them, but he didn't like leaving loose ends. "Maybe we'd better. No telling if the hombre might go in for some back shooting."

Smoke opened the tack room door and asked the old hostler, "Are you all right in there, *tio*?"

"*Sí, señor*," the man replied.

"You know who those fellas were, don't you?"

The old man emerged tentatively and nodded. "Señor Shawcross and his men. They come here to Espantosa from time to time. They do as they please because everyone is too afraid to stand up to them."

"Well, you won't have to worry about that anymore," Smoke said. "Do they stable their horses here?"

"*Sí*. This is the only place in town for the *caballos*."

Smoke nodded. "Preacher, you and Dog stay here in case the fella tries to double back and grab a mount."

Preacher didn't argue with the decision. Even though he had mentored Smoke for many years and taught the younger man practically all he knew about surviving on the frontier, there was no denying that Smoke was a natural leader and usually knew the best thing to do.

"The rest of us will see if we can find him," Smoke went on.

"Should be able to," Matt said. "This settlement isn't much more than a wide spot in the trail. There aren't that many places he could have gone."

The three of them holstered their guns, buttoned up their slickers, and slid Winchesters from saddle sheaths. They worked the levers on the repeaters, then stepped out into the rain, moving quickly so they wouldn't be silhouetted in the doorway for more than an instant.